TO THE
PRINCESS
BOUND

TERMS OF MERCY:

TO THE PRINCESS BOUND

SARA KING

Published by
Parasite Publications

ISBN: 1942929056
ISBN-13: 9781942929055

DISCLAIMER

At the time of publication, the human race did not have faster-than-light travel, psychic genetic mutations (that I know of), or colonies on other planets. In case you're still not sure, yes, you are reading a work of fiction. The people and places in this story are not real, people. Really.

DEDICATION

For Kim Fangel Burling,
Who has a way with plastic spoons.
And who, with the help of her co-conspirators,
snuck this book behind my back,
read it, loved it, and gave it life.
This one was all her, folks.

For Amy Breshears,
A wannabe copyeditor with some seriously mad skillz.

For _____,
Who would rather remain anonymous because his buddies would
mock him mercilessly if they found out he was reading and edit-
ing a romance novel. He pestered me for *weeks* (don't you have
ANYTHING else for me to read?) before I dug this one up off my
harddrive for him. Turns out, we were both pleasantly surprised.

Table of Contents

Disclaimer · v
Dedication · vii
Chapter 1 – The Last Emp · 1
Chapter 2 – The Princess's Return · 12
Chapter 3 – To the Princess Bound · 21
Chapter 4 – Understanding · 41
Chapter 5 – To Entertain a Princess · · · · · · · · · · · · · · · · · · · 66
Chapter 6 – Reliving the Past · 80
Chapter 7 – Touched by an Emp · 93
Chapter 8 – The First Bath · 112
Chapter 9 – The Golden Rule · 137
Chapter 10 – Whip's Close Call · 157
Chapter 11 – At Home with an Emp · · · · · · · · · · · · · · · · · · · 174
Chapter 12 – The Core Rama · 186
Chapter 13 – Village Life · 197
Chapter 14 – A Plan Foiled · 237
Chapter 15 – The Womb Rama · 244
Chapter 16 – An Open Heart · 260
Chapter 17 – A Man Without Mercy · · · · · · · · · · · · · · · · · · · 276
Chapter 18 – Trust · 294
Chapter 19 – An Imperial Decree · 315
Other Titles by Sara King · 317

CHAPTER 1

The Last Emp

Dragomir watched the violet monkshood flowers and grainy white flecks of water hemlock swirl in the cup of amber mead. His wife had made the warped earthenware vessel two years ago, after a trip to the clay-mines down in the valley with the village women. He could still see the gentle impressions that her delicate fingers had scored into the edges of the mug as it had spun on the potter's wheel. He traced them idly, remembering the graceful way her hands had worked the blue glacial clay. Once put into the village kiln, the cup had come out lopsided and orange, with black stripes where her glaze had accidentally run.

Guess I'm a goatherd, not a potter, she had laughed, upon seeing the half-crumpled, deformed result that she had pulled from the kiln. She had thrown it away, but Dragomir had pulled it from the trash pit the next morning and filled it with flowers. She had found it on the window-sill and given him a scowl of disapproval, but he had seen her love and happiness overflowing in washes of green and pink within. *Can't lie to me, missy,* he had said, kissing the wrinkle out of her forehead. *Should know better than try to lie to an Emp.*

Dragomir ran his fingers around the drooping edge of the cup, tracing the paths her fingertips had taken. The liquid inside had been made by her, too. Almost eight months ago, now. One of the last batches in the fall, bottled only days before she had gone up into the

mountains with him, to pick berries for winter. The monkshood floating within the mead began to blur as he remembered the way she had
worn her hair that day. He'd asked her to leave it loose for the trip.
Loose and free, because he loved the way the mountain air played
with her beautiful auburn locks. She'd complained for almost an hour
before he agreed to brush out all the tangles when they got back.

True to his word, he'd brushed her hair for hours, afterwards. He'd
combed the blood and bone away and braided it lovingly down her
back…

Voices in the front yard made him jerk. A moment later, his door
began rattling in its frame with a heavy fist. "Got a sick horse for the
healer," the no-nonsense Brigamond Borer called from the front door. A
moment later, he opened the door and peered inside, silhouetted against
the brilliant sunny day outside. "You in there, Emp?"

Heart hammering, Dragomir jumped up and grabbed a pot from
where it dangled above the stove and dropped it, upside-down, over
the cup of mead. The sudden motion was too fast, and the *clunk* drew
Brigamond's attention. The old man peered into the darkness of
Dragomir's living-room, obviously trying to make out the source of
the sound. Quickly wiping his face, Dragomir composed himself as
Brigamond's ancient eyes adjusted to the shadows.

"Hey there, Emp," Brigamond said, finally spotting him. "We got
some business for you."

Dragomir nodded, not trusting his voice as he left the cup of mead
behind. "I heard," he managed, walking to the door. "Whatcha need,
Brigamond?" Every ounce of him felt wracked with exhaustion. He was
too tired for this. Soul-tired. Just walking to the front door took every
ounce of energy he had.

Brigamond Borer and his two eldest sons stood in his front yard with
a sick horse. Dragomir could tell it was sick by the way its earthy lines
of gi seemed stagnated in its bowels, coagulating there, creating a ball of
murky darkness that was rapidly spreading outward, into the creature's
heart and lungs.

He winced, recognizing the animal. A pretty gray, the Borer's new
prize filly, traded just a month ago from a village down the valley.

Barely a year old, she was already full and heavy in the shoulder and rump, destined to be an excellent draft animal. She walked with her head down, having to be pulled forward, with none of the bounce that Dragomir had seen a week ago, when he'd visited Borer Farm to get Thunder shoed.

The big man at the door glanced at the pot on the table, then up at Dragomir, a little frown on his face. "You okay in there?" Brigamond pressed, trying to peer past him. "Thor told me to keep an eye on you while he's up in the mountains."

Immediately, Dragomir felt himself stiffen. Damn Thor and his meddling. Eight months of meddling, and now he had the entire village intruding on Dragomir's affairs like they had every right to do so. He stepped through the entrance and pulled the door shut behind him, forcing the old man gently backwards with his body. Despite the fact that Brigamond and his two boys were six feet tall and built like gene-spliced oxen, they were still dwarfed by Dragomir's six and a half, and today, Dragomir used it. "You said you've got a sick horse?" he said, with as much pointedness as he could manage without being rude.

While the two Borer boys always carried an aura of awe and respect around Dragomir, the old man's *au*, as always, was like a stiff sledgehammer of control, painful to be around. With a grunt, the old man said, "Yeah, sick. She stopped eating last night. We think she's got colic."

"It's worms," Dragomir said, seeing the malignant energy lines balling backwards up the filly's intestines and into the stomach like a blood clot. "How long's she been like this?" When he got closer, he could see the sickly red-brown gi of a mass of roundworms in the filly's small intestine, stopping up the flow of the horse's bowels.

Brigamond Borer gave him an irritated look. "She's too old for worms. 'Sides. We dewormed her, just to be safe. She's got colic. Just ate something she shouldn't have and we need you to help her pass it." The old man sounded impatient and disgusted that he'd had to drag the horse up the road to see Dragomir in the first place. It was the fourth time this year that Brigamond had been forced to bring a horse to Dragomir's farm to save it from certain death. Each time the old man had come trudging up his road, Dragomir could see the shame rolling off of him in great, unhealthy yellow waves, and he had been brusque and irritable and cantankerous in general.

Dragomir knew that the self-sufficient jack-of-all-trades hated the fact that he had to seek out his help, and Dragomir suspected the Borer Farm rates of colic were actually a lot higher, but the old man could only bring himself to come to Dragomir when it was an especially valuable animal—like a prize mare. In fact, unlike most of the villagers of Sodstone—who would routinely bring him such tiny things as sick kittens and baby birds—horses were the *only* animals that Brigamond ever brought to him. After all, with all the other animals on his farm, Brigamond could just force saltwater down the creatures' throats and make them retch up whatever was troubling them. Unfortunately, with horses, there was very little—if anything—a normal person could do to make them vomit.

"So just make her vomit like you did the last one and I'll be on my way," Brigamond insisted. His fist was white-knuckled fingers as he shoved the filly's reins at Dragomir. With the other hand, Brigamond dug into his pocket, then pushed a coinpurse at him. "There's for your troubles." Like Dragomir had set a price for his services, and Brigamond was disgusted because it was too high. As Dragomir gingerly reached out to take the reins and the purse from the farrier, the old man struck a posture of agitation, checking the sky.

Dragomir grimaced down at the purse. He always found it difficult to deal with Brigamond. While the Dormuthian had been raised with a healthy respect for healers, the old man was proud of his independence, and didn't understand the intricacies of an Emp's sight. Clearing his throat, Dragomir glanced again at the malignant mass of dead and dying worms plugging up the horse's gut. "Okay, Brigamond. What do you think she ate?"

Of course, deworming the horse had probably loosened enough of the worms from the horse's intestines that she was having a physiological reaction—an herbivore suddenly exposed to several pounds of rotting worm-meat—but he knew from experience he would not be able to change the old farrier's mind.

"Who knows?" Brigamond snorted disgustedly. "The headstrong hussy keeps jumping the fence and running off. Weeds, wood, metal—the monkshood just started flowering, too. Might've gotten a mouthful of the stuff."

Dragomir flinched at the last. He cleared his throat, hoping Brigamond hadn't noticed. "There's definitely a lot more monkshood up here than those villages lower in the valley," Dragomir offered delicately. He patted the sick filly's shoulder. "Maybe the poor girl never got acquainted with the stuff. Different climate down there in the lowlands. Terraforming took better, I hear."

Brigamon rolled his eyes. "Come on, Emp," the old man said. He waved a hand at the big gray animal. "No need for pleasantries. Let's get this over with."

Like he was a cobbler who was trying to talk him into buying shoes he didn't need. Dragomir sighed and glanced down at the tufts of spring grass at his feet. He knew without asking that the old man was going to tell him to make his horse throw up, regardless of what he was seeing. He also knew that using up that kind of energy at the wrong end of the problem might kill the horse. He thought about it a moment, then nodded. "All right. I'm gonna need three wild geraniums, a bag of willowbark, a fistful of fireweed root, about fifty elderberries, and about a pound of pinecones from a white spruce. *Must* be a white spruce. Black spruce would have the opposite effect."

Brigamond made a face, obviously not looking forward to a jaunt through the woods. "I thought you just need to think about it real hard and she'll vomit."

"I can," Dragomir agreed, "but she's eaten recently and this'll help it come up smooth. We *need* it to come up smooth. Horses aren't made to throw up. This'll keep it from bunching up in the esophagus and choking her."

Brigamond grunted, then turned to his two boys. "You heard the healer. Go get—"

"You should probably go with them," Dragomir said, too tired to really care about decorum any longer. "It's important to get it right. I'll keep her alive until you and your boys get back."

The white-haired farrier gave the horse an irritated look. "Keep her *alive*, huh? She close, then?"

"Close enough," Dragomir said, running his hand down a long gray flank.

Brigamond shook his head. "Some fine damned breedstock she's turning out to be. Last time I buy from *those* bastards." He gestured at his two sons. "Let's go." He turned, then paused a moment, turned back, and said, "*Fifty* elderberries?"

"Thereabouts," Dragomir said. "More would be better, in any case."

Brigamond grunted and led his two boys away.

Dragomir let out a breath of relief once the old man's agitated, rigid energy had retreated. He glanced at the filly. "Better?"

The filly, of course, did not understand him—communing with beasts was the realm of a Psi, not an Emp—but it relaxed nonetheless. *Both* of them breathed easier without the Brigamond's au to agitate their gi lines. The filly lowered her head a bit further, completely uninterested in the green grass by her feet, panting. Dragomir could feel the hurt rolling off of her, and it was building into a sharp pain in his own gut.

"You're a lucky horse," Dragomir said, tracing his hand down the horse's side, to the area of the blockage. "Life got plans for you, girl?" He felt through the gi lines as he spoke, feeling out which ones were disturbed. "Got here just in the nick of time. You an important horse, eh? You gonna save some soldier from the Imperials someday?" He ran his hand down her ribcage, feeling the stagnated energy there, drawing it outward with his fingers, getting it moving again.

For her part, the filly just shuddered under his touch, but didn't fight him. Animals rarely did. It was the humans who got scared. Animals, despite the pain he put them through, knew he was there to help, and held still.

He found the center of the problem, the two gi lines on either side of the blockage. They were turning black and shriveling from contact with the rotting wormflesh. His forehead touching the filly's flank, now, Dragomir considered. The horse he could save, but this wasn't the first time that Life had tried to stop him. He still remembered his brother in the middle of the night, running up the road in his underwear to cut him down.

Softly, Dragomir said into her fur, "All right. But this will be the last. One last healing before I go." Then…peace. No more nightmares. No more loneliness.

When he received no Sign that Life would try to intervene again, Dragomir took a deep breath, closed his eyes, and sank his consciousness into his core. The crystalline roar that followed left his body flooding with energy, pouring out his ramas and through his gi lines, setting his whole essence abuzz. Immediately, he drew that energy outward, sinking his mind into the horse's stomach-rama.

Immediately, the filly jerked and lifted her head high, eyes beginning to show white.

"Shhh," Dragomir whispered, eyes still closed. "Easy." He gently rubbed his hand against the filly's side as he infused her au with a rush of calm from his heart-rama. "You'll be fine, girl. Just another minute or two."

The horse snorted in alarm as Dragomir began pumping energy into the lines of gi running along her intestines, forcing the lines back into place, spasming the muscles, loosening her bowels. Yet, despite the horrible feeling roiling through her insides—and the sudden fear rolling off of her—she held absolutely still under his touch.

"It's working, girl," Dragomir murmured, still in trance. "Just hold on." He watched as the blockage of dead worms began to spasm and squish as the intestines there clenched, then followed the mass with his eyes as it began to move through the horse's system, jerky at first, but then with increasing rapidity, like mud being squeezed down a sausage wrapping. "Almost done…"

With an indignant whinny, the horse lifted her tail and let out a long string of nuggets that became more and more runny as her bowels continued to release, eventually becoming a watery green slurry. A few moments later, the clump of worms slid free and spattered to the ground, a white mass of dead, rotting parasites about three times the size of Dragomir's fist.

The filly, for her part, was standing with her legs splayed, head low, panting.

"I know," Dragomir said, dropping to rub the animal behind the ears. "That felt real bad. But you'll get better."

You'll get better, Meggie...Immediately, Dragomir stiffened at the memory that followed. He ducked his head to the horse's neck and closed his eyes, tears threatening again. She hadn't gotten better. She had died, in his arms, and all his precious Emp powers that everyone loved so much hadn't even made her lifeless body twitch, after the Praetorian had shot her in the face.

"You'll get better," Dragomir whispered, once again seeing the scene. Beneath his grip, the gray started tugging at grass.

Two hours later, when Brigamond and his two sons returned with the items Dragomir had specified, Dragomir was still squatting in the yard, staring down at the reins in his fist as the filly cropped the tufts of grass nearby.

"What did you do?" the old man bellowed, before the three Borers were even within comfortable earshot.

"Nothing," Dragomir said, waiting until they came close enough to explain. He stood and handed Brigamond back the reins—and his purse. "Poor thing just took the biggest dump I've ever seen over there." He gestured. "Think she got whatever it was out of her system, though."

Brigamond frowned at the horse, then at Dragomir, but made no move to take the items he was being given. "You didn't do anything?"

Dragomir shook his head. "Sorry I couldn't help."

Brigamond frowned at the horse, then at Dragomir, then reluctantly took the purse back. Squatting over by the gigantic horse-patty, one of the two Borer boys cried, "Holy crap, Dad, it was *full* of worms!" He lifted a clump of them with a stick and they clung in limp, ivory-white strands, much like a morbid wad of spaghetti.

Brigamond grunted. "Worms, huh?" He looked up at Dragomir, and for a split second, Dragomir thought he would try to give the money back. Then the curmudgeony old farmer shook his head and tossed the elderberries and bark he had gathered aside. "*Knew* I didn't need to come all the way up here. Good breedstock, my ass." He gave a disgusted snort and started to turn. Then, to Dragomir's frustration, the old man hesitated and turned back. His cloudy old eyes fixed again on the door that

Dragomir had pulled shut behind him. "You ain't gotta be alone up here, Emp."

Immediately, Dragomir bristled. "I'm fine alone."

"My daughter's looking for a husband. She knows the ways of a farm."

Dragomir could barely suppress a snarl when he said, "I'm not looking for another wife."

The old man laughed. "What, you're just gonna *sulk* up here, waiting for the next girl of your dreams to what, wander through your front door? Handed to you on a silver platter? You gotta go *look*, boy. You ain't been *lookin'*. You been up here mopin'. Like that halfbreed was the only fish in the sea."

Dragomir felt every muscle in his body stiffen at the word 'next,' but the last made his anger rise. "Brigamond," he said stiffly, "get off my property."

"Leslie's of good original stock," Brigamond insisted. "All the Borers are. She ain't too smart, and she ain't got no problem with chores. She can cook, she can sew—"

"She can pluck a chicken in like a minute flat," one of the man's boys laughed. "Have it on the table in two."

Brigamond nodded. "She'd bear you strong babes, unlike that barren half-Imperial weakling you marrie—"

Dragomir, whose rage had been rising over the course of the conversation, grabbed Brigamond by the throat and lifted him off the ground with enough force that the old man was almost at eye-level with him, standing on his tiptoes. "*Never*," Dragomir whispered, lowering his face to meet Brigamond's, "assume I want your opinion. Ever. Again. If you don't get off my property, *now*, I'm going to cut a few gi lines and leave you pissing yourself every time a rooster crows. "

Brigamond's eyes widened and Dragomir shoved him backwards, away from him.

"*Boys!*" Brigamond cried, stumbling backwards, deathly pale. His two sons were standing nervously beside the horse-patty, wide eyes on Dragomir, the worms forgotten. "We've got lambs to shear. We're going. C'mon!" Then he was backing away from Dragomir, one hand clutching his throat. His boys fell in beside him and the three of them put distance between themselves and Dragomir, looking pale.

"The offer's open, Shipborn," the man called, from a good fifty feet away. "All alone up here…Seems a real waste, you not passin' on that genetic. At least go dally around in the village a bit. Make a few girls real happy. You ain't gettin' any younger, and the village is gonna need another Emp—"

"*Go!*" Dragomir roared.

Brigamond turned and led his boys away at a run.

Dragomir watched them go, so angry he was shaking. He'd heard the same argument a thousand times from well-wishers, snoops, and even his own brother: Go make some bastards to pass on the lines. Like he was a prize damned stud.

He waited until the Borers' backs disappeared down the road back to the village before he turned back to his home and threw the door open again. Thor was up in the mountains on an ore run. Gold, tin, copper. His brother wouldn't get back until nightfall three days hence. When he did, he—and all the other idiots in the village—wouldn't have to feel obligated to tell him to spread his seed.

Dragomir slammed the door shut, draping his home in darkness once more. Without Meggie, it had been a cold and desolate place. They had never managed to afford the windows she had wanted, in life, so there was still a horrible draft. Thor had tacked blankets over the openings, but Dragomir had torn them down. Meggie liked the sun.

No curtains in my home, she had told him firmly. He'd hated that certainty, called her 'bossy.' He had complained every morning he could remember, waking up with the sun in his eyes. He'd wanted to put curtains in, and more than once, they had ended up sleeping in different rooms over the subject. Now, Dragomir couldn't even stand anything sitting on the window-sill to block the light. The sun reminded him of her.

He sat down at the table and lifted the overturned pot, revealing his brew. Without another moment to think about it—two hours had been more than enough—Dragomir wrapped his fist around the little warped cup, lifted it from the worn wooden table, and put it to his lips.

I'll see you soon, Meggie…

The sudden blast of energy through his heart rama launched Dragomir backwards over his chair, dropping him to the floor in a wash of mead and flower petals. He lay there, dazed, staring up at the rough-hewn rafters of his ceiling, overwhelmed by the sudden rush of energy, wondering what the hell had just hit him. Like someone had reached out and grabbed him by the heart and tugged. He was pretty sure it hadn't been the mead—his lips weren't even wet.

"Meggie?" Dragomir whispered, trying to feel for her spirit. "Was that you?" He didn't think so. Meggie had never been a very strong being, and he doubted she had enough power, even dead, to hit him that hard. She'd been a younger soul, one he had shared only two previous lifetimes with out of thousands, and didn't have the richness and depth that he felt in on that other end. Richness and depth and…hurt? Terror? Whose terror? It was slamming into him down the tendrils lashed to his heart. Dazed, disoriented, he weakly tried to grab the table-leg to pull himself back up, but his arms failed him and he slipped back to the wet earthen floor.

"Who's there?" Dragomir asked hoarsely. Silence answered him. His chest, always feeling pressured and burdened by the energy around him, now felt like it was roaring with power. Dragomir frowned and felt out the new gi pathway carved out of his heart-rama, twined out into the ether. More vast than anything he'd ever experienced before, yet infinitely delicate and…desperate. He groaned and dropped his head back to the earth.

As the full force of the initial blast died down, Dragomir felt the power drain from the channel, leaving it an open sore, a dormant link between him and some stranger. He knew it wasn't Meggie. Though ghosts could certainly touch the living lightly here or there, they could never leave the massive, vibrating lines that he now felt spinning out into the ether, connecting him to someone on the other side of the planet.

11

CHAPTER 2

The Princess's Return

Adjudicator Keene looked up as his son stepped through the expensive double-doors of his war-chamber at a brisk walk, slamming the huge portal wide and marring the exquisitely-carved mahogany trim. Seeing that, Keene made a face.

For all its landmass, Mercy was cold, rocky, and grew very few lumberworthy trees. Despite repeated imperial timber-farming experiments, Keene had been forced to import his mahogany, maple, and cherry from a planet closer to the central core at a cost of sixty slaves a ton, and that had been at an imperial discount. Regularly priced, the wood in his doors, end-tables, shelves, bed, and desk alone would have cost him an entire freighter of natives. The void-like marble floor, the soaring white marble pillars, the polished granite bathtub, and the carved jade statuary, however, had been free.

Living betwixt the glittering granite spires and towering marble cliffs of Mercy, stone was the one thing the planet had in excess. Stone… and slaves.

"What now, Matthias?" Keene sighed, lowering his pen to his desk. "You know I am not to be interrupted between the evening hours of five and nine."

Prince Matthias slowed with a grimace. Keene knew the prince had no more love for his father than Keene had for his son, and it showed in the distaste marring his handsome visage.

His son, as a Second Generation Royal, unfortunately shared all the physical characteristics of Keene's late wife, including her too-pale skin, her unruly black hair, her fine bones, and her deep green eyes. With such a striking outward physical resemblance to the useless woman, Keene could only hope that the boy retained the intellectual capacity of his First Generation sire, as opposed to his Fourth Generation dam.

"We found her, milord," Prince Matthias said. He stopped some distance from the desk, obviously reluctant to share breathing-space with his father. Good. All the best leaders cultured hatred for something. Keene was more than willing to fill that role for his son, if it gave him the discipline he needed to become Adjudicator when the time came.

"Found *who?*" Keene demanded, irritated at the interruption. He didn't remember sending the boy to find anyone. "Can't you see I'm managing reports?" He gestured at his mass of paperwork.

His son seemed shocked by his words, then angry. "Your *daughter?* The one who was captured by rebels?" Matthias's green eyes seemed to have a dangerous glint in them, and his anger gave his pale features a healthy flush. It was exactly the type of deadly poise that would be required from the boy as the future ruler of Mercy.

Then Keene realized what his son had said, and he frowned. His *daughter?* It took him a long moment to make the connection, so long ago had he lost that particular spawn to the war. It had been six years since the princess's transport had been accosted by rebels, her escort murdered, herself captured. Once he *did* make the connection, Keene carefully set his glasses upon his priceless table, the vast mechanisms of his mind coming to a sputtering halt. "You found *Victoria?*"

His son gave a stiff nod. "She's been back a couple months. Thought you would want to know." The prince turned brusquely to leave.

"Stay here," Keene barked. "Where was she? And why wasn't I told?" He was infuriated at the boy's impudence, hiding such a thing from him.

Prince Matthias turned, a tenseness to his heavy shoulders that Keene didn't like. "One of the villages in the Blackrock Hills. And you *were* told. I sent six different missives in the time she's been back. The courier said you threw them in the fire."

Hmm. So he had. Keene made an indifferent gesture. "If you had wanted to talk to me, you could have done it in person," he replied. "And burn the village that had her. Kill everyone. Then do the same to every village in a fifty-kilometer radius. Don't bother taking slaves. We need to make a statement this time."

Prince Matthias's face darkened as he turned back to face him fully, his broad shoulders almost filling the doorway. "One would think a father's first question would be how his daughter fared her capture."

Keene waved a dismissive hand. "Just bring her here. I'll question her myself."

His son's face blackened to a thunderhead. "She was raped, Father. Staked out in one of the barbarians' villages to be entered at will by anything with a cock."

"That happens in war," Keene said. "You've taken a few women in your forays yourself, no doubt." He retrieved his pen and went back to his charts, noticing a discrepancy between two of his balance-sheets.

Prince Matthias's disgust was thick in his voice as he softly said, "Victory's eyes were glazed the entire voyage home. I don't think she realized she was back in the palace until she was sitting on her bed and her maids were trying to pull her out of the tattered and...stained...rags she was draped in."

"Did you end any unwanted pregnancies?" Keene suggested, correcting one of the scribe's transcribing errors. "Wouldn't want a rebel bastard running around."

His son stared at him so long that Keene had to look up from his paperwork.

"Are you even human?" his son asked.

Keene laughed and went back to his work. Between figures, he said, "Remember to send your sister to speak with me. I must determine if she acquired any inside information on the rebel cause."

"No," his son said.

Adjudicator Keene paused and lifted his head, curious. "*No?*" He hadn't had anyone tell him such a thing in thirty years.

His son stood straighter, reaching almost six feet—still sadly well below Keene's six-three. Yet another unfortunate indication of his Fourth

Generation heritage that was painfully impossible to ignore. "She locked herself in her room and is refusing to come out. She's been there two months. She screams and goes into shock when a male comes within fifteen feet of her." When Keene looked, there was dampness in the corners of his son's green eyes. "Even me."

Keene grunted, the news surprising even him. "You and your twin were very close."

Prince Matthias narrowed his eyes. "You have no idea."

"Tell her it's an order." Keene flipped a page in his ledger and compared it to a chart representing Mercy's strongest areas of cash-flow. "If she is to be a ruler, she certainly can't be afraid of men. Tell her that."

His son stepped forward and slammed both heavy fists into his paperwork. "Listen to me, you bastard. Victory is teetering on insanity. I've looked into her eyes. I've seen her. She's at the brink. Is that what you want? An insane Adjudicator to succeed you?"

Keene eyed his son's gloved fists in irritation. "I'll be dead, so I don't really care. Now please remove your hands before they blot the ink." Already, he was going to have to have a scribe produce duplicates where the boy's motion had smudged his ledger.

"You need to give Victory time to heal," Prince Matthias said. "If you try to bring her here, now, she's only going to go into shock. She's done it every time she's seen a man in two months, with no change. The doctors think it's permanent. Psychological trauma."

Keene had to laugh. "Permanent." Seeing his son was going to make no move to obey, Keene retrieved his glass of wine—also imported—and took a sip. He peered into the deep crimson liquid, considering. If there was one thing that Keene enjoyed, it was a psychological puzzle. "You say she's afraid of men?" he asked.

His son straightened and gave him a sneer. "Wouldn't you be, in her position?"

"No," Keene said, setting his glass down. "And no daughter of mine will be allowed to entertain such ridiculous fears."

Prince Matthias's mouth dropped open. "Not *allowed*…?"

"Go to the stables," Keene said, his powerful mind already made up. "Find the biggest, most fearsome brute you can get. Affix a belt to

15

Victoria's waist and chain him to it. Naked. Make her drag the beast around everywhere she goes. Hobbled and restrained, of course. That should make her realize her fears are unfounded."

His son flushed red, fury starting to bubble within his green eyes. "I told you she was *raped*!"

Keene frowned and wiped a blemish from the edge of the glass. "Make the chain eight feet long." He went back to his paperwork. "Oh, and stop allowing food to be brought to her room. If she wishes to eat, she will emerge and face the world."

"She needs time to *heal*," his son sputtered.

"You said yourself she's had two months. And that there's been no sign of recovery."

"Yes, but she screams—"

Keene snorted. "I've raised four children. If I've learned one thing from the experience, it's not to humor a child having a tantrum." He motioned at the door. "Go see to it. She's to wear her new slave until she overcomes her fears. However long it takes."

In the silence that followed, Keene could feel his son staring at him. He looked up. "That's a command, Matthias."

"Some days, Father, I hate you."

"Not surprising," Keene said, returning to his figures. "Royalty isn't allowed the luxury of familial endearments enjoyed by most commoners. It is one of the drawbacks to being royalty."

Matthias whirled and stormed from the room, slamming the priceless door behind him.

Keene shook his head, amused, and dipped his quill for another calculation.

• • •

Victory sat in a corner of her bedroom, arms wrapped around her knees, shuddering at the sound of booted footsteps against stone in the hall outside.

Here he comes, she thought, trying to fight down the animal panic that was beginning to claw at her throat. Father was going to chain her to a man. For days, *months…Oh gods oh gods…*

Sure enough, the door opened and four Praetorian women stepped inside, a monstrously big man hobbled between them. He was easily six and a half feet tall—a hulking brute whose head almost hit the door jamb as he shuffled inside. His ebony hair had been shaved down to his scalp, and had an odd streak of white—*scarring?*—along his right temple. His muscles rippled when he moved.

He was naked.

When her eyes found that place between his legs, open and exposed, terror hit her like a surge of lightning. Victory whimpered and tried to crawl further into the wall, but the metal ring around her waist only ground into the marble.

Oh no, she thought, trembling, as the House Praetorian located her huddled in the corner of her room and moved closer. *Oh no, no, no…* Pulled between the four women, the man kept his eyes on the ground, away from her.

Knowing what they planned, knowing she *had* to stop it or it would kill her, Victory forced herself to her feet, her entire body trembling. "Praetorian, as the Adjudicator Potentiate, I order you not to do this."

The women only hesitated a moment, glancing at each other nervously. Then one of the black-clad women uncoiled a heavy chain, and in horror, Victory realized that one end was already hanging from the man's metal collar, dangling against his broad, brown native chest. Seeing that, it took every ounce of willpower Victory had to keep her voice steady. "I am the next Empress of this planet, and I'm *commanding* you to stop."

"Sorry, milady," the Praetorian said, sounding sincerely apologetic. "It was the Adjudicator's orders." When the Praetorian woman reached for the band of metal her father's smiths had sealed around Victory's waist, her nerves finally failed her. Letting out a terrified cry, she tried to bolt. Two of the four House Praetorian lunged and caught her, then held her easily as the woman fed the chain through the loop in her belt.

As the tether rattled against the titanium band encircling her hips, Victory felt the world shift, felt herself on a cold dirt floor, naked, hands bound painfully behind her back as a huge form grunted over her. A huge form much like the one standing before her, with similar brown, sun-darkened skin and long, lean face. Feeling the Praetorian retrieve the flash-welder from her pocket and start sealing the leash binding them together, Victory whimpered and clung to the women holding her, putting them between herself and the native. "Please don't leave me with him," she whimpered. "Please." Her breath was starting to burn in her throat, and she couldn't seem to get enough air.

"I'm sorry, Milady," the Praetorian woman said. Her words sounded genuine, even anguished.

They're going to leave me alone with him, she realized. With it, came a new wave of horrible sensations. She could feel their big bodies moving against hers, hunched over her, their fingers probing, penetrating. Their demonic faces were wet with sweat, her thighs wet with their remains. She felt her own anguish welling back up from within, her own terror choking her through the gag.

Shivering all over, Victory caught the man watching her.

It was only for a second, his deep blue eyes flickering across hers before he quickly dropped his gaze back to the floor, but it was enough to break what little hold Victory had on her body. She lunged and fought like a wild thing, biting and clawing, screaming curses as she tore at the House Praetorian that held her.

She might as well have been battering statues.

The women efficiently finished welding the chain in place, then released Victory, bowed, and turned to go.

Seeing them retreat, Victory went utterly still, her terror ratcheting up another notch. So terrified she couldn't move, couldn't breathe, couldn't think, she managed, "Wait!" She found herself suddenly frozen in place, with the stranger between her and the door. "Please don't..." she swallowed, hard, forcing out the words through bile, "leave me...

with him." *Oh gods, please, no...*She swallowed again, fighting a building animal terror that was clawing its way up from within. "Please." It came out as a barely-controlled rasp, and she hated the way it sounded like begging.

One of the House Praetorian slowed and gave the huge slave an uncomfortable look. "Your father's orders, Princess. The Adjudicator says at least a couple weeks." The woman licked her lips, looking up at the slave's massive frame. "Just endure for a couple weeks and I'm sure your father will tell us to take the brute back to the stables."

A couple weeks? Victory's startled mind screamed. She'd die. She couldn't survive a *day*, let alone a *week*.

But then the woman bowed and followed her brethren from the room, passing by Victory's scowling personal Praetorian on the way— four women wearing the symbol of the Phoenix-and-Egg, instead of the House Phoenix-and-Dragon—and bowed again before yanking the door shut, leaving Victory alone with the looming stranger.

Though she had spent the last five days preparing herself, only eight feet from his massive body, Victory sank against the wall in terror, her breath speeding up in her chest. *Oh gods,* she thought, drawing the chain tight as she tried to crawl backwards across the wall. *Oh gods oh gods.*

As soon as the chain went taut, and she got a feel of just how *close* the man would be to her, permanently, something within her snapped and Victory began scrambling like a wild thing, tugging and pulling, panting, screaming as her mind evaporated in terror.

The man stepped forward, loosening the chain.

Victory's entire world narrowed to the line that had slackened between them.

"Stay back!" she screamed, clawing to get back to her feet, a hand up between them. "Stay *back!*" She started backing away, looking for some weapon, some tool.

"Sorry," he whispered to the floor.

The sound of the native tongue drove a nail through Victory's chest. She sank to the floor, remembering what happened when those sounds were made. She was once more chained to a post, exposed to the elements, begging for food or clothes, hoping the man who brought them didn't want something in exchange. Whimpering, she drew her knees up to her chin and wrapped her arms around her shins and started to shiver.

"Please don't hurt me," she whimpered, watching the scene in her mind. "Please, please, please…"

CHAPTER 3

To the Princess Bound

S o this was why he had been taken from his home at gunpoint. They wanted him to serve a royal woman. Naked, humiliated, Dragomir stared at the floor with bitter resignation as the black-clad Praetorian led him into the room. He knew what they would want him to do, and he despised the thought. He'd heard of similar things happening all over Mercy. The Imperials looked upon the Mercerians as little more than animals, and abducted them from their villages at a whim. It had probably been his size that had attracted Imperial attention. Most Mercerians were much smaller, care of cold winters and wartime malnutrition, and Dragomir had stood almost a head over most of the men in Sodstone. With the Imperials taking millions of slaves throughout Mercy each day, Dragomir might as well have painted a neon target on his back and danced through the front lines—sooner or later, they were going to find him.

Hopefully, the royal woman would grow tired of him and he could somehow find a way home. With the Imperial invasion in full force, there was much sickness in the Silversand Mountains. The village of Sodstone needed its healer.

Besides, as long as Life was going to stubbornly keep him alive despite his wishes, Dragomir wanted to get back to Sodstone to meet this soul that had been teasing him across the end of that massive link. A woman. In pain. It had been almost a month, now, and he felt no closer to meeting her than he had when the connection had knocked him out of his chair.

As they led him toward the woman huddled against the wall, he kept his eyes down, as he had been told to do between the beatings leading up to this. The man's blazing green stare still haunted him. *You will do exactly as she tells you, instantly, without hesitation.*

But Dragomir had been close enough to feel the man, and his green-eyed tormentor had been in great anger and pain inside, so much of it leveled against Dragomir that it made no sense. In between lashings, he had snarled dire warnings of what would happen to him—and his village—if he hurt her in any way…

…and then he had told Dragomir to help her.

Dragomir was still bitterly puzzling through that when the Praetorian tugged him to a halt about six feet from the jewel-clad woman on the floor. As he stood there, tense, he blinked when he felt the fear feeling washing off of the royal woman in cold, *rama*-clenching waves.

…Fear?

Dragomir kept his head down, but frowned. She was afraid of the Praetorian? Her own royal guard?

Then she stood up, and in a commanding voice, said something in Imperial. The Praetorian responded with a polite bow and a few crisp words, then the room suddenly exploded in a blast of gut-wrenching terror. Dragomir choked on it, having to shield himself from the energy before he was washed away in it.

Out of the corner of his eye, he saw the royal woman try to bolt. The Praetorian caught her, and the fear in the room began to build, radiating from the robed woman like blood spilling from a severed limb thrust into a bath of water. Soon the room was awash with it, so thick Dragomir was having trouble breathing. He heard the woman whimper and babble in Imperial.

He had a sudden, strong vision of a man atop him, pinning him to the ground, grunting with the sounds of passion. His eyes flickered toward the woman in shock. *She thinks I'm going to…?*

Their eyes met, and her emerald eyes went wide. In that moment, Dragomir felt like he'd been hit by a sledgehammer. He *knew* this woman. He didn't know from what time, or place, but he knew her. The feeling went all the way to his core. He felt a connection buried there, something very old…

No. His heart began to hammer like a sledge in his chest. The soul-link, made from across an entire planet, completely dormant, yet *still* radiating residual fear to him for an entire month…It was *her*?

A thousand questions pounded through Dragomir's mind with each thunderous beat of his heart. Had the Imperials found some way to trap Emps? Was the woman a decoy? Was she faking her terror? How had they found him? How did they even *know*? Was she, too, an Emp? A royal Emp? Or a betrayer? An Emp seeking out other Emps, turning them over to the Imperials for land and money, forging connections with strangers to make it impossible for them to hide? Had she located him in trance, then sent her minions out to find him?

Dragomir was about to throw up a shield around himself and fight in earnest when the woman suddenly started screaming and battering at the Praetorian, wrenching him back to the present. Her terror amplified, slamming Dragomir out of his light trance, seeping into his *au*, its raw power threatening to overwhelm him.

Whatever the fear was, it was genuine. Not an Emp, then. A royal? One of the legendary brainiacs that the Imperials put on pedestals and worshipped as demigods? One of the mutant descendants from early cryogenic space travel who, using their increased brainpower, had wrested control of the Imperium from the other Gifted? That could explain its strength. And magnified by the dormant connection they shared…

Oh gods, he thought, when he realized that even his strongest shields weren't going to be enough. The connection was so strong that it was impossible for him to hide from her emotions, there being a direct channel—however dormant—between himself and the woman for the energy to tumble down. In a moment or two, her fear was going to seep into him, and he was going to try and bolt.

If he did, it would probably earn him another week on the rack, enduring the green-eyed man's fury. If they even let him live at all.

In desperation, Dragomir did what he did back in the village, when trying to determine the root cause of an illness. He opened himself fully to the terror. He threw each *rama* wide-open, so he could fully experience her emotions with her.

He grunted with the impact.

Men. Many of them. They suffocated him in a wash of pain, brutality, and horror. He heard their voices—in lies, in passion, in violence, in disdain. They told him they were going to kill him, that he was not worth the time it took for them to use his body, then took him anyway, violent and painful. They told him he was dirty, that he needed perfume. He felt the rotten fish on his back, chest, his knees. He felt the cold, the rain, the snow.

He whimpered, but somehow kept his feet steady, knowing that the visions were not his own.

Then whose are they? he wondered. The woman on the floor was dressed in the greatest gems and finery that Mercy could produce, and she smelled of perfume and flowers. Her bedroom was lavishly appointed with rugs, silks, furs, tapestries, curtains. She lived in a palace crafted of solid black marble, with gold and silver designs inlaid into the floor, ceiling, and walls. Thousands of Dragomir's brethren had been enslaved to cater to her every need.

The Praetorian got up and left, and, when the woman tried unsuccessfully to stop them, more visions assaulted him. His body was bartered and sold. He was paraded by a metal collar around his neck, brought into roomful after roomful of lewd, dirty men, and was only allowed to eat his meager ration for the day after the last one had taken their fill of him. He saw his belly swell up, experienced the horror of an impassive old man reaching inside, pulling his baby out, dropping it into the trash. He felt a shot in the arm, was told it would never happen again.

Dragomir gasped and opened his eyes as the chain started yanking tight against the metal collar around his neck. Again and again, the princess slammed into it, screaming and wailing and thrashing like a wild thing.

He stepped forward, despite himself.

The woman on the other end froze, and he felt the terror of the room crack outward like a rifle retort. She screamed something at him in Imperial, holding her hand up between them. Then she was sliding backwards on the end of the chain connecting them…

…connecting them?

What is going on here? he thought, deeply disturbed upon seeing the metal belt encasing her waist, the loop in its center holding the chain linked to his collar. *Why doesn't she just take it off?*

It took him a moment to realize that she couldn't. The Praetorian had welded the chain in place.

He saw her scramble backwards, her panicked green eyes obviously searching for some weapon she could use against him.

"Sorry," Dragomir whispered. He wanted to say more, but, even if he hadn't been admonished by the green-eyed man not to open his mouth, the spasm of terror that followed his voice was enough to stop him. He kept his eyes down, the healer in him trying to decide just what was happening. The connection was puzzling enough, but the horrible visions left him disturbed.

Bad dreams? Night terrors? Dragomir didn't think the explanation was so simple. Perhaps the cause was deeper. Was she remembering some former life? Some horror-ridden existence on Mercy, many years ago? Or was she simply serving as the channel to another lonely woman, experiencing what the woman was going through? Perhaps this Imperial royal had a split-Gift—and the habit of forging connections with random strangers. Dragomir felt for a link to another woman, some sort of conduit that could be powering the visions, but found that every one of the woman's energy centers were bound, if not completely closed. Most of her links to others had been cut off long ago by the closing of her heart-*rama*.

In fact, with the blockages stopping up her gi, he only found two connections. The first was withered, emaciated from years of disuse, but it still had loving emerald *gi* flowing down it, trying in vain to push past the clamped rama petals to feed the center's malnourished core. It was a small, but steady trickle. Like a hand-pump or garden hose.

The second connection wound straight to his heart.

It was much larger, like a massive river-channel, but shadowy and inactive. Beside the tiny trickle of the emerald gi-link, Dragomir's link to the princess was deep, a vast, empty canal. It had no flow of *gi*, but the potential was there, and its power breathtaking, strong enough for Dragomir's heart to skip. The translucent, dormant link was an open connection just aching to be realized. He had no doubt that, the moment she relaxed enough to open her *rama*, the connection was going to knock him completely to his knees.

Oh no, Dragomir thought, feeling a welling of dread as he watched that massive, humming connection, just aching for its mate. *I can't do this. Not again.* The way the link was vibrating in his mind's eye, Dragomir knew that it was close, that any tiny trigger could set it off. He tried to shy away, to pull back.

But the visions kept bombarding him, shattering his defenses. They kept getting stronger, more violent, and they didn't appear to have an outside source. *They must be coming from within*, he thought, confused. He saw the visions emanating from her throat, her heart, her liver, her womb, her core…About the only *rama* unaffected was her mind-*rama*, and it was completely shut down, the terror and images spiraling up from the lesser *ramas* making it lock itself away, leaving the lower *ramas* of instinct and emotion in charge. Above it, the soul-*rama* had withdrawn, leaving the body to stagnate in its own emotions without the guiding hand of previous lifetimes of soul-knowledge.

Without a healthy window into her spirit's great wisdom and calm, she was trapped in the growing cycle of panicked silver *gi* building and spiraling within her lower *ramas*, crashing within her like a full-force hurricane.

She was rocking back and forth, now, babbling something under her breath.

On instinct, Dragomir closed his eyes and found the humming crystalline core that was his center. He sank his mind into it, allowing the terror rushing through him to disintegrate under its power. Then, gathering this calm, he gently reached out to her with his heart-*rama*, surrounding her with the tranquility, peace, and love that made up the essence of that energy center.

He tried to forge a new link—*not* the dormant one, which he knew was in danger of exploding into being with the slightest touch—to feed his *gi* inside her body, but with her *ramas* all cinched shut on the tornado within, all he could do was give her external peace. He concentrated on that, flooding her *au* with gentle, reassuring heart-*rama* energy. The color changed from panicked flashes of sickly orange, red, and brown, to a warm gold as his own energy began to seep into the outer edges of the *au*, then slowly spread deeper, until it was touching the edges of her physical body.

Her rocking slowed, then finally stopped. Dragomir let out a pent-up breath as he felt as the *ramas* slowly stopped pouring their poison into her being. A few moments later, her heart rama unfolded a tentative petal. Then another. As gently as he could, Dragomir brushed it with the golden energy of his core. A tiny, needle-sized passage opened within it, and the emaciated, emerald-laced *gi* link he had seen before jumped to push energy through it, into her center, instinctively trying to re-activate the neglected rama with a flow of emerald *gi*.

The other connection, Dragomir's, the bigger, dormant one, had started to almost keen with the intensity of its hum, almost painful to Dragomir's mind as his soul ached to make the connection and help her. *Life*, it seemed, wanted him to seal that connection and surrender to her. For whatever reason, this royal, like that pretty gray filly, had been chosen for healing.

No. He actually had to avoid looking at that massive channel in his mind's eye, just to keep from getting sucked in at the *need* buried there. Life had guided Dragomir to this woman, but he would help her on his own terms. He would not be surrendering to a royal, opening his heart to one of the invaders of this planet. After Meggie, he would rather die.

But he was a healer, and the healer in him instinctively wanted to help this woman. To do that, he had to figure out what was going on. Avoiding the massive, dormant connection lest he accidentally trigger something he couldn't take back, Dragomir gently grabbed the tiny green tendril woven through the rama's petals and used it as a tether to carefully ease his consciousness into the swirling energy beyond.

He was staggered by what he found.

Unlike the screaming visage of terror that her body portrayed, the woman was a well of depth and passion. He saw the loving, nurturing experiences of thousands of rich lifetimes stored within, all caged by the cold, brutal set of memories that had erupted only a moment ago. Her trust, her love, was bound. He tested the cage gently, found it firm. The ramas themselves were utterly choked with the visions that plagued her, but he could find no outward connection that could be producing the images other than the emerald gi-line. Troubled, he backed out of the heart-*rama* and turned to follow the emerald strand to its owner.

An old soul. One who, like this woman, had experienced many, many lives in the past. A man…

Dragomir froze when he realized which man. He was ringed so heavily in worry and fury that there was no mistake. It was the green-eyed general who had took him from his home, humiliated him, and whipped him bloody. The shock quickly launched Dragomir back to his body, and he jerked with the impact.

They're siblings, he realized.

• • •

Victory had felt her mind shutting down, her consciousness disconnecting from the sensations roiling within her body, when it had suddenly felt as if someone had taken a warm blanket and draped it over her shoulders. She froze, checking to make sure the brute hadn't moved.

He remained where he was, tethered at the end of his chain, head down, his manhood pointed at the floor, eyes closed.

She sucked in a shuddering breath as she felt the warmth spread around her, easing the pent-up pain in her chest. She slowly let her breath out through chattering teeth, feeling the panic slowly drop away.

When she looked up, the man was watching her again.

Instantly, his blue eyes widened and his heavy jaw flinched as he lowered his gaze, biting his lip.

Victory felt a surge of panic try to rush through her again, but it seemed sluggish, less insistent. The fear lasted a few heart-pounding moments, then slid back to where it had come from. Her alarm faded faster than ever before. She once again found the courage to look at his body.

He was every bit as big as she had first feared. Easily six and a half feet, with heavy muscles padding his bronze chest, shoulders, arms, and torso. When she brought herself to bring her gaze downward, she found that, with his arms shackled behind his back, his nakedness was displayed for her there, hands useless to hide it. Like his body, his genitals were large and brown, and rested gently upon two great thighs. His highly-defined calves led into strong ankles, around each was a sturdy band of metal, linked together by a short chain.

Victory knew he was aware of her perusal because he bit his lip and looked away; the side of his face that she could see flushed in shame.

For the first time in years, Victory felt a rush of triumph. Unlike so many times in her past, when she'd been stripped, fondled, licked, entered, this time *she* was the one who could look. *She* was the one who could do as she wished. *He* was the one absolutely helpless to stop her.

Excitement and anger overcame the last vestiges of Victory's fear. She stood up, slowly. At the movement of the chain, the man's eyes flickered, but he kept his head down.

He's mine, Victory thought, a thrill of vicious anticipation rushing up her core, riding the back of a furious need for vengeance. *I can do anything I want with him.*

He met her eyes, then, and there was understanding, there. And fear. "When did you start having the visions?" he asked softly.

All of her newfound confidence shattered instantly at the sound of his crude native tongue. Victory jerked away from him, yanking the chain tight between them, making him grunt with the strain on his neck. She screamed, out of instinct, and yanked again, turning to scramble for the bed.

"I'm sorry!" the man cried. "I'm so sorry. Please." He stumbled after her.

"*Stop talking!*" Victory shrieked, climbing backwards over the bed, putting it between them.

The man hesitated at the edge of the bed, looking down at the obstacle with trepidation. Even as big as he was, with as little room the chain gave his stride, he would have trouble crossing it.

Victory huddled at the edge of the chain on the other side, dropping to the floor once more, taking comfort in that small barrier between them. *What do I do?* she thought, her entire body shuddering with fear and adrenaline. The panic was spiraling upwards again, and her breath was beginning to come in fast, short heaves. With the panic, came the memories.

Victory cringed as she once more found herself chained to a pole, her back cold against the wet ground, a warm body pressing into her, licking her face, twisting her breasts, calling her his 'imperial slut.' She let out a miserable whimper, trying not to watch the flashing memories, unable to stop herself.

She was on her stomach in the dark. Her head was covered, her hands lashed behind her back, her ankles tied. She was still wearing the red and black Imperial Academy uniform she had put on that morning for the two-month, sixteen-jump journey to the Core. She remembered a jolt in the ship, fire, a horrible shrieking sound, and the sound of men's voices, yelling. Gunshots, her bodyguards dropping around her...

The warm-blanket sensation wrapped her once more, restoring that sense of security she hadn't felt since that first, horrible night.

Across the bed, the man got to his knees, then lowered himself to his rear, back against the bed. At first, Victory's panic surged again at the movement, but when she realized she could no longer see him, she slowly relaxed, leaning her ear against the edge of the mattress.

Somehow, the bed between them helped to alleviate some of her fears. The tightness in her chest was no longer an overwhelming, all-encompassing terror. Instead, it began to settle in her gut once more, taking the images with it. Within the next few minutes, Victory's breathing and heart-rate slowed, until she was simply staring at the delicately-embroidered blanket, following the silver and gold patterns with her eyes.

She watched the antique dials on the cherrywood grandfather clock as several hours went by, the two of them separated by the width of the bed. Victory heard absolutely no sound on the slave's end, and wondered if he was asleep.

What am I going to do? she thought again, miserable. Just *looking* at the brute sent her into an uncontrollable spiral of pain and memories. And somehow her father wanted her to spend weeks like this? *Months?* It wasn't possible. She would die of heart failure before that.

Victory heard the man shift on the other side of the bed and she froze, her eyes riveted to the chain as it moved slightly over the covers. When it stopped, she let out the breath she had been holding and balled her trembling fingers into the blankets in relief.

"Sorry," he said, as if he could feel her spike of panic. "I had to move. My hands—"

"*Stop talking*," Victory bit out in the native tongue. She hadn't had to use the language of her captors for two whole months, and when she did, every muscle in her body began to shake, remembering.

He fell silent, but only for awhile. Softly, he said, "When did your visions start?"

Victory froze. *Visions?*

"I think I might know what's happening," the man ventured. "Sometimes past lives resurface into current ones, interrupting the flow of—"

His words choked off when Victory grabbed the chain and yanked it, hard. "Be *quiet*," she snarled.

"I can help you," the man said.

Victory felt a desperate surge of hope, warm and unusual in her chest, but then dashed it aside in anger. "Quiet."

"I really can," the man whispered.

Victory yanked the chain again. "I *own* you, slave," she snarled. "I told you to be *quiet*."

And he was.

A half hour before dinnertime, there came a polite knock on her door. A maid's voice called tentatively, "Supper will be in the great hall in thirty minutes, milady."

Victory's stomach tightened, but she said nothing. She had learned to live with hunger. She could out-wait her father.

Twenty minutes later, another knock. "Dinner will be in ten minutes, milady. Will you be joining us?"

"No!" Victory screamed, adrenaline powering her lungs. "Leave me alone!"

Fifteen minutes later, another gentle knock on the solid wooden door. "They are eating, milady. Your lord father the Adjudicator has decreed that you shall not eat unless you do so at his table."

"*Leave!*"

She heard footsteps bolt down the hall.

Dinnertime came and went, and Victory never moved from where she squatted beside the bed. Sure enough, as promised, there were no more knocks on her door. Victory relaxed her head against the bed with a whimper. Hours passed like that, and she fell into a light doze.

"You were a slave in another life," the man said softly, making her jump. "You were on a ship, headed to a school, when your ship was attacked. You spent many years humiliated and scorned."

Victory jerked awake and frowned. Her family had taken great pains to keep her capture a secret. The fact that someone had told a humble slave, and a native, at that, was degrading. Probably yet another 'lesson' her father had decided she needed to learn. "Shut up."

But he kept talking. "For some reason, you were a great prize. They took you to large meeting-places and let everyone there laugh and spit on you while others violated you. They raped you and rubbed rotten fish into your skin. They chained you to a post and left you out in the cold, to face the elements in rags. You probably died like that, because that's where the memories end."

Victoria tensed. She had never told anyone about the fish.

"I think this must have been your last life, because it is so powerfully connected with this one," the man said softly. He rustled on the floor, the chain jerking against the bed. Then he was kneeling, his big body large enough to allow him to look over the lip of the bed at her. His blue eyes were kind. "It's also probably why you're a princess in this life. The wheels of Spirit make beggars out of kings, and emperors out of slaves. You experienced one extreme, thus you were given the other. The spirit thrives on contrast. It helps us to grow. It is the Cycle."

Victoria huddled further beneath the side of the bed, out of sight, her heart hammering. "I told you to be quiet."

"I'm not going to hurt you," the man said softly.

Those words were like razors in her mind. Instantly, she saw a blue-eyed man hovering over her, a knife in his hand.

"Shhhhh," he said, kneeling beside her bound body. He unzipped her Academy jacket and pulled it aside. Then he slipped his knife under her Academy blouse. "I'm not going to hurt you, Princess," he whispered, the scar on his lip puckering with his grin. She felt the cold back of the blade press into her skin, heard the fabric rip…

Victory screamed and started clambering backwards, snapping the chain taut as the blue-eyed man's foul breath filled her face. "I'm not going to hurt you," he said again, as his filthy hand found her breast, kneaded it. "Shhhhh." She screamed through the gag as he slid his hand toward her pants.

"That man isn't real!" her slave shouted, over the bed. "He's meaningless to you! He's from another life!"

His booming voice shattered the stench of the scarred man's cloying breath and Victory, seeing herself back in her room, laying on the thick woolen carpets instead of on the cold metal grate of a raider's ship, sucked in a huge breath and let it out in a long, horrible sob, sinking into the floor.

A loud knock sounded on the door, and her head Praetorian's commanding voice shouted, "Is everything all right in there, Princess?"

Victory hunched on the floor, whimpering, the remnants of the vision draining with her tears.

The Praetorian captain opened the door, then looked inside. Seeing Victory curled on the floor, Lion quickly stalked inside, unsheathing her blade. An instant later, her blade was pressed against the slave's throat, and Victory felt the belt around her waist tighten as the man tensed backwards to the end of his tether.

"Did he hurt you, milady?" the gray-haired Praetorian demanded. "I heard shouting."

Victory whimpered and pushed her face into the floor, rocking it back and forth, allowing the intricate weave to soak up her tears. She knew, beyond a doubt, that if she allowed Lion to kill the man, her father would see to it she would be chained to a *corpse* for a few years, instead. If only that didn't seem the better alternative…

For a long time, Lion stood there, looking from Victory to the slave, then back. Finally, she bowed deeply. "I apologize for the intrusion, milady." She sheathed her sword and stalked back outside.

"No," Victory whimpered. "Come back."

Then the door was shut, and she was once more alone with the slave.

Victory squeezed her eyes shut and sobbed into the rug.

"When did you start having the visions?" the man asked, for the third time.

"What visions?" Victory asked in misery from the floor.

"Like the one just now, with the man cutting open your blouse. When did they start?"

Victory froze, every muscle in her body going utterly still. She twisted slowly on the floor, then carefully got to her feet, every single hair on her body prickling with goosebumps as she turned back to look at the slave.

The man was sitting up, watching her.

"You're a Psi," she whispered, on a surge of horror. She backed to the end of the tether, staring at him.

The man nodded, slowly, blue eyes searching hers.

Her breath tightened in her chest. Long-term space travel—jumps, in particular—produced strange effects on stored embryos and sperm, and the original colonists to Mercy, over five hundred years ago, had found their destination planet to be uninhabitable, and had struck out on a desperate-man's voyage deep into the galaxy back when long-term space travel was still a new and dangerous frontier. Consequently, when they by chance found a rocky planet with a habitable atmosphere, they dipped heavily into the cryogenic genetics database to help replace the numbers they had lost on the voyage.

Due to that, Mercy had left an overabundance of Psi, as well as Kin, Shi, and other unnatural human-base mutations. Once the original Liberated Assemblage of Planets sponsoring the colonies failed, almost four hundred and fifty years ago, Mercy was left to survive on its own, and the Psis were allowed to reproduce in the gene pool. When the Imperium emerged, three hundred and fifty years after that, it began re-claiming the colonies that had survived.

Then, once the jump-mutations were recognized, the Imperium had given every sub-Empire orders to exterminate on sight. Eliminating Psis and other human-base mutations had been the Imperium's first order of business, once her father had landed with his fleet. Psi natives had been hunted for decades. They thought they had got them all.

Victoria, seeing a way to remove the man from her belt permanently, opened her mouth to scream for the guards.

She saw the man's blue eyes drop, saw the resignation in his face.

He just put his life in my hands.

Victory hesitated, frowning at him. Softly, she said, "You know I could have you killed."

He gave her a tired, tentative smile. "Princess, from the looks of things, you could have me killed at any time."

Instinctively, Victory glanced at the nick in his throat left by the Praetorian's blade. It was still oozing a slow line of crimson down his neck.

She bit her lip, once again glancing at the door. *If I have them take him away*, she thought, *Father would just find someone else.*

And a Psi was...

...*interesting*. She had always wanted to meet one. As children, she and Matthias had planned to go out and capture a Psi and bring him back to be their playmate. Their father, upon hearing of their plans, had been furious, and had claimed that, had the Imperium learned of their antics, it would have had them both removed as Adjudicator Potentiates. Speaking of Psis—or any of their genetic kin—had been absolutely forbidden from that point on, which had only made her and Matthias more determined to find one.

And now she had one, not eight feet away. The only problem was that his every move made six years of terror stir within her.

He started to get up, exposing more of his big body to her.

Victory quickly huddled down behind the bed again. "Stay where you are!"

On the other side of the massive bed, the Psi stilled. Victory listened to his breathing, watching his knees under the bed. After another twenty minutes passed, he said, "Princess, if you're not going to have me killed, I need to relieve myself. I've been holding it since this morning."

Victory closed her eyes and drew herself into a fetal position on the floor. She had been dreading this. The lavatory was immense, the toilet located a good ten feet inside the doorway, trapping her inside with him. She said nothing, hoping that his urge would go away.

"This is a very nice rug," the man commented.

Victory winced. Slowly, carefully, she sat up and peered over the mattress at him. She swallowed at the thought of crossing it, once more leaving nothing but chain between them.

"Are you really a Psi?" she whispered, searching his cerulean eyes. Somehow, with their bodies hidden from each other by the bed, it was easier to cope with his presence.

His face twisted in a strained smile. "A Psi that's about to pee himself."

A third of her wanted to tell him to pee—that she wasn't going to get anywhere near him. Another third of her didn't want to deal with the smell of urine until one of her maids came to clean it up. The last third was caught between the horror of seeing his body again, and the horrible bad form of not even giving him a proper place to relieve himself.

"I'm not going to hurt you," the man said softly. "I can't." He jingled the shackles holding his arms behind his back.

Of course he could. A Psi could destroy one's thoughts, change one's memories, speak inside the mind...

Then a more disturbing thought occurred to her. *A man doesn't need his arms to hold a woman down and use her.*

"Is there a chamberpot on your side?" the man asked, desperation in his voice. "You can just slide it over to my side of the bed and I'll make do."

Victory frowned, struck from that thought by the barbarian's provinciality. "This is a civilized household. We have a composting toilet."

The Psi whimpered and dropped his head to the bed, face down. "I'm gonna have to pee the rug, aren't I?"

Victory gnashed her lip between her teeth, considering. Finally, she said, "I'm going to come over there." Then, as his head darted up in gratitude, she growled, "But don't *move* until I'm on the other side."

He nodded, his blue eyes pleading.

Victory swallowed and started to crawl over the bed, but stopped when more of his body was revealed. She shrank back, fear and dread wrenching her gut.

The Psi said nothing, just remained absolutely still, like a woodsman trying to tame a wild animal. "Would it help if I looked away?" he asked softly.

He knows I'm afraid of him, Victory thought, fighting humiliation. She was a *princess* and he was a *slave* and she couldn't come within six feet from him without bawling like a terrified child.

She yanked a sheet off of the bed and threw it over him, so that it covered his face, head, and body. He remained motionless, a black mound of embroidered cloth.

"Stay there," Victory said, hating the trembling in her voice.

He nodded against the sheet.

She bit her lip, watching the fabric move with his breathing. It didn't hide what it concealed, but at least it made it easier to stomach. Reluctantly, Victory began crawling across the bed. The last two feet before the other side, with the man's big body only a couple feet away, her nerves finally failed her and she made a panicked scramble, lunging to her feet and hitting the end of the chain, hard.

The man grunted, but otherwise remained silent.

"Get up," Victory managed, every nerve humming. "Leave the sheet where it is."

"I don't know how well it will stay on," the Psi said, "But I can try." He eased backwards over his feet, then stood up.

Victory gasped. She had forgotten how big he was. "Get low," she babbled, looking away. "Gods…" She stared at the floor, feeling like she was going to vomit.

He hunched under the sheet, so it looked like he was barely taller than she. "Better?" he asked.

"Much," she whispered, trying to keep her utter gratitude from showing. She looked at the door to the lavatory, her heart-rate already starting that frenzied climb. "Follow me." She led him, shuffling and hunched under his sheet, to the restroom. She opened the door, and only then did she realize her problem. The toilet was far in the back, near the large stone basin tub. She could let him step inside first, but then he would have no idea where to go with the sheet over his head. And she was not about to take his hand and guide him.

The second problem was that the toilet seat lid was down, the room ever-so-thoughtfully maintained by her household staff.

If she led him into the room to lift the seat, she would be trapping herself. A spike of terror began worming its way through her gut as she considered being pinned against the wall by his massive body while he—

"I just want to pee," he promised. "I don't care where or how at this point."

She flinched, glancing back at the lump of sheet. *He can read my mind,* she thought, unnerved. Then, biting her lip, she snatched a heavy golden mermaid-statue off of the shelf beside the door. With it in a fist, she found the confidence to continue. "I'm going to lead you in. When I tell you to stop, you *stop.* Understand? You don't, and I'm gonna cave your skull in."

He nodded, a bobbing in the sheet.

Swallowing hard, Victory moved into the lavatory, pulling him with her.

He never stumbled, never slowed. When he reached the shift from carpet to tiled stone, he didn't flinch or hesitate. He walked through the door and kept moving.

It's almost like he can see through the sheet, Victory thought, frowning. As far as she knew, Psis couldn't see or affect anything but another mind.

She backed to the toilet, then, still watching him carefully, squatted to lift the seat. Then she backed up, crawled over the edge of the huge white marble tub, then climbed onto the shelf on the far side, against the wall, gripping the statue in a white-knuckled fist. *You're trapping yourself,* a frantic voice in her mind started to babble. *You've got nowhere to run...*

"Stop," she said.

But he was already turning, and she watched as he squatted forward over the toilet, sheet blocking her view. At the first sounds of liquid hitting the bowl, she swallowed and looked away.

"Ohthankgods." The big man let out a huge sigh and thumped his sheet-covered forehead against the wall.

"Done?" Victory demanded, disgusted by her father's cruelty. When *she* was Adjudicator, she would make an Imperial decree that slaves could not be chained to living beings. Such was barbarism of the highest degree.

"Yes," he said, sounding utterly relieved. "Thank you."

"Turn around and walk out," Victory snapped, to keep the desperation out of her voice. What if he didn't turn? What if he didn't obey her? What if he decided to, instead, step into the bath with her and—

He turned and shuffled back towards the door.

Once he was well out of reach, Victory followed gingerly, but hesitated at the toilet, the thought of revisiting the whole nerve-wracking experience again in an hour making her feel sick. And yet, the thought of performing a function so private, within eight feet of a naked man, left her nauseous.

The Psi, once the chain went taut between them, stopped.

Seeing him wait there, patiently, Victory made her decision.

"Don't turn around," Victory whispered, her voice thick with shame. She squatted and, as quickly as she could, finished her business, then sent the result to the composter. She was shaking by the time she got back to her feet.

The Psi waited, motionless, hunched over as low as his big body could go without falling over.

"Back to the bed," Victory said, too mortified to speak more than a whisper.

The Psi moved flawlessly towards the bed, then, without being told, knelt again on the floor at his side.

Once she was sure he wasn't going to try and move, Victory rushed past him and flung herself across the bed, then dropped into a huddle on the other side. She grabbed her ankles and, bringing her knees up under her chin, closed her eyes and started rocking against the images that began invading her consciousness from having come within arm's reach. Men, their big arms reaching out, with her chained, nowhere to run…

"They're not real," the man said softly, from under the sheet. "They happened in another life."

Victory's eyes narrowed at the edge of the mattress. "That's where you're wrong." She hadn't meant to say it, and wasn't sure she had, but she felt the man's breath catch.

"Oh my gods," he whispered.

CHAPTER 4

Understanding

Her voice had been low and quiet, but it had also been laced with bitterness and contempt. "That's where you're wrong."

Dragomir felt his breath catch, losing control of his emotions for the first time since the prince invaded his home and dragged him, alone, back onto the ship. He felt the energy around him spike with horror even as his heart rama flung itself wide open, releasing a floodgate of compassion. "Oh my gods."

She said nothing, hunched in silence on the other side of the bed.

Suddenly, everything he had seen within her heart-rama began to make sense. Automatically, he found himself feeding his consciousness back through the tiny needle-entrance to get another look. The cruel visions of pain and humiliation were strangling the rich silver *gi* inside, choking the rama to a tiny shadow of what it could have been.

"They *took* you," he managed, shocked. "The rebels took you."

She didn't respond physically, but her heart-rama slammed shut and her energy solidified around her, forcing his consciousness back outside her *au*. He heard a small sound, low and quiet. Dragomir, frustrated, twisted his hands in their shackles. She needed to be held—every inch of him could feel it. Chained and hobbled like he was, though, any movement he made would only scare her.

"I'll hold you, if you want," he finally offered. Perhaps, if he had any luck, she could feel the dormant connection between them. If she did, it might make her more willing to trust him. If she didn't, he was walking on glass. Most non-Gifted, he had noticed, rarely felt such things, or even believed they existed.

The crying stopped for a moment, and he winced. When she didn't scream disgusted curses at him, as he expected, he allowed himself a bit of hope.

"Stop talking," she said. Her voice was ice.

Once again, he was reminded that the woman had the power of life or death over him, and that she was very close to exercising it. Again, Dragomir wondered what had he been thinking, telling her—a *royal princess*—that he was a 'mutagenic anomaly,' as the Imperium liked to call it. The Imperials *killed* people like him. By all rights, she should have called in her guard the moment he let it slip what he was. Yet, for some unknown reason, this girl who was so obviously terrified of him had let him live. Why?

Unhappily, he closed his eyes and focused on reaching into his core and sending what warmth he could, in his own humiliated state.

After a moment, she quieted. Her rama petals ticked open a bit, once again allowing a thin stream of his golden *gi* to pass beyond its protective shell.

She gasped. "*You're* doing that, aren't you?"

Dragomir froze. He had long ago learned that the Imperials feared what they didn't understand. And one of the things that Imperials could not seem to grasp was that Emps *could not* hurt people. It was against their nature. Yet, by Imperial decree, Emps were cancerous tumors of society that needed to be excised before they murdered whole villages 'as they had on the core planets.' Official Imperial policy, last he heard, was that Emps were mass-murderers.

Yet, if Emps were psychopathic serial-killers, how did the Imperials manage to snatch them from their homes and drag them to the heads-man's block without losing hundreds of soldiers in the process? It was a small thing for Dragomir to cut a few gi lines and prematurely end a life. He assumed that his brethren—those who hadn't been hunted and killed by the invaders—could do the same. Yet, despite the capability,

Dragomir never had. Even the Praetorian who had deserved it most had died by Dragomir's fists, instead. He'd never *heard* of an Emp hurting someone with their gift. It just wasn't done.

"Answer me," the princess grated.

Dragomir lowered his forehead to stare at the blanket, dark beneath the sheet. He felt his own life balancing on his next word. "Yes," he managed.

She hissed, half snarl, half rage, and fisted her hand in the tether at his neck, pulling it tight. "You dare?!" He knew then that she was going to kill him. He could feel it rolling off of her in a sick, black rage. Pinned by the chain, arms fixed in helplessness behind him, he was utterly incapable of defending himself, and the experience left him humbled...and more than a little terrified. Even when hanging from the rack, screaming his rage as her brother whipped the objections out of him, he hadn't felt so utterly at another's mercy.

He felt her get up onto the bed, putting her knee on the chain to pin it in place to the mattress, felt the tide of emotions clash around her as she approached him with a heavy golden statue grasped in a fist. Then, silence. For long moments, he waited for her killing blow.

"I was wrong about you," the woman finally whispered. Dragomir lifted his head and looked at her nervously from under the sheet. Her green eyes were stony, her normally pale skin flushed, her freckles tightened in a scowl. She had a thundercloud of negative energy swirling around her like a winter storm, and her pert chin was jutting out imperiously. "You can't actually read my mind, can you?"

Dragomir shook his head.

"Then you're an Emp," she said. She hefted the golden mermaid thoughtfully. "If you were a Psi, you would've known I had planned on killing you just now."

"I was getting that general idea," Dragomir whispered up at her.

Her eyes were cold green emeralds. "I still haven't decided yet."

"I know." He swallowed.

"Close your eyes. Turn your head away."

Oh gods, a part of Dragomir's mind screamed. *That's what they say before they execute you.* Once, as a small child, he had witnessed an Imperial squad line up a group of village men. They shot all of the ones that were huddling, backs to the soldiers, but one of them refused to look away. Even after his fellows were dead on the ground around him, he kept peering into the eyes of the soldier who was to kill him. The soldier kept screaming, *"Close your eyes. Turn around!"*

And, eventually, he did. And the soldier shot him.

They buried their bodies in a shallow pit in a mountain meadow. They used Imperial tanks to fill it in.

Looking into the princess's eyes, Dragomir remembered Meggie. He remembered what had been done to her, remembered being unable to save her, remembered the rope that had been strangling him when his brother had come hurtling up the road, at night in his underwear, to cut him down, remembered lying on the ground in his brother's arms, willing himself to let go, when his brother had loosened the rope and pounded on his chest, forcing him back.

He remembered this Imperial's connection hitting him like an avalanche, rocking him out of his seat, sloshing the poisoned mead across the table, leaving him in a daze for hours, lying in a puddle, staring at the rafters in his ceiling as he tried to understand what had hit him.

A month later, an Imperial ship had set down on the grass outside his home. The green-eyed devil—flanked by twenty black-clad Praetorian—had put a gun to his head and told him to get on the ugly black vessel. Dragomir had almost fought them. Almost. Something, though, some nagging tug, had told him to cooperate. So, instead of infusing the Praetorian with terror long enough to escape into the mountains, Dragomir had allowed the green-eyed devil to put him in chains.

Now he was wondering why.

Dragomir had spent many sleepless nights trying to understand why the Universe had spared him. Brought to a *princess* like he had been this morning, after being shackled in the hull of a ship for two days in the dark, bound for for some unknown destination, then hung from a rack and tortured for another three days for crimes that were never specified, he had harbored a faint hope that perhaps it had all been to help this soon-to-be ruler heal, that she was the reason why Life had sent Thor up the road that night, instead of leaving Dragomir to stiffen in the breeze.

Reluctantly, Dragomir turned his head, and for long heartbeats, he expected her to smear his brains across her mattress. But, after minutes had passed in pounding silence, she eased closer, then gingerly lowered her hand to his shoulder. With each movement of his breath beneath her hand, he felt her body struggling against a deep, rising panic that was infecting his own *au*, making it difficult for him to breathe.

"Do it again," she said.

Dragomir's mind gave a startled twist of surprise, realizing she *wanted* him to work with her *gi*. "Uh. Are you sure?"

"Hurry," she whimpered. "It's coming back." Indeed, the flood of images was once more rising from her ramas like a tornado.

I'll do my best," he whispered, stunned. He knew from experience that most Imperials would rather stick their head in a blacksmith's furnace than willingly place themselves in the hands of an Emp. He'd once wandered the remnants of a battlefield, offering to help the wounded soldiers of both sides. Rebels had either stabilized or passed in peace with his touch. But the Imperials, to a man, had screamed and tried to shoot, stab, or, in one man's case, beat him to death with the broken, cast-off tread of an Imperial tank when he offered his help.

Dragomir closed his eyes, concentrated, and somehow managed to slip to the crystalline core through the cloud of fears, worries, and distractions roiling through him. He bathed in the energy, sank into the calm power he found there, then began feeding it outward, spiraling it around them, infusing her *au* once more.

She let out a little gasp and he felt her hand tighten on his shoulder. "You want me to stop?" Dragomir whispered, hesitating.

For a moment, she said nothing. Then, "Keep going. Please."

Still unable to penetrate her core, Dragomir fed every good, nourishing emotion he could think of to her *au*, pushing it out through his heart-rama, wrapping the two of them in it like a swath of warm, moving cotton.

He felt the woman relax against him, slowly. He felt another petal of her heart rama tentatively tug free of the stale energy that bound it, widening the needle-fine passage by a fraction of an inch. She felt her tense, heard her inhale sharply as a tiny thread of his energy began to filter through to her center to join the emerald tendril of her brother.

As he watched with his mental eye, his gold began to make the woman's rama shudder and the petals shift, stretching against the energies binding it in place. Sensing his opportunity to free her from her prison of fear, Dragomir began to gently push, increasing the amount of energy he was feeding her. The rama shuddered, straining against the net of trauma that held it.

The princess's hand tightened on his shoulder, fingers digging into the muscle, and for a moment, Dragomir thought he might succeed. The old energies, however, were too strong, too ingrained. After a moment's struggle, the net simply tightened, drawing the petals back to a close.

He let out a frustrated sigh.

For the course of several minutes, neither of them spoke. Then, softly, she whispered, "What did you just do?"

He flinched and turned his head to her anxiously. "Did it hurt?" Often, working with *gi* blocks—especially pushing against a longtime locked-down rama—ached, like stretching an atrophied muscle. And that was just getting the rama open again. Had he actually managed to break the old energies free, they would have flooded outward and engulfed her, and she would have experienced them all anew as their energies dissolved and passed through her *au*.

Next time, he chastised himself, *Think before you do something that stupid.*

But she was staring at him in awe, green eyes stunned. "It felt wonderful."

"I tried to help you re-open your heart rama," Dragomir said.

She frowned at him. "Tried?" Then her frown deepened, wrinkling her freckled brow. "What is a rama?"

Dragomir opened his mouth, trying to think of some way to explain the seven energy centers to an Imperial who insisted such energies did not exist...yet tried to kill everyone who used them. Finally, he said, "Think of your body as machine floating within a vast vat of liquid energy."

When she didn't snort and turn away, but instead watched him with an acute, intelligent stare, he tentatively continued, "Your body is controlled by spirit, which gives the machine orders. The ramas are like conduits that allow the body to suck in the energy all around it, so that the spirit can make the machine move."

The princess's frown was deepening.

Unsure if he should continue, yet afraid to stop, Dragomir blindly pressed on. "The ramas allow many good things to pass into the machine that help it, though some bad things can get through, too... It all depends on the energy in the vat. Sometimes, if the energy is bad enough, it will block the rama, and slow down the body's ability to digest energy from outside. In very bad cases, when trauma blocks the flow of *gi*, or when the spirit has decided the energy outside is too painful to absorb any longer, the rama will close completely. This is when illness develops."

She frowned down at him. "You really believe that, don't you?"

"It's what I see," Dragomir whispered, following the lines of gi through her body, noticing the shifts in her au as her emotions came and went, the dull glow of her closed and blocked ramas. "All the time."

"What are you seeing now?" she asked, looking curious.

His eyes stopped on her chest and the dormant tendrils twining there. In his mind's-eye, they sang, begging to be acknowledged. The princess wouldn't be able to link with him unless her heart rama opened, but Dragomir could feel the *need* of that connection humming under the verdant petals, begging for its counterpart. Like a trapped prisoner, screaming for help, it called to him. Wincing, he tore his eyes from it and said, "I see lines of energy. Ebbs and flow. Like cables and fire, but everywhere, and different colors. Constantly moving."

She gave him a long, considering look. Holding her hand up to his face, she said, "What about this?"

He looked at the lines of gi running through her fingers, the points in the joints where they wove back and forth, the small, secondary rama in her palm. He cleared his throat and looked up at her. "What do you want to know, exactly?"

She had been watching him all-too-carefully. "Tell me what you're seeing."

Dragomir sighed. "How can an artist explain color to a blind man?"

Immediately, he realized it had been the wrong thing to say to an Imperial royal, who prided themselves on their mutagenic mental prowess. Her beautiful eyes narrowed. "Try."

He returned his gaze to her hand. "The human body has a webwork of gi lines that run through it that is constantly providing energy to the muscles and organs. I can see them, kind of like spiderweb glistening in the sunlight. Real fine, but absolutely beautiful. There's some big ones, like the main one running up your spine. That's all different colors, though most are kind of a neutral bluish color." Then he took a deep breath, lifting his eyes back to her face, fixing his attention back on the violet ramas within her skull. "Then again, it's not really a color. It's more a *feeling* of color, you know? Like the way a pretty red rose feels. Or the deep blue of a glacier feels when you're standing beside it." He raised an eyebrow at her. "You understand so far?"

She nodded warily.

Now for the big question. Dragomir cleared his throat and ventured, "I also feel other things, like the links between a mother and her baby, or the ties between husband and wife, or best friends…" He licked his lips and, eyes on the massive, thrumming connection still dormant between them, he said, "You might actually be able to feel one of them, if you wanted to. Like, maybe a month ago, you started feeling a buzzing in your chest? A heaviness? Or a heat?" When she said nothing, only frowned at him slightly, he quickly went on, "The same feeling you're feeling right now, like hot water vibrating within your heart and lungs, overflowing and rushing out…" And here was the real leap…"…connecting us?"

For a long moment, she just gave him a little frown. Then, "You realize that whatever you're seeing is just psychosomatic, right? Your brain is just trying to find a way to make sense of neuron pathways that have never before existed in the human body. That's all any mutant is. You're taking your own excess energy and inflicting it on others. The only *safe* mutation is that of the Royals…that's why the Imperium puts us to good use serving the people."

"I hadn't known that," Dragomir said. He was disappointed, but not surprised. He'd heard many of the same things, almost word-for-word, in the propaganda chips that the Imperium distributed all over Mercy, urging residents to turn in 'mutogenetic anomalies' for their own safety.

The princess shrugged. "You're a native. The colonies haven't really had a chance to fully study it. The Imperium has." She cocked her head at him. "What's your name?"

Dragomir dropped his face back to the bed. Not only did she not feel their dormant link, but she thought he was insane, to boot. "Dragomir," he said, trying not to let his despair show.

She squinted at him as if he were an insect. "Dragomir. How'd you get the scar?" She gestured at his right temple, almost brushing the silver hair there with her fingers.

Dragomir stiffened, remembering the circumstances behind the wound. "I fell."

She narrowed her eyes at him, obviously sensing the lie. "How did you escape Imperial sweeps?"

Dragomir grimaced. He knew of three other 'mutants' that were living in nearby villages, and the last thing he was going to do was tell an Imperium Royal Princess how he managed to evade the years of persecution.

The princess's face hardened. "I asked you a question."

"And it's one I might someday answer," Dragomir said, "once I can trust you."

Her mouth fell open. "Once *you* can trust *me?!*"

He looked her dead in the eyes and said, "Yes."

She snorted. "I *own* you, slave," she said. "You will obey."

Dragomir narrowed his eyes. Glaring up at her, he said, "You have me bound and helpless. You do not own me."

Her mouth fell open and she stared at him like she could not believe the words she was hearing. Finally, sputtering, she said, "I am a Royal Princess of the Imperium and I am giving you an order."

Dragomir gave her a flat stare. "Miss, until five days ago, I was quietly serving my village in the foothills of Skitwater Pass. It's a farming community—about two hundred people who eke a living out of the Silversand Mountains. We dig in the dirt for a living. Our ancestors were the original crew of the original colony ship who landed here and claimed this world as our own. Five hundred years ago, our charter established this as a free world, ruled by free men. And, until the Imperium showed up on Mercy's doorstep forty years ago, our lives were very good. Ever since, it's been nothing but hell, anguish, starvation, and brutality." He paused, allowing some of his anger to show in his eyes. "So if you're asking if I give a crap whether you're an Imperium princess or a highly poisonous frog, not really. Either one could kill me. I'd actually prefer the frog, though, because the frog would have the decency to do it quickly."

For a long moment, the princess simply stared at him, fury billowing around her. Then, in a rush, her face darkened and she raised the golden statue, aiming at his face.

Spoiled brat, Dragomir thought, furious. He refused to look away.

• • •

Victory hesitated, paused mid-swing by the look in his eyes. He was *angry* with her. At first, she was flabbergasted. How *dare* he? She was a *princess* and he was her *slave* and she could do what she *wanted* to him!

Regardless of what he thought, she owned him. Legally. The Praetorian had delivered his papers the moment his brother had purchased him from the stables.

Then it clicked. She frowned, slowly lowering her weapon. "My brother didn't buy you from the stables?"

"No," the man said, his eyes flashing anger. "He took me from my home five days ago. Personally."

"That can't be right," Victory said. "He doesn't waste his time capturing slaves."

"Funny, isn't it?" He didn't look like he was amused.

She narrowed her eyes. "You must not have paid your taxes."

"No one in that village has paid their taxes," Dragomir growled. "The only places on this entire planet that pay your 'taxes' are the big cities along the ocean, and half of those are relocated Imperials, anyway."

"Only criminals don't pay their taxes," Victory said, though she found herself a little taken aback by his growing anger and her words weren't as strong as they could have been.

"Really?" Dragomir demanded, sitting up. "And when was the last time *you* paid taxes, Princess? Do you even know what the levy *was* for this year?"

Sitting up like that, the sheet started to slide down his body, revealing his powerful shoulders and chest. Victory cried out and scooted backwards, falling off her side of the bed.

"It was sixty percent," Dragomir snarled. "Sixty percent of anything grown, produced, or harvested was to be transported—at taxee's expense—to a collection station. The nearest collection station is four hundred miles away, through mountainous terrain, and maybe one in fifty families owns a skimmer."

Victoria frowned at the absurd number. *Sixty percent can't be right…*

"I know what you're thinking," Dragomir said. "That number sounds too high, right? It's probably because you've never overseen any collections, or checked any books. It's because it's sixty percent for natives, only twelve percent for Imperials." His eyes narrowed. "It's for your father to have an excuse to take slaves, for 'not paying taxes.'"

"*Slaves are our biggest cash-flow, Victoria, dear,*" her father had told her when she was a very small child. "*This barren rock has stone and slaves, and slaves are a hundred times more valuable than stone. Which do you think we export?*"

"Slaves, Daddy," had been her excited reply.

He'd ruffled her hair. "*That's right. We just need to make sure our exports never exceed our resources' ability to replenish themselves.*"

Victory felt sick. "You're lying."

"Go look it up," Dragomir growled. "If they'll even let you look at the records."

Victory straightened. "I'm the next ruler of Mercy. They can't stop me."

Her slave made a pointed glance at the chain linking the two of them together. "One of them can."

Victory narrowed her eyes. "You stay right there." Getting up, she turned to the door to her servants' quarters and shouted, "Kiara!"

The prim and proper woman who had once been one of Victory's tutors, before her fateful trip to the Imperial Academy, opened the door. She now functioned as her butler. "Yes, milady?" She was wearing her nightclothes, obviously about to go to bed.

"Tell the Constable of Numbers that I wish to see this year's copy of the current tax order. Now."

If her butler found anything out of the ordinary with Victory's request in the middle of the night, she didn't let it show. Bowing, she said, "As you say, milady." Then she quickly shut the door once more. Victory heard a few thumps in the second room, then the outer door open and shut, with whispered words in the hallway as a set of stockinged feet ran down the corridor at a sprint.

Victory turned back to the man kneeling on the other side of her bed. "Talking about trust…If you're lying to me, you're dead, you know that."

He sighed, looking more perturbed than fearful. "Lady, you have every reason to trust me."

Victory snorted. "And why's that?"

"Because," the man growled, "If I'd wanted to, I could've shut off your flow of gi the moment I stepped into this room. Could've done the same to your brother, when he was beating me senseless, and to your Praetorian, when they tugged me along by this pretty titanium chain like I was a dog on a leash."

Victory froze. "You're lying."

"You know why I didn't?" the man growled. He pushed his feet underneath him and stood, his massive naked body growing ever-taller. "I didn't because I don't believe in coincidences." He was glaring down at her, now. "And, no matter how frustrating, painful, or utterly unfair and humiliating the last five days have been, I believe Life has a reason for it, and I'm going to see that reason through. Whether that reason is to help you, or kill you, or merely find a more dignified way to end my miserable existence than swinging from a tree, I'm going to figure it out and do it."

Victory stared at him. "Did you just threaten to kill me?"

"No," Dragomir stated. "I simply told you I could." He cocked his head at her chest. "But looking at your ramas right now, I'd say that your time is already pretty limited. You're barely taking in any outside energy at all. You feel tired a lot, yes? Exhausted?"

Victory stared at him. Suspiciously, she nodded.

"That's because most of your ramas are closed," he said. "I can see the energy in there right now. It's stagnant and…chunky."

Peering at him, Victory said, "…chunky."

He shrugged. "It clogs the gi-channels. Probably residues from your trauma as a captive this lifetime, but it could belong to a past life. I'd have to get a better look to be sure."

Curious, despite herself, Victory said, "You can see my past lives?" Her father had never allowed her to meet with any of the fortune-tellers that her maids had so giggled about.

Dragomir gave her an irritated look and snorted. "It's just my own delusion, anyway, so what does it matter? Just psychosomatic. My brain trying to make sense of new energy pathways." Grunting, he flopped himself onto the bed and used his shackled feet to scoot himself backwards until his back was pressed against the headboard.

"Get off my bed!" Victory cried, horrified that he was touching it with his naked body.

He gave a huge, pleased sigh and leaned his head back against the wall. "It's just as nice as I thought." Giving a pleased smile, he said, "Cushiony." Then a small frown as he looked down at his feet. "But mine is still better."

"Your *posterior* is touching my *pillow*," Victory said, aghast.

"Good thing you let me relieve myself, then, eh?"

Victory was so furious with his audacity to ignore her commands that all she could do was blurt, "You lived in a *village*. How could your bed *possibly* be better than mine?"

He slid his head sideways along the headboard to look at her. "I'm not a midget."

She blushed furiously. "I'm five-one."

He gave her a flat look. "I'm not."

Indeed, he was approximately the same size as an aurochs. "Uh," she said, embarrassed, "Maybe I can have Kiara arrange something larger."

He raised an eyebrow at her, his blue eyes surprised. "You mean you're gonna let me sleep in your bed with you?"

Victory flushed burgundy. "On the *floor*," she growled. "Something on the *floor*."

He sighed and turned to look at the room opposite his toes, seemingly picking through the lavish furnishings and statuary, evaluating them. "You have a pretty room," he said. "I like all the mermaids."

Still on the floor, Victory blushed. Reluctantly, her eyes flickered to the thousands of statues she had collected before her departure to the Academy. Porcelain, gems, and polished stone glittered back at her from hundreds of different lighted nooks, shelves, and backlit glass displays. "I was still a child when I left," she said softly. "I haven't had time to redecorate."

The Emp gave her a look that said he understood much more than Victory wanted him to. Victory looked away in shame. Eventually, he said, "So even Royal Princesses of the Imperium have to eat, don't they? Are they going to feed us?"

Victory realized then that he didn't speak Imperial. Grimacing, she said, "Apparently, my father decided that, if I wanted to eat, I would have to leave my room to do it. He ordered my maids to stop bringing me food the moment they welded you to my waist."

Dragomir frowned and jerked his head around from where he had been eying a gold-thread-and-mohair mermaid tapestry. "Is your father insane?"

Yes, Victory thought, at the same time she said, "Of course not. He's just…" She hesitated.

"…a callous brute," Dragomir finished for her.

Victory stared at him, stunned that he could be brazen enough to speak harsh words about her father in his own palace. "Did you just insult the Adjudicator?"

"From everything I can tell," Dragomir said, nodding at the chain, "I just stated a fact."

Swallowing, she glanced at the door, then said, "When did you realize you were an Emp?"

Dragomir shrugged. "Didn't really realize it. Mercy's not like the Imperium. There were a *lot* of us before you showed up." He gave her a quick sideways look. "Being an Emp was like having red hair, instead of black or brown. Like being good at sports, or arithmetic. Instead of reading books, I was good at reading people. I could look inside, see what made them tick, and help fix things that had gone wrong."

Victory felt her curiosity rising again. He had information she had wanted her entire life, and it was all so tantalizingly close…"Do you really see…energy?" she whispered.

"All around me," he said.

"And mine?" she insisted again. "You see that, too?"

"Of course," he replied, looking a little exhausted. "I've been dealing with it all day."

Victory's curiosity was piqued. She eyed him and moved a little closer. Again, she asked, "What do you see?"

"When?" he asked. "When I'm just looking at you, or when I'm centered and pushing my consciousness outward?"

"Uh," Victory said, "Both?"

Taking a deep breath, he let it out slowly and his body relaxed. He glanced up at the air around her head, then his gaze went to her forehead and moved slowly down her body, stopping at her feet. After a moment, his gaze seemed to clear and he blinked. "I'd say you've probably got asthma or heart problems due to the chunky energy around your heart-rama, and I can't tell without getting inside, but not all of it seems to be fresh. Some of it is much older." He gestured at her torso with his chin. "I'd say you get ulcers a lot from the feelings of helplessness that got balled up in your liver rama. Your periods are probably either very sporadic and unpredictable or incredibly heavy and painful, due to the heavy residual fear that's stagnated there. Your core rama is completely closed—no real surprise, there—so you probably experience repeated yeast and bladder infections. Your legs might not circulate well in cold weather, and the joints of your ankles are currently hurting you—I'm guessing because you were probably chained by your ankles, and your subconscious mind felt that they betrayed you—the normal gi-flow there is completely disrupted. Oh, and because of that, your feet are probably cold. All the time. You probably get things like plantar's warts and fungal infections."

Everything had been so right-on that it made Victory freeze. She had heart palpitations and trouble breathing at night. When she ate more than a handful of food at a time, she started getting ulcers. Her periods were heavy—very heavy—and painful, leaving her entire abdomen wracked with cramps for days on end. She blushed at his dead accuracy concerning the workings of her internal plumbing, then grimaced and looked down at her ankles.

As always, they were throbbing. Most of the time, she completely forgot about the ache; she'd been dealing with it so long that she had learned to ignore it. When her attention was returned to it, however, it came back in full force, as if to get back at her for forgetting it was there.

"The ankles would be easiest for me to help," Dragomir said, watching her. "But I'd have to have my hands free."

Victory blinked. "Why?"

He gave her a sheepish grin. "A master can manipulate and dissolve old gi with just the power of his mind, but I find I work better with a crutch."

"Your hands?" Now that he had mentioned it, her ankles were throbbing like someone had cut them off at the widest point. The doctors had prescribed arthritis medications and pain relievers, but none of it had helped.

He wiggled his fingers behind him pointedly. "There's a smaller rama in the palms of the hands, though they're not so much a gathering center, as a conduit."

"I'm not freeing your hands," Victory said. "Do you think I'm stupid?"

Dragomir stared at her for a long moment, then sighed and *clunked* the back of his head against the mahogany headboard once more.

But now that Victory was thinking about them, the sharp throbbing in her ankles were excruciating. She lowered herself to the floor to get the weight off of them. It worked, but only for a moment. She winced, trying to put her mind elsewhere.

"I could help," Dragomir said, still staring at the ceiling across the room from his feet.

Victory glanced at her ankles, then at the huge slave seated naked in her bed. Her joints *hurt*, but when she looked at the man's huge hands, she knew he could hurt much, much more. "If I release your hands," she finally demanded, "what would stop you from wringing my neck?"

"Well, the four Praetorian Guard standing watch outside your room, for one," he said. "If I kill you, I'm dead. That simple." He glanced at her, his blue eyes sincere. "Look, Princess. I told you once already, but I'll say it again. If I was gonna kill you, I would've done it already, in some way that was *not* traceable back to me. The line of gi running to your heart, maybe. You're so afraid of men you had a heart attack...Or the lines following the veins in your brain. A little tweak could make one of the blood-vessels weak enough to explode when, say, you take your next dump."

No wonder the Imperium wants to get rid of them, Victory thought, in horror.

"But I'm a *healer,*" Dragomir said. "I help people. That's why I'm here, this life. That's why I didn't join the rebellion. That's why your brother's still *breathing,* after torturing an innocent man for three days straight."

"Matt didn't torture you," Victory said, automatically defensive of her twin brother.

Dragomir gave her a long, piercing look.

She swallowed. Quickly, she said, "How do I know you're not just trying to get me to untie your hands?"

"I *am* just trying to get you to untie my hands," he laughed. Dragomir leaned forward and shifted his arms behind him, a pained look on his face. "My goddamn wrists and shoulders hurt like hell. I'm willing to work on your ankles, in exchange."

Well, at least he's honest. Victory glanced down at her ankles. The joints now felt as if someone had poured raw acid into the cartilage, and the piercing heat was working its way into her feet.

"Basically, what I'm seeing," Dragomir said, "Is that you cut your own feet off, mentally." He cocked his head at her. "*Did* they use ankle shackles?"

She grimaced and looked away.

He nodded. "My guess is that you hated your feet for keeping you trapped, so you forgot that they existed. Gi flows according to thought, so it started puddling just above the middle of the ankle bone. What I would do is start re-establishing the old pathways, help pull it down into your feet."

"I didn't 'hate my feet,'" Victory sneered, but it felt like a lie on her lips. "That's nothing but delusional Emp garbage."

Dragomir shrugged his big shoulders. "If you want to deal with the pain without my help, that's your prerogative. You have me bound and helpless, after all." He yawned and, leaning back against the headboard, closed his eyes.

"What are you doing?" she demanded.

"Going to sleep." He said it as if it were the most obvious thing in the world.

Victory frowned. "I'm talking to you."

"You're not interested in anything I have to say." Dragomir said, "So I might as well just keep it to myself."

"I *am* interested," Victory blurted. So interested it hurt. "If I were to release your hands—and I'm not saying I'm going to—what insurance would I have that you would allow me to shackle them again, once we were done?"

He sighed, deeply. "My word, I suppose. Though it won't be necessary, I swear to you."

Victory watched him carefully. "You are telling me on your honor that, if I free you, you will willingly allow me to put you back in shackles at any time?"

"I'm saying it's hardly necessary, but yes. If it would help you sleep better tonight."

Victory grimaced. "I'm not going to sleep tonight, thank you."

He raised a heavy eyebrow at her. "Why not?"

The question was so absurd that she just gaped at him, then laughed. She gestured at her bed. "Because there's a...a..."

"Huge naked man practically the size of a house sharing the room with you?"

Victory lowered her hand, nervously, once more reminded of the fact that she was trapped in the room with a *male*. She felt the old panic begin to rise, and she took a step back, tightening the chain.

"Have you thought about the fact," Dragomir said, "that for most of the last couple hours or so, you've been chatting with me like a normal human being, instead of screaming and cringing and trying to run away like a scared little kid?"

Victory flushed, anger wiping the panic away. "I am the Royal Princess, and you will not speak to me like that."

Dragomir snorted. "Right now, I couldn't care if you were the Royal Turd Receptacle. My arms hurt, I'm hungry, I'm naked, and I'm being told I'm an idiot even though it's obvious I know what I'm talking about. It's making me more than a little cranky."

Victory stared at him. "You're an uncouth ass," she managed finally.

"Yeah," Dragomir said, "but until we figure out how to get this chain off my neck, I'm *your* uncouth ass, so get over yourself and unshackle me, all right? I'll fix your ankles, you'll feel better, then we can go to sleep."

Victory narrowed her eyes at him. "Or I could have the Praetorian string you up for the night." She gestured at the eye-bolt in the top of the headboard, which had been made for just that purpose.

Dragomir tilted his head back to look at it, then sighed. "That, too."

But Victory's curiosity was eating at her. The idea of being able to heal someone with a *touch* was beyond anything she had ever been taught. The doctrine of the Imperium was one of hard science and time-tested medicine—the romantic mind-over-matter philosophy of the Liberated Assemblage of Planets was one of the reasons why it fell apart. Too much hand-holding idealism, not enough practicality and discipline.

Yet this Emp was sitting not eight feet from her, telling her the Imperium was wrong, and claiming he was willing to prove it.

...All she had to do was pull the key from between her breasts and unlock his cuffs.

"What do you know of my past lives?" she asked, trying a new approach. "Was I ever poor?"

Dragomir looked at her, then snorted. "Most people ask if they were ever rich."

"Was I?"

He looked at her a long moment, then sighed and closed his eyes. "Only about a few thousand times," he said, after a moment. "Which life of poverty are you interested in?"

Victory's eyes widened. "A few *thousand?*" she breathed. As a child, she had idly entertained the fanciful thought of ten, maybe a dozen.

Dragomir lifted his head to squint at her. "You say that as if you are surprised."

"I *am*," she managed. "I guess that's why I was born a princess, right? Because I've had so many?"

Dragomir snorted. "Princess, pauper…Your spirit gives you what you need at the time to grow. You, apparently, needed to grow up wealthy and secure, then have your world shattered by a bunch of small-minded assholes."

Victory's mouth fell open at the sheer *audacity*. "Are you trying to *insinuate* that I was…" she swallowed, unable to say the word 'raped', "…kidnapped because I *wanted* to be?!"

He gave her an analyzing look. "Actually, you were probably pretty nervous entering this life, knowing what would befall you. But we're always growing, ever-changing, and we do what we need to do to keep expanding. Like jumping in a cold creek because you know you need a bath."

She gave him a dubious look. "I've never jumped in a creek."

He stared at her as if she'd grown bat ears. "We'll have to change that."

"I thought you just said it was cold," she growled.

"It is." He grinned. "But it's fun."

Victory lifted her chin. "They are infested with bacteria and protozoa."

"Germs and whatnow?"

"Bugs," Victory said, not about to try and explain the characteristics of an entire phylum of organisms to an uneducated post-colonial primitive.

He grinned. "Oh yeah, there's those, too. Some as big as your toe." He wriggled his big toe and held it up for her to see.

"Your feet are dirty," Victory said, disgusted at his black soles.

He set his foot down and gave her an irritated look. "Well, normally I wear socks, but somehow I seem to have misplaced them, along with the rest of my clothes."

Victoria stared at him, unable to comprehend his sarcasm due to the sheer audacity required to deliver it so perfectly. "Are you *mocking* me?"

He gave her an innocent smile. "You have an extra pair of socks?"

She snorted, despite herself. "It would take half a rhino skin to clad feet like those."

He gave her another bewildered look. "A whowhatnow?"

"It's a very large single-horned ungulate native to the Old Country. Not many were exported during the Building Times due to their general bad temper and lack of serious domestication potential, so they're considered an exotic and are protected under the Natural Species Act. We have a pair in the menagerie, if you wish to see them." Then she caught herself, frowning. "Well, we *had* a pair, but that was six years ago."

He was still staring.

"I'm saying you've got big feet," she said. "And that there's no way in the Twelve Pits of Hell that I'm going to let you destroy a pair of my socks."

"Huh," he said. "Guess I'll just have to destroy your blankets, instead." He pulled his legs up and started rubbing the soles of his feet on the covers.

"No!" Victoria shrieked, rushing forward, shoving his knees back down. "Ugh!" she cried, staring at the streaks. "That's so disgusting! I have to *sleep* in that!" She grabbed a pillowcase, yanked it off, and started rubbing at the smear.

He chuckled and *thunked* his head back against the headboard.

Only then did Victoria realize she was within a foot of a large, naked man, and that she had left her golden mermaid on the floor behind her. Panic surged within her, cold and icy, and she slowly put down the pillowcase, every inch of her screaming at her to get the weapon back in her hands.

"Not gonna hurt you," Dragomir said, almost idly. He wasn't even looking at her. "Now stop being a royal chickenshit and figure out how to get me something to eat. Or you plan on starving me to death, as well as leaving me naked and sockless?"

Victoria frowned, indignant. "You act as if you think this was all my idea. I had *nothing to do* with your capture, and if I *had* had the choice, I would have left you in the wretched little hovel where you belong!"

"Good," he said, "Then we're on the same page, because personally, I find all the wealth you stole from this planet a little tacky. I mean, hell, even your *toilet's* got gems in it. Who needs emeralds in their toilet? That somehow help you concentrate? I mean, *come on.*"

Victory found herself so furious she could only sputter. "You—you—" She froze, realizing that he was grinning.

"Feel better?" he asked, still looking across the room.

Victory's mouth fell open. "You've been making me *angry.* On *purpose.*"

When he turned his shaggy head to look at her, his blue eyes were dancing. "How else you think I managed to keep you talking for three hours straight?"

She stared at him in utter flabbergastation. "You were *provoking* me? Trying to get me to *bludgeon* you to death?"

He was grinning widely. "Better than you screaming and running away like I'm gonna somehow grab your head between my toes and twist it off."

Victory glanced at his toes with apprehension.

"They're big," he said, giving the appendages an appraising look, "But not that big." He wiggled them, cocking his head to watch them with a small frown. "I could probably only manage a small child, at best."

Victory laughed, despite herself. "You're a cad."

He blinked at her. "A what?"

"A boor."

He continued to peer at her.

"An oaf, a lout, a fool, a scoundrel, a heel, a rake, a rascal, a—"

"Okay," he said, grimacing, "I get the point."

"A barbarian, a buffoon, a churl, a philistine—-

"Oy!" he cried. "Ignorant native gets lesson in humility by well-learned Imperial, showing off words he didn't even know in his own language." Then he cocked his head. "How do I even know that's my language, and you're not just making it up?"

"You want me to pick a different language?" Victory demanded, crossing her arms. "Which one? I know six." Then she cocked her head. "Well, nine, if you consider Latin, Greek, and Mandarin, but no one but scientists use those these days."

He sighed and thunked his head again, hard. To himself, he said, "I want to go back home. At least there, I could show off my big muscles and cool Emp powers to pretty girls and feel special. Here, the pretty girl just thinks I'm an ill-informed, harebrained oaf with bouts of delusional schizophrenia."

Victory narrowed her eyes. "You knew what a cad was, didn't you?"

"People have used it on me a time or two," he said. "Though most weren't in this lifetime."

Victory's interest was piqued. "Who were you?" She cleared her throat. "Last lifetime, I mean?"

"Me?" Dragomir sighed. "I was a violent, war-mongering bastard. I needed to be an Emp this go-around to balance things out a bit. Lots of black marks on my Karmic tablet, so to speak." He laughed disgustedly at the ceiling. "Hell, I probably signed up to be dragged from my home by Praetorian, beaten within an inch of my life, screamed at by an asshole, and chained, naked and helpless, to a pretty young woman who hates my guts."

"You're not helpless," Victory growled.

"Ah yes," he said, lifting his head to look at his feet, "Completely forgot." He wriggled his toes. "My secret weapons."

She giggled, despite herself. "You don't really think I'm going to unshackle your hands, do you?"

He rolled his head against the headboard to look at her. "How badly do you want to find out what I can do with them?"

Victory froze. *I know what you can do with them.* She repressed a shudder, the revulsion working its way back to the surface.

"I killed a rapist, you know." His eyes had never left her face. "This Praetorian went on leave, decided to go on a hike through the Snowback chain. Fancied himself a mountaineer. He caught one of the girls in my village out in a meadow. Had his way with her, continued on his hike. Once I was finished repairing the damage, I went after him."

Victory watched him with a wary look.

"Tracked him by the energy he left behind. Kind of like a wolf tracks a deer through the woods, except this deer smelled like pain and violence. I caught up with him when he was camped up in the pass. And, well, I'm here and he isn't."

"You killed a Practorian?" She couldn't hide her disbelief. Praetorian were trained from *birth* to be the Imperium's best…

Dragomir gave her a sheepish grin. "Don't know if you noticed, but I'm a big guy." Then his face took on a thoughtful look. "Though it helped I shot him a few times, first."

"You shot a man in cold blood?" she demanded, offended.

"Uh," Dragomir said, "I wasn't about to walk up to him and say, 'Gee, I'm pretty pissed off about what you did to Meggie the other day. Would you please engage me in hand-to-hand combat?"

Victory stared at him, utterly shocked. "You really *are* a boor," she said. "That man trained his whole life—"

"—so he could go rape some girl in a mountain meadow?"

Victory shut up.

"The way I see it," Dragomir said, "You've got nothing to fear, so stop pussyfooting around, unshackle me, and let me help you."

The way he said 'help you' left Victory to believe he meant more than just her ankles. "What are you saying?" she asked, wary.

"I said your ankles were the easiest," Dragomir said. "But there's other gi blockages, some in some rather…uncomfortable…places. So you'll have to learn to trust me before I can work on those."

Victory went utterly still. "You mean you think I'm actually going to let you—" She couldn't finish. Had to look away, clear her throat. "*Touch* me?" A squeak.

He snorted. "You're going to have to, if you want me to work on your ankles." He made a dismissive shrug. "As for the rest…eventually, we'll work up to it."

Victory could only stare.

"Now," Dragomir said, jingling the shackles behind his back, "Would you *please* take these off of me?"

"No," Victory said.

He made a disgusted sound and thumped his huge body back against the headboard. The bed shook with the impact. "Fine," he said. "I'm going to sleep."

Victory frowned. "What about me?"

Without opening his eyes or turning to her, he said, "Sleep beside me or sleep on the floor or, hell, go get your Praetorian buddies to fling my huge ass outta bed and make me sleep on the rug, I don't care. I'm tired and irritated as all hell and my shoulders really hurt. I dislocated them both doing something stupid when I was a kid and all the ligaments are torn and shredded and it feels like someone's ramming stakes through my back every time I breathe." He heaved a huge, frustrated sigh. "Good night."

Victory nervously watched his breathing settle, watching the rise and fall of his big chest until it had fallen into a slow, easy rhythm. He began to snore, and it was obvious as his body relaxed that he had been utterly exhausted, but doing well to hide it. Feeling a bit guilty, she cleared her throat and asked, "How did you hurt your shoulders?"

CHAPTER 5

To Entertain a Princess

Dragomir was dreaming of a one-eyed woman from the past, a torrid love affair many lifetimes ago, when he heard someone speak. He opened his eyes blearily. For a moment, he thought he was back in his home, having fallen asleep in his chair. Then he saw the gauzy purple curtains, the roaring fireplace, the black marble walls and ceiling. His heart sank when he felt the strain in his shoulders, the cold steel around his wrists and ankles. He turned his head, searching for his captor.

It took him a moment to locate her—he hadn't been allowed much sleep in the last five days—and when he did, he found it difficult to focus. "Huh?" he asked, more a grunt than a word. His exhaustion was definitely catching up with him.

She cleared her throat and said, more loudly, "How did you dislocate your shoulders?"

He gave her a long, mouth-open look. Was she closer than she had been before?

She touched his shoulder. "You said you dislocated it?"

He looked down at the crest of his arm, then grunted again. He licked the drool out of the corner of his mouth. "Someone bet me I couldn't jump off a tree-fort and catch myself holding the climbing-rope behind my back. Think I was like eight, and pretty sure I was invincible. Wrapped it around my fingers real good, then jumped."

She winced at him. "Sounds like it hurt."

"Not as much as hanging there did, once my shoulders came out." He yawned. "Got caught around my wrists. Couldn't make my fingers work to unwrap themselves. They had to cut me down."

She grinned at him, and Dragomir actually forgot how tired he was. She was *beautiful*. Alabaster skin, freckles, green eyes, and the most raven-black hair he'd ever seen on a woman.

"Sounds like something my brother would do," she said, beaming. "He was always doing stupid things like that."

Dragomir gave an indignant grunt. "I said I was invincible, not stupid."

She peered at him like he was a poor, flattened bug on the sidewalk. "That sounded pretty stupid to me."

Dragomir sighed. "Maybe a little. Taught me something, though."

She cocked his head at him in curiosity. "What's that?"

"Taught me not to jump off a tree and catch yourself with a rope behind your back, that's what." He grunted, wishing he could ease the strain in his shoulders. "Uh, miss, is there *anything* I can do to assure you I'm just a harmless, six-foot-seven poodle?"

She raised both eyebrows. "Poodle?"

"Poodles are funny, not ferocious." He grinned weakly. "I think of myself as being funny."

"I used to own a poodle," she said. "It bit the butler on the rump. A lot."

Dragomir grinned. "Well, I'm more the fluffy, primped-up, lazy version of a poodle."

She snorted, but gave him an appraising look. "Tell me about one of my past lives. Then I'll think about it."

Demoted to entertainment for a princess, Dragomir thought with a sigh. Still, it was worth a try. Anything to relieve the growing ache in his shoulders. He closed his eyes and concentrated, seeking out the residual images and drifting emotional tags that, once he snagged with his consciousness to examine deeper, revealed a door into the past.

He randomly pulled one of the stronger ones from her *au* and began to delve deeper. He ducked through the door of that particular soul-bead and watched her life replay before him like one of the Imperium's vid-chips, looking for something interesting to tell her.

He watched her born to a hard life in a mining-family on some unknown planet. He wasn't even sure that, throughout her life, *she* ever knew the name of her planet, so backwater was her home. He watched her grow up, watched her build forts with the boys and run through the upper mine shafts, playing. He watched her poke out her eye on a broken branch, while playing tag. He watched her grow into a beautiful woman, with sleek curves and long, flowing red hair. He watched the village boys ridicule her, turn away from her because of her missing eye. Then he frowned, watching the land darken in the valley below, a mass of soldiers. He watched villagers scream and run for the rocky clefts above their home. People marching, by the thousands, their armor gleaming in the sun. He watched a man on horseback thunder up, sweep her, screaming, onto the back of his horse. He felt her hands bound behind her back, her ankles lashed together. He watched her turn, saw the man's face for the first time…

"Oh shit."

The princess perked up, leaning forward intently. "You saw something?"

"Uh," Dragomir said. "No."

She frowned. "No?"

"I mean yes," he said quickly, "But you don't want to hear it."

The princess growled. "Tell me."

"Uh," Dragomir said, frantically trying to come up with something that would satisfy. "You had one eye. You were very ugly and dirty and people laughed at you."

She scrunched her face. "One eye?"

"Uh huh," he said. "One eye. Yep. That's it. That's all I saw."

She gave him a long, narrow look, but let it go at that. "You going to go to sleep, then?"

"Plenty of room for two up here," Dragomir said.

Snorting, she said, "No, thank you. I'm not sleeping tonight."

"Suit yourself," Dragomir grunted, sliding down to lay on his stomach, trying to ease some of the pressure in his shoulders. "Would you mind tossing a cover over me?"

For a long moment, she gave him a suspicious look, like he had asked to see her underwear. Then, slowly, she inched forward just far enough to flip the cover over him before she quickly backed away.

And, miracle of miracles, a Royal Princess of the Imperium sat there on the floor, watching him in silence as he fell asleep on her bed.

• • •

When Victoria opened her eyes, she was in a fetal position on the sheepskin rug, her body being bathed by the warmth of the sun. She groaned and sat up slowly, her body aching from sleeping on the floor.

She froze when she saw the deep blue eyes, watching her.

"Morning," the man said.

Victory screamed and flailed backwards across the rug.

The Emp yawned and flexed his huge shoulders. "Hope you had a better night than I did. Feels like someone's tearing my arms off." He cocked his head at her. "Hungry? I think they were calling for you to come eat, earlier. You slept through it."

Victory blinked. She had fallen asleep? With a *man* in the room? It was beyond comprehension. "Did you coerce me?" she demanded. "Force me to relax with your powers?" Yes, that's what had to have happened. The Emp had manipulated her.

Dragomir laughed at her. "With how exhausted I was yesterday?" He snorted. "Princess, I was passed out. Completely. You could've come up here and picked my nose with a fork and I would've slept through it."

She narrowed her eyes at him. The thought of being compelled into sleeping beside a man was more acceptable to her than the idea of doing it by *accident*. "You're lying," she stated firmly.

But he wasn't listening. He was peering down at the bedding between his legs. "You know, I was thinking about it while you were snoring, and we could fashion some sort of sarong out of one of the sheets."

"I was *not* 'snoring,'" she cried.

"Okay, Princess. You were 'expelling large quantities of air through the back of your throat while you painstakingly created a puddle of saliva on the stone under your face." He chuckled. "But honestly, a sarong would make us *both* feel better. A sheet is a hell of a lot better than getting paraded around stark-ass naked with an entire kingdom to gawk at you."

"I'm not wrapping a sheet around you," Victory blurted. The mere thought of getting that close to him left her trembling.

He shrugged. "Then have your Praetorian do it. They opened the door this morning to check and see if you were alive, and if I was being a good boy. *Gods* those women scare me. Like looking into the eyes of a phoenix."

"The phoenix is their emblem," Victory said. "The female units, anyway. The males use the dragon. Combined, the phoenix and dragon is the symbol of the Imperium. It's an ancient symbol, borrowed from the ancient empire of—"

Dragomir grunted. "You ready for some food?" The way he said it, he was about as interested in Imperial symbology as he was in paying taxes.

Victory's eyes narrowed and she sniffed. Now that he mentioned it, she *was* hungry. Her gaze once again fell upon his big body and she swallowed and quickly averted her eyes. "I'll call my maidservants," she said. She turned over her shoulder and called for Kiara.

"Speaking of that, funny how you never got those records you wanted, isn't it?"

Victory frowned, even as Kiara stepped into the room, towels and clothes in hand, flanked by Jolene and Carrie, Victory's two handmaidens. The thought, however, was quickly shattered the moment she realized what Kiara planned to do.

"I'm not in the mood for a bath," she said, quickly glancing at the huge brute sitting upon her bed. And, for that matter, she wasn't in the mood to change, either. Grimacing, she said, "Leave me in my current garb, brush my hair, wash my hands and feet, and bring me some slippers."

Kiara frowned slightly, but with one look at the massive slave, she bowed low. "As you command, milady. Will you be requiring your medications?"

"Please," Victory said, grateful to have the women in the room with her. "With a glass of orange juice."

70

Her servant flushed. "I meant at breakfast, milady. I have been given strict instructions that no edible substances of any form to enter your bedchamber. The Adjudicator…"

Damn, Victory thought. She sighed. "Very well. Tell the cook to have my breakfast prepared within the hour. I fancy duck eggs. Soft boiled. Sausages. Elk, I think. The bison had an unpalatable flavor last time. A cup of hazelnut and cinnamon coffee, foamed. And one of those pastries she does so well…the ones with the lemon filling?"

"And him?" Kiara said, nodding at Dragomir, who was watching them alertly, but with a tiny frown of uncertainty. "Will your slave be fed this morn?"

"Take my meal and double it for him," Victory said. Then she looked him up and down and said, "Make that triple. With scrambled eggs. I'm not watching some fool try to spoon soft-boiled egg into his mouth, thank you. I fear that might destroy my appetite."

Kiara gave her a slightly startled look that, coming from the well-trained woman, was approximately the same as saying she thought Victory was completely out of her mind. "I was thinking more along the lines of porridge, milady."

Victory snorted. "Eggs. Sausage. Pastries. And a servant to feed him."

Kiara bowed low and hurried off, leaving Victory to sit in the chair that the maids dragged over beside the bed while they primped her as well as possible without removing any of her slept-in garments. They poofed the four-ply, embroidered silken sleeves and fluffed the matching ivory pants, lamenting the wrinkles that Victory refused to let them iron out. They affixed jingling golden anklets with emerald mermaid clasps, then did the same with each wrist.

She waited as they wove jewels into her hair, then lifted her chin as they placed a large, complimentary emerald necklace around her throat. The aging Adjudicator of a failing colony had given it to her as a birthday present when she was fourteen, over six years ago, claiming that it matched her eyes. It had been a blatantly desperate attempt at courtship, but Victory had kept it, anyway, to use on days like this, when she felt the need to shield herself in her wealth.

Victory despised painting her face, and the makeup they used was just enough to cover up the dark rings of emaciation under her eyes that the doctors had insisted would go away with time, food, and rest.

Once they had finished, they carried her silver, ermine-trimmed cloak over to her and draped it around her shoulders, fastening it in place with gold-and-emerald clasps. Her slippers were last, silver to match her cloak.

When she was done, Victory stood and turned to the slave on her bed.

Dragomir's mouth was open. At her raised brow, however, he quickly shut it and looked at the embroidered black bedcovers between his legs.

"Wrap him in a sheet," Victory ordered. "Pin it closed with something nice."

Carrie, the more outgoing of her two handmaidens, giggled and moved to the other side of the bed to pick up the sheet that had fallen to the floor. Dragomir turned, warily, watching her.

"Stand up," Victory told him. "She's going to give you something to wear."

Gingerly, he inched his way across the bed on his knees until he could slip his legs off the other side. Seeing the object swinging between his thighs, Victory quickly averted her eyes.

Jolene, on the other hand, stared. "Oh my gods, milady, he's…" Then she blushed and caught herself. On the other side of the room, Carrie giggled and stroked her hand across Dragomir's rump. Dragomir stiffened, looking nervous. "…huge," she finished, stopping to stand in front of the massive slave with an approving look. "Look at the muscles on him. Like an ox." She reached up and casually slapped a big bicep, making Dragomir wince. "And his *bits*…" She reached for crux of his legs, and Dragomir tensed.

Seeing her handmaiden grab the man's genitals and heft them with no more concern than if she were judging the freshness of an apple, Victory fought a sudden rush of anger, remembering similar treatment at the hands of her own captors.

"You forget yourself, girl," Victory growled, not liking the anxious lines in Dragomir's face. "That slave is mine."

Carrie gasped and quickly curtseyed low. "My apologies, milady. I just thought that—"

"Whatever you thought, you were wrong," Victory growled. "Finish affixing the sheet and leave."

Red-faced, head down, Carrie hurried to complete the task that had been given to her, fumbling three times with the little mermaid pin as her trembling hands tried to fasten the sheet to the man's hips, then quickly excused herself.

"I want it made clear," Victory told Jolene, "That no slave of mine will suffer through what I once did."

"Yes, milady," Jolene said, bowing low to follow her friend out. Then she paused at the door, a shy smile on her face. Her blue eyes drifted back to the slave and she nodded at him. "It's good to see you so much… better…milady." Then she turned and fled.

Victory considered. She *was* doing better, wasn't she? She glanced over her shoulder at the slave, considering.

"What was that all about?" Dragomir asked. He had let out a breath once the sheet had been securely cinched around his waist, and some of the edge had left his stance.

"Misguided staff," Victory said. "It won't happen again."

He gave her a look filled with such gratitude that Victory felt ashamed that she hadn't given the order sooner. She cleared her throat to hide her embarrassment.

"Let's go," Victory said. "My Father, damn him, is not going to let us eat until we face the world." Even as she said it, she cringed at the open door and the Praetorian beyond.

"I'm here," the man said softly.

Victory swung to face him, her irritation seeping into her voice despite her efforts to control it. "You have no idea what this is going to do to me. I'm a *princess*, and I'm probably going to end up bawling in a corner halfway to the breakfast table."

"No, you won't," he said.

At the plaintive way he said it, Victory froze. She looked him up and down, hope starting to work its way into her chest. "You can do that?" she asked, tentatively.

"Would be better if I had my hands free, but I'll do my best." He gave her a shy smile. "Just make sure somebody feeds me soon. That kind of work uses up a lot of energy. Eggs would be nice. Sausage would be better."

"You keep me from embarrassing us both," Victory said, "And you can have all the eggs and sausage you want."

He chuckled. "I'm going to hold you to that, Princess."

"My name is Victoria," she said, hesitating as she tried to work up her courage to walk out the door. "You can call me Victory. My brother does." Victory closed her eyes, steeled herself, and stepped through the threshold.

• • •

Dragomir did his best to shuffle behind the princess, trying not to gape at what he saw. He had been blindfolded when the Praetorian had led him through the palace, and now that he was seeing it for the first time, he was suddenly feeling very provincial, indeed.

The four Praetorian stationed outside the princess's chambers fell in behind her on either side, flanking Dragomir, and together they walked down the hall to the spiral marble staircase leading to the next floor.

Like everything about the palace, the staircase was composed of polished black marble, with white marble accents running along the walls and inlaid in fanciful dragon and phoenix designs on the floors. Gold laced the walls and ceiling in filigreed designs and patterns, each different for each wing of the palace. While the princess's hall bore golden images of the ocean and mermaids lounging upon rocks, the next hall down—the prince's, he guessed—was decorated in a thousand different dragons, each golden shape carefully inlaid into the black marble with such precision that it seemed that the gold was standing out against the Void, leaving the dragons almost appearing alive.

The craftsmanship was simply unbelievable, and left him gawking at the fantastical images. Dragomir had never seen such art before, and it left him humbled to realize that such things could be produced by a human hand.

As if the walls, ceiling, and floors were not enough, every twelve feet, a statue had been placed along the balustrade overlooking the lower floor. In the princess's hall, the statues were of mermaids in every possible position, each scene a breathtaking thing of beauty.

"Like I said," Victory said with a grimace. "I was fourteen when I was captured. I haven't had time to redecorate."

The idea of removing the walls, ceiling, and statuary as 'redecorating' left Dragomir stunned. "I think they're beautiful," he blurted.

Her face grew bitter. "Yes, well, I'm not a child anymore." It was then that he saw the strain in her face, realized how much trouble she was having holding in her growing panic.

"You'll be fine," he reassured her, sending her a wash of energy. "See? That Praetorian up there is clearing the way." At the bottom of the stairs, six more black-clad, phoenix-emblazoned Praetorian had met them, and two had stayed to flank the princess, while four had run ahead to empty the halls.

Victory gave the path ahead a dubious glance, but said nothing.

Sure enough, the halls were clear all the way to the great dining hall, which was empty except for a long, ebony table, thirty-foot-long woven tapestries of forest and mountain scenes, and about a hundred jet-black ironwood chairs. Several plates of food sat upon the end of the table closest them, and a woman clad in black was waiting quietly beside it at attention, facing the far wall.

It was the food on the table, however, that caught Dragomir's attention. His stomach lurched hungrily.

The princess, however, did not seem pleased. She barked a few comments to one of the Praetorian in Imperial, and the woman bowed deeply and replied with an apologetic look.

"What's going on?" Dragomir whispered, twisting again at his wrists, trying to ease the ache from his shoulders.

"I was asking why they decided to serve me breakfast in the great hall, instead of the sun-room," Victory told him. "Apparently, one of my father's orders was that my meals be served to me here, and only here." She made a disgusted sound, as if being served an elegant breakfast in a majestic dining hall, surrounded by servants, was somehow highly disappointing.

"You really should come visit me sometime," Dragomir said. "I'll sit you at my kitchen table and serve you roast chicken." He started rolling his shoulders as he twisted his hands, trying to work out the nagging feeling that someone was driving nails through the joints there.

One of the Praetorian slammed a fist into his elbow, almost breaking it. Dragomir hissed and jerked away from her, then stared down at the woman in incomprehension as she barked at him in Imperial while pointing to his hands and making a cutting motion at her neck.

Victory snapped something at the woman, who immediately bowed and stepped aside, face utterly neutral.

"Uh," Dragomir asked, once the shouting had stopped, "What just happened?" His shoulder and elbow were both throbbing, but now he was afraid to move.

"Lion was telling you to stop trying to escape," Victory said. "I was telling her to mind her own damned business."

"My shoulders are killing me," Dragomir said. "I don't suppose you'll free them so I can eat?"

"The servant standing beside the table will serve you," Victory said. She moved into the room and elegantly sat at the table head. Dragomir shuffled to a chair beside her and sat down.

Immediately, a Praetorian jerked the chair out from under him, dropping him on his ass on the stone floor.

"What the *hell?!*" Dragomir shouted at the woman, who was guarding the chair as if he had somehow stained it with his rear. He realized instantly that it had been a mistake. The woman—he thought of her as Loud Mouth—dropped the chair behind her and stalked toward him, her mailed fist ready for a swing that he knew was going to knock out teeth.

A soft word from Victory stopped her. As quickly as a machine that had been shut off, the woman went back to stand beside the wall.

"What the hell?" Dragomir asked the princess, softer.

Victory sighed. "The Adjudicator's table is only for those of noble blood or those loyal to the Imperium."

Dragomir felt a welling of shame within him. "So I've got to eat on the floor."

"You are a slave," Victory told him.

He glared at her, humiliated at the simple way she had said it—and the fact that she wasn't going to try and correct his seating arrangements. "I'm bound and helpless," he growled. "Not a slave."

She gave him a patronizing smile. "You'll learn."

The words burned like coals in his mind. *She honestly thinks I'm her property*, Dragomir realized, disgusted. *Just like that pretty necklace, or her fancy cloak.* His lips formed a tight line and he scowled down at the floor, once again feeling shame burn through his chest. "You know," he said, unable to stop himself, "That's probably what they thought about you, when they took you off your ship."

The princess, who had been politely tapping the shell of an egg with her spoon, choked. She turned on him, giving him a look that would have singed off his shirt, had he been wearing one. "You *dare* to suggest...?" she began.

He just raised an eyebrow at her.

Red-faced, the princess went back to cracking at her egg, much more violently, now.

It was at that point, however, that the servant who had been waiting beside the trays carefully lifted a food-covered tray into his lap, and the savory scents of egg, cheese, sausage, and pastry hit him at once. Dragomir groaned and waited impatiently as the servant knelt beside him and started cutting tiny, delicate chunks off of each item of food, then carefully began putting them in his mouth.

At the first taste of a real meal in almost a week, Dragomir moaned. "Tell her to cut bigger chunks," Dragomir said, impatient with how slowly the woman was feeding him.

The princess spoke a few words and the pieces of food halved in size. She gave him a smug grin.

Dragomir narrowed his eyes. "You are a pain in the ass."

The princess raised an eyebrow. "And you are lucky that none of the Praetorian speak your primitive native brogue, or else you would probably be dead for the comment."

Muttering, Dragomir returned his attention to his food. He ate as quickly as he could, with the tiny pieces that were being offered to him, willing the woman to speed up. She continued to be infuriatingly slow and methodical, however, and by the time the princess had finished with her meal, he was still only halfway through his.

Grinning, the princess spoke another string of Imperial at the woman feeding him, and the bites quadrupled and sped up. Dragomir, giving the princess an irritated look, wolfed them down, eating until every dish was clean.

"All right," Victory said, "Let's go. I've had about as much time out in the real world as I can handle, at the moment." She turned to go.

Two Praetorian were in the process of standing him up when doors slammed open on the other side of the hall and a man in black and red armor came striding through the far side, his body surrounded by the greenish haze of an energy shield. Behind him came a dozen male Praetorian bearing the golden dragon-and-phoenix insignias upon their breasts.

Her father, Dragomir thought, *The Adjudicator himself.* The man was about six foot-three, but he carried himself as if he were nine. His eyes were a sharp, arrogant gray and his blonde hair was streaked with white.

And, if it weren't for the hazy green energy bubble around the man's body, muddying Dragomir's second sight, he could have saved Mercy a century of heartache by working a couple simple knots into the man's flow of gi.

Then he realized that Victory was frozen behind him. He could feel the fear welling up within her, and Dragomir frantically tried to wrap her in calm, wishing he could reach out and touch her.

The Adjudicator bellowed something in Imperial and never slowed in his approach, and Victory shrank back against the wall, whimpering, her terror swirling upwards despite Dragomir's attempt to calm it. He cursed, wishing he could get a hand free. Physical contact was the easiest, most direct method of pass calming energy to his patients, but his hands were literally tied.

Just hold on, Dragomir said, closing his eyes infusing her *au* with as much peace as he could. *Whatever's going on, you can deal with it, Princess.*

The man strode up to Victory as if he didn't even notice the way she was shrinking into a corner, dragging Dragomir with him. The man glanced at Dragomir, then began shouting something in Imperial, gesturing at his body.

The male Praetorian behind him marched forward and, with a violence that snapped the pretty golden mermaid pin that the handmaiden had used to fasten it to his waist, yanked the sheet from Dragomir's body, once more exposing his nakedness for all to see.

Hot shame coursed through Dragomir under the stares of so many dispassionate eyes. The Adjudicator, in particular, made him feel as if he were a cow or a sheep up for perusal. The man walked around him, utterly unconcerned by the way that Victory was now screaming in the corner.

Victory! Dragomir realized that the intensity of his shame had drowned out his feeling for her terror, and she had fallen into a full-fledged panic. He hurried to kneel beside her—if he could just get a hand on her, he knew he could help—but was brought up short and hard by a Praetorian's sudden grip on the chain at his neck.

Behind him, the Adjudicator barked a command. An instant later, a kick in his exposed manhood brought him gasping to his knees. Arcs of pain drove through his body as the Praetorian took turns kicking him, driving him into the stone floor with their blows. Dragomir groaned and tried to apologize, tried to explain, but if anything, his words made their attack more brutal. He heard his ribs snap, felt the explosion of pain and the sick feeling in his gut as their boots connected with his stomach. He tried to scrunch into a ball in desperation, but with his arms stuck behind his back, he could do little to protect himself. His face, chest, and groin were completely exposed to their assault.

And, through it all, Victory screamed. *I'm sorry*, Dragomir thought, as he began to lose consciousness. *I'm so sorry…*

CHAPTER 6

Reliving the Past

"Who told you that you could clothe the slave?" her father demanded, as Victory sank deeper into the wall, wildly trying to get a hold on her panic. She could feel Dragomir helping, but with so many men, so close, she was starting to lose control, and they both knew it. She started to whimper, unable to fashion an intelligible answer to her father's question.

"My orders were for the slave to be *naked*," her father snarled. "Is this a *game* to you, Victoria?" He gestured furiously at a Praetorian. "Remove it from him. Now."

Victoria gasped as the first images started flooding her from within, triggered by her father's angry face.

Cold meat, untouched on a plate, congealed in grease, smelling of rancid rot. A furious face. *"What, is my food not good enough for you, Princess? Maybe if you don't wish to eat it, you can wear it, instead."* The cold, rancid meat sliding down her shirt, between her legs. Laughter at her cries. *"Or maybe you'd like to use it, instead."* The feel of it rubbed back and forth, sliding between her delicate lips, until her own body had warmed it and the juices ran freely down her legs. The feel of it in her hair, on her skin…

Distantly, she saw Dragomir stumble towards her, and, seeing his naked body, she was taken to another place, another time. She screamed for him to have mercy, that her baby was due within weeks.

Distantly, she heard her father snort. "What's she saying? She's *scared* of that brute? Then give her a show. I want him groveling on the ground. Make her understand she's being stupid."

Victory heard thumps and grunts, and watched as a dozen men held her down and used her, their wet scrotums slapping against her as she whimpered up at the falling snow.

She lost herself to the horror then, weeping for mercy as their heavy forms moved over her, while at the same time she was grateful for the warmth…

Victory opened her eyes sometime later, her body still shaking with leftover adrenaline. When she looked around, she was surprised to see that she was back in her chambers, laying comfortably in her bed, the blankets wrapped around her.

For an instant, she thought that perhaps she had experienced another nightmare, that her father truly hadn't given the order to chain her to a man. Then she felt the hardness of the metal belt biting into her back, saw the chain loop under the covers and down onto the floor.

Frowning, Victory sat up and looked over the edge of the bed.

Dragomir was there, face down on the stone, his body a mass of ugly red bruises. Aside from a shallow breath now and again, he was absolutely motionless. His wrists and ankles were bleeding where the metal had bitten into his skin, obviously due to some struggle. She stared. Then she cried out for her Praetorian.

"I gave orders that this slave not be harmed!" she snapped. "What happened?"

The captain of her guard, a lithe, powerful woman who had aptly chosen the name of 'Lion' once she finished her training, looked irritated. "Your father's guard, milady. You went into shock and screamed. The lord Adjudicator decided to prove to you that there was nothing to fear."

"By *beating him senseless?*" Victory was so furious she could hardly breathe. "Bring my doctors in here. *Now.*"

The woman actually looked relieved. "Thank you, milady. As much as your father's ways are blunt and brutish…we're all glad to see the changes the slave has brought about in you. We all think your brother made a good choice."

The changes? Victoria thought, frowning. *It's only been a day.* Then her eyes went wide. "You know what he is?"

Lion smiled. "We accompanied your brother, looking for him. Your brother's personal guard, and yours."

"And you're not afraid of him?!" Victory demanded.

"Milady," the Praetorian said, "I believe that if he was going to harm someone, he would have done it during your brother's beatings. It's why Prince Matthias was so brutal—he was testing him. Three others failed the test." She nodded her head at the native on the ground. "He passed without even a ping on the meter."

"What happened to the others?" Victoria whispered, dreading the news.

"Your brother sent them home, milady."

Victory froze. "He did *what?*"

But the Praetorian bowed her leave. "If you'll excuse me, I will go get him some medical attention." Turning on heel, she jogged from the room, her heavy, steel-shod boots clicking on the marble floor.

Victory hesitantly dropped down beside the unconscious man and, after a long moment of watching him breathe, gingerly touched a hand to his battered brow. She bit her lip. The last time she had seen anything so gruesome, it had been on her own face, after the first man had taken her virginity on the raiders' ship and left her naked and shivering, chained to the toilet in the tiny lavatory.

Her eyes slipped down his back, gingerly touching the bruises along the spine. *They could have paralyzed him*, she thought, horrified by the huge black bruises she saw there. Her fingers moved on, and they stopped on the bands around his wrists. She bit her lip at the crusted blood she saw there, recognizing the marks for what they were. *He tried to protect himself,* she thought, remembering a time when she had done the same.

"You could release them, you know," came a weak rasp from the floor. "I'm pretty sure it'd be easier for me to shit nails than it would be to get my ass off the ground right now."

Victory jumped and slid away from him, though only halfway to the end of the chain. She sat there, just out of reach, watching him warily. "I've got doctors coming. They'll give you nanos, painkillers."

Dragomir made a wry sound into the black marble floor. "My arms don't hurt so much anymore."

Victory winced at what he left unsaid. When the doctors arrived, they lifted Dragomir off of the floor and laid him out in the bed, the relocation dragging a ragged moan from his throat. They analyzed him, injected him with nanos, wrapped his ribs tight in bandages, and cleaned and covered any visible wounds.

"Ribs are broken, milady," one of the doctors said. "Should be a simple fix, though, and the healing process will be greatly increased by the nanotech. Bruises should fade within a day and a half. You'll be able to remove the bandages within a week." The woman nodded at Dragomir's sleeping form. "We've given him a sleeping draught, as well as painkillers. He should be asleep for the next five or six hours."

"Thank you," Victory said, nodding their dismissal. Already, on the bed, the native's huge chest was rising and falling in a deeper, more even rhythm, and the lines of pain had faded from his face.

"I'm sorry," she told the sleeping man, once the door had closed behind them.

"Not your fault," he slurred.

Victory smiled, despite herself. "Go to sleep, stubborn cad."

"Working on it, wench."

She raised an eyebrow. "Did you just call me *wench?!*"

His reply was a soft snore.

She let a slow grin play upon her lips, despite herself. Once she was sure he was asleep, she crept forward. Somehow, the fact that there was nothing powering the brute made it easier for her to cope with his presence, and she found her curiosity taking hold of her. Even bruised and bloody, his body was glorious. She reached out and traced the bandages of his ribs, gingerly feeling the rise and fall of his chest.

She remembered her father's arrival, his bellow of, *"I'm tired of you disobeying me, girl! I've told you to come to my chambers six times, now, and*

83

you've ignored me. What do you think my empire must think of me, if I cannot even control my own child?"

Victory squeezed her eyes shut against the vision.

"I see you were properly fitted with the beast. Are you beginning to see that your fears are ridiculous?"

Victory slammed her fist into the headboard. *I hate you,* she thought, wishing she could have had the presence of mind to say as much. *Matt and I both. You are a prideful, small-minded fool.*

She thought of Matt and her heart ached. She hadn't seen her brother but once, when he had quietly slipped into her chamber after Victory realized she had somehow come to be taken back home. She had seen his great body, the size of his shoulders and hands, and had screamed herself hoarse.

He had quickly backed away, tears in his eyes.

She glanced again at the Emp, misery welling up within her. *He said he could help me,* she thought. She allowed herself a little hope. Twice today, she had received comments that she was getting better. In less than a day, he had somehow begun to do what an army of doctors had not.

And, for his troubles, her father had beaten him bloody.

Victory dropped her forehead to the bed beside his shoulder, stifling a wretched laugh. "I'm sorry. You must be very unimpressed with my family. Two heartless bastards and a woman who goes into screaming fits for no reason."

He did not respond.

Gingerly, she crawled up onto the bed beside him and pulled the covers over herself.

"You have a reason," he said.

Victory sat up quickly, her heart beginning to pound. Dragomir's eyes were closed, rapidly moving against the lids as if in a dream. She watched him for several minutes as he continued to snore softly. Then, slowly, she lowered herself back to the bed.

• • •

When Dragomir opened his eyes, it was to the tingling wash of Imperial nanos working their magic within him. Usually, he would have removed the disturbance within his tissues immediately, much preferring to heal normally than to use the Imperium's dispassionate tech. He hated the odd feeling, the strange energy the tiny machines left behind that was so foreign to his own, but at this point, feeling bones in his back and ribs and arms mending, he was willing to put up with their internal buzz. His ribs were killing him, and his shoulders felt like they had been hacked off and their bloody stumps used to pound at his empty sockets. He groaned and tried to roll off his arms.

Too late, he found himself face-to-face with the sleeping princess.

He froze.

She was beautiful. Body and soul. When she slept, her ramas opened slightly, allowing some of her deep silver energy to flow through, setting her *au* aglow.

Dragomir knew he should probably roll back aside quickly, before she could catch him staring at her in her sleep like some morally-deprived letch, but he found himself enraptured by every curve of her face, the gentle lines of her nose and chin. Against his better instincts, he settled back to carve every detail into his memory. Her smooth face, completely devoid of fear or anxiety, was an exquisite work of art, and the gentle curve of her neck as it disappeared into the hem of her nightgown, the way her raven hair lay across her chest in luxurious ripples, took his breath away. Had he had his sketchbook, he would have taken pleasure in drawing her freckles, her alabaster skin…

Her green eyes popped open suddenly, startling him.

Instantly, she sucked in a huge breath and—

"I'm rolling back over!" he cried, fighting the wash of panic she was throwing out. "See?" He flopped onto his back and winced at the way his shoulders started to pound again. He rolled onto his other arm, scooting himself away from the edge of the bed.

"Why were you staring at me?!" she demanded. She had crawled out of bed and was at the other end of the chain. He knew, because he felt it go taut.

"My arms hurt like hell, Princess," he said honestly. "I rolled off of them when I woke up and you were there."

He could feel her squinting at the back of his head. "Then that's what woke me? You rolling over?"

"Probably," he lied. He wasn't sure how long he had been staring at her, but he was pretty sure it had been upwards of fifteen to twenty minutes. He wasn't about to tell *her* that, though. She'd probably think that he had been planning some nefarious deed, or something else equally as ridiculous.

After a moment, she tentatively said, "I had an interesting dream. Very vivid."

Sensing an olive-branch, still facing the opposite end of the room, Dragomir gingerly said, "What about?"

"It was about a one-eyed woman."

He froze. Trying his best to sound disinterested, he said, "Really?"

"She was taken from her village by a handsome soldier. A general of some sort. For some reason, I kept feeling like I knew him from somewhere."

Dragomir winced. "Probably your brother, then."

There was a long pause. "You're hiding something."

Oh crap. "No I'm not," he blurted.

"Sit up," she growled. "I want to see your face."

"I'm comfortable right here," Dragomir said.

"Now."

He sighed, deeply. Lancing agony through his ribs at the contortions necessary to get into a seated position, he let out a huge breath of relief as his head came to rest on the headboard.

She squinted her emerald eyes at him. "There's something you're not telling me about that past life."

Dragomir tried to keep his face utterly straight, the picture of sagely, knowing wisdom. "What makes you say that?"

"You want your hands unshackled?" she demanded.

He sighed and slumped forward, the scholarly façade vanishing in an instant. "Lady, you sure know how to dangle a carrot."

"Tell me what you forgot to mention last night. Don't think I didn't catch the way you babbled like an idiot trying to change the subject. What did you find? Was I a mass murderer or something?"

He looked up at her, scanning her face. *She's going to think I'm lying.* Softly, he said, "Your village got taken by an invading army. I was one of the officers. I grabbed you and threw you over my horse. You weren't pleased."

She stared at him, clearly in disbelief. "That man was *you.*"

Dragomir allowed himself a nervous grin.

She narrowed her eyes, her face darkening. "You took me against my will."

Dragomir reddened. "Uh. From your home, yes. But, uh," he said, remembering the dream, "Not sure how much of the life you saw, but you were more than willing by the time I took your virginity. Took a couple months of coaxing you. Was hard to get you to trust me, considering."

Her mouth fell open. At first, she started to blush. Then her hackles went up, and anger started boiling up from within, making his skin ache where it radiated outward. "I didn't get to that part," she growled.

"I warned you," Dragomir said, glaring. "I wasn't going to say any-thing, but you got pushy."

"Tell me of another," she snapped. "Something I can believe."

Once again, he felt as if he had become the passing entertainment for a bored princess. Dragomir sighed and closed his eyes. "Very well," he said. One of the curses of being an Emp was that people always wanted insight onto their past lives, always too fascinated with what had once happened, and not with who they were now, and what they planned to do. Fortunately, until today, he had been able to simply tell them, 'Not right now,' and they would bob their heads and babble their thanks that he would consider it, someday.

Here, with the princess, he had the feeling that he'd get the same result telling the princess 'Not right now' that he would get telling God to halt the tides.

Settling himself, Dragomir focused on her *au.* Within moments, he found another strong soul-thread drifting through the embarrassment and irritation that was her current state of being. He narrowed his consciousness to that single image, then followed it back to its soul-bead.

She was a merchant's son who grew up in his father's footsteps. He watched him count every credit, watched him save up the money for a new mansion and a retirement at a very young age, watched him sell his empire and move to the colonies for adventure. He watched a great catastrophe befall the colony's supply lines, watched much of the colony deteriorate to primitivity within a few short years. He watched a band of desperate raiders attack his manse, take his food, and cart off his property. He saw the raiders force him to the ground, hogtie him, saw them put a gun to his head. He saw a fiery redhead stop them, saw her step forward and lift his chin, a warning in her deep blue eyes…

Dragomir's mouth fell open as he watched himself claim the young merchant, take him for his own.

"What?" the princess demanded, wary.

"Uh," Dragomir said. He replayed the lifetime, trying to find some evidence that it wasn't *him* carting the merchant off to work her fields. But he knew. There was no mistaking the fiery redhead…or the passion they shared between the sheets. "Uh." He swallowed, his mouth suddenly very dry. *This can't be happening*, he thought. *Coincidence.*

"Tell me, slave," the princess growled.

The word 'slave' got under his hackles just enough to make him tell her. Dragomir grinned, all teeth, and said, "You were a merchant's son who inherited a vast trading empire. You sold out, went out to the colonies, claimed yourself a huge swath of land, had a mansion built. The colony's supply lines failed—I got the feel maybe it was an exploding star that rendered one of the jumps unusable…" He paused, frowning. "Stars can explode?"

"Probably a supernova," she said dismissively. She was watching him hungrily. "What else?"

Still frowning at the idea of an exploding star, Dragomir haltingly continued, "Well, you were a practical man, and rich, so you had plenty of stored foodstuffs. You did well for yourself, right up until the point where some starving colonists raided your mansion and put a gun to your head."

When he stopped there, the princess frowned. "They killed me?"

"No," Dragomir said reluctantly.

"What happened?" she demanded. When he didn't respond, her look was utterly cold. "I have seen horrors that you can only imagine, slave, and if you think to spare me some shock to my sensibilities, you're wasting your time."

Dragomir narrowed his eyes. "You're going to unlock the cuffs?"

She bit her lip and eyed his hands warily. "We'll see."

"I want your word."

"You'll tell me what I want to know and I'll think about it." No threats. Just a statement of fact. Once again, Dragomir was reminded of just how much power the princess had over him in his current state. Life or death. She could deliver either, with a single word.

Sighing, he said, "A redhead woman told them to hold their fire. Saved your life. Raiders told her to take him home with her, 'cause they weren't leaving evidence for the government to find, if it ever did get back on its feet. She trussed you up, threw you in a wagon. Took you back to her farm to work her fields. That was me, too."

Victory stared at him so long that Dragomir began to wonder if something inside her brain had snapped. Finally, she laughed and said, "Another."

"What do you think I am?" Dragomir growled, "your personal storyteller?!"

The princess narrowed her eyes. "Until I say otherwise, that's exactly what you are."

And Dragomir realized she was right. He found himself feeling very much like he was facing off an annoyed tigress. Nervously, he searched through her *au* for another powerful soul-image. He found it and followed it back to the lifetime-bead.

He watched her born a chieftain's daughter on one of the forgotten colonies. He watched her people struggle for resources, watched her grow to a life of war. She was raised a warrior, a glorious Valkyrie amongst a militaristic people. He watched her lead raids on countless towns and villages, watched as she accumulated a vast wealth, blossoming into a chieftain in her own right. He watched her fall to a peasant's shovel, watched her men pushed back in retreat. As the village finished routing the attackers, searching back through the fields of wheat looking for raiders to put on display and execute, he watched her thrown over a shoulder, quickly scurried off the field by an anxious villager. He watched her trussed up to a barn post. He felt her defeat, felt her acknowledge the laws of combat and victory's spoils. He felt her not care. He watched her open her eyes, take in her captor's face for the first time…

Dragomir stared at the man's face, recognizing it from his own memories. *This can't be right*, he thought.

"Well?" the princess demanded. "Another one of the two of us?"

Dragomir fumbled through the lifetime. Finally, he just stared at her. Suddenly, the dormant connection was beginning to make a lot more sense.

"Let me guess," she sneered. "I captured you, brutally whisked you away to my home, and tied you to my bed."

"Uh," Dragomir said. "Not quite."

She raised a brow, waiting.

Reluctantly, he said, "You were a great warrior princess. You led many successful raids on nearby towns. You were very wealthy—a sign that you were good at what you did—and beautiful, in an 'I'm Going To Crush Your Scrotum For Looking At Me Sideways' sort of way. You were in the middle of a raid when a peasant snuck up behind you and hit you in the head with a shovel."

She frowned. "A shovel?" She cocked her head. "He killed me with a shovel?"

"No," Dragomir said, "But he did save your life. The villagers routed your party—on the way to the raid, you and most of your men caught the flu, and you made the decision to push on anyway, but you did so sick, and there were more villagers than you had anticipated…Anyway, they routed you, and they were combing through the remains of the battle, looking for survivors to put on the rack, when the villager who flattened you threw you over his shoulder and scurried you off to his homestead in the woods."

She gave him a dark look, obviously knowing where this one was going. "Tell another."

"You were a pirate," Dragomir said, no longer bothering to filter as the images came up. "Big. Male. You took pleasure in raiding government ships. You captured yourself a galleon, found yourself suddenly rich. You took the galleon's captain—a nice little brunette, about 5'2"—and chained her to your bed to entertain you as you fled that sector of space. You settled down in a mansion outside a pirate colony, had great sex with the woman you'd captured, and eventually married her." He turned to scowl at her, the truth beginning to settle painfully into his stomach. "And oh, yeah, that was me, too."

The princess laughed. "I knew you were lying."

"I'm not lying," Dragomir said, frustrated. Irritated, he reached to his core, began sorting through his own memories. He found the connection their souls shared, watched it spiral between their soul-beads, every once in awhile tying them together, interweaving their lives throughout the ages. He found the same theme, again and again. Each time they met, it was under duress, with a knife to their throat or a gun to their head. Each time, it ended in the deepest, most earth-shattering passion he could imagine. Each powerful lifetime for him, each time he remembered dying old and happy, she was there.

"Um," Dragomir said, caught between the joy of finding her and the irritation that she was a spoiled princess that wouldn't give him back his hands even after being beaten half to death, "All things considered, will you just trust me that I'm not going to hurt you?"

"You won't?" the princess sneered. "Surely you harbor hard feelings for me chaining you to my bed and using you for my entertainment."

Dragomir glanced up again at the eye-hook bolted into the head-board above him. "Well, no hard feelings yet. But you string me up there and there's gonna be a few."

She blinked, obviously not having considered that she was, in essence, doing just that. She cleared her throat, sounding embarrassed. Finally, she said, "Since you are such a good storyteller—and because I am letting you live despite the fact you're an Emp—perhaps you could tell me the story of your life."

She's gonna be stubborn. Dragomir groaned and leaned back against the headboard. *Gods*, his shoulders hurt. Even sitting up, the pain was lancing down his arms, setting his elbows and wrists on fire. "Lady," he said, "We've both had a miserable week, and my arms feel like someone is jamming a red-hot rebar through the marrow, so it's hard to concentrate. Take off the shackles, then maybe we can talk. Until then, I'm gonna try and sleep." Then, desperate to find some way to relieve some of the pressure in his arms, he scooted down the bed, rolled onto his stomach, and closed his eyes, trying to push the throbbing into the back of his mind.

He had fallen asleep again when he felt a hand gripping the back of his neck, hard.

CHAPTER 7

Touched by an Emp

"Just stay where you are," Victory cried, when the man jolted awake and started to sit up beneath her. Seeing the huge muscles in his back flexing, fear lanced through her like an unwelcome jolt of hot ice. She spasmodically tightened her fingers on his neck, digging her nails into his vertebrae and jamming his face back into the blanket. Into his ear, she snarled, "You *move* without my permission and I'm going to put this thing through your skull, do you understand?" She hefted her statue where he could see it, her fingers clammy on the mermaid's golden tail.

"You know," he said, his voice muffled by the covers, "I need to add this to my list of Least Favorite Ways to Wake Up. I think I just peed myself."

Victory swallowed, hard, trying to find the same force of will that had put her on the bed in the first place. "Just don't move," she said, trying to fight the terror building within her. Quieter, she said, "I'm going to release your hands."

She knew he heard her, because he went absolutely still.

Oh gods, she thought, holding him down, horrified at the way their bodies were touching, yet too terrified to let him go. *What am I doing?!*

But her greatest foible—the greatest foible of anyone with the Royal gene—was curiosity, and the stranger had piqued it beyond endurance. "Just stay very still," she said. She looked down at the key dangling from where her fingers were wrapped around the statuette. Ever so slowly, she released his neck.

He remained stock-still, only the rise and fall of his bandaged ribs giving any indication he was still alive.

"You make any wrong movements and I'm going to make the world less one Emp," she warned. Then, before she could change her mind, she ducked down, grabbed the short chain holding his wrists together, and started undoing the locks.

The shackles fell off, and he groaned as his arms slid off his back to rest on either side. "Oh my gods, thank you," he moaned into the blanket.

Suddenly, seeing his big arms free, it was all Victory could do not to curl into a terrified ball. She slammed her palm back to the base of his neck, pressing down hard. "Just don't move," she whispered, her knuckles aching around the statue. Terror was driving upwards again, and the images of six years of brutality began filtering through her consciousness. She remembered big hands, on her breasts, between her legs, holding her down.

"I'm not going to hurt you," he said. "I swear."

"I'm the Royal Princess," she babbled. "Of course you're not going to hurt me."

"You may be a princess," he said, "But you're also scared shitless, otherwise you wouldn't be trying to press my spine through my esophagus."

She couldn't do it. He was too big, too close. She was beginning to shake with the images pouring from within. "Put your hands back. I'm going to shackle them again. Maybe you can work on my ankles later."

This time, he stiffened. "Princess," he said, "You're going to have to trust me." He left his big hands at his sides.

He's not going to do it, Victory thought, her panic rising like a hurricane within. "Please," she whimpered, scared, now.

Instead, his big shoulders bunched, and his arms slid forward, slowly, under him.

"What are you *doing*?!" she gasped, unable to get enough air. "Lay down. Stop."

Slowly, like a big cat, he pushed himself to his hands and knees and slid away from her, dark blue eyes fixed on her face. In moments, his head was out of range of her statue.

Seeing him, naked, free, disobeying, with his manhood dangling low between his legs, the switch in Victory's brain tripped. She felt herself slide away, distancing her from her body even as it began to rock back and forth, crying. She closed her eyes against the image of him on her bed, watching her like a wary predator.

Just call the Praetorian, a voice within her demanded. *Just call them and tell them he's an Emp. They'll get rid of him for you.*

Then, in misery, *They already know he's an Emp, and they chained me to him anyway.*

She started to sob in despair, the terror becoming too much.

She felt the warmth settle around her again, making her feel safe and secure despite the way her chest was sucking in too much air, the way her hands were tingling from fear and over-oxygenation.

That's him, she thought, horrified. She started to pull away.

Her terror ratcheted upwards when she felt his big hand settle on one of her ankles, holding her in place.

"Sorry I've gotta do it this way, Princess," he said softly, "but there's something I have to show you."

Sorry I've gotta do it this way...She shuddered and froze, staring at where he was grabbing her, so wrapped in terror that she was unable to even call for the Praetorian. A whimper escaped her lips as she felt his warm fingers move against her skin.

"Shhh," he whispered. "Feel that?"

Something was flooding through her ankle, washing up her leg, leaving exquisite golden warmth in its wake. Despite her terror, it relaxed her almost instantly. It swept through like a ball of glorious sunshine, brushing the horror out, burning the fear to dust upon contact. It flushed her from head to toe, then settled into her chest, a pleasant, tingling heat.

"You still afraid?" Dragomir asked softly, after a moment. His blue eyes were worried, his big, tawny body tense.

Victory stared at him, her mouth open. "What did you just do?"

His big hand still on her ankle, he grinned shyly. "I opened up your gi meridians."

For the first time in six years, she was totally and completely without fear. Tensions she hadn't even realized her body had seemed to melt into the blankets, and she kind of slumped backwards onto her elbows to stare at him, lest she fall over completely.

"It's only temporary," he said quickly, "a quick fix until we can get your ramas working again. Basically, you're not getting the outside energy you need, so I fed you with some of my own. I can do it once a day, if you'd like, though I've gotta have my hands free."

She continued to stare.

"I'd do more, but I'm using up my own reserves to do it," he said quickly, obviously growing nervous under her stare, "They should be built up again by tomorrow, though."

Victory fought to find something to say, and failed, finally giving up to just soak in the delicious relaxation within her. *The Imperium kills Emps...why?* Suddenly, the fact that they were genetic freaks didn't seem all that important. Only the peace—after so many years of fear—seemed important.

"So," Dragomir said, starting to sound uneasy. He sat back and pulled a pillow over his crotch. "Still want me to work on your ankles?"

Her...ankles? Come to think of it, they were still throbbing, and it seemed a different sort of ache than the rush of relaxation that had flooded her. Victory flopped onto her back and stuck a foot in his lap. "Could you have done that all this time?"

"Yes," he admitted, gingerly picking up her foot with hands that dwarfed it, "but it really *is* hard to concentrate when they're twisted behind me like that."

She peered at him with one eye. "You lied to me."

"Uh, stretched the truth a bit, maybe." He closed his eyes, and she jumped as she felt spikes of warmth lash downwards through her ankle, into her foot. It started to soothe the throbbing, there, and within a minute, she felt the blood in her toes start to circulate again, driving cold up her leg as her heart carried it away.

"It's going to take a few weeks," he said, once he came out of his trance, "But eventually, your mind will start recognizing your feet, again, and forgive them."

In any other situation, Victory would have tilted back her head and laughed until she was hoarse at the ridiculously sentimental idea that she subconsciously hated her feet. But lying here, one foot warm while the other was still ice cold, pain-free when none of the doctors' medications or procedures had helped, she simply nodded.

Dragomir's big hands moved to the next foot, swallowing her ankle between them. She watched this time, fascinated, as he closed his eyes and the spikes of warmth began pulsing down through her bones once more. "What I wouldn't give to be able to see what you see," she whispered, as the ice began flowing up her leg and her foot began to throb with blood-flow.

"Maybe someday," he said, setting her foot back on the bed, "I can show you." He leaned back against the headboard, looking exhausted.

Victory muttered something to herself about uncouth native cads, but savored the feeling in her feet. She fell into a light doze, reveling in the warmth and calm she felt within.

"I'm hungry," he said, making her jump. "What are you going to feed me?"

Victory blinked at him. Clearly, he had been making some sort of joke.

But then, seeing his raised eyebrow and his impetuous pout, she realized he was serious.

"*Me?*" she managed. "Feed *you?*" She snorted. "Now that your hands are free, slave, *you* shall be feeding *me*." She waved a dismissive hand. "Grapes and such."

His mouth fell open. "You can't be serious."

She pushed herself up onto her elbows, giving him an appraising look. "Cheese," she decided. "And apples."

He narrowed his eyes at her. "You put cheese and apples into my hands, and they're going down my gullet. I'm starving. That dinky little meal you fed me didn't do jack."

It was her turn for her jaw to drop. "I gave you three servings of everything!"

He raised an eyebrow and jabbed a finger at his stomach. "You hear that? She is telling me that she's hungry. And yes, it is a 'she' because more often than not, she's chewing me a new hole."

Victory could not believe what she was hearing. "You insult women… in my presence?"

"Just stating a fact," he said, glancing at the door. "Did we miss dinner?"

"You…" Victory sputtered. "You, sir, are a pompous chauvinist ass!"

"Better than being a slave." He got off the bed, headed for the door.

"Where are you going?!" Victory cried, sitting up all the way.

"I'm hungry," he said. "I'm going to go find something to eat."

Faced with such grace and power, all she could think to say was, "What about me?"

"You're coming with me," he said, grinning. He gave the chain between them a gentle tug. "Obviously."

Bruised and battered as he was, Victory knew he could still drag her, kicking and screaming, wherever he wanted to go. And the Praetorian, damn them, would probably let him do it. She swallowed, trying desperately to think of a reason to stay in the room. "My hair and makeup need to be done," she babbled. "I'm not presentable."

The man gave her a look like she were growing popsicles from her ears, then snorted. He turned and started shuffling to the door, one hand gripping the chain around his neck.

"Wait!" she screeched, when the chain went tight, dragging her out of bed.

He stopped and looked back at her. "Yes?"

"I'll call my chambermaids," she insisted. "I need my wardrobe—"

He raised a heavy eyebrow at her. "Lady, I'm so hungry I'm about to walk out there naked as a jaybird. You and your wardrobe can wait." He turned back to the door and put his hand on the latch.

"I'm not presentable," she moaned, realizing he was utterly serious. She started patting at her hair, which was loose and snarled from sleep.

He glanced over his shoulder at her. "You're beautiful," he said. Then he yanked the door open and smiled at the Praetorian outside. "Now please tell these nice ladies we're just going out to eat, and that the swords at my throat are completely unnecessary."

"Leave him," Victory said, not knowing what else to do.

The phoenix-clad Praetorian quickly dropped their weapons and stepped back.

Dragomir grunted and stepped forward, a big fist gripping the tether at his throat. The chain went taut again, and he tugged her out of the room by the band around her waist. The Praetorian gave Victory a dubious look, but said nothing, falling in behind her, allowing the slave to lead the way.

"This is not proper!" Victory cried, as he tugged her down the hall and started to descend the steps. "*I'm* supposed to be leading *you*."

"Then *lead*," the man said, stopping on the stairs. He made an irritated gesture at the steps in front of him. "I'm telling you, wench, that she's about to eat a hole through my spine."

Victory stared at him. 'Wench' again. In public. It was so utterly horrifying that she just stood there.

"Fine," Dragomir grunted, turning back to the stairs.

"No!" she cried, running up to get in front of him. "If my father saw you leading me around like a mule, he'd do much worse than last time."

Dragomir glanced down at her, and she saw a flash of something soft in his eyes before he hid it. "Then by all means, Princess. Lead the way. I'll follow along like a properly trained pet, if it means I'll get my dinner."

"Fine," Victory said. At the bottom of the stairs, the squad of house Praetorian were watching her curiously. She took a deep breath and reached up to rearrange her hair.

"Oh for the gods' sakes!" Dragomir cried, waving his arms in disgust.

Several of the house Praetorian frowned and started coming up the stairs, darkness in their features.

"Keep your voice down," Victory growled, motioning at the Praetorian to stay back. "The house Praetorian are not allied to my brother or I, only to the Imperial House. These women around us wear the phoenix egg—it symbolizes my personal crest. You can trust them. They were sworn to me at my birth, and have served me since they were able. The ones down there belong to the house, and the phoenix upon their chests bears no nest or egg."

Dragomir frowned down at the black-armored women. "Now that you mention it, I recognize the one who tried to break my elbow."

"I have given orders for my personal guard not to hurt you," Victory said. "That will not carry over to the house guard, as my father's orders will overrule mine for those allied to the house."

Dragomir narrowed his blue eyes. "So keep my mouth shut and my head down around them. Gotcha."

"I also discovered while you slept that you can trust my brother's guard, as well," Victory said. "If you see a Praetorian wearing a dragon with his feet wrapped around an emerald blade, it means that the man was sworn into his service, personally. If he gives the man an order, he will follow it, even if it means his death."

Dragomir turned and gave her a long stare. "This is not putting food in my gut."

Provincials. Making a disgusted noise, Victory brushed past him down the staircase.

"How many Praetorian in your personal guard?" he asked, as he followed.

"Twenty," Victory said, before she caught herself. Frowning, she glanced back up at him suspiciously. "Why?"

He shrugged. "I only ever see four at a time. Thought I saw different faces. Was just wondering if there were more."

She watched him a moment, suspicious, then continued her march down the staircase, spine as straight as she could make it go. Once the house guard tried to fall in around her, however, she said in Imperial, "The slave and I will be sightseeing. I will be bringing my personal guard. The rest stay."

The house guard gave each other nervous looks. "We were instructed to guard you on your journey, milady." Which meant that her father had told them to ensure she didn't eat unless it was at regular meals, at his table.

"You will stay here," Victory said. "It is late, and I am not interested in a great parade." She started moving forward, and watched with falling hopes as the Praetorian started to fall in behind her anyway.

Then Lion, captain of Victory's Praetorian, stepped forward and snapped, "You heard the princess. Back to positions."

There was a tense moment between the two factions, as her house guard and her personal guard faced off. As if she weren't nervously awaiting the result, Victory kept moving.

With Lion being the ranking Praetorian, however, the house guard stepped down.

"Thank you," Victory whispered, once they were out of earshot.

She thought she saw the glimpse of a smile cross Lion's no-nonsense face as she marched beside her. "I live to serve, Princess."

After a moment, Dragomir leaned down and into her ear asked, "What was that all about?"

"Technically, we're cheating," Victory said. "My father stated that I would only eat if I came out of my room for meals. He meant, of course, that I eat every meal at his table, during mealtime, or not at all. I'm taking him a bit more literally." She winked at Dragomir. "It's a habit my brother and I got into, as kids. Often, my father's bane is in the details. He completely overlooks the small stuff sometimes."

"How far to the kitchens?" Dragomir asked.

Victory made a disgusted sigh and peered over her shoulder at him. "You really do have a one-track mind, don't you?"

He patted his chiseled—and bruised—abdomen. "She's hungry."

"Ugh!" she cried. "Men!" She had turned on heel and taken three steps before she realized he was chuckling behind her.

"Do you realize," he said, "That we've passed three different males in the hall so far, and you haven't even noticed?"

Victory opened her mouth to tell him he was an ignorant native fool, then froze. She glanced behind them at a quickly-disappearing form in the darkened hall.

"That was one of them," Dragomir confirmed. "He saw you coming and bolted."

Victory stared at him. "You *healed* me?" Gratitude began welling up from within, mixing with the delicious warmth that still heated her chest.

Dragomir made a sour face. "Unfortunately, no. Your body's going to run out of energy again here soon, and I'll have to repeat the treatment. You'll never be truly fixed until we get those ramas open and working again."

The thought of falling prey to the horrible images of her past once more left Victory feeling sick. "Slave," she said, "You keep that from happening again, and I swear to you that your hands will stay free."

Instead of grinning, like she expected, he simply glowered at her. "Bound and helpless," he growled. Then he looked down at his hands. "Well, not so helpless." He gave her an evil grin.

Victory blinked, suddenly terrified that she wasn't terrified. He was *huge*, he was a *native*, he was *naked*, and he was bound to her *waist*, and his arms were *free* and…

Dragomir whistled a pleasant tune and shuffled past her.

Victory stared until he paused and gave a slight tug on the chain, jerking the belt around her waist. "You coming, Princess?" he asked. "'Cause that offer to drag you's still open." When she only gaped at him, he shrugged and started walking again.

Fuming, Victory trotted up beside him before he toppled her over. "You are a *cad*," she growled. "An absolute—"

Dragomir twisted and kissed her. On the face. His big hand wrapped in her hair, his big body pulling her close.

Time stopped for Victoria, and all she could think was that her Praetorian were going to kill him.

Then Dragomir released her and grinned. "But thanks, Princess. I think I can manage that." Whistling again, he kept walking, big arms swinging.

Victoria's heart was hammering in her chest so hard that she didn't hear her Praetorian's question at first.

"Are you all right, Princess?" Lion asked. "Did he hurt you?"

She glanced blankly at her Praetorian, who was watching Dragomir depart with something between astonishment and Death on her face. "Huh?" Her brain was still fuzzy.

"Did he *hurt* you?" Lion demanded.

Flushed, Victoria said, "Uh…" Then she realized the chain was about to snap taut again and, letting out a squeal, raced to catch up, giggling. "You cad!" she cried again, whacking him on the arm. "I'll lead."

"Probably better if you did," Dragomir said, "'Cause I have no idea where the hell I'm going." He didn't slow his shuffle at all.

Victory had taken another few steps before she realized that her Praetorian were not following. When she looked back, she saw four mouths agape, four hardened, lifetime-soldiers staring at her like she'd grown a foot between her eyes.

Seeing their stunned expressions, Victory giggled again. "This way." She grabbed Dragomir's arm and tugged him through a smaller hallway, toward the kitchens.

Shaking themselves, her Praetorian jogged to catch up.

They found the kitchens shut down, the stoves and grills cold. Victory snuck in and flipped on the lights, half-expecting to get scolded by the cook. Seeing the thin woman's domain unguarded, Victory grinned and started rummaging through bins.

Dragomir glanced around the kitchen like a panther that had suddenly been dropped into a den of lions. "Uh," he said, "this place is huge."

"Just start opening up cabinets," Victory said. "There's crackers and things."

Dragomir turned to stare at her as if she had lost her mind. "You've got a kitchen like *this* and you're going to eat *crackers?*"

Victory frowned at him. "Well, I'd eat pastries, but I don't know where Cook put them. Probably gave the leftovers to staff."

"By the gods' stale nutsacks, woman, get out of my way." He brushed past her and grabbed one of the skillets from the rack. She watched as he set it down on the burner and went rummaging through the wall of cool-boxes, picking out foodstuffs here and there as he went.

Nervously, Victory said, "Um…What are you doing?"

"Feeding us," Dragomir said. He held up a chunk of raw flesh sitting in a glass dish, in a pool of blood. "What kind of meat is this?"

Victory gagged. "I don't know!"

Shrugging, he tossed it on the pile. "You know where the cook keeps his spices?"

"What spices?" Victory said, with a small frown.

But he had already started sifting through the cabinets, plucking out bottles here and there.

Victory watched him, curious, as he rubbed butter into the bottom of the skillet and flicked on the burner. Behind her, the Praetorian had come inside, probably to assure that the Emp wasn't going to start playing with knives.

When he *did* start playing with knives, they quickly positioned themselves between the man and herself, blocking her view.

"Oh would you just get out of the way!" Victoria cried, pushing past the Praetorian to see the vegetable that Dragomir was chopping. "What are you making?"

"Spaghetti," he said, popping a mushroom into his mouth, then rolling his eyes with pleasure as he chewed it.

Obviously, Victory thought, he had lived a sheltered life. She told him as much.

He shrugged and went back to work dicing. "We usually only make spaghetti on feast days, and it's a whole village affair. Everybody chips in a little bit of everything. I usually throw a goat or two into the pot."

Victory's stomach twisted. "*Goat?*" she demanded, in disgust.

He didn't seem to hear her. "It's gonna probably take an hour or so, so snack on something if you need to." As he spoke, he handed her a slice of red bell pepper.

Victoria stared down at the pepper. She saw no dip, no oils or cheese within reach. "What am I supposed to do with this?"

"Eat it," he said, already chopping up another onion.

She sniffed it, then took a tentative nibble. Without dips, cheese, or oils to accent the flavor, she wrinkled her nose and managed politely, "It's...fresh."

He dumped the onion into the pan and started cutting olives. "Considering the Imperium steals two thirds of the crops of most of Mercy, it better be."

Victory made an indignant scoff. "You have yet to prove that the tax rates are so high."

Dragomir pulled a pot from the rack and started throwing tomatoes and vegetables into it. "That snooty woman with the stick up her ass didn't bring any records back with her, did she?"

Victory frowned. "Don't be rude. Her name is Kiara." But now that she was thinking about it, Kiara hadn't brought the subject up again, and it wasn't like Kiara not to be on top of things. Eight years under her watchful eye as her student had taught Victory that the woman had an amazing eye for detail, and she never forgot a task.

Dragomir shrugged. "I don't like her. I can't understand what she's saying to you, but I don't like the feel I get off of her."

"Don't be ridiculous," Victory snorted. "I've known Kiara since I was a child. She helped raise me."

"Raised by wolves doesn't make you a wolf," Dragomir said.

Victory, uncomfortable, nodded at the food. "It smells okay."

He grinned at her shyly. "It's not often I can cook for someone. Even when I was home—" He slowed, his voice dropping soberly. "Even when I was at home, I didn't have anyone."

Strangely, she got the sense that he was lying.

He glanced at her, his face clearing. "You're right, you know. Being an Emp in the colony isn't just like having blonde hair, instead of brown. People look at you differently. They give you a wide berth. They..." He gave a soft chuckle down at the meat he was cubing. When he looked up at her, there was pain in his gaze. "They don't want you around their daughters unless it's to cure them of some ill."

"*You?*" Victory snorted. "You're harmless."

He raised a thick black brow at her. "That's not what you were saying yesterday."

"I changed my mind," Victory said, plucking a mushroom out of the sizzling skillet. She blew on it carefully, then tasted it. "I never watched anybody cook before," she said, peering around his elbow as he finished browning the meat and dumped it into the pot with the rest of the veggies. She leaned against the counter, enthralled, as he dumped a couple cups of wine into the pot and started to stir. "How do you know when it's done?"

Dragomir rummaged for a lid and dropped it atop the pot, then turned toward her to lean against the counter, facing her. He had a handful of walnuts in one hand, and was popping them into his mouth. He glanced at the clock above the exit where the Praetorian stood. "If my calculations are correct, it will take exactly one hour, twenty-three minutes and fifty-two seconds for the sauce to finish simmering. Then he cocked his head. "Give or take three seconds."

Victory was impressed. "Wow, that's pretty—" She bit off the word 'precise' at the flash of amusement in his eyes. Narrowing her eyes at him, she growled, "You're lying."

"Maybe a little." He grinned and tossed the rest of the walnuts into his mouth.

Wrinkling her nose, she looked around the kitchen. She found herself a little taken aback at all the numerous weapons hanging from racks, sitting in blocks, lying on counters…And was even more surprised that it hadn't even occurred to her that he would try to use one of them.

"Whatever you did to me," Victory said, "You're going do it again tomorrow."

The Emp raised a single eyebrow. "That so?"

"Yes," Victory stated. "First thing."

He dropped another walnut into his mouth and chewed thoughtfully, watching her. "How about a trade? I energize your meridians, you unlock the ankle cuffs."

Victory laughed. "You'll do what I tell you to do."

Dragomir hesitated, a walnut half-lowered into his open mouth, a single eyebrow raised.

Remembering that she was dealing with an Emp, and that her brother had supposedly beaten him half to death without so much as a blip on the meter, Victory grimaced. "We might be able to work something out."

Dragomir laughed. "Sounds like you were choking on something when you said that."

Victory sniffed and went to examine Cook's huge copper pot where it hung from the ceiling. Easily big enough to cook a whole Praetorian cavalryman, horse and all. Twenty minutes later, the savory smells issuing from the top of the Emp's pot were becoming too much for Victory to bear. "It smells good. Let's eat it now." She reached for the lid.

"Wait. Not done yet." When she ignored him, Dragomir frowned and smacked her hand.

Instantly, four Praetorian had him backed over the stove, their swords at his throat.

"Um, Princess?" he asked, sounding nervous. He looked at her over the folded steel blades, swallowing hard.

Victory lifted the lid of the pot and looked inside. She inhaled, then set the lid back down with a grunt. She dug into the bag of walnuts that the Emp had found and started munching them thoughtfully. "You know," Victory began conversationally, "you should be more careful. They're trained to kill anything that touches me without my permission."

"I think they broke another rib," he muttered.

Victory sighed and dismissed her Praetorian with a wave.

Dragomir patted at the bandages around his torso. He lifted his head and glared at the Praetorian, who glared back. Their hands started to slip under their cloaks, for their swords.

"I wouldn't stare," Victory warned, popping another walnut into her mouth. "They're getting agitated."

"They're *jumpy*," he growled, looking them dead in the eyes. "Like small, annoying dogs with metabolism issues."

She lifted both brows at him. "You just raised your hand to a member of the royal family. By all rights, you should be dead."

He swung to face her, scowling. "I smacked your greedy little fingers away from my food."

She choked on a walnut. "*Greedy*? It befuddles me that you think you can speak such to a member of the royal family."

He narrowed his eyes. "Be glad I didn't use a spoon, wench."

Victoria choked. "Be glad my Praetorian don't flatten you to the floor. They would in a heartbeat, if they knew you were referring to me as such. You may address me as Princess or milady or mistress or, on a very good day, Victory. Not 'wench.'"

"You know what, wench?" Dragomir said, glaring. "You're right." He snatched up his spoon and pointed across the kitchen. "Go stand over there and find your own food. I don't want them getting the wrong idea and thinking I'm force-feeding you."

And, true to his word, when his meal was finished, he took out an enormous serving-platter from the cabinet, heaped a tangle of noodles in its center, and then dumped the entire pot of sauce atop it. Then he took out a fork and a knife, moved his heaping platter to an island counter, and started eating.

"I want some," Victory said, eying the pile. Her stomach was rumbling.

"Sorry," he said, stuffing noodles and sauce into his face. He didn't sound sorry at all. "We can't let the Praetorian take the chance that my cooking is so sub-par that your royal ass might suffer the ill-effects of food poisoning."

Victory stared at him. "You're really going to eat that without me?"

His answer was a loud slurp of noodles.

Victory stomped over to the nearest fridge, yanked it open, and stared at the contents. She found a wedge of cheese, which she mutilated in an attempt to get it out of its rind, and yanked some crackers from a shelf in the pantry, then sat down opposite the island from Dragomir, eating with her back facing him.

Behind her, he slurped like a pig in the trough.

"Would you *please* not eat so loud?!" she cried. "You're making me lose my appetite."

If anything, the slurping sounds grew louder.

"Ugh!" Victory growled. She hunched over her plate of cheese and crackers, trying to pretend the disgusting creature behind her didn't exist.

When they were both finished with their meals, Victory stuffed the leftover cheese and crackers into a bag and then stuffed it between her breasts. The Emp, for his part, looked ill. He had cleaned his plate, but she had watched him force the last bites down with all the stubborn determination of a feral boar.

"Did you enjoy eating *all* that food?" Victory asked pleasantly. When he gave her a dark look, his face pale and sweating, she gave him a polite smile. "Let's get going, then." She gestured at his clean plate. "Now that you've had such a *filling* meal, perhaps you would enjoy a tour of the palace?"

His blue eyes flashed with challenge. "I feel great."

She smiled at him. "Why, slave, I never said you didn't." She cocked her head at him. "Though now that you mention it, you *do* look a little pale. Are you sure you're all right?"

"Fine," Dragomir bit out. "Enjoyed every bite."

She gave him a knowing grin. "I'm sure you did." She turned and started out the door, the Praetorian falling in beside her. "Which part of the palace would you like to see first? I was thinking a trip to the Vanishing Spire, so that we get the spectacular view of the two-thousand-foot drop off the Gorgarian Cliffs.

"Sounds fine to me," he said, much too forcefully.

Delighted, Victory led him to the base of the Vanishing Spire and, because she was feeling malicious, decided to make them walk up the long, spiraling staircase instead of taking the elevator hidden in the wall.

"Don't know what kind of view you're going to get at this time of night, anyway," Dragomir muttered, about halfway up.

"The moons should be out," Victory said. "At their peak, they highlight the entire valley." She continued up the stairs cheerfully, as Dragomir shuffled along behind.

She was actually beginning to feel sorry for him, shackled the way he was, by the time they reached the door to the viewing deck. She opened it and stepped outside to an immediate gust of wind.

At the exit, Dragomir balked. "Those railings don't look big enough."

Oh my gods, Victory thought, delighted, *I think he's afraid of heights…*

"Well," she said with a disappointed sigh, "I suppose if it unnerves you, we may find our entertainment elsewhere."

He straightened like someone had rammed a pole down his spine. "Didn't say it unnerved me," he said tightly, stepping out onto the deck with her.

Oh this is too perfect, Victory thought, absolutely thrilled with this interesting new discovery. She clapped her hands, and the lights on the viewing deck dimmed at her command. The stars were out, and the twin moons lit up the cliffs around them in dazzling shades of blue. Wind whipped past the great cliffs into which the Imperial Palace had been built, and each gust sucked her breath away.

Dragomir, who had followed her reluctantly to the edge, stumbled backwards, grabbing the wall behind him like he was afraid the deck was about to rip off and fall into the ravine.

Victory clapped the lights back on, unable to hide her grin. "Enjoyable, no?"

She'd never seen a man look so green. "I think I need to go lay down."

Chuckling to herself, she led them to the elevator.

As soon as he saw the doors slide open and realized what it was, Dragomir shot her a dark look.

"I was in the mood for a stroll," Victory said, grinning.

"A stroll up sixteen flights of stairs?" he growled.

She waved a dismissive hand. "It was only twelve."

Dragomir muttered something under his breath and followed her back through the winding corridors to her chambers. Victory giggled to herself and led him in a few extra circles around the castle.

"Are you sure you know where you're going?" Dragomir asked, giving the walls and corridors a dubious look.

"I grew up here, didn't I?" Victory said sweetly.

"Yeah," Dragomir said, "But this whole place looks the same. And I'm pretty sure I've seen that elk statue three times already."

He *had* seen that elk statue three times already, but Victory quietly left that part out. Once she felt she had thoroughly made him regret eating her dinner, Victory finally took a small service corridor to start them back on their way to her wing.

They turned a corner on a hallway and Victory almost stumbled into four young men having a hushed conversation in a huddle around a game of dice. They stood up suddenly, giving her and her entourage a wary look.

And, to Victory's horror, one of them looked just like the man who had taken her off of her father's ship. The man who had taken her virginity and left her to bleed in the dark, the man with the crystal blue eyes and scarred lip...

Something about his face triggered something deep within Victory, and she felt her terror surging again, violently shoving its way to the surface.

"Easy, Princess," the Emp said behind her.

"I think it's wearing off," she whimpered.

"I know it is," he said. He grabbed the nearest Praetorian and shoved her at the boys. "Get them out of here!" he snapped.

Lion tore her arm out of Dragomir's grip and turned in a snarl, reaching for her dagger. Dragomir merely gestured at Victoria, then at the boys. Lion followed his gesture warily. She caught the look on Victory's face and seemed to take in the four men in the hall for the first time. An instant later, she was unsheathing her sword. "By order of the Royal Princess of the Imperium, *clear the path!*" She and Victory's other captain, a no-nonsense, willowy woman who had chosen the name of Whip, started toward the men, and they scattered.

Despite the fact that they were suddenly alone in the corridor, the young man's wary face continued to haunt her, clamping down on her throat in terror. *It's him*, Victory thought, remembering the scar upon the man's bottom lip. *That's the man who took me.* She felt a strangled sound coming out of her mouth, the images of her first, horrible night flashing back into her awareness. She saw him tie her legs apart, spread between two bunks. She saw him settle himself on top of her, his ice-blue eyes only inches from her face as he told her how much he was going to enjoy his first royal lay...

Dragomir put his hand on her shoulder.

Instantly, warmth began rushing through her body from his touch, driving out the fear in a wave of clean, hot light. It surged through her with an almost angry violence, seeking out the images boiling up within her and burning them away, leaving gentle, fuzzy warmth in its wake. The sunny energy didn't vanquish all of the darkness, leaving some small corners of herself for her nightmares to hide in, but it managed to stop the images that were bubbling up from the Void.

"Thank you," Victory whispered, looking up at him.

Dragomir's face was ashen, his hand trembling as it fell from her shoulder. When he met her gaze, there was panic in his features. "I need to lay down. I used up too much—" At that, his eyes rolled up into the back of his head and he slumped to the floor at her feet.

CHAPTER 8

The First Bath

D ragomir didn't wake for two days. During those, Victory endured a quick, half-hour food excursion once a day in which a half dozen Praetorian carried his unconscious body in a sling through the halls behind her.

It was Kiara who finally posed the question of what had happened to the slave to cause him to be so thoroughly incapacitated for so long.

"Ask my father," Victory growled at the woman. "The doctors had to medicate him for his injuries."

Kiara's eyes narrowed slightly, but it was just for a moment before the woman bowed and turned to go. Before she reached the door, Victory stopped her.

"Yes, milady?" Kiara asked politely, though there was something in her eyes that Victory didn't like.

Could the Emp be right about her? Victory wondered, studying her butler's face. Finally, she said, "What of those taxation records I requested?"

It could have been Victory's imagination, but she thought she saw a dark look flash over the woman's features before it was hidden behind her stiff mask once more. "The taxation records you requested will take several weeks to gather, milady. It is an entire planet, after all."

Victory didn't like the woman's immediate response—it almost sounded as if had been pre-planned, awaiting for Victory to spring the question—but thanked her and dismissed her anyway.

"She's lying," a weak voice rasped from the bed.

Victory spun, feeling a surge of excitement within her. It was the first time that Dragomir had moved in days.

"I don't know what she was telling you," Dragomir said, his eyes closed, facing the ceiling, "But she was lying. I could see it, plain as the pounding in my head and the horrible need to take a piss."

Victory flushed. "Will you require help?"

"To take a piss?" Dragomir slowly heaved himself out of bed, groaning. "I'm afraid I've got a few more years on me before I need someone to hold my hand when I pee and wipe my ass when I fart."

"You're a cad," she muttered, embarrassed at his colloquialisms. "I'd request that you curb your crass aboriginal language in my presence."

Dragomir dropped his hand from where it was pressed to his forehead and gave her a flat look. "And I'd request a pair of pants, socks, and some undershorts, but we know just how far that's going to get me, don't we?" Muttering, he started trudging to the lavatory, the chains strung between his ankles clinking on the stone with every step, once again giving Victory the choice of following or being dragged.

To Victory's horror, he broke wind as he stopped over the toilet. She quickly turned her back as he lifted the lid, door still wide open to the outer chamber. "Hold on!" she cried, pulling him forward to yank the door shut, blushing again.

He grunted. "Lady, the only two people in here are you and me. Now could you *please* try not to jerk me around right when I'm about to pee like a fire-hose?" He started dragging her back to the toilet.

"You are uncouth," she muttered, listening to the tinkle of his stream hitting the composter.

Dragomir did not reply, instead triggering the composter and moving—*deeper?*—into the room. Victory turned to look.

"How do you get this thing to work?" he asked, peering at the many knobs and nozzles of the enormous bathtub.

Victory felt a sudden spasm of panic. "You can't."

He lifted an arm and stuck his nose in a massive armpit. "Yep," he said, wrinkling his brown face. "It's time." Without waiting for explanation, he turned on the water and set the plug. He started swishing his fingers through the water and fine-tuning the temperature with the individual nozzles.

"You...you..." Victory gulped. "You are a barbarian!"

"Why?" he asked. "How many days have you spent in that set of clothes?"

Victory grimaced. Too long. Then she caught his inference and her eyes widened. "You can't be trying to imply—"

"I can smell you from here, Princess," Dragomir grunted, fiddling with the nozzles as the tub began to fill up. "Fear stinks, you know."

She felt her jaw drop open even as her heartbeat began to speed up. "I am *not* taking a bath with you."

He raised a brow as the tub filled. "Why not? I've been naked not eight feet away for, what, three days now?"

"Four," Victory squeaked. Then she hurriedly added, "But that doesn't matter. You are a slave. It is your lot in life to be naked at your master's whim."

He paused, then, and slowly looked at her over his shoulder. In the dark silence that followed, Victory realized that they were in an enclosed space, with two closed doors, a wall, and fifty feet of space between them and her Praetorian. Her eyes widened and she spun to run, even as he grabbed the chain at his throat.

"I," he growled, tugging her an arm's length-closer, "Am getting," another tug, dragging her backwards, "tired," another, "of hearing" another tug, "that word."

Suddenly, they were face-to-face, and she was held tight against his massive body by his grip on the chain. Softly, into her face, he said, "I'm here of my own will. If you'd open your damned eyes, you would see that."

"Unhand me, slave!" Victory snapped, pushing at him, squirming. "Before I have my Praetorian flog you bloody."

His face darkened, and she saw a decision flash through his features. He reached for her waist, and suddenly, he was tugging her shirt over her head, yanking her pants from her hips, pulling her undergarments from her thighs.

With the startling, sudden roughness of his treatment, Victory screamed and thrashed as memories came flooding back, driving her into an animal panic as he picked her up and…

…lowered her into the bath, opposite him.

"Soap?" he asked, offering her a bar.

Victory yanked her knees to her chest and wrapped her arms around her shins, shivering. "What are you going to do with me?" she whimpered, hating herself for the fear crawling up within her. Naked. She was naked with a man…

"Wash your back, if you're not careful," Dragomir growled. "I told you I'm not going to hurt you, Victory. Now." He soaped a sponge and held it out to her, water swishing around his elbows as he moved. "Are you going to do the honors, or should I?"

"I could have you killed for this," she said, trembling. She felt so humiliated, so debased. It was her capture all over again.

He heaved an enormous sigh and dropped the sponge on the edge of the tub beside her. Then, soaping another, he began lathering his body.

Thinking his attention elsewhere, Victory slowly began to climb out of the water.

Dragomir caught her by the chain. "Where do you think you're going?"

She felt a spasm of old terror snake up within her and she whimpered against the images that started to push up from within. Disrobed, this close to a man, unable to escape, her deepest fears were once more laid bare. She felt her body tremble in a whimper.

She heard the water swish as he moved toward her. Suddenly, every part of her was aware of how exposed she was, how utterly vulnerable. She let out a tiny sound of terror and flinched down into the water, trying to use it to hide.

He seemed to hesitate, then a big hand grabbed the soapy sponge and slapped it into the water in front of her. "Wash," he growled.

Victory recoiled from him, curling into the far corner of the tub, unable to hold in the terrified whimpers were building within. Her mind was going numb, once more detaching itself from the feelings of her body.

He had gone back to his own washing. "I'm not gonna ask again," he insisted. "I'm tired of your crap, Princess. You don't start cleaning yourself up, I'm gonna do it for you."

She only heard him in some distant part of her brain. The rest of her was falling apart, taken over by the terrible fact that she was naked, chained, and utterly helpless to stop him from doing whatever he wanted to her. Though she hated herself for her weakness, the terror was too strong—she squeezed her eyes shut and started babbling, begging that he wouldn't hurt her.

A big hand touched her knee. "Shhh. We'll get you fixed, Princess."

"Please let me go," Victory whimpered. She could not meet his eyes, her whole body trembling with her fear. "Please."

His face melted in a wave of anguish. "Oh, Victory." He hauled her into his arms, rocking her against his chest.

She shuddered and felt him grab her in some distant corner of her brain. *Too close,* she thought. *He's too close.* It was then that her mind simply began to shut down, seeing nothing but the soapy water swirling against the far wall of the tub.

As she had done countless times in the past, Victory prepared herself for the horror that she knew would come.

• • •

Too late, Dragomir realized that his own anger had clouded his sensing of the princess's oncoming panic. Holding her tightly in his arms, Dragomir tried to push the raging hurricane back out of sight, but the princess's *gi* meridians were completely stagnant, locked down by a mind-rama that had switched her body on autopilot.

Oh gods, he thought, pulling her back, looking into her vacant eyes. *Oh gods, you fool…What have you done?* He wished he could take the last few minutes back, wished he could somehow repair the damage that he could already see in her empty stare.

"Victory?" he asked, gently setting her on a ledge in the tub. "You've gotta come back, love."

She stared at a point across the wall, rocking slowly.

Oh gods, he thought. He glanced at the soaped-up sponge, then at the water. Knowing he had already come this far, he decided to save her the horror of another bath.

"Okay, Victory, love, I'm going to wash you up so we don't have to go through this again for awhile, all right?"

Her gaze never shifted, fixed on some random point on the far wall. He could see the silver core of her energy, detached and disassociated, hovering at arm's-length from her physical form, just within the outer shell of her *au*.

Anguished, not knowing what else to do, Dragomir grabbed the sponge and, as quickly as he could, washed her limp body. Then, once she was rinsed and clean, he dumped a fistful of shampoo in her hair and started massaging it through her scalp, all the while talking to her, trying to bring her out of her trance.

She never moved, never spoke, never reacted in any way.

Gently, Dragomir held a clean rag over her face as he poured water over her hair to rinse it. She never blinked.

"I'm so sorry, sweetie," he said, lifting her to sit on the rim of the tub. She didn't fight him in any way—her arms hung at her sides, her eyes unfocused and staring.

Grabbing towels, he wrapped her in them, then lifted her from the tub and carried her out of the bathroom and back to the bed. There, he slid her under the blankets and tucked her in.

"Victory?" he asked softly.

She stared at the canopy, unresponsive.

Finally, Dragomir settled himself on the floor, still wet and covered with goosebumps, watching her *au* for some sign of change.

It came four hours later, when her mind-rama slowly began to open again, and the energy mass that was her consciousness began to slide back into place at the seat of the brain. She heard her sharp inhalation, saw her eyes twitch to the blankets.

For a long time, he said nothing, dreading the next words he knew were coming out of her mouth.

"I'm having the Praetorian replace your cuffs." Her voice was cold, calculated, utterly emotionless.

Dragomir hung his head. He said nothing.

Without sitting up or moving in any way, Victory said, "If you touch me like that again, I will tell the Inquisitors about you and take a front seat at your execution."

"I'm sorry," he whispered.

She didn't respond. She sat up and raised her voice in Imperial.

A moment later, two Praetorian marched inside. Dragomir didn't struggle as they grabbed his wrists and wrenched them behind his back. He felt the cold bite of steel snap shut around them and he closed his eyes against tears. "I'm sorry, Princess," he said.

She ignored him completely.

• • •

Victory let her chambermaids dress her, no longer caring about the slave on the floor. He hadn't moved in hours, nor did she care. For all intents and purposes, he no longer existed for her—he was a piece of furniture, that was all.

"I'm sorry," he said again, once Carrie and Jolene had curtsied and taken their leave.

Victory peered at her reflection in the mirror, tracing the dark rings that were the only remaining physical sign of her years of captivity. Her body had regained its lost weight, her skin had lost the sickly boils, her hair had started growing again. It was just the rings, dark and brown, that was a daily physical reminder her of six years of starvation, torture, and rape.

"I'm sorry, Victory," he said, for the thousandth time.

Picking at a stray hair to rearrange it behind her ear, Victory said, "You may refer to me as mistress or Your Royal Highness. I hear that word uttered from your lips again and I will have my Praetorian come in here and gag you."

Setting the mirror down, she turned to the nightstand. On it, she found a porcelain figurine of a beautiful mermaid, swirling amongst a school of fish. The workmanship and detail were exquisite, the piece an acquisition from an Imperial museum. She picked it up, thoughtfully. Then, twisting so that it was hovering over the bare marble floor, dropped it.

The white porcelain shattered over the black stone with a thousand tinkling shards, and the slave winced where he sat on a rug. "That was pretty," he said.

"It was useless," she said, picking up another one. This time, it was of a mermaid playing a harp. She turned and dropped it with the other.

The slave watched the second statuette shatter and turned away. She felt a warmth begin tracing around her, trying to cradle her.

Victory seized a third statuette and, whirling, flung it at him as hard as she could manage.

It missed, streaking past his head to shatter on the wall behind him. The slave jerked, his eyes flashing open, startled.

"*Don't*," she said, trembling in her fury. "Don't *ever* do that again."

He bowed his head to look at the floor between his knees. For a long time, he said nothing, and Victory went back to relieving her room of unwanted pieces of her past.

Behind her, he softly said, "You were a mermaid, many lifetimes ago. You enjoyed that life very much."

Victory stopped, a statue in one fist. She turned to him, slowly. "What did you say?"

He must have seen the rage, there, because he lowered his head and whispered, "They were a genetic mutation created to help colonize a water planet."

"Let me guess," Victoria sneered. "You were in that one, too?"

His lack of response was all she needed. "Stop *lying* to me!" she snarled, hurling the figurine at him. It caught him full in the chest and he grunted. The tiny statue fell into the rug between his knees, where its delicate tail snapped off and tinkled across the floor. She turned back to her dresser and, with her arm, slid her entire collection off of the surface, flinging it across the room in a scream of rage.

There came a gentle knock on the door. "Are you all right, Princess?"

"*Stay out!*" she screamed. She went to another shelf, threw the mermaids across the floor, and went to another. She went to every shelf, every open surface, and swept the clutter of useless artifacts of her past onto the black marble floor. Then she plucked up a wooden mermaid statue that hadn't shattered on impact and threw it across the room. It bounced harmlessly off of the wall, skittering under the bed. In a fury, she snatched it out from under the bed and started toward the fire with it.

Just before she threw it in, she hesitated. It was an ironwood carving of a mermaid reading a book, something that her mother had given her in the last months before she had packed up to fly to the Academy.

Victoria felt her hand spasm around it. *Mother,* she thought, remembering her loving arms, her warm embrace. Her mother had died within the first year of Victoria's captivity. Heartbreak, her maids had said. Sorrow that ate at the heart. The doctors hadn't been able to establish a cause. She had simply...died.

Victoria glanced at the destruction behind her, then again at the statue.

Slowly, her legs gave out beneath her. She sank to the floor, clutching the statue to her chest. She closed her eyes and leaned over it, a low moan of despair sliding from her lips. She felt tears of loss, then, the first tears of loss since she had realized she was in her own bed, her body an emaciated jumble of bones and protruding ribs.

Mother, she thought again. She had asked for her repeatedly in those first few days. She had called out her name in her sleep, babbled it in her bouts of terror. They hadn't told her she was dead until she'd been home almost a month. By then, that last avenue of hope had closed, and, without her mother's shoulder to whimper her fears into, she had simply retreated further into herself.

Victoria cried, then. All the tears that she had waited to shed in her mother's arms, they came pouring out of her in a wave of grief and loss. *I miss you,* she thought, *I miss you so much.*

She felt the soft golden warmth blanketing her again, but she ignored it, too carried away by her anguish to care.

When she could finally find the will to wipe the tears off of her face, she called for her chambermaids and watched in a numb silence as they swept up the scattered remnants of her childhood collection. Many of them had been priceless relics from before the Fall, and she felt a pang of loathing at herself for destroying such treasures in a tantrum.

She knew what her mother would say. She would shoo the maids out of the room and make Victory clean it up herself. Then she would order her gifts from family and suitors diverted, donated to some charity while Victory suffered through an empty room for a year or two.

Victory pushed the grief back down and stood up, a new strength flooding her. She wasn't a child anymore. The last six years had taken that from her as brutally as the blue-eyed weasel had taken her virginity. She was done hiding. She was going to find her father and tell him he could take this slave off of her or she could cut off his head and remove the collar herself.

She was also going to find Matt.

Pacing to the doorway, she gave the slave just enough time to get to his feet before yanking the door open and striding through it, forcing him to struggle against his hobbles to keep up.

She found her father first. She pushed through the outer hall, ignored the two male house Praetorian standing at attention outside his chamber, and threw the doors open, despite the babbling protests from his butler.

"Father!" she snarled, storming up to him, where he was working over his desk, a goblet of wine at his right hand. "You will take this man from my waist. Now." She grabbed the chain and tugged hard, making the man on the other end grunt and stumble.

Her father took his time in finishing the marks he was making on his ledgers before carefully setting his pen aside, taking off his reading glasses, and looking up at her. "So," he said. "The rabbit has finally come out of her hole."

Victory narrowed her eyes. "Don't you dare call me a rabbit, you insensitive pig."

Her father raised both blonde brows. "And quite feisty, it seems." He leaned back in his chair, reaching for his wine. "Tell me, dear. Are you quite done with your tantrum?" He took a sip, eying her over the lip of his glass.

"That was not a tantrum, father," Victory said, so full of rage that all she could get to come out was a whisper.

Her father cocked his head, a smile playing upon his lips. "I'm sorry. What was that?"

Victory swallowed her fury and tried again. "You are going to remove this slave from my belt."

"My dear," her father said, swishing his wine, "You're trembling."

"That's because," Victory managed, "I'm trying very hard not to slap that smile off your face, you pathetic old man."

Her father's gray eyes darkened to the color of storm clouds. Slowly, he put his goblet down and leaned back in his chair, idly tapping his fingers upon the tabletop. "Though I must admit that this latest change in your demeanor better behooves a Princess of the Imperium than a whimpering coward," he finally said, "It would be in your best interest to watch your tongue, girl."

"I am a *woman*, not a *girl*," Victory snapped. "I haven't been a *girl* since a group of rebels took me off my ship and raped me until I had their seed puddled between my legs."

He gave her a distasteful grimace. "That disgrace would never have happened to Matthias."

Victory could only stare at her father in utter flabbergastation. "Are you trying to imply I could have stopped them?" Her voice was a tight whisper of rage.

Her father snorted. "He would have fought to the death before he surrendered to rebels."

For long moments, Victory found she could not speak. She was so utterly furious that she couldn't even think of a way to form a response.

Casually, her father continued, "Women are not meant to rule. They don't have the heart for it. If the Imperium didn't have such strict rules regarding succession, I would have put your brother in your place twenty years ago.

"*I* am the next Adjudicator," Victory snarled. "Whether you like my brother better or not, it is going to be *me*, and you are going to die knowing I'm taking your place."

She thought she detected a hint of amusement in his face. "My," he said. "You *are* feeling better, aren't you?"

"I'm fixed," Victory snarled, slamming the chain onto the table between them. "Take it off."

Her father met her eyes and watched her closely. "No, I don't think you are." He leaned forward, smiling, and tapped her upon the side of the skull. "That frightened little child is still in there somewhere, hiding, waiting for a chance to get out. Until you've burned her silly antics from your memory, you're still going to lapse into tantrums." He leaned back, waving a dismissive hand. "Give it a month or two. Then come back to me."

"It was *not a tantrum!*" she screamed.

He tisked. "That's not what your staff told me, when I caught them disposing of your collection," he said, and tilted back his goblet to drain his cup.

Victory slapped it out of his hand, hurling wine and goblet across the room.

Her father tensed, looking down at the crimson spatter upon his embroidered silk shirt. For a long moment, neither of them spoke. Then, very softly, he said, "You walk a very delicate line, Victoria." His voice was cold, emotionless. In her childhood, that voice had terrified her. Now, it only made her laugh.

"What are you going to do to me?" Victory laughed. "Throw me in a cell? Starve me? Disgrace me in front of the masses?" She flicked a bit of wine spatter from her arm. "Sorry, father. You're too late for that. It's *been done*." She gave him a cruel smile. "I will see you at dinner, you disgusting waste of human flesh. I'm sure I can find some interesting stories to tell your guests."

Then she turned and stormed from the room, dragging the slave with her.

She found her brother reclining on a couch in the sunroom, enjoying the afternoon rays as he looked thoughtfully out over the valley below, a pitcher of mead on the table beside him.

"You!" Victory shouted, stepping past his Praetorian. "How the *hell* could you let him do this to me?!" She jerked the chain at him, making the slave stumble behind her. "Were you a part of this madness? Whose idea was it? His or yours? Did you actually think it would *work?!*"

Matthias scrambled to his feet, his green eyes wide and shocked. "Victory, you're—"

She bowled over him. "I know you had something to do with it. I know you picked him. I know what he is."

Her brother's eyes widened and he glanced at the slave. "He *told* you?"

Victory narrowed her eyes. "I want him gone, Matt. Send him *home* goddamn it."

Matthias gave her a nervous look. "I could find someone else. A non—" He glanced at the exit and lowered his voice. "A normal man."

"That," Victory snarled, "Is not the problem." She yanked the slave closer, forcing his big bulk to bend down beside her. "The problem," she snarled, "Is that there is something slow and heavy connected to my waist, and it is limiting my freedom of movement."

Matt looked uncomfortable. "I just got a courier from Father. He said you are to remain in the belt for three months." He glanced at the Emp. "I could switch him out, though, if he has displeased you."

Victory screamed and kicked an ancient ceramic pot off of the end-table, spilling plant, soil, and decorative statuary onto the floor, breaking open the root-ball contained within. Panting, she picked up the plant by its long wooden stem and, wielding it like a bat, started slamming it into the wall, throwing dirt and leaves everywhere.

Matt caught her wrists gently. "Victory," he whispered, when she dropped the plant and started kicking at it. "Dear," he said, tugging her away from the plant. "Should I call for a doctor?"

"*I don't need a doctor!*" she screamed, shoving him. "I need this *slave* off of my *waist!*" She grabbed the tether and held it out to him, fury burning like fire within. "I know you can do it, Matt. Take it off. Now."

Matt gave the chain a nervous look. "You know the way Father thinks. If you find a way to take it off, he's only going to make it worse."

In a scream of frustration, Victory picked up the pitcher of mead and hurled it at the window. Instead of cracking the bullet-proof glass, however, it simply shattered against the barrier, mead and stoneware dripping down to the window-seats below. Furious, Victory slammed herself backward into the seat that her brother had just occupied and kicked the coffee table out of her way.

Matt watched it go crashing across the room, his nervous look growing. "Did the slave do this?" he asked.

"The slave did *nothing*," Victory snarled.

Matthias's face seemed to fall. "Oh. But I heard—"

"Your reports were *wrong*." She stared at the opposite wall, feeling bad about the plant, not wanting to destroy anything else, yet boiling with anger inside. Years and years of fury, all twisting within her like a cyclone. She was finding it hard to breathe through her hatred.

"Perhaps," Matthias said, gingerly taking a seat beside her, "He truly did help, after all? You are out and facing the world…"

Victory gave him a cold look. "That was my doing. Not his."

"Oh." Her brother looked confused. Then he seemed to search for words before saying, "Is there anything I can do for you, then? Aside from relieving you of your burden? Not even I am willing to brave Father's wrath for that. The courier said he was having trouble dictating, he was so angry."

"Good," Victory said, feeling a small flash of triumph at making her infamously cold and analytical father angry, despite the desperation rising from his edict.

"It's not wise to make him angry," Matthias said. "He has a long memory."

"I couldn't care less about making him angry," Victory snapped.

"I can see that," Matt said. He looked concerned. "Do you want me to call a doctor?" he asked again.

Victory turned to him and met his eyes. "I don't. Need. A *doctor*."

Her brother blinked and looked away. "Sorry. You're just…" He swallowed. "Not what I expected. Last I heard, you collapsed into a ball when father walked into the room and had his Praetorian pound your slave senseless. Now you're…" He obviously struggled for the right word. "…different."

"I realized I was being childish," Victory said.

Her brother frowned. "Is that what Father said? You don't actually *believe* that, do you?"

Victory frowned at him, reminded of what else she found hard to believe. "Matt, what is Father charging the natives of this planet by way of taxes?"

"Twenty percent," her brother replied. He gave a small frown.

Victory glanced at the Emp, then at her brother. "How long would it take to get a copy of the reports?"

Matt shrugged. "An hour. Two. Mother would have known. She was constantly hounding the Constable after you disappeared."

After I disappeared… Victory frowned. "Why was that?"

Matt grunted. "She told me something once about discrepancies in the staff wages."

The staff wages. Victory once again remembered the ice-blue eyes of the young man from the hall, his scarred bottom lip. His sneer as he looked her up and down.

"What are Mercy's biggest exports?" Victory asked.

He frowned at her, curious, now. "Is this a test, sister?" he asked, giving a chuckle.

"Tell me," Victory growled.

"Slaves and stone," he said, his frown deepening. "Everyone knows that."

"How many slaves a year?" she asked.

He gave her a curious look. "I'm not sure. Somewhere in the millions."

"And our slaves are all obtained legally?" Victory demanded.

"Of course." Then his eyes flickered to the Emp and he said, "Well, most of them."

Victory ignored that. "There are only a hundred million people on this planet, brother."

"So?" He seemed perplexed. "The planet is in a state of rebellion. Has been since the occupation."

"Forty *years* have gone by since Father landed with his Imperial fleet," Victory said. "It takes most new Imperates four years to restore order. A few have taken six. Why would the planet still be rebelling after so long, unless there was a root cause behind it?"

Matthias sighed and slumped back into the sofa, staring out over the valley. "That's what I've been trying to figure out." She knew he was the

General Commander of the Imperial Fleet, acting as her father's right arm in everything military ever since his father had forced him to take the job when he was fourteen.

She also knew that the war had been wearing at him. While his sigil was a sword—chosen for him by his father—and while he inspired a loyalty in his troops that most leaders would give their firstborn children to obtain, he much preferred to wield a pen.

Victory stood up. "I'm going to go figure it out. If you see Father before dinner, give him my *warmest* regards."

"Wait!" Matt said, jumping to his feet with her. "It's been so long since I've talked with you. Perhaps you would walk through the gardens with me—"

"Not now," Victory said. "I have business that needs attending to."

And then, despite Matthias's protests, she stalked from the room, dragging her slave with her.

She found the office of the Constable of Numbers deep within the bowels of the palace, near the treasury. When she stepped to the door, the soldiery guarding it stepped quickly aside, their eyes round as they watched her and her entourage pass. This deep in the palace, they probably only saw a Praetorian a few times a year, from a distance. They gave her a wide berth, which was probably a life-saving measure for them, considering Victory's mood.

The Constable himself was a large, flushed fat man sitting behind a desk stacked with sheets of numbers and built-in computers. When he saw her, he straightened rigidly, sweat breaking out on his overly-red brow.

"I want to know why my request was not fulfilled," she growled.

The Constable of Numbers licked his lips and glanced down at the reports on his desk. "Request?" he asked. "What request, Princess?"

"The one that Kiara made at my behest," Victory snapped, tired of the games.

"Oh, I'm sorry," he said, looking genuinely perplexed. "There must have been some mistake. I never received a request from your staff."

"Then do it now," Victory said. "I'd like to see tax documentation for the native populace of Mercy."

"I'm sorry, milady," he said, making a nervous chuckle. "Such a monumental task takes time."

She smiled at him, though Victory didn't need the Emp to tell her the man was lying. "How much time?"

"Weeks," the man said. "Months."

Victory cocked her head at the Constable, then at the electronics on his desk. "I was under the impression that the numbers I seek are all in electronic format. Burn me a chip. I will take them back to my chambers and sort through them myself."

He balked, his jowls quivering. He opened and closed his mouth several times before sputtering, "Would that I could, milady, but they are so scattered…What is it you would like to know?" He tried to smile, but his eyes were flickering between her and her Praetorian uneasily.

What is *it I want to know?* Victoria thought. Was she here simply to prove to herself that the slave had been lying? Or was it something else? She remembered again the scarred man in the hall, who had looked so much like the man who had boarded her ship…

Then she noticed the Constable's nervous look, the piggish eyes of a cornered boar. *He's hiding something.* She narrowed her eyes. "I'd like to see the tax documentation on the native populace of Mercy. Right now."

His blubber seemed to shake around him with the strain that was working its way across his smile. "I understand your impatience, Princess—I find myself having to wait months for even the preliminary numbers. I assure you—"

Victory took a step closer, squinting down at the papers on his desk.

Then she saw the man lick his scarlet lips, saw him glance at the paperwork on his desk, saw him start to sweat. As if she could not see him, he began slowly sliding the papers aside, slipping them into a folder. "I might be able to find you some taxation records, now that I think about it," he said slowly. "Let me check my computers."

"Praetorian," Victory said softly, "Move him aside."

"No!" the man jabbered, his jowls jiggling with the effort. He snatched up the folder and held it to his chest. "The records are very sensitive documents, Princess. I would be happy to guide you through them…"

As the man babbled and pled, the Praetorian pulled him away from his workstation.

"And bring me the folder," Victory said.

The man cried out and tried to fight the Praetorian, which was his mistake. A swift knee to the stomach and he was on the ground, choking. Lion appeared a moment later, the folder in her mailed fist.

Victory took it and opened it.

"Nooo," the man on the ground wailed to the floor.

Inside, Victory found a sheaf of numbers that immediately made her frown. Most, she knew, couldn't have read it, because it was in a crude form of code. Her enhanced Royal blood, however, allowed her to analyze and translate the document in a matter of seconds. It showed one of the chef's assistants due an eight-hundred-thousand credit lump payment—eight times the yearly wage of the Cook himself—the date set for fourteen days hence. The money was to be transferred from the Adjudicator's personal account, along with fuel and staff costs for a six-day pleasure cruise, to begin in one week.

Father doesn't take pleasure cruises, she thought, frowning. He was constantly at work, an insomniac who spent all day and night running over facts and figures in his chambers.

"What is this?" she asked, peering at the papers like she was absolutely confused. "These numbers make no sense."

"It's just some notes on various accounts, milady," the man said. "Nothing you would understand.

Victory narrowed her eyes but pretended she hadn't heard him. Why did her father's men all seem to underestimate her? The way they acted around her, she was nothing but a feather-headed dimwit who liked to wear emeralds and dress pretty. She looked again at the employee identification number for the eight-hundred-thousand credit payment. She sat down at the Constable's system and, reading from the paper, put in a search query for the same number.

The last payment to that particular employee had been five years ago. Then another, six years, three months ago.

Victory's heart began to pound.

"What are you doing?" the Constable cried, trying to wriggle around to see the screen.

"I'm looking up taxation amounts for the native populace of Mercy," Victory lied, trying to look as calm as possible. "But I'm having trouble… This system is so confusing." She attempted to open the employee's file, but when she did, the screen was empty. No picture, no finger-prints, no vital statistics.

"You say you never received a message from Kiara?" Victory asked, backing out of that search and starting a new one.

"No, majesty," the man whimpered. "I *swear* she never came to me."

And Victory believed him. When she opened Kiara's file, the woman was receiving a stipend far and above anything a butler should make, being paid directly from her father's account. It had begun approximately one month before Victory's scheduled flight to the Imperial Academy.

Victory thought again of the day she had found out that Kiara would not be flying with her to the Academy, but instead taking another, later flight to rendezvous with her once she had had time to settle in. "It's my mother," Kiara had said, tears in her eyes. "She's dying. Cancer. The doctors tell me it's incurable, at least for our means. I need to be with her for a month or two, before she goes."

A growing dread beginning to well up within her, Victory checked the files for Carrie and Jolene.

Both of them were receiving stipends from her father's account.

Disturbed, furious, Victory searched her brother's manservants' accounts. All of them were at least eight years in service, and all of them were receiving monies strictly from her brother's account.

"If you would only tell me what you're looking for," the Constable of Numbers babbled, "I could make your search much easier, Princess."

Victory did a search for native accounts.

She found four hundred and sixteen registered native taxpayers, all with vast holdings in the several millions of credits.

Frowning, she searched for Imperium citizens.

She found six hundred forty-two thousand and sixteen.

For some time, Victory could only stare at the screen. Thinking perhaps that the peasant accounts were in another section of the system, she initiated another general search by monetary income, starting at the lowest and working her way up.

The list started with Imperium citizens. She found not a single native account within the first three minutes of scrolling down the list.

This can't be right, she thought. "Tell me, Constable," she said, "How do I access the native accounts for this planet?"

Quickly, he gave her the method she had already used to obtain the four hundred and sixteen files.

Frowning, Victory said, "And where are the rest of them?"

Silence.

When she looked back, the Constable of Numbers was pale and sweating, slumped between two Praetorian, looking as if he wanted to slink into the wall. "I was ordered not to waste my time with the smaller accounts, Princess. The Imperium collectors are too few and too well-paid to waste their time traveling to villages that might produce, say, a cow, or a handful of chickens. We have to manage our resources, Princess."

"You have *no* accounts for natives, aside from these four hundred and sixteen?" she demanded.

"The natives are poor," the Constable whimpered. "It costs more to record them than they can offer up in taxes." The tension in his deathly-pale face, however, told her he was lying.

Scowling, now, Victory did a search for the last slave freighter destined for auction on the core planets. Thirty thousand souls. Under each name was the demarcation, DELINQUENT ACCOUNT. Time and time again, the same reason. There were no criminals, no self-bonded men. Regardless of age, sex, or stature, it was 'Delinquent Account.' Three-year-olds were cited for tax evasion. Even slaves whose entry under the NAME column was 'NAME UNKNOWN' were cited for years of tax fraud.

Eventually, Victory closed the file. To the Constable, she said, "Thank you, I found what I was looking for."

He hesitated in his babbling, giving her a perplexed look. "You did?"

"Of course," Victory said, frowning at him. "I was looking for the largest native revenue-center on Mercy. I would like to schedule a visit, to evaluate a possible troop increase that my brother has proposed."

The man's relief was so stupidly vivid on his face that it made her gut clench in anger. "Oh, well, why didn't you say something?" he chattered, his fleshy jowls jiggling. "I could have supplied you with that information without even looking it up."

So could I, Victory thought, disgustedly. *I am of Royal blood, a Second Generation mutogenetic anomaly. I have eleven times the acquisition and storage capacity of your cholesterol-blotted cranium.* Not only that, but she had been tutored for fourteen years by the empire's best historians, scientists, linguists, and accountants. She could probably do this man's job with more efficiency than he himself could, with decades of experience. The fact that he had underestimated her so thoroughly made a new rage uncurl within her gut. She was the next ruler of Mercy, yet so many of the officials at the palace had treated her as if she were just a poor, delusional kitten. She began to wonder if that, too, was part of her father's doing.

Still, she smiled pleasantly. "I enjoy being able to do things on my own, though I have to admit all the numbers were so horribly perplexing...I think I found the right one, though. Merephit?"

"Yes," the Constable cried, his relief thick in his voice. "Merephit. You were looking for Merephit." He almost sounded like he was reassuring himself.

She cocked her head politely. "Why? What did you *think* I was looking for?" She smiled through her teeth, still burning with fury at the man's insulting stupidity.

"Nothing," the man babbled quickly. "Nothing, Princess. It's just so odd that you would arrive so soon after..." He caught himself, reddening. His eyes flitted to the desk, then away again, too quickly.

"So soon after what?" she asked. She glanced down at the papers on the desk. She saw her father's royal seal on the blank remains of a courier message—a ribbon and a wax stamp all that was left of a self-erasing missive. She glanced again at the folder, considered the numbers therein.

A cold chill began working its way up her spine.

"So soon after your return," the man said. "I was told you were so very sick after your capture..."

Victory felt her mind sharpen. The only ones who are supposed to know that she never made it to the Academy were her Praetorian, her father, her brother, and her maids. The latter, she was told, had given vows of silence on pain of death to keep her secret.

"Yes," she said slowly, yawning, "I'm still very tired." She got up, leaving the folder haphazardly open on the desk. She paused, gesturing at the folder. "What did all that mean? It was all very confusing."

"Your father is scheduling a celebration for your return," the Constable said. "A pleasure-cruise across the continent."

Victory forced a smile through the cold feeling in her gut. "How *sweet* of him! It must be a surprise."

The man hanging between her Praetorian nodded, panting. "A very nice surprise, very nice, so you cannot tell him or he would simply kill me for ruining it."

I'll bet he would, Victory thought darkly. But she made a delighted giggle. If there was anything she had learned from her mother, it was how to act like the stupid airheaded princess in order to relax minds and loosen tongues. "I'll be sure not to say anything," she said. "Thank you for your time, Constable." She gestured at her Praetorian to release him and walked from the room.

Once they were into the hallway, well out of earshot, she told Lion, "I believe there is going to be another attempt on my life, sometime within the next two weeks."

Still walking at her side, the Praetorian stiffened. "*Another*, milady?"

"From what I just found in the accountant's files, my capture was not an accident. A nameless individual was paid, very handsomely, days after my disappearance. That same individual was paid about four days after my mother passed. And the Constable of Numbers is planning another payment to him, fourteen days hence."

Lion stiffened and turned, obviously intent on going back and arresting the Constable.

Victory caught her arm. "He takes his orders from my father. The money came directly from his personal accounts each time."

Lion went pale. Then her face hardened. "I will increase the guard. You will not leave your room. You—"

"My father has already paid for a pleasure-cruise in my honor," Victory said. "I will be ordered to attend, I'm sure."

Lion frowned. "I have not been told of a pleasure-cruise."

Remembering the royal missive on the Constable's desk, Victory said, "It was scheduled today, immediately after my chat with him."

For a long moment, Lion looked torn between seeking out her father and ending the problem and going back to the Constable anyway and arresting him for interrogation.

"You will act normally," Victory said.

"I will be increasing the guard," Lion said stubbornly. "Eight on at a time."

"It must not look as if I suspect," Victory said, "or he will merely set a different date."

Lion's face was hard. "I will come up with some plausible excuse." Then she hesitated. "But milady...If the Adjudicator wants you dead, you are not safe in this building."

Victory gave a disgusted snort. "If he wants me dead, I'm not safe anywhere within the Imperium."

"Then what will you do?" Lion asked.

"The Adjudicator is a criminal," Victory said. "I'm going to stay alive long enough to prove it."

She ate dinner at her father's table, and ordered a bowl of pig slops for her slave. To her surprise, he didn't complain. When he wrinkled his nose and asked for help to eat it, however, she ignored him. It was the delight of many of her father's dinner-guests to watch his antics as he tried to bend over far enough to eat his slops without falling into it, face-first.

She watched the slave's face burn, watched his body stiffen at their laughter, but throughout it all, he never complained. He simply ate his dinner, then sat back, staring at the floor, waiting for her to finish.

Several times throughout the night, Victory caught her father watching her. Each time, the darkness in his face left a cold spot in her soul before she pretended to turn her attention to a nearby conversation.

By the time Victory finally made it to her room, her anger had all but washed away under her father's ominous stare, and without its strength to propel her, she felt deflated, hollow.

He's going to kill me, Victory thought, the cold truth settling into the pit of her stomach like a stone. *Just like he killed Mother.*

Suddenly, the enormity of what she had done came crashing down around her, and her world seemed to collapse under its weight. She looked to her slave, who had quietly stood near the center of the room in silence, then to the door and the Praetorian beyond, the only things standing between her and an assassin in her sleep.

She had to tell her brother.

Then she hesitated. Victory was more or less sure that her brother was safe—he was her father's favorite, after all. And, if she told her brother now, she was sure that he would try to do something drastic. As the General Commander of Mercy's Imperial Fleet, he would more than likely try to start a war with her father. A war that, as soon as news of it reached the Core, the Imperium would send a fleet to execute him. Inter-familial power-struggles were not tolerated by the Imperium, and were dealt with brutally and efficiently, the stability of the planet its upmost priority.

Feeling alone, scared, not knowing who to trust, she slumped to the floor against the wall, trying to ignore the throbbing in her ankles. As her slave had promised, the pounding had come back over time, and, now that she had had a taste of what it had felt like to have them working perfectly again, it made the agony all that more excruciating.

She sent her Praetorian for a painkiller, but when the little pills came in their tiny cup, she reluctantly set them aside. The doctors had found no cause for her mother's death. Who was to say that her planned assassination wasn't a simple switch in medication, and her father's surprise pleasure-cruise was simply a distraction to avoid suspicion from Imperium investigators?

It was too much. The fury that had powered her through the day had thoroughly dispersed, leaving her mind free to be haunted by her creeping fears once more. She once again recognized that she was alone with a naked man, once again found herself balking at the idea of leaving her room, of running into the men in the hallways.

"Gods," she whimpered, dropping her face to her knees. In a single tornado of a day, she had destroyed everything. Her ankles throbbing, she carefully got up and moved around the slave, keeping at the end of the chain, and went to her bed. Before crawling into the covers, she took the chain near his throat to a locking clasp on one of the head-posts of her bed. It would force him to stay on his knees all night, but it would also allow her to close her eyes without worrying that he would try to assault her again.

And, with the many worries piling up around her, the last thing that Victory needed was to worry about her slave.

He knelt and let her clip him to the post without struggle, and didn't bother to complain when he saw her settle under the covers for the night. Still, Victoria had trouble falling asleep. Every now and then, she heard him shift on his knees, obviously uncomfortable on the stone floor. In addition to the small sounds of his discomfort, her ankles were like throbbing masses affixed to the ends of her legs, and it kept her awake long into the night.

A small, guilty part of her wondered if the slave was feeling something similar, in his shoulders.

Then she remembered the bath and decided she didn't care.

CHAPTER 9

The Golden Rule

D ragomir kept his head down and followed the princess through her daily routine for the next few days, feeling numb and defeated.
How could I have been so stupid? he wondered, as he watched her icy mask go up whenever she looked at him. She hadn't said more than four words to him in as many days, and aside for the quick trips to the kitchen, to eat foods that she had her Praetorian prepare for her, and the one evening meal each night, she simply sat on her bed and stared off into space.

Something was bothering her, and it had something to do with the lying fat man behind the desk. Dragomir, however, had not understood the conversation, and the princess had failed to enlighten him. And he, quite convinced by the violence rolling under her surface that one false move would cost him his life, had kept his questions to himself.

Instead, he gritted his teeth and allowed himself to become the laughingstock of the palace. Every time they went anywhere, now, servants would walk past him and make oinking noises, then run off giggling. Dinner, however, was the worst. He was fed a bowl of what looked like pig slops, and was given no way of eating it gracefully. The one time he had asked for assistance, he had been completely ignored, so he had gritted his teeth and endured, his face crusting with dried food that no one bothered to wipe off.

Debased, humiliated, Dragomir still felt it dwarfed in comparison to the wrong he had done her. Everything that he had been hoping to achieve in days past, every bit of progress that he had made at winning her trust, all of it had been utterly destroyed in those few moments of anger.

At the end of the day, he watched her step inside her chambers and lean against the door, relief flooding off of her in a cold wave. Dragomir was beginning to think that she dreaded their nightly meal even more than he did.

He watched her prepare for sleep, stepping out of her clothes and into a robe, giving him no more regard than she would a piece of furniture. As she walked to the bed, however, he watched her hobble, saw the blocked energy in her feet, knew it was hurting her more than she wanted to admit.

"Come, slave," the princess said, pointing to the spot where she had begun chaining him to the bed while she slept.

Dragomir almost hesitated. It hurt. Hell, it was *excruciating*. To kneel on a stone floor, with only an inch of wiggle in any direction, for eight hours at a stretch...By morning, he had trouble getting back to his feet.

But then he remembered how badly he had failed her trust, remembered her dead stare as she let him move her body about like a doll, once again saw Meggie's eyes as the Praetorian ravaged her in front of him, and he went to the spot and knelt.

He did wince, though, when he heard the snap lock into place.

She must have been watching, because he thought he saw her hesitate, thought he felt a spasm of guilt jolt through her system, but then it was gone. She climbed into bed and lay facing the ceiling, once more beginning her slow descent into sleep.

He heard her shift under the covers, saw the discomfort roiling in her ankles with his mind's eye. He had known for awhile what was keeping her awake, but had been too wrapped in self-pity to say anything. Now, listening to her contortions throughout the night, he finally found the will to speak up.

"I can work your ankles again, if it would help you sleep."

The tossing in the bed stopped. For a long moment, the princess said nothing. Then, in a sneer, she said, "If you think that I'm going to unshackle you again, *ever*, then you are deluding yourself."

Dragomir lowered his forehead to the bedpost in despair. "I can do it without. Just put your foot in my hands. I'll work with them behind me."

For a long time, there was utter silence from the bed. Then, softly, he began to hear her slip from under the covers. When he met her eyes, he saw raw determination there—as well as fear. For a long moment, she simply sat beside him on the bed, saying nothing, just watching him.

"If you try anything, you are a dead man," she finally said.

"I know," he whispered. He was so stricken by the coldness in her gaze that it tore at his heart. "I'll just make the hurt go away. I swear."

She watched him warily a moment longer, then stuck her foot into his hands.

With his shoulders and knees ablaze, it was all Dragomir could do to find his center. Somehow, he sank to that crystal core and immersed himself in its humming song, then gingerly spread it outwards, through his hands, into her ankle. Being unable to physically see the appendage, he had to go completely by feel, working the energy through the long-disused gi-lines, restoring the old patterns that had been cut off.

When he finished, he gently released her foot and waited. After a long, wary moment, she dropped her other ankle into his grasp. He repeated the process, renewing the old lines of gi, invigorating the energy there. Then he let it drop. "Done," he whispered.

Without a word, the princess slid back under the covers.

Hopeful that he had gained some favor, unable to face the dread of another night on his knees in silence, Dragomir quietly asked, "Would you please allow me to stretch out on the floor, Princess? You have my word that all I want to do is sleep."

He watched her shut her eyes, heard her settle in to sleep. Moments later, he heard her breath slow, felt her mind and body relax.

Dragomir lowered his head to the post and tried to not to feel the throbbing ache in his limbs.

• • •

That morning, Victory woke feeling more rested than she had in days. In contrast, her slave was already awake, dark rings under his eyes, staring at the floor. She wondered if he had slept at all in the last four nights, then quickly pushed that concern from her mind. Why should she care if he slept or not? Whatever feelings she might have felt for him had been utterly destroyed the moment he forcibly disrobed her.

Still…

With his talents, she knew he could help her. Perhaps if she offered him a trade…

"Slave," Victoria said.

When he lifted his head, there was exhaustion and defeat there.

"I'm going to offer you an exchange."

She thought she saw hope flash in his eyes before his expression grew guarded. "What kind of exchange?" He had yet to add the 'mistress' or 'Your Royal Highness' to any of his statements, but he seemed cowed enough that Victory let it slide.

"My father is trying to kill me," Victory said. When the man didn't laugh or look even remotely surprised, she squinted at him. "But you already knew that, didn't you?"

He lowered his head until his forehead was resting against the bed-post. "I saw something in his *au* when you were yelling at him. I was hoping that wasn't what I saw." He sounded miserable and tired. Very tired.

Victory *refused* to feel sorry for him. "My exchange is this: Aside from my brother, I have no allies that my father cannot bribe or control. I have nowhere I can hide where he doesn't have eyes and ears. But I do have something he hasn't foreseen. I have you. An Emp. If you can keep me alive long enough for me to prove to the Imperium that my father is a murdering criminal, I shall send you home with enough wealth to turn your little village into a kingdom."

His deep, pained sigh was not what she expected. "It would be easier to keep a rabbit alive in a den of lions with the tools that you've given me, Princess."

Victory's mouth fell open. She hadn't actually thought he would refuse, and hearing it from his lips was a whole new humiliation. "You mean you won't even *try?*"

For some time, he didn't reply, merely stared at the chain connecting his throat to the bedframe. Then he turned his head where it rested on the post so that he could see her with one eye. "I have another exchange for you, Princess."

She frowned at him. "You didn't think mine was reasonable?"

"Disappear for awhile, come back to my village with me, and live there under my care and protection until such time as your father is brought to justice."

Victory's heart stopped. That was an alternative she hadn't considered, having automatically written off all native territories in her mind as possible places of refuge, and hope suddenly rushed into her being. Considering what had been done to her, the *last* place her father would look would be one of the native villages. She felt excitement threading through her being, the first real optimism towards the whole affair that she had encountered since realizing her father was going to assassinate her.

Then she realized what living with the Emp would entail, and her eyes dropped to his arms. She felt herself stiffen. "You can't be serious."

"You can even bring a couple of your Praetorian," the Emp said softly, watching her reaction. He gave her a weak grin. "Just to make sure I don't do anything stupid like slap a princess's hand away from my food."

"Or tear off my clothes?" Victory growled.

He flinched and dropped his head back down to face the chain.

She hated to admit it, but he had given her the best alternative she had seen yet. Reluctantly, she leaned forward and unclipped him from the post. "Tell me more about your village," she said, as she released the chain.

The slave groaned and slumped forward, his massive body stretching out on the floor on his stomach with a moan. He took several deep breaths, letting them out in relief, before he craned his neck to look at her. "It's small," he said. "About thirty families. Lots of children. We Mercerians have much larger families than those of the Imperium."

"Because you breed like rabbits," Victory snorted.

He gave her a long look. "Because we have to."

Victory remembered the freighter's cargo list, packed with over thirty thousand slaves, all for 'Delinquent Account.' With each slave worth a good two hundred thousand credits—often three-fifty to five-hundred for healthy males or attractive females—that one freighter alone would have been worth at least six billion credits.

She cleared her throat. "The people in your village…Would they not suspect something if three foreigners simply showed up with you?"

He shrugged his massive shoulders on the floor. "I'll tell them I was rewarded for services rendered, a healing of one of their princesses. The Imperium deals in slaves."

Victory frowned at him, not understanding. "My father would know instantly if I paraded you around as my slave in some native village."

He gave her a sheepish look. His face reddened. "Uh."

Suddenly, Victory understood what he was suggesting, and she lunged to her feet. "*Never*," she growled.

He sighed. "It's not like you haven't done it before, Princess. At least a dozen lifetimes. I didn't hurt you then, I won't hurt you now."

Lying there on his stomach, trussed up on the floor as he was, his promise was almost laughable. But Victory didn't laugh. "You're *insane* if you think—"

A heavy knock on her door stopped her. It was followed by a Praetorian stepping inside, a nervous look on her face. Victory frowned. "Yes?"

Lion was sweating, and worried. "As you commanded, milady, I have been keeping someone at the kitchen to watch it at all times, in plain-clothes, registered as a cook's assistant."

Victory nodded.

"The woman died last night, inside the kitchen. It was said that she was stealing food and choked on a cherry. Her face was blue. It was found blocking her esophagus."

Victory fought a horrible welling of dread. "She didn't choke on a cherry."

Lion shook her head. "Milady, she was allergic to most fruits. She couldn't even touch them without a reaction."

"Were there marks on her throat?" Victory demanded.

"Yes," Lion said. "But the doctor said that such marks could be made by a woman trying to remove the object from her throat as she panicked. The case is being dropped, as no one is going to look deeper into the death of a servant."

Victory's eyes narrowed and she wondered if the doctor, too, might be taking payments from her father's accounts.

"If we revealed she was a Praetorian, though…" Lion suggested.

"No," Victory said. "We can't let them know we suspect."

Her captain's mouth tightened, but she nodded. "The cherry was stemmed," she growled. "Who puts a stemmed cherry into their mouths?"

"She was murdered," Victory said. The coldness of her voice surprised even her. "Any idea what was disturbed in the kitchen?"

Lion's face darkened. "The death was labeled an accident, milady, and no investigation took place. There was a great uproar about the new assistant stealing food, and the Cook made much ado about finding good help. He shooed everyone from the room and refused to let anyone linger."

It pained Victory to think that Cook was part of the conspiracy, but she nodded.

"I slipped back when he was off to the privy and had left the kitchen to his assistants. I entered the kitchen saying that milady was hungry, and that she needed a snack. No one would dare stop a Praetorian in full regalia. None of those fools, anyway. Your favorite cheese, milady. It was laced with tiny syringe-marks."

Victory stood up. "I need to speak with my brother."

Lion flushed. "He was out on a barracks inspection, but he's on his way. I hope you don't mind, milady. I figured that you would want to speak with him."

"I do," Victory said, then she hesitated. The thought of her brother, coming *here*, was triggering another bout of nerves. She hadn't been able to meet with him alone since she had caught him in the sunroom, still powered by raw fury. Aside from dinner, when she specifically chose seats at the table surrounded by women, she hadn't seen him. In fact, aside from the slave, she hadn't had to converse with a man in over three days.

She glanced again at Dragomir. She needed her wits about her for her brother's visit, and there was only one way she knew to ensure that…

"Wait for him outside," Victory told her Praetorian. "Don't let him in until I am ready. I will…" She bit her lip. "…prepare."

Lion followed her glance to the man on the floor, then her eyes widened and she bowed and backed away. A moment later, the door shut, leaving her alone with the native again.

"My brother is coming," she said stiffly. "I will require my full faculties for my dealings with him. In return, I will allow you use of the bed while he and I talk."

Hearing his native tongue once more, the slave craned his head again to glance at her, his blue eyes tired. He seemed to consider a moment. Then, softly, he said, "I'll need my hands."

Victory snorted. "You've proven you don't."

"That was before yet another nine hours of crouching on my knees while you slept," he snarled. For the first time, Victory saw bitterness in his eyes.

Victory straightened, not about to be manipulated by a slave. "I *command* you to flush my fears aside for my brother's visit."

He snorted and dropped his chin back to the floor. To the stone, he said, "You can capture an artist, put a gun to his head and command him to paint, but he can do nothing if you leave him tied."

Facing his disdain, Victory's face hardened. "If you hate me so much, why did you fix my ankles again?"

He twisted to look up at her, his blue eyes gentle. "Because you were in pain, Princess," he said. Then, more softly, "And I don't hate you. I hate myself, for being stupid, and I hate your father, for being cruel. Doesn't change the fact that I'm too tired to work that kind of energy without full use of my hands. Even with them free, it might be a stretch. I'm exhausted."

And, even as Victory watched, he fell into a light doze. Victory examined him, caught yet again by how beautiful he was. Like one of the great cats in her father's menagerie. She hesitated a moment, then nervously found the key between her breasts, knelt beside him, and began unlocking the cuffs.

As his big wrists slid free, they slumped to the floor and stayed there. He started to snore.

Victory crawled around in front of him. "Hey," she said, gently putting a hand on his shoulder. His body dwarfed hers, and she was once again aware of how much larger a creature he was than she. "Dragomir." When that didn't wake him, she gingerly shook his huge shoulder, calling his name some more.

He continued to snore, oblivious to her touch.

Victory narrowed her eyes. "*Slave.*"

Dragomir jerked and opened his blue eyes, startled. He put his hands on the rug in front of him and started pushing himself into a sitting position, then stopped and stared at his arms, then at her.

"You're free," she said, trying to ignore the fears that were building within her. She gestured at her ankle. "I'm waiting."

Instead of rushing to do as he was told, a slow grin spread over Dragomir's face. He moved forward and, before she could pull away, took her hand in his.

Seeing her fingers swallowed by his big palms, Victory cringed. "I'd prefer you use my ankle," she said, trying to tug her hand away. "I'm not sure I'm comfortable with—"

He kissed her knuckles, gently but firmly keeping it in his fist. She was just about to call for her Praetorian when she felt the rush of energy flooding through her arm, washing into her core. She felt herself go limp under the golden glow, reveling in the total relaxation it left behind.

The Emp's power blazed through her, burning away her fears, leaving her utterly calm and secure. Then he opened his eyes and gave her a weak smile.

"Thank you," Victory managed. "I—"

He tilted forward, falling face-first onto her lap, where he started to snore. Victory was still staring at his huge body, pinning her to the carpet, when she heard the knock on the door.

"Victory?" her brother shouted.

Startled, Victory scrambled to get out from under him. She was only halfway free when her brother threw the door open and stepped into the room. He glanced at the slave, then at her, then at the slave again, a startled expression on his face.

Victory flushed until she thought her face would explode. "We didn't do anything," she growled, wriggling the rest of the way out from underneath his huge form.

Her brother lifted a hand to his face and coughed, obviously hiding a smirk. "Your guard said you needed me?"

Victory finally worked her foot free and stood up, brushing herself off. Looking him in the eye, she said, "I need you to make me disappear."

Her brother laughed. Then, when she did not share his amusement, he blinked, looking as if he thought he may have misheard. "…disappear?"

Victory told him what she had found in the Constabulary of Numbers.

"He always liked you more," Victory told her twin, as her brother's face reddened. "I think he's been planning for you to be on the throne since I hit puberty."

Matthias's look was darkening to a stormcloud. "If only this wasn't making perfect sense." He balled up a mailed fist and slammed it into his thigh. "I *thought* it was odd that he was planning a pleasure cruise. Seemed like a real spur of the moment kind of thing, and Father doesn't do that."

"He does when you make him angry enough," Victory said dryly.

Matthias shook his head. "The Imperium needs to know about this. The records should be easy enough to track…"

Victory snorted. "We're talking about Father, here. He's probably got a completely separate set of accounts that he shows to Imperial auditors." She gestured in the general direction of her father's chambers. "He's an insomniac. What do you think he's been doing in there every night?"

Matthias raised both brows. "You think he's in there falsifying accounts for the entire kingdom?"

"He's got the royal blood," Victory said bitterly. "His brain works just as well as yours or mine."

"Yes," Matthias said, frowning, "But even Father isn't infallible."

"His assassin killed one of my Praetorian last night," Victory said. "He poisoned the cheese I told Cook to set aside for me." She then told him about the man with the ice-blue eyes and scarred lip that she had recognized from the hall.

Her brother paled. "You're sure?"

"Lion has been looking for him," she said. "Everyone's seen him, but no one knows what his job in the castle is."

Matthias frowned. "Have your Praetorian buy everything you eat or drink from now on from the marketplace. Don't go anywhere without a full guard. At least eight. Ten would be better."

"That doesn't address the root problem, Matt," Victory growled. "We need to figure out how to uncover what Father is doing to the Imperium, and we need to do it fast. The assassin is a distraction. If Father is removed from the equation, then the assassin will follow."

"Well," Matthias said, "I know they're already investigating him for the war. It looks really bad that he hasn't settled the rebellion yet." Then he looked at her, his green eyes concerned. "But proving it to them will take months."

"That's why you're going to help me disappear," Victory said.

Matthias frowned at her. "You can't stay in the palace. Even the lowliest servant has been given the entire royal family's pictures to memorize and identify, in case one of us decides to go wandering around in our nightrobes in the middle of the night. You would be recognized instantly."

"We have friends," Victory said. "Nearby planets. The old bachelor who gave me the emerald necklace…"

"He died," Matthias said. "And any friend we send you to, Father would have spies in their homes. Word would get back to him."

"I could take a vacation to the Core," Victory growled.

"On whose account?" Matthias demanded. "If you're dead and someone is spending your money, they're going to try and figure out who."

"What about your account?" Victory demanded.

Matthias snorted. "Mine? I use mine for a set of clothes once a month, a few puzzles I pick up at market, and to pay my Praetorian. A voyage to the Core would definitely stand out."

And Victory had determined as much, long before ever calling for her brother. Reluctantly, she glanced at the sleeping man on her rug. She swallowed, hard. "Um. There's another solution."

Her brother frowned at the Emp. "Him?"

"Dragomir had an idea," Victory managed. When her brother only waited, she blurted, "I, uh, could stay with him."

Her brother laughed. "As if the natives aren't going to gossip when a princess and her royal guard get dumped in their village, guests of their local healer."

Victory's face reddened. "I, uh, could pose as his, uh…" She swallowed, hard.

Matthias frowned. "His *wife?*" He snorted. "That would be just as suspicious. He was captured at swordpoint, carted off and has been missing for almost two weeks. What do you think they will say if he comes back married?"

"No," Victory squeaked, her throat suddenly seeming to close on her. "His…" She swallowed, tried to force the passage open. "Slave."

Matthias's brow hit his hairline. "I'm surprised that you would even consider it."

"Father has his hands in every pie on this planet," Victory said quickly. "The only real safe place for me is up in one of the mountain villages, where the Imperium is like a distant boogeyman."

"I know that," Matthias said. "But to trust him like that…"

"Trust him like what?" Victory demanded. "We drop me, Lion, and Whip off with him, he tells everyone that he healed a princess and the Imperium is paying him in slaves. That simple."

He chuckled. "And you're just going to act the cowed and demure little slave girl for a couple months while I cooperate with Imperial investigators, is that it?"

Her face reddened, but Victory stood straighter. "If that's what it takes. I have done it before. I can do it again."

Matthias snorted. "And your collar?"

Victory froze. "What?"

"The Imperium collars its slaves. You would have to wear a collar."

The thought was so horrifying that she could only stare at him.

Matthias shrugged. "It probably wouldn't have worked, anyway. I know you, sister. You would have opened your mouth in front of one of his guests, berated him for being a cad, and the gig would have been up. I think I might be able to hide you in a ship hold for a few weeks. Then maybe set you up to earn your keep in a stone quarry. A camp cook, maybe?"

Victory shuddered. "I'll take my chances with the Emp."

Matthias looked at her carefully. "You realize that, when he walks you off of the ship, you will be in shackles. Slaves are delivered in shackles. Period. You would be putting yourself at his mercy."

Victory lifted her head high, though the idea left her feeling sick with terror. "And you will station a squad of Praetorian in the woods outside town, to rescue me if he decides to take advantage of it."

"I could," Matthias said, "But the fewer people who know about this, the better, and if a squad of my Praetorian suddenly weren't showing up in the palace anymore, then I think it would raise suspicions." He shook his head. "Like I said, sister. We can find something else for you. How about a chambermaid to a native baron?"

"I'll go with the Emp or not at all," Victory snapped. "The only reason I'm even able to function with you standing so close right now is because he worked his energy through me, not moments before you arrived."

Matthias gave her a shocked look, and she realized what he thought she meant by 'energy.'

"No!" Victory snapped. "You *cad*. His power. His consciousness. His love."

"Is that what you call it," Matthias chuckled.

Victory narrowed her eyes at her brother. "The psychic anomaly that makes him an Emp."

"I know," Matthias said, grinning. "I'm just enjoying the look on your face. It's too cute." He sighed, looking down at the Emp. "You trust him enough to put your life in his hands like that?"

No, a part of Victory whimpered. Then, "Do I have a choice?"

Matthias considered. "Yes."

"That *doesn't* involve washing someone's laundry or cowering in a back room in fear that another man might walk through the lunch line?" Victory demanded.

Matthias gave the sleeping Emp a curious look. "So he really did heal you, then? I've heard conflicting reports."

"It's temporary," Victory growled. "He spouted some native nonsense about energy puddles and machines and told me he'd have to have me trust him before he could truly fix the problem."

Matthias grunted. "He was the most talented Emp on my list, according to our accounts. Possibly the best on Mercy, but my staff has only documented about half of them."

Victory's mouth fell open. "You've been documenting Emps and letting them live?"

Matthias's face darkened. "I've been protecting them." At her shocked look, he said, "The jump mutations are a fact of life. And, as your friend has proven, they can be an extreme benefit to society. Hell, the royal lines themselves were caused by jump mutations."

"But if one were to become an assassin…" Victory began.

Matthias wrinkled his nose. "The only *violent* jump mutation that I've seen has been the one that initiated the royal lines. Too much brainpower, not enough empathy. Just look at Father. You look at the average Psi or Emp or Kin or Shi and you're going to find someone who just wants to be left alone."

Victory stared at him. Finally, she broke into a grin. "Brother, I love you."

Matthias's frown faded slightly. "Then you approve?"

Victory glanced at the man on the ground. "After meeting him? Absolutely."

He peered at her much too closely. "And you're so certain of his good intentions that you're willing to tromp off a ship in shackles and watch while I and my Praetorian leave you there."

No, Victory thought, even as her mouth said, "Yes."

"You're lying," her brother said, his green eyes full of understanding. "You're scared to death."

Victory looked away. "Do I have any real choice?"

He grunted and looked at the man on the floor. "If I were to have to make the decision, right now, with my life on the line, I would say that you can trust him. I had him on the rack for three days trying to provoke him enough to attack me. We didn't even get a blip on the sensors."

Victory jerked her head to give her brother a sharp look. "Then it was true? You *tortured* him?"

Matthias shrugged. "I didn't enjoy it, and I'm sure that the men I released are simply going to spread more hatred for the Imperium, but it was necessary. I needed to determine what kind of man he was, and whether he was going to try and use his powers to harm you." Then Matthias cocked his head. "He hasn't, has he?"

Victory bit her lip. "No," she whispered. But, like her brother, she had given him every reason to do so.

"Huh," her brother said. He glanced at the sleeping man. "I was told by your Praetorian that they suspected he had done something, though you refused to talk about it. It was around the same time you came flying from your room in a rage...I heard you smashed all your statuary?" He glanced at the shelves, dressers, and tables now all empty but for the wooden statue of a reading mermaid that her mother had given her. He grunted. "That much seems to be true."

"Our plan is simple, then," Victoria said, ignoring him. "I will stay in my room until you've made proper arrangements. My excuse will be that I feel suddenly very ill, and that it came on rather suddenly after my last foray to the kitchens, where I once again stole some cheese. In the meantime, my Praetorian will buy my food from the market and deliver it to me."

"We'll need to move fast," Matthias said. "Father will expect you to board the cruise in two days, and I've reviewed its flight path. There are plenty of places where it could flounder and never be found. It crosses the Boiling Rift, weaves through the Voidstar Mountains, and shoots up over both poles."

"Some pleasure-cruise," Victory said bitterly.

"That's what *I* thought," Matthias said. "My first thought, seeing its route, was that it takes every possible pathway to set itself up to be ambushed."

Victory frowned. "But Father is going to be on the cruise. He said so himself."

"He'll be on it when it sails," Matthias said, "But I'm willing to bet that he gets called away sometime before the cruise starts entering dangerous territory."

"And you with him," Victory said, scowling.

"It will be a military emergency, I'm sure," Matthias said bitterly. "Something that the General Commander must drop everything to attend to."

"And then I cruise on, alone, and my ship is attacked and I'm killed," Victory said. "And he has another excuse to prolong his war."

Matthias's green eyes sharpened, and she watched her brother's frighteningly quick mind formulate a plan. "I think," Matthias said slowly, "That we're going to let him kill you."

• • •

Victory spent the rest of the next two days more or less watching Dragomir sleep. She hadn't yet told him that she intended to follow through with his plan, and was afraid to even mention it.

Finally, however, the night before the cruise, Victory knew she had to tell him. As he woke, she told him of her brother's plans, and how they would be faking her death on the cruise. "I'll be going with you to your village," Victory said. Then, when he hesitated, mid-yawn, to blink at her, she quickly explained, "Just as long as it takes for my brother to bring my father to justice."

Dragomir raised an eyebrow of disbelief. "You would go as my slave?"

"I would wear a collar for show," she said, flushing. "I am *not* a slave."

Dragomir chuckled and leaned back against the bed, crossing his dark, native arms over his muscular native chest. "Sounds familiar, doesn't it?"

Victory felt her face redden. "I would *never* demean myself so, if not in the name of keeping up the illusion."

He watched her for some time. "Do you trust me?" Dragomir asked finally, scanning her face.

Victory's mouth fell open. Of course she didn't trust him. "I'll pay you well, once I've been instated as the next Adjudicator."

"That's not what I asked," he said.

"Trust has nothing to do with it," she babbled. "You will be well-rewarded for your services."

"You put that collar around your neck," Dragomir said, his blue eyes flashing, "And you're putting yourself at my mercy."

"You're not that stupid," Victory growled. "I'll have my Praetorian."

"It's a fact," Dragomir said. "Your Praetorian will also be chained, and I'll have an entire village at my back, should I need it. How does that make you feel?"

"And *I'll* have my brother's entire armada," Victory babbled. "You wouldn't *dare*."

"Put a collar around your neck and hand me the leash," Dragomir said. He smiled sweetly. "Then I guess we'll see."

"My brother would check in on me eventually," Victory snapped. "And when he did, you would be a dead man."

"Unless I decided to take you somewhere else."

Victory froze, the idea not having occurred to her. *Oh gods*, her panicked mind thought. *He could make me disappear again.*

"Unchain my ankles," Dragomir said. When Victory simply stared at him, he grinned. "You want an exchange? The trade begins now." He shoved a shackled foot at her, arms crossed, waiting.

"My brother's already made his plans," Victory snarled. "If I'd known you were going to be ridiculous, I would have told him to set me up with the quarry."

"How is this ridiculous?" Dragomir demanded, shaking his foot, making the chain rattle. "I'm going to have you at my mercy—for *months*, it sounds like—and you seem to expect me to treat you no differently than I would a house guest. Would it kill you to return the favor as a show of good faith?"

Victory felt her heart beginning to pound. He was right. All the money and influence that she brought to the table meant nothing if he decided to take advantage of the situation.

And I've given him every reason to hate me, Victory thought, remembering chaining him to the bed, remembering the jeers of the dining hall as he ate his slops.

Dragomir jiggled his foot again. "Well?"

I can't do this, Victory thought, looking at the man's shackles, feeling the key resting between her breasts. Then, a disgusted part of her said, *Then why would you expect him to do differently?*

Slowly, reluctantly, Victory inched forward across the floor, until she was within reach of his shackles. At the way her throat seized at his nearness, however, she hesitated. "I think I'm going to need another cleansing first," she said, as her nerves started to betray her. "The fear is coming back."

"Unshackle me," Dragomir said. He made no move to reach for her and work his energy through her body, only waited.

Victory gave him a shocked look. He hadn't refused until now.

"Someday, Princess, I intend for you to discover that, despite your every belief otherwise, I'm not going to hurt you." He shook his foot. "So unshackle me. I won't have you drugged as I prove it to you."

For some time, she could only stare at him.

Dragomir dropped his foot with an irritated look. "Then don't bother taking us to my village."

He's serious, she realized, in horror.

Victory's hands were trembling as she reached into her shirt and retrieved the key. One by one, she unlocked the titanium bands, her heart jumping at each metallic click.

When she was finished, Dragomir's hand snatched out and he grabbed her wrist. Victory gasped and froze, peering at the dark hand encircling her pale skin, every muscle caught in growing horror.

Uncoiling like a big cat, Dragomir moved forward over her, forcing her to the floor as his big body came to rest above her.

"So," Dragomir said, lowering his weight atop her, pinning her to the carpet. "Do you trust me?"

Victory was so terrified she couldn't scream. She started panting, hyperventilating as her mind began to shut off.

She felt something grab her mind, force it back into full awareness.

"I'm not letting you go anywhere this time," Dragomir said. His blue eyes were intense as he looked down at her, his face only inches from hers. "I want you to really think about it. Do you trust me?"

Feeling all the tiny places where his great body melded into hers, Victory squeezed her eyes shut and tried once more to separate her awareness from her physical body, but something was holding it tightly in place. Realizing she was trapped, she started to panic. She opened her mouth to scream.

"Didn't think so," Dragomir said with a sigh. He raised his weight off of her and picked up the shackles from the floor. These, along with the ones from his wrists that she had looped over the hook in the headboard, he carried to the window. He yanked it open and, with a heavy grunt, hurled the shackles out into space.

"I can get others," Victory blurted.

Dragomir closed the window and turned to her. "You can," he agreed, his legs spread wide, his arms crossed across his big chest, "But from now on, considering your plans, Princess, I think you should really start taking to heart the Golden Rule."

"Is that a *threat?*" she squeaked.

He shrugged. "It's a fact. You want my help. I may or may not be inclined to give it."

The cruise was scheduled to depart the next morning, and Victory was cursing herself for waiting this long to determine that Dragomir was going to be uncooperative.

"From what you told me," Dragomir said, as she stared at the floor in frustration, "We are getting on a ship tomorrow morning, where your father intends for you to die. There may or may not be an assassin onboard, and if there is, I would like to have my hands and legs free so I can kick him in the face the moment I see him."

Victory blinked and looked up at him. "What?"

"I can tell a sociopath or a psychopath at a hundred yards," Dragomir said. "Like that guy in the hallway, right before you had your breakdown. He had an *au* like I've never seen before. If I hadn't been trying to calm you down, I'd have tried to get you to sic your Praetorian on him. That one has done very many bad things with his life, and the world would be a better place if he took a dive off of your Vanishing Spire."

Victory's jaw fell open. Until now, she had thought that maybe she had just been seeing things, a figment of her panicked mind. "You *saw* him?"

Dragomir gave her a curious look. "Saw who?"

"The blue-eyed man with the scar on his lip," Victory cried. "Can you recognize him again, if he were wearing a different guise?"

Dragomir snorted. "I could see that one coming a mile away."

"He's an assassin," Victory babbled. "He sabotaged my ship, on its way to the Imperial Academy. He took my virginity and handed me over to the rebels.

Dragomir's face hardened in a scowl. "You recognized him and said nothing?"

"My Praetorian know," Victory said. "They've been looking for him, but it's like he's a specter. Everyone has seen him, but no one knows where he works or sleeps."

"Then," Dragomir said, "If I see him again, I have your permission to end his miserable existence?"

Victory gave a bitter laugh. "Only if I get to watch you do it."

Dragomir grinned and tugged the chain hanging between them. "Unfortunately, I don't really see how you could miss it."

156

CHAPTER 10

Whip's Close Call

Dragomir slept on the bed that night. He was actually surprised that she offered, though it left him chuckling inside. *Remember the Golden Rule*, he thought, grinning at the ceiling. *You sly dog.*

The princess, quite adamantly, had taken up residence on the floor—along with half the blankets and most of the pillows. Dragomir let it pass. Someday, she would trust him. Whether that day came sooner or later, it didn't really matter in the cosmic scheme of things. He *wished* it was sooner, rather than later, but whenever it happened, it would come in time.

Probably sooner than she would like, he thought, thinking of the days ahead. He felt himself hardening at the idea of having the princess as his own, finally giving her no choice but to open up and trust him.

He was tired of having his hands tied, both literally and figuratively. If her brother's plan carried through and they came off of the cruise alive and her brother dropped them into his village with her and her two Praetorian as make-believe little slaves, he was going to take full advantage of the situation.

When it was over, perhaps she would never speak to him again, but by the gods, he was going to open her ramas. One by one. He was going to restore balance to her energy-starved system, and if she took offense, then that was too damn bad.

He was tired of watching helplessly as her past overtook her. He could fix it, and he was going to, and if she didn't like it, she could kill him after he was finished. He was a healer. He would *heal* her, or die trying.

At dawn, they ate a big breakfast that the Praetorian brought to them, then he watched as her maids came and packed enough luggage to clothe an entire army for a week. Once the princess's belongings were safely secured and on their way to her chambers upon the cruise ship, her Praetorian came—all nineteen of them—and herded the both of them through the palace, out into the courtyard, and onto the ship in a huge fanfare of song and celebration from the observers.

That many people, all in one place, had always made Dragomir nervous. He shielded himself from the barrage of scattered emotional energy and trusted the wall of black-clad bodies around them to keep out any poisons or daggers.

They made their way quickly to the princess's suite, and once they were out of the chaos of the courtyard, Dragomir finally allowed his shields to come down.

It was then that he saw the woman step from the princess's chamber, dressed in a maid's stark black and white. He froze, however, upon seeing the roiling black mass of energy billowing around the woman.

The woman's ice-blue eyes met his stare and he thought he detected amusement there. Then she curtseyed and, ducking her head, hurried down the hall.

The princess hit the end of the chain and turned back to him, frowning.

"That was him," Dragomir said. "I'd recognize that *au* anywhere."

"Who?" Victory demanded. "The *maid?*"

"Unless your father employs two assassins," Dragomir said, "That was the man from the hall." He refused to move further down the hall, despite the Praetorian pushing at him to continue. "Either way, Princess, I'm pretty sure you don't want to stay in that room."

Victory frowned, but then turned to chatter in Imperial at her Praetorian.

Four of them took off at a run down the hall, turning the corner after the maid. Four others entered her chambers while the rest remained stationed around her in the hall. Dragomir could hear thumps and crashes from inside as they searched.

Finally, they came back with a needle, clasped between a Praetorian's fingers like she were holding a viper. The princess's other captain, Whip, stumbled out of the room and leaned against the doorframe, pale and sweating, staring at the needle. Her *au* was flickering, like a candle flame that was burning low.

The one called Lion muttered something in Imperial, gesturing at her pale companion, who was rapidly starting to slide down the doorframe, to the floor. The princess narrowed her eyes and replied in a growl. Immediately, the Praetorian started herding them down the hall, away from the chamber, towards the front of the ship.

"What happened?" Dragomir asked, once they were moving again.

"I told them to put me in another room, one with a better view," Victory said.

"No," Dragomir said, "to the woman." He nodded at her. Something was wrong with her steel-gray energy—it seemed to be slowing down, pushed aside by an inky blackness.

Victory grimaced. "They found a needle in my bed," she said. "Nano-poison, I would guess. It sank into Whip as she swept the sheets back. They don't think she's going to make it."

The tall, lean Praetorian in question was panting, her face becoming a very dull gray. She was strung between two of her companions, head down, wheezing. Watching the energy within her stagnate on her *gi* meridians, a black energy overpowering them, Dragomir frowned. "Tell them to set her down."

Victory frowned at him. "I told you they used nanobots. We need to get her to a doctor."

"Do you want her to *die*?" Dragomir snapped.

Hesitating, Victory gave the command to lay the woman out on the floor. As she did, Dragomir saw her eyes start to glaze as she went into shock. He dropped to his knees beside her and, without taking the time to think about it, put one hand over her core rama and another over her soul rama. The Praetorian gasped and tried to struggle away, but Dragomir tightened his grip and held her in place.

Immediately, several Praetorian unsheathed their swords and made to use them.

Dragomir ignored them. A palm on her groin, the other on her crown, he shoved energy through her from both sides, catching the blackness before it had a chance to enter the ramas, then shoving it back out through the roiling black wound in the meat of her hand.

Beneath him, the Praetorian gasped and arced her back. Dragomir kept working, hunting down every last shadow, burning it away.

Once he had scoured all the blackness from her central body, he moved his consciousness down her arm, squirting it from her *gi* lines like ink from a pricked water-bag. When he finally reached the wound itself, the Praetorian was panting underneath him, alert gray eyes fixed to his face, but holding entirely still. Dragomir sought out the blackness in her palm, isolated it.

"Tell her to hold up her wounded hand," he said, maintaining his trance, monitoring the flow of energy.

Victory did, and slowly, reluctantly, the Praetorian lifted her hand to Dragomir.

He took his hand off of her core rama and, still pushing energy through her soul rama to keep the roiling black energy in her wound contained, grabbed her wrist.

Then, feeding energy through her wrist from his hand, he released her crown and, still focused on the woman beneath him, held up an open palm to the Praetorian around him. "I need a knife."

It was Lion who offered her blade.

Dragomir took it, and, while the Praetorian on the floor watched nervously, brought the knife to the meat of her hand.

"Tell her I've got to cut it out," Dragomir said.

Victory must have relayed his message, because the woman's eyes went wide. Instead of flinching or trying to pull back, however, she simply nodded.

Dragomir made it quick. He sliced into the woman's palm at an angle, just deep enough to collect the source of the roiling black material, then came at it from the other side. The woman winced and gritted her teeth, but did not so much as whimper. He tossed the scrap of skin and flesh aside and looked again to make sure he had gotten all of the voidlike darkness. After ascertaining that the wound was clean, he grunted and handed Lion back her blade.

"Tell her that the blade should probably be destroyed, in case it carries any infection," Dragomir said. He stood up and gestured at the bloody flap of skin on the ground. "And the piece of her hand, as well."

For a long moment, everyone in the hall simply stared at him. Victory didn't relay his words, and Dragomir frowned at her. "Tell them."

"You *healed* her?" Victory said, instead. She was staring down at the woman, who was cursing and wrapping her hand in her shirt, but whose color had already returned to her face, the sweating stopped, her breathing back to normal, if a bit faster than standard. Her steel-gray *au* was shimmering, brighter than Dragomir had ever seen it, and it contained traces of his own golden energy in patches here and there.

All of the Praetorian seemed to be glancing from their companion, then back to him, awe forming in their battle-hardened eyes.

Embarrassed, Dragomir looked at the ground. "Can you ask her how she's feeling, at least?"

Still staring at him, Victory uttered something in Imperial. The Praetorian woman hissed something back, and, using the wall as leverage, started getting to her feet.

"She says her…" Victory hesitated, "…*blessed* hand hurts." She gave him a small frown. "But aside from that, she's never felt better. You even cured her head-cold, or so she seems to believe."

"Probably," Dragomir said. "I wasn't being specific."

Victory frowned up at him. "You can cure the sick?"

"That's what I did back in my village," Dragomir said. "In between cutting hay, herding goats, digging potatoes, and plowing fields."

"You never said that," Victory growled.

"I'm pretty sure I did," Dragomir replied. "You just didn't believe me."

Victory looked at him for several more breaths, flicking her attention between him and Whip, then silently gestured at her guard to continue.

The Praetorian led them to a new chamber, and for the rest of the day, as they waited for the passengers to load and the ship to get underway, Dragomir caught the black-clad women staring at him. When they brought out food for their first meal, one of the sleek, armored women handed him her hunk of cheese, saying that she didn't need it. Another gave him a half-loaf of bread. A third offered him an apple she claimed she didn't want. Dragomir, blushing, took it all quietly, getting the very distinct idea that he would be pounded flat for the insult of refusing.

As the ship finally powered up its engines and shuddered as it left dock, Dragomir felt the tension in the room increase tenfold. A disagreement began, and for the first time, he saw Victory and her Praetorian argue.

"What's going on?" he asked, watching the Praetorian snarl amongst themselves.

"Father will want me to make an appearance at dinner," Victory said. "They are insisting that one of them eat before I do, to test my food for me. I am telling them 'no.' I know it's their jobs, but it's not right that they sacrifice themselves that way."

"Then don't eat at all," Dragomir said. "You're supposed to be feeling very sick, right? Use it as an excuse to not partake in dinner. I saw the amount of food your Praetorian brought along. You have plenty of stores to keep you from starving."

Victory sighed. "You don't understand. This cruise is in my honor, supposedly celebrating my return from the Academy. I will be expected to—"

"This cruise is orchestrated to *kill* you," Dragomir growled.

Several of the Praetorian stiffened at his tone, but didn't interrupt.

"You do whatever you need to do to stay alive until we can get off this ship," Dragomir said. "If that means hiding in your room, pretending you're sick, then so be it, I'll hold you here myself. The less you are out and about, the less opportunity that sly little bastard has to slip you something deadly."

The princess gave him a look like he had suddenly sprouted antlers. Scrunching her face disgustedly, she said, "And just what makes you think you have *any* say at all in—"

Dragomir raised an eyebrow.

He could almost *see* the Golden Rule flash across the back of her brain in huge, neon red letters. Her eyes widened. "Uh," the princess said. "I mean." She swallowed, hard. "Thank you for your input." She grated out every word, and it sounded like she was cracking teeth in the process. Dragomir had to suppress a chuckle.

Keeping a straight face, he said, "So, we are in agreement? You will claim you are still too ill to move around, but will be out just as soon as you can stop vomiting all over the place."

The princess gave him a look like she would rather take instructions from a moldy dumpster, but she nodded.

"Good," Dragomir grunted. "Then get me some clothes. I'm tired of running around in my birthday suit. Too many pretty ladies around here to gawk at me." He winked at her. "I might feel like I'm being taken advantage of."

The princess wrinkled her face and opened her mouth. "There's no way I'm—" She caught herself, swallowing, the Golden Rule again blazing like a warning beacon in the back of her head. "Uh," she said. "Right away."

Dragomir was actually surprised that she didn't add, "Sir," so cowed was her expression.

This is going to be so *much fun*, he thought, suppressing an inner giggle. He stretched out on a couch, watching as Praetorian departed at a run to find him clothes. They returned with a too-tight servant's outfit, but he wasn't going to complain. He shrugged it over his shoulders and yanked up the pants, so utterly ecstatic to have clothing again that the pinch in the chest and the calf-length legs didn't bother him.

The Praetorian, for their part, seemed thrilled at his idea to keep the princess abed, and immediately took up positions around the room, the argument settled. Even Whip, with her bandaged hand, stood at attention beside the door.

"There's going to be hell to pay for this," Victory muttered, but she ended her complaints and instead entertained herself with the view out her suite window.

Dragomir, who had never even been on a skimmer before Prince Matthias had abducted him, went to sit beside her. He found himself awed by the view, by the mountains and rivers passing beneath them. Then, suddenly, a towering black cliff was passing outside, not fifteen feet from the window, and he jerked back, staring out the glass in awe.

At his gasp, Victory quirked a curious eyebrow at him. "Have you never been on a cruise before?" As if it were the most natural—and common—thing in the world to sail around in a massive ship for weeks on end, wasting enough fuel and supplies to keep a thousand villages powered for the next ten millennia.

He had known such diversions existed, but it had been in a distant corner of his brain, his thoughts instead going towards his daily existence, and how he was going to put away enough food for winter. To be faced with it now, after living in a cottage eating eggs and potatoes his whole life, Dragomir found it very overwhelming. "I knew it was possible," Dragomir admitted, "But I never thought I'd actually experience it myself."

She frowned at him as if she didn't believe him. "*Never?*" As if everyone had the opportunity to sail around the world because they were bored.

At her stare of pitying disbelief, Dragomir felt himself bristle. "Until two weeks ago, Victory, I had never left my village except to go to the next town over, to trade goats."

The princess stiffened at his use of her name, but, with a sideways look, she did not mention it.

The Golden Rule, Dragomir thought, unable to stifle his grin that time.

Victory narrowed her eyes at him, but turned her attention back to the passing scenery.

A courier came a half hour before dinner, telling them that the Adjudicator required the princess's presence. The Praetorian took his message, then told him that the princess was ill, and that, while unfortunate, the Adjudicator could more or less get stuffed. Another arrived ten minutes before dinner, again insisting that the princess's father demanded her attendance. He was sent away with just as much fanfare as the first.

The third messenger arrived, mid-meal, with a note scribbled by the Adjudicator's own hand. Victory, who had been snoozing, sat up, read it, grunted, and tossed it into the fire.

"He says I am humiliating him," Victory said, "And that if I am not at his table within five minutes, he is going to send his Praetorian to retrieve me." She glanced around the room. "Considering that I've got nineteen of them with me, and he brought only sixteen, ten of which must stay with him at all times, I'm not seeing how he's going to follow through on that particular threat." She yawned and went back to sleep.

Two hours later, there was a commotion in the hall, and Dragomir heard someone shouting Victory's name in Imperial.

"Sounds like he's here," Victory said. She gestured at her Praetorian to let him inside.

• • •

As soon as the door was open, Victory's father strode in, red-faced and furious. His blonde eyebrows stood out on his crimson face like fresh snow upon a bloodstain. "I *commanded* you to attend me," he snarled. "How *dare* you disobey?"

"I sent a response message," Victory said, still lying in bed, "but since my brother tells me you rarely read your messages, perhaps you didn't catch the fact that I would politely vomit all over your table and shit all over your chair. I'm sick. Have been since eating in Cook's kitchen the last time. I think I found some bad cheese. I can't move without my world spinning and my bowels spilling themselves like pudding from a sack."

Her father narrowed his eyes, but she saw a flicker of recognition there.

You bastard, Victory thought, her hopes that her father was not responsible for her assassination attempts dashed by the calculation on his face.

"I was told you weren't eating from the kitchen anymore," her father finally said.

165

"I'm *not*," Victory snapped. "If this is what I get?" She snorted. "I'll eat my own food, thank you. Whatever disease is plaguing his kitchen can stay with Cook."

"Have the doctors attended to you?" her father demanded. "You don't look sick."

Victory gave him a grim smile. "Would you like me to demonstrate?"

Her father gave her a distasteful look. "No, I am quite content with—" He froze, his eyes on her slave. His face darkened to a thunderhead. His voice was utterly cold when he said, "You clothed him."

"Yes," Victory said. "He is *my* slave, after all."

"I ordered him to be naked."

"You also ordered me to dinner," Victory said. "We saw how well that worked."

Her father stared at her as if she had lost her mind. Then, slowly, she saw his anger rise again, like a volcano that was slowly increasing pressure from the inside. "Praetorian," he said, his eyes still fixed on Victory, "Beat her slave to death. She can drag around a corpse for the rest of the trip."

As three of his house guard stepped forward, ten black-clad women stepped between, swords out and resting on the men's throats. Behind them, nine more women drew swords, the sound of ringing steel sweet to Victory's ears.

"Turns out," Victory said, as her father sputtered in rage, "My personal guard have taken a liking to the brute. Now get out of my chambers."

For a moment, she thought her father would actually be stupid enough to pick a fight. He had twelve Praetorian with him, the other four probably stationed at his chamber door. She had nineteen, and they already had their blades bared and ready, their hands on their energy weapons.

"If you don't leave now," Victory said softly, "I think I might decide to inherit my empire early, father." She plucked a piece of her dinner from between her teeth. "After all, the house Praetorian serve the ruler. If you are dead, then that will be..." She cocked her head, pretending to think about it. "Why, that would be *me*."

For what seemed like an eternity, her father merely glared at her over the shoulders of her guard. Victory met his gaze with one of her own, refusing to be cowed by the lying, selfish bastard any longer. Finally, her father's lips stretched in a small smile.

"You'll be dead before this cruise is complete." His words were soft, so full of fury that they came out only as a whisper.

Victory smiled, showing teeth. "We'll see, Father."

"You will. I'll make sure of it." The Adjudicator had Death in his eyes as he turned and stalked from the room. His twelve Praetorian, looking nervous and conflicted, eventually backed from the room, eyes on their sisters' swordpoints.

"Close the door and stay together," Victory said. "None of you go anywhere alone. I doubt he'll try anything overt, but he might have his men take potshots, should you give them the opportunity."

Then, nerves on edge, she sank back down to her couch and tried not to think about just how utterly dead she and all of her Praetorian would be if her brother's plan failed.

Her brother came to her chambers about an hour later, looking disturbed. His green eyes flickered over the Praetorian, then back to her. "I heard that you threatened Father's life."

"He told his guard to beat my slave to death," Victory said. "I told him to back down, or I might decide to inherit my empire early."

Matthias sighed and glanced at the Emp, who was currently lounging in a sofa like a big cat. "Well, at least it's assured that this ship is doomed to crash."

Victory raised an eyebrow. "Have you made arrangements?"

"A little mining village out in the Twinbrook Range. Completely surrounded by about three hundred miles of mountains in any direction. They're building cells in the mine as we speak."

"What did you tell them?" Victory asked.

"Uncooperative slaves," her brother said. "In return for housing them for a few months, we will gift their village with a freight skimmer. As they have it now, they've been packing their minerals and supplies back and forth on donkeyback. Their mine is actually quite productive—they are simply bottlenecked at how much they can haul, not how much they can pull out of the ground. One good freight skimmer and that town could be booming by next year."

Victory gave Dragomir a wary look. "Could I stay there, too?" she asked. "Perhaps we could rent a villager's house…"

Her brother shook his head. "They have a much higher chance of being found, simply by the numbers involved." He gestured at the ship around them. "It takes two hundred people just to keep this place running. If you add all the guests that father leaves behind, as well as staff for those guests, we're probably looking at somewhere around four hundred people. I'm going to have to ship food into that town on a weekly basis. Sooner or later, the Constable of Numbers is going to take another look at the odd charges I've made to my accounts lately. Someone's going to talk. I estimate they will find the prisoners before they manage to pull the ship from the Boiling Rift, though I can hope for longer."

"Then you discovered the ambush site?" Victory asked.

"Two days beyond the Boiling Rift," her brother said. "There's a cluster of ships gathered in the mountains directly overlooking our flight path. Aside from our route, there is nothing interesting in that area for seven hundred miles in any direction."

"When do you figure Father will depart?" Victory asked.

Her brother shrugged. "After your display? I wouldn't be surprised if he leaves tomorrow."

• • •

Matthias was wrong. Their father departed that *night*, and left Matthias with standing orders to be prepared to leave at a moment's notice, because it was looking as if the uprising that had demanded his attention might require the General Commander to put it down.

A day and a half later, as they were sailing over Mercy's largest ocean, nearing the Boiling Rift, Matthias got the call. Victory made a show of walking him to the ship that came to get him, then waving and wishing his safety in the war as he departed.

Four hours later, as evening was settling over the ocean, Victory saw the mass of steam and rippled water on the horizon. Even through the ship's filtration systems, she began to smell ammonia.

Thirty minutes later, the ship's alarms went off. The intercom light came on, and the captain said, "Ladies and gentlemen, this is the captain speaking. Don't panic, but it appears we are being attacked by pirates. They are attempting to board, but our ship's crew is well-trained in these matters, and can easily stand against a few ragtag rebels. Stay within your cabins and everything will be handled by our expert crew."

Ten minutes after that, "Ladies and Gentlemen, this is the captain. It seems our attempts to repel the invaders failed, and they have taken the bridge. They intend to drive the ship into the Boiling Rift as a warning to the Adjudicator. They will free the crew and any non-royal guests in the closest port city, and are currently opening their ship to boarding. I repeat. They are going to scuttle the ship. Please retire to the upper deck and *please* do not hide from their searchers. I repeat. There is no surviving the Boiling Rift. Its temperatures are over three hundred degrees at the surface. Jumping ship would be fatal. Please, go quietly to their ship and this will all be over soon."

"Well," Victory said, gesturing at Dragomir. "Let's go."

She and her Praetorian stepped into the hall, where they were met by one of her brother's men. He bowed deeply, shouldering his energy rifle, and led them down the corridor towards the upper deck of the ship. "The skimmers were all sabotaged?" she asked him, as they walked.

He nodded. "There is no way that the traitor could have escaped, milady, unless he had left with your father's staff."

It was possible, Victory thought, but not probable. More likely than not, her father had given his man the order to see the job finished, this time, so that she could not come back to haunt him.

"This way," the man said, leading her out onto the upper balcony and sweeping around to the front of the ship. As they approached, they saw the invading ship—large and sleek, with guns poking from every surface, it was one of her brother's best warships, albeit with a hasty make-over and a sloppy paint job. Still, Victory was a bit disappointed that the captain mistook it for a raider ship. She would need to remember to increase wartime training requirements for ship captains, when she took the throne.

At the base of the warship's gangplank, a mass of frightened, expensively-dressed guests were gathered and milling, herded into place by a few dozen of her brother's heavily-armed soldiers. More were being added by the minute, as searchers brought up the stragglers in the bowels of the ship.

"You see him?" Victory asked the Emp, as they came to stand beside the base of the gangplank, flanked by another dozen of her brother's soldiers.

"Not yet," Dragomir said, frowning. "Start letting them on the ship."

Slowly, the men at the gangplank allowed a trickle to filter from the mass of people, up into the open maw where another dozen heavily-armed soldiers stood at the top, waiting.

"And now?" Victory demanded, as the last stragglers were brought from the ship's bowels, the captain was brought down from the helm, and the exit doors were sealed.

"No," Dragomir said, through a frown of concentration.

Four fifths of the cruise ship's occupants had boarded the gangplank by the time Dragomir's fist tightened on her arm. "There he is," he whispered. His eyes were riveted to an arthritic old woman hobbling up the plank.

Victory looked up at the old serving woman, saw the woman's ice-blue eyes dance nervously over her brother's men from under her thin white bangs, and she knew.

"Stop," Victory commanded, gesturing at the woman.

A dozen men retrieved the assassin from the gangplank, to her loud and agitated struggles. They took her off to the side and held her there as Dragomir watched the rest of the men board. Her bottom lip, Victory noticed, was scarred.

"Take off her disguise," Victory ordered.

Six men started stripping the old woman, trying to pull off her wig, removing her clothes, and when they revealed withered old breasts and knobby knees, she frowned, feeling her first traces of doubt.

"What disguise?" the woman cried, the picture of ancient indignance. "I don't know what's going on!"

Could he have been wrong? Victory thought, glancing at Dragomir. He was still scanning each person as they boarded, the men guarding the plank waiting for him to shake his head before allowing the next to board. Dragomir hesitated at a couple—most of them single-minded courtesans with aspirations of power—but eventually let them each through. Victory turned back to the old woman. *Or could there have been two of them?*

Victory caught the woman watching Dragomir with a frown. Then her ice-blue eyes flickered with shock. "He's an *Emp*," she snarled, fury clear in her voice.

"Of course," Victory said, smiling sweetly. "How else do you catch an assassin who seems to disappear into the walls themselves?"

Her brother's men, who had already been informed, did not even bat an eye.

It was at that point that the woman began to panic. Victory saw the shimmer in the woman's flesh, saw the slight shift in proportions before she got her fear back under control. Her eyes narrowed.

"And you're a Shi," Victory said softly, trying not to let it show how the assassin's presence was giving her goosebumps. To her brother's men, she said, "Make sure *it* doesn't escape."

When finally the last passenger had boarded the ship under the shake of Dragomir's head, her brother's men retracted the gangplank and the warship departed. A moment later, a smaller courier ship slipped in behind it, taking its place. As the bow opened and the ramp extended, the Shi watched it with hungry eyes.

"Are you going to kill me, then?" it asked. Neither male nor female, an inShi—a Shi with the power to make internal changes in the base structure of matter, rather than external—was born hermaphroditic, with the ability to change shape between the sexes at will. And, with much practice and dedication, could eventually change the appearance of age and features, as well.

They were the perfect assassins. Victory cursed herself for not thinking of it sooner. It simply hadn't occurred to her, due to her father's outspoken hatred of anything mutogenetic.

"I'm not going to kill you, no," Victory said.

She saw the flash of cunning in the ice-blue eyes. "You are going to turn me in to the Imperium?" she—*it?*—asked. Though the Shi was the picture of fear, Victory didn't need to be an Emp to know that the assassin was laughing inside.

"And return you to my father's service?" Victory snorted. "No, I don't think so."

Again, Victory watched her flesh shimmer with fear. This time, several of her Praetorian saw it, too, because their hands tightened on their weapons. She sighed. "Drop the guise, fool. We know who you are."

The image of the woman seemed to slough away, leaving a familiar young man with ice-blue eyes staring back at her, his face contorted in a sneer.

Victory swallowed the fear that was forming in her gut, seeing him again.

"Oh, you remember me?" the man jeered. "I don't suppose you want to go for another round, Princess?"

Lion stepped forward and punched him in the gut, doubling him over. Then she briskly stepped back, letting him wheeze into the ship's deck.

Coughing into the deck, the Shi gasped, "If you idiots aren't going to kill me and you're not turning me over to the Imperium and you're not sending me back on the cattle car with the other passengers, what are you going to do with me?" He looked up, smiling. "Let me guess. You want to make a deal."

"I didn't say we weren't going to kill you," Victory said, gesturing for Whip. "I said that *I* wasn't going to kill you."

At that, she stepped out of the way as Whip, carrying Lion's bloody dagger, rammed it into the assassin's throat. Even as he was grabbing for the weapon, trying to pull it free, three Praetorian lifted him and threw his body overboard. They heard it splash in the boiling waters far below. Victory, Lion, Whip, and several others went to the railing to look down, watching until the body stiffened and went still.

"They are efficient," Dragomir said, looking ill. He had stayed well away from the edge of the railing, giving the ocean beyond a wary look.

Afraid of heights, Victory remembered. "It's their job," she stated. "That Shi was dead the moment you pinpointed him on the gangplank. He just didn't know it yet."

"If you will follow me, milady," her brother's man said, gesturing to the courier's gangplank. "The vessel is set to start losing altitude in three and a half minutes."

Victory glanced up at the open maw of her brother's ship. Knowing what awaited her on the other side, Victory took a deep breath, then led her entourage into the breach.

CHAPTER 11

At Home with an Emp

"**I** don't like it, milady," Lion said, glancing again at the Emp, who was watching them carefully from a bench across the ship's hull from them. He was wearing a good set of four-layer embroidered black silk, and above the fine ebony cloth, his blue eyes seemed to almost glow.

Two Praetorian now stood between her and him, casually making sure he kept his distance. Ever since they had cut away the metal belt and removed his collar, Victory had been exercising her newfound ability to be as far from him as possible.

…and here she was about to put herself into the exact same situation, but with their positions reversed. Victory wondered if the doctors were right and she had simply lost her mind.

"It's not smart," Lion insisted. "You'll be putting your life into his hands."

"And?" Victory demanded. "What choice do we have?"

"Allow me to station my Praetorian outside the town," Lion said. "They will make daily checkups, ensure that he is not abusing his privileges."

It was oh-so-tempting. Victory considered it, strongly. Then she finally shook her head. "My brother was right. Tales of Praetorian wandering the woods might get back to my father, and you know he would investigate."

"They would dress as common peasants!" Lion objected. "Please, milady."

"Seventeen common, light-skinned female peasants, all setting up camp in the middle of the mountains?"

Lion flushed. "We could send less. Five or six."

"We stick to the plan," Victory said. "Your girls will help my brother with his investigation, as plainclothes agents in the palace."

"I don't trust him," Lion growled, meeting the Emp's blue eyes with her challenging gray.

I don't, either, Victory thought. But she knew that if she showed lack of resolve now, that Lion would balk, most likely hijack the ship, and fly Victory to some place that she deemed to be safe, regardless of her brother's plan. "You seemed to trust him well enough the other day," Victory stated, "When you stood against my father to spare his life."

"Yes, but that was a favor owed," Lion said quickly. "He saved our sister's life. We saved his. It was an even trade. *This,*" she waved to the shackles and collars laid out on the floor between them, "is madness, milady."

"How better to hide?" Victory demanded.

Lion opened her mouth, but closed it again with a frown. She turned to glare at the Emp, who had been watching their conversation in a wary silence. "There must be a better way."

"Well, if there is, you have approximately two minutes to figure it out," Victory said, glancing down at her clock. "The pilot said we'd be arriving in his village at two-oh-four." They'd already been flying for two days and fourteen hours, and the change of scenery was going to be a welcome—if nerve-wracking—experience.

Lion continued to object, refusing to don the garb of a slave.

"Just do it," Victory snapped, finally losing patience with her guard captain. "Either that, or find another who will."

Lion went utterly stiff, then lowered her head in defeat. She picked the collar off the ground and snapped it around her neck. She winced as it flash-welded in place. Then, giving the Emp a look of defiance, went over to sit at the exit beside Whip, who was already wearing both her collar and cuffs.

Victory snatched up two sets of cuffs and tossed them at Lion. "Those, too."

The woman snarled profanities under her breath, but she allowed her sisters to help place the restraints.

Victory may have been imagining it, but she thought she saw the Emp smirking as he carried a leash over and snapped it to Lion's neck. He snapped another to Whip's collar, then let them both drop between their linen-covered breasts. They were garbed in a standard one-piece slave shifts, without weapons, armor, or decoration—typical slave fare, and even then, the rough cloth felt itchy upon Victory's body. Itchy...and familiar.

I can't do this, Victory thought, staring down at the collar in her hands. She felt the engine's rhythm change, felt the G's shift as it began to slow. *I can't.*

She didn't notice the Emp until he squatted down beside her. When his big hands reached for the band of metal in her palms, Victory jerked away, glaring.

"Trust me, Victory," Dragomir said softly. "There's something between us..." He swallowed and glanced at his hands, where they touched hers. "We're...connected...in a way that most people could only dream." He seemed to be struggling for words, and settled with, "You were always safe with me, as I was with you."

Scowling, Victory peered into his eyes, wanting to ask him what he meant by that, yet not finding the courage. When she said nothing, he gingerly reached down and took the collar from her hands. He lifted it, slowly, until it was level with her throat. Seeing it, Victory balked.

"Trust me," Dragomir whispered again. "As you have before."

As she had before...in other lives? All the Emp's sentimentality about other places and other times almost gave her hope...Victory squeezed her eyes shut, wishing she could believe him.

He gently settled the band around her neck and clapped it shut.

Victory flinched at the sudden hot-cold sensation as the metal band flash-sealed around her throat. She let out the breath that she had been holding in a shuddering, nervous laugh.

"Wrists, now," Dragomir said. He picked up a set of shackles.

Shaking, yet trying not to let the Praetorian see how afraid she was, Victory turned to give the Emp her back.

She felt the cold steel when he snapped them into place and squeezed her eyes shut against the first pangs of terror.

"Ankles," he said softly. He picked up a shackle and set it around her ankle. Instantly, the memories came flooding back to her and Victory let out a tiny whimper that only Dragomir could hear.

His voice became gentle. "You won't be in them long, Princess." He waited, watching her face.

She searched his blue eyes, saw the sincerity there. Slowly, even as her stomach twisted with terror, Victory nodded.

The ankle shackle snapped shut. A moment later, the second one followed it. Knowing the Praetorian would put an end to the plan if she didn't, Victory repressed her shudder.

"Now this," Dragomir said softly. He reached under her chin and clasped a leash to her throat. A moment later, she felt him padlock it in place. Victory squeezed her eyes shut against tears. It was then that she felt the warm blanket sensation once more, wrapping her, leaving her feel as if she were sitting in a titanium-reinforced fortress, instead of the bowels of a courier ship, about to be dropped as a slave to a man whom she had forced to eat pig slops and sleep on his knees.

Outside, Victory heard the landing gear slide into place, felt the *thump* as the ship settled onto the village's central square.

Above her, Dragomir stood up to face the gate.

When it opened, revealing a cluster of tiny stone hovels and filthy farm animals, Dragomir's face lit up with a relieved smile. "I almost didn't believe it," Dragomir whispered. He motioned at Victory, his hand holding her leash. "Come on, Princess," he said softly. "Your new home awaits."

"My brother will be back to check on me," Victory warned him.

Dragomir sighed and waited.

Victory reluctantly got to her feet and, shuddering at the cold tug around her ankles, shuffled after him. At the gate, Dragomir bent to pick up the leashes of her two Praetorian, then together, they shuffled down the gangplank.

Seeing the crowd of dirty faces that had begun to emerge from their hiding places behind buildings and rain barrels, Victory glanced again at the gangplank leading back up to the ship. *Oh gods*, she thought, watching it as it retracted behind her. *They're really going to leave me here.*

Then the ramp slammed up into the courier's belly and the ship's engines powered up.

"Wait!" Victory screamed, unable to hold in her terror any longer. "Please don't leave me here!"

If the pilot heard her over the roar of the engines, he didn't respond. A moment later, the Imperial courier ship was rising out of sight, disappearing over the gnarly limbs of the cottonwood trees, leaving her alone in the native village.

Victory was finding it hard to breathe through her panic. Tears were burning at her eyes, and she was backing away to the very extent of the leash. More natives began to creep from the woodwork, collecting around them in a dirty, smelly crowd. *I want to go home*, she thought, tendrils of terror beginning to strangle her heart as she caught all the villagers staring at her, their dirty faces curious, like she was a piece of strange meat. *I can't do this…*

A warm, sunny blanket broke through her panic, wrapping her tightly in its soothing embrace. Victory closed her eyes swallowed several times, finding the strength she needed to fight the terror.

"That you, Drago?" one of the larger men of the village demanded from the crowd. He had cerulean eyes similar to Dragomir, the same muscular build, with a big, easy smile and tousled, curly black hair. Though Victory hadn't thought it possible, she guessed the man was even larger than Dragomir, perhaps an inch or two taller. Then something alarming occurred to her.

Is that his brother? Victory thought, so stunned that she forgot about the hundreds of eyes that were gawking at her.

Dragomir chuckled. "Who else do you think it is, Thor, you prick?" The way Dragomir stepped forward to wrap the man in a huge bear-hug confirmed her suspicions.

Oh gods, she thought, cringing. *Oh gods oh gods, I can't do this.*

Dragomir went through a long round of hugging—it seemed *every-one* in the village wanted to receive an embrace from the Emp—and spent what seemed like a couple hours chatting and telling his story to the crowd.

In that, Victory realized with relief, he kept to the plan. He claimed he had been captured to heal a sick princess, beat half to death just to make sure he wouldn't hurt her out of spite, and then, after being chained naked to her bed for a couple weeks while he tended her, fed nothing but pig slops and groped humiliatingly by her attendants, he had finally been given a pretty new set of clothes and his choice of reward for healing her, then sent home as if nothing had ever happened. The villagers, of course, ate it up with wide eyes and open mouths. Victory, on the other hand, found herself scowling at the Emp.

"They ask for your help after they hunt you down and kill ya for no reason," a big, pudgy woman demanded. She spat. "Imperial hypocrites. Should all be killed to a man an' their carcasses fed to the ravens." A round of agreement followed her.

Looking a bit uncomfortable, Dragomir returned his attention to his brother once more. "So what happened while I was gone?"

"Quite a lot, apparently," the blue-eyed devil said, eying Victory and her two companions. His gaze came to stop on Whip and he frowned. "What is this?"

"Slaves!" Dragomir laughed, giving a gentle tug on their leashes. "I healed an Imperial princess. They asked me what I wanted in return and I said some livestock. They gave me slaves."

Thor frowned, eyes still on Whip. "And you're keeping them?"

"Why not?" Dragomir asked. "My bed could use a few Imperial play-mates." He glanced back at Whip. "Why? You want one?" He turned to grin back at Victory and her Praetorian. "There's only so much room in my bed."

Victory's jaw dropped at Dragomir. *He wouldn't dare. It's just a show.*

But then Dragomir handed over Whip's leash to the big man named Thor, and then slapped him on the back. "I'm so glad to be home."

Whip, who had gone utterly stiff at the transaction, was watching the two men with alert gray eyes. She had not, however, demeaned herself by struggling.

Thank the gods, Victory thought, utterly grateful that the Praetorian was so well trained in the control of her emotions. Had it been *her* leash that Dragomir had handed to his brother, she would have screamed and flailed like an animal. Already, he was not sticking to the plan, and already, a sinking feeling was building in Victory's gut that he had never intended to follow it in the first place.

"What's going on, milady?" Lion asked softly. Her voice, while quiet, held the sound of Death in every syllable.

"Uh," Victory managed, "I think he just gave Whip to his brother."

She saw fury flash in the Praetorian's eyes. "I'll kill him."

"Never fear, sister," Whip said softly. There was quiet murder in her gaze as she continued to watch the two men. "We have keys. If he tries anything stupid, we will simply free ourselves and kill them both."

Victory knew that her Praetorian were trained in a thousand different ways to end a man's life, yet looking up at their huge bodies, comparing them to the much smaller forms of her two Praetorian, Victory began to have her doubts.

And, with her doubts, came another wash of terror. She started to have to fight to control her breathing. She felt her skin crawl, remembered the cold around her ankles, the stares...

Eventually, Thor's eyes fell on her. "That one's terrified."

Victory was surprised that she had let it show.

Dragomir glanced at her, raised an eyebrow, then shrugged. "Probably. Poor little thing. Big guy like me. Unable to speak the language...She probably thinks she's in for a trip through Hell."

"Maybe she is," someone in the crowd jeered, and there was a round of harsh laughter. "How much for the green-eyed one?" another called out.

Victory lowered her head in shame and fear, her legs starting to shake. To her surprise, the Emp's energy-blanket tightened around her.

"Sorry," Dragomir laughed. "She's not for sale, folks."

"What about lease?" someone laughed.

Victory let out a shuddering breath and stared at her feet, knowing now what the Emp had meant. He could sell her, give her away, lend her to his friends…

…And there was absolutely nothing she could do about it.

"These two are mine," Dragomir said, tugging their leashes. "You want to work out a trade, talk to my brother."

His brother grunted, then looked down at Whip as if he was trying to piece together a puzzle. For her part, Whip stared back at him with all the ferocity of a wolverine.

"She looks like she wants to cut out my throat with her teeth," Thor chuckled.

"Probably does," Dragomir said. "From what I heard, she and the other one were Imperial soldiers. Maybe even Praetorian."

What is he doing? Victory thought, horrified.

Thor's eyebrows went up and he seemed to tense. "Praetorian?"

Dragomir shrugged. "Just a warning. Not sure if it's true or not. Just what the handlers told me before they dumped them in my lap." He sighed. "I'm hungry enough to eat my horse. How'd he hold up while I was gone?"

"Thunder's fine," Thor said, "Though a stubborn shit, as usual. Takes after his owner."

"You just don't know how to properly ask his help," Dragomir laughed. He glanced at the hundreds of faces around them, then turned and looked up the mountain valley. "And the rest of my place?"

"We cleaned it, packed it up," Thor said. Victory saw a flash of emotion cross the man's bronze face before he hid it again. His booming voice was low when he said, "We weren't sure you were coming home, brother."

Dragomir glanced back at Victory. "I wasn't sure I was, either." When Victory looked away, he grunted. "Well, let's go see the damage." He started down a path that led from the village.

When the entire village tried to follow them, however, Thor rounded on them with a roar. "Get back to your own business," he snapped. "Let the healer find his own way home, fools!"

People scattered like startled deer.

Once they were alone, Thor grunted with irritation. Gruffly, turning away from the departing crowd, he shook his head and said, "Like a damn wandering circus had come to town."

"In a way, it did," Dragomir chuckled, as they walked. They were following a dirt track out of the village, deeper into the valley beyond. They went at an easy pace, slow enough for Victory and her Praetorian to keep up, but Dragomir made no motions to free any of them of their restraints.

As they walked, Victory caught Thor eying the three of them. He grunted. "What do you plan to do with them, Drago?" His eyes stopped on Victory. "That one there looks like she's gonna bolt for this hills, first chance she gets. We both know how long an Imperial would last up there in the snow…"

Dragomir glanced back at Victory, then shrugged. "Haven't decided yet."

Victory stumbled, so great was her shock. He hadn't *decided* yet? She fell to her knees, glaring up at him.

Dragomir reached down and gently helped her back to her feet, then went on chatting with his brother as if nothing had happened. They talked about the weather, the house, the livestock, the news…

And all the while, the lump of dread was growing in the pit of Victory's stomach.

About an hour later, they stopped at a crude wooden fence, where Dragomir paused to open the gate. "Let's leave them here for a couple minutes," he said. "Let them catch their breath. I'd like to walk around the property a bit. See what's new."

And then, to Victory's horror, like they were no more than horses, he clipped their leashes out of reach around the crux of a heavy birch branch. Thor did the same. Then Dragomir turned his back to them and he and Thor walked on down the fence, chatting casually between themselves.

Once he was some distance away, Victory saw her Praetorian slip their keys into their palms and start working at the locks.

"Don't," Victory muttered, watching the Emp's back disappear

"But milady!" Lion cried. "This is ludicrous. He hasn't yet removed the shackles, and he has us strung up here like beasts of burden!"

"He's keeping up the charade," Victory said, praying that it was true. Her gut, however, was telling her otherwise. Every instinct was screaming at her to get free, to run, run, run, *run*.

"What if one of those villagers comes along and finds us like this?" Lion growled.

"We knew going into this that we'd have to trust him," Victory managed. "So just calm down and let him chat with his brother."

Muttering, Lion watched the line of the fence where the Emp had disappeared. "He has one hour," she snarled. "If he's not back by then, we're taking you home, Princess."

"Home?" Victory snorted. "I think my father made it clear that I don't have one right now."

"We're taking you *somewhere else*," Lion amended. "He has one hour."

With the finality in the Praetorian's words, Victory knew that an angry bear wouldn't be able to stop her from carrying out her threat, if the Emp arrived a minute later.

• • •

"You ask for livestock and they give you slaves." Thor shook his head, sounding mystified. "Don't they realize that's more mouths to feed?"

Dragomir shrugged, trying to decide how much to tell his brother, now that they were alone. "It's the way the Imperium thinks. I suppose they were doing me a great honor, giving me their finest livestock." He sighed and glanced back in the direction of the gate. "Now I just need to figure out what to do with them."

"Don't give them to the village," Thor said. "We have a few thoughtless men who would enjoy breaking an Imperial." He cocked his head, his blue eyes fixed on Dragomir. "But then, you already knew that. That's why you gave one of them to me."

"To look like I wasn't being greedy," Dragomir agreed. "Less chance there will be hard feelings if I'm not holed up on my farmstead with three beautiful women."

"True enough," Thor said. Then he slowed, watching him. "What are you not telling me?"

Dragomir took a deep breath. His younger brother had no love for the Imperium, but when asked a direct question, he found he couldn't lie. He glanced over his shoulder at the tree where they'd left the women. "That green-eyed one is the Royal Princess and the evil-looking ones are two of her Praetorian. I've been asked to watch them for awhile."

Thor's eyes widened. "Asked by *who?*" And then, his voice rising, "Somehow, brother, I think you might be serious."

"Dead serious," Dragomir said. "There's a power-play going on in the palace right now. She's next in line for the throne, and her father has made several attempts on her life. She needs a place to lay low for a bit. Stay out of sight."

Thor turned to stare in the direction of the gate, hidden behind a copse of trees. "You have a Royal Princess of the Imperium and two of her Praetorian strung up in a tree like slaves?"

"Thought it was fitting, didn't you?" Dragomir said, grinning.

His brother stared at him like he'd gone mad. "And you somehow think you're going to *live* through the next couple days?"

"They'll be here a couple months, at least." Dragomir eyed their backtrail thoughtfully. "If I were you, though, I wouldn't release the Praetorian. I've seen what she can do, and you give her her hands or her feet and you're going to be on your back in two seconds flat."

"You're insane, brother. We should turn them over to the rebels. We—"

Dragomir felt fury surge through him in a rush. He had lunged at his brother and slammed him into a tree before he could finish his sentence.

"Listen to me carefully," Dragomir growled into his brother's face. "We are being given an opportunity to change things here on Mercy. Her father has the power now, but she stands to inherit the throne from him."

"*What* throne?" Thor roared. "What they've done is illegal! Mercy is an independent colony. They are invaders. You are *helping* the *invaders*."

"Believe me," Dragomir said, "She is a better alternative than her father. Can you think of another royal princess who would willingly put herself at her subjects' mercy?"

"Then she's insane as well as an outsider," Thor growled.

Dragomir glared at his brother. "Mercy has tried war. We've tried war for forty years, and *look* where it's gotten us."

Scowling, Thor turned his head in silence.

"I think it's time we tried something else, instead," Dragomir said. "Don't you?"

"You know I belong to the resistance," Thor growled. "By all rights, I should report this."

Dragomir shrugged. "If the resistance gets her, then it will only be more fuel for her father's fire. He will use it to request more troops from the Imperium, and you certainly can't use her as a bargaining chip. The Adjudicator's wanted her dead since she came out of her mother's womb ahead of her brother."

Thor looked back at him, and Dragomir saw the desperation there. "Do you really think she can change things?" he asked softly.

"I do," Dragomir said. "And before I send her back to represent Mercy to the Imperium, I'm going to do something that should be done to every ruler, before they are allowed to take the throne.

"What's that?" Thor snorted, "Starve her, dress her in rags, make her work the fields, and show her what it's like to be common?"

"I'm going to make sure all of her ramas are fully functioning," Dragomir said. "The heart, especially."

His brother's eyes widened slightly. For a long moment, he said nothing, his breath caught in his throat. Then, softly, he whispered, "You just convinced me, brother."

CHAPTER 12

The Core Rama

Dragomir appeared around the copse of trees a good thirty minutes later, coming from the same direction he'd left.

"What do you think he told him?" Lion growled, obviously assuming the worst.

"He said he wanted to walk the grounds," Victory said, but she wasn't so sure. If he *had* walked the grounds, they had only seen a small portion of it.

When the two men neared, Victory thought she saw the brother's eyes come to rest on her before they flickered away and he cleared his throat. "Well, I need to be getting back. Have to buy a sack of salt before heading out to the homestead." Almost tentatively, the man reached up and unclipped Whip's leash from the tree. To Dragomir, he said, "It's good to have you home, brother." He rested a hand on Dragomir's shoulder. "If you need anything, let me know. I'll keep the channel open."

"Come over for dinner tomorrow," Dragomir said, leaning his big body against the fence. "I should have settled in by then." He looked at Victory and Lion and grinned, making the Praetorian bristle.

Grunting, Thor gave Whip one last frown, then gave a gentle tug on her collar and started back down the trail.

As Whip passed, Dragomir grabbed her by the wrist suddenly and pried one of her hands apart. Then he slapped her on the rump and

186

shoved her after his brother, Whip gasping and suddenly looking very pale.

Did he just…? Victory thought, stunned.

"He just took her key," Lion snarled. Already, the Praetorian was starting to work at her own shackles. Chuckling, Dragomir came up behind her and wrenched the key from her hands, as well. "You didn't actually think I'd believe you'd leave yourselves *completely* at my mercy, did you, Praetorian?"

Lion bared her fangs at him, and probably would have sunk them into his flesh, had he not chuckled and backed away. Then, as Victory's world started to crumble, he reached out and, holding Lion's head steady with one hand, dipped his hand into the Praetorian's shirt. He came back with a string of keys, which he snapped off of her neck with a tug.

"You are a *dead man!*" Lion snarled up at him.

"You know," Dragomir said, "I think that's one of the few times I haven't needed an interpreter." Smiling at Lion, he said, "Please inform your Praetorian that she will be civil or I will sell her to the village and use the money to feed my horse."

Then, as Lion snarled curses, Dragomir stepped around Victory and touched her shackles.

Victory shuddered as she felt his big body move behind her. She was helpless. Just as she had been in that village, just as she had been for six years of her life, she was utterly helpless. Her eyes began to burn with tears. She dropped her head, waiting for the humiliation to end.

She felt a click in her wrist-shackles, then jerked her head around to stare as they fell to the ground. Behind her, the Emp squatted and began tinkering with her ankle-shackles. "You hold up okay, Princess?" he asked, releasing her feet. Then he stood, his blue eyes kind. "I was worried about you there for awhile."

"What is that man doing with Whip?" Victory demanded, straightening.

The Emp raised a single ebony brow. "Whatever he wants with her, would be my guess."

Victory felt a sickness crawl through her gut. She looked away. "Take this chain off of me."

"Hmm," Dragomir said. "How about no?" He unclasped the leash holding Lion to the tree and, carrying their leashes and both sets of shackles, started walking towards the small stone hut. Victory grabbed her chain and dug her bare feet into the soil, but she might as well have been fighting an Imperium freighter—all she succeeded in doing was scraping the skin of her heels.

"Let me *go*, you cad!" Victory shouted, as he dragged her to the house. "What are you *doing*?!"

He grinned at her. "Chaining you to my bed."

Victory forgot how to speak. Her body went rigid, and she almost toppled to the ground as he continued tugging her along.

"What did he say?" Lion asked, watching the man with a deadly scowl. She looked somewhat mollified that he had released Victory's hands, but not by much.

Victory was so shocked she found she couldn't reply. She stumbled after him as he opened the rugged wooden door and pulled them inside.

The interior of the shack was depressingly small—perhaps only a thousand square feet—and smelled strongly of leather and wood-smoke. Dragomir took them to the middle of a dingy living-space no larger than several couch-widths, then he got up on a chair and clipped Lion to a rafter. "Stay there for a second," he told the Praetorian. "I have to deal with your mistress." Victory's heart began to speed up when he started dragging her deeper into the house.

When she saw the bedroom, she balked. "You *can't* be serious," she snarled at him.

As if he hadn't heard her, he pulled an extra padlock from his pants' pocket and moved to wrap her chain around the heavy wooden frame of his bed.

Victory froze, every muscle going stiff, eyes on the padlock. "Where did you get that?" she asked.

"I stole it," Dragomir said cheerfully. Then he snapped it into place around her chain and she was, quite thoroughly, chained to his bed. "Wait here while I make up a place for Lion to sleep, okay?"

"My brother will come looking for me!" Victory shrieked, yanking at the chain.

"And I intend to be finished with you by the time he does," Dragomir said.

...*Finished* with her? Victory froze at that, a thousand different scenarios playing havoc with her mutated brain cells.

Then, leaving her with that ominous statement, he left her in the bedroom and retreated deeper into the house. Victory heard scuffling in the living-room, followed by Lion's curses. Then, suddenly, a loud *thump*, followed by silence.

Oh my gods, Victory thought. She backed away from the sounds until she hit the length of her chain, then scrabbled along sideways until her back was against the wall.

The quiet coming from the other room was eerie. Victory strained to hear over the sound of her own heartbeat, desperate to know that her Praetorian was all right.

Then she heard footsteps in the hall, big and heavy. Victory cringed and started frantically jerking at her chain again, the memories rising around her in a flood of terror.

"Okay," Dragomir said, as he stepped into the room. He smiled at her. "Finally. It's just the two of us." Seeing her huddled against the wall, he frowned.

"Please don't hurt me," Victory babbled. "I can pay..."

Growling, Dragomir strode across the room to her, plucked her off the floor, and deposited her in the bed as she flailed and screamed herself hoarse. He moved over her a horrible instant later. His heavy body pinning her beneath him, his blue eyes only inches from her own, he rumbled, "Just so we're clear, Princess, if I'd wanted to hurt you, I would have done it a long time ago."

Victory whimpered and started to hyperventilate, but suddenly a rush of golden energy drove the fear back home. "Now," his husky voice said, against her neck, "Let's think about this a moment, Princess." He shifted above her, so that he was looking into her eyes. "We both agree I could take you at will right now, yes?"

Victory shuddered against the horror and squeezed her eyes shut. "Look at me," he commanded.

She shook her head, able to feel every inch of him above her, trapping her with his warm body.

"I can wait all day, Victory," he said, his chest vibrating above her with his deep voice, much too close. Almost touching her face with his own, he whispered, "I didn't want to say anything earlier that might discourage your plans, but that's the beauty of this particular setup, Princess. I'm finally being given the time I need to work with you...on *my* terms. So open your eyes. I'm a healer, girl. Not a rapist."

Trembling, she met his blue eyes for an instant before she looked away in shame.

"We're going to start with trust," Dragomir said. "Are we both in agreement that I haven't violated you, despite the fact that I can?"

Victory trembled under him, so wrapped in the terror of his massive presence that she couldn't respond.

"Okay," Dragomir said softly, his blue eyes gentle. "Let me put it this way. I could pull down my pants, lift your shift, and drive myself into you, if that were my intent. Does it look like that's what I'm doing?"

Victory stopped trying to twist from under him. In truth, he was just lying there, holding her in place with his body. "No," Victory whispered, though she didn't allow herself a shred of hope. Hope was what destroyed the mind, once her captors found it, and crushed it.

"That's right," Dragomir said, "I'm not. I'm just squishing you to the bed like an ill-bred oaf." He paused, watching her. Softly, he said, "My name is Dragomir Shipgrown. I am a healer for the village of Sodstone, in the Skitwater Pass. I have the ability to see and feel emotional energies, and the life energies that precede them. Some would call me an Emp. I'm really just a farmer who's lucky his crops didn't fail while he was gallivanting across the planet with a royal princess."

"What do you want?" Victory whispered, not daring to look at him.

"I want to help you," Dragomir said, never moving from his position atop her. "But in order for me to do that, I need you to trust me." He was too close. Much too close. Victory could feel the memories at the edge of her awareness, visions of times when other men had been this close...

"But you're...you're..." Victory couldn't find anything truly horrible about what he was doing. "You chained me to your bed!" she finished, anger seeping up with her words.

"Yes," Dragomir said. "And?"

She blinked at him in dismay.

"Have I hurt you in any way?"

She could find nothing to say.

"Have I touched you or otherwise assaulted you in any way, aside from simply hold you down so we could talk?"

Victory narrowed her eyes at him, much too aware of every inch of him, and where it was touching her. "You didn't have to hold me down so we could talk."

"Oh?" He raised a single ebony brow, looking amused. "Then you are going to tell me that you were being perfectly reasonable, just now."

"Perfectly," Victory growled.

He grinned at her, his blue eyes twinkling. "Good. Then maybe you'll hear me out, instead of screaming and thrashing like I was coming in here to molest you."

"You're not?" Victory sneered.

Dragomir sighed deeply and rolled off of her, staring at the ceiling. "Gods," he whispered as Victory scrambled away from him, "How the Fates must laugh at me." He cocked his head at her, still lying on the bed. "Do you remember when you first discovered I was an Emp, and I told you about ramas, and how yours were frozen shut?"

"Why did you chain me to your bed?" Victory demanded. She tugged on the chain, trying to get more distance between them, but he was laying on it, pinning it to the thin, lumpy mattress with his big barbarian body.

Dragomir rolled onto his side, still lying on the chain. He propped his head up on an elbow and watched her. "Well, for one," he said, "I'm going to work on your ramas tonight, and I don't want you running off."

"I *command* you to release me!" Victory cried, tugging on the chain in frustration. "I am a Royal Princess of the Imperium and you are nothing but a *sla*—" Victory choked off the rest as Dragomir's face darkened.

The Emp grabbed a fistful of the chain and dragged her inexorably closer. With their faces almost touching, he said, "What was that, Princess?"

Victory tried to lean away from him, but there was nothing she could do to avoid his penetrating stare. "Um," she whimpered. "Please…"

He leaned back on the bed, dragging her with him, until her body was stretched out over his. Victory froze, suddenly aware of where their bodies were touching, and how. It sparked something within her, something long-buried and forgotten, and she quickly squashed the sensation, refusing to feel anything like that for a man, ever again.

Like a panther, he lay beneath her, his gaze sharpening. *He knows*, Victory thought, horrified. "Um…" she said, trying in vain to pull away from his iron grip around the chain.

"I take that back," Dragomir said. "I'm going to work on your ramas right now. Starting with your core." He closed his eyes and leaned back into the bed.

Victory grunted and stopped struggling when she felt heat building between her thighs. *What in the hells?* She hesitated, feeling the warmth in her groin spread outward, until it felt like someone had set hot rocks against her mound. "What are you doing?" she whispered, trying to pull away.

"Something I should have done a long time ago," Dragomir said. "I'm opening your core rama."

Victory suppressed a moan as the heat reached her abdomen, caressing her thighs, slickening her—

"No!" she cried, realizing what he meant. She renewed her struggles to get away from this strange new sensation building in her groin. When the sensation continued to build, heat pooling between her legs, Victory started pounding at him in her desperation to get free.

Dragomir merely rolled on top of her, once more pinning her to the bed. And this time, with no way to escape the building pressure, Victory felt like she was going to explode. She bit down a gasp, panting.

"It's about to go," Dragomir warned, his eyes still closed. "When it does, think of it like a dam breaking. Everything that cluttered up the dam is going to flood outward, and you're going to re-experience everything that shut the rama down in the first place. This time, though, instead of bottling it up and keeping it inside, you're going to let it go. It will only be like this one time per rama. Understand?"

Victory frowned, wriggling beneath him as she tried to inch away from the building warmth. "I don't know what you're—"

Then the feeling detonated within her, and Victory revisited her last moments of virginity, saw again every horrible time they used her for their pleasure. She let out a low, wretched wail as the disgust overpowered her, as men lost all interest for her, becoming nothing but depraved animals that wanted what she carried between her legs. She saw it all over again, every rape, every act of violence. She felt her hatred wash outward, brought under the microscope of her awareness, then dissipate as if it had never been, flooded away by the golden wash of energy behind it.

Sometime afterwards, Victory found herself sobbing in Dragomir's arms, clinging to him as she cried into his chest.

"There," Dragomir said, looking down at her. His blue eyes were gentle. "Feel better?"

"No," Victory whimpered. "What did you do to me?"

He released her slowly. "I opened your core rama. The place where all your sexual hatred is stored...as well as your ability to feel physical pleasure."

Victory peered at him, wiping away tears. "I don't understand," she whispered.

Dragomir considered. Then, softly, he said, "Perhaps a demonstration would serve better. You once craved the touch of men, yes? As a young woman, you would fantasize about being whisked away by the man of your dreams and giggle with your maidservants over the well-built Praetorian in your House guard?"

Victory frowned, vaguely remembering such childish antics. Reluctantly, she said, "I suppose..."

"Yet since your abduction, you have felt no sexual urges, right? Absolutely no longing for the male form?"

Victory didn't like where this was going. She tried to inch away.

Dragomir surprised her by setting her aside and...

..taking off his shirt.

Victory watched the muscle move in his chest and shoulders and immediately felt a warmth pool between her legs. Her eyes widened and she looked down, stunned.

Dragomir was grinning like a fool as he pulled his shirt back over his head. "See? Fully functioning, now. Probably better than you'd like, even, but you'll get over that."

She jerked her head up, frowning. "But I've seen you naked for *weeks*!"

He shrugged, and it brought with it a tingle of appreciation at the crux of her thighs. "Your rama was blocked."

"Oh my gods," Victory whispered. "You take it back. Take it back *now!*"

Chuckling, Dragomir caught her by the chain and pulled her close, and instantly Victory felt herself throbbing down there, aching for…

"Let me go," she squeaked.

"And what if I don't want to?" Dragomir asked, rolling back atop her, pinning her yet again with his huge body. Softly, into her ear, he whispered, "You are my captive, after all."

This time as their bodies touched, Victory gasped at the sudden building of pressure at the place where their groins met. "Oh," she whispered, as the heat increased between them.

Then Dragomir bent to sweep her away in a kiss. His tongue met her lips, parted them, seeking. She moaned as he explored her, the aching between her thighs becoming an unbearable, throbbing agony. By the time Dragomir retreated with a groan, she was panting.

"Gods how I want to open the rest," Dragomir whispered huskily. She saw the desire in his blue eyes, felt the need he carried there.

He kissed her forehead and sat up. "Tomorrow, though. I try to do another tonight and I'll be useless for a couple days."

As she was still gasping for breath, he stood and, with one last longing-filled look at her, disappeared back through the hallway to the rest of the building.

Victory slumped back against the bed, staring at the ceiling in both shock and horror. The feeling in her womanhood was a hot, throbbing ache, and it was leaving her heart pounding, her face flushed. She wasn't sure if she was relieved he was gone or anguished he had left.

This isn't possible, she thought, trying to sort through her thoughts. *What did he do to me?*

· · ·

Dragomir walked past the sleeping Praetorian and out into the yard. It had started to rain while he had settled the Imperials, and he welcomed the cold, grounding droplets as they showered his skin and drenched his clothes.

You fool, he thought, slumping against the fence. He had done it all wrong. He had meant to open up her heart-rama first, so that she could *love* him before she could desire him in that way. He was a healer, not an abuser of women.

Yet his passion had gotten away with him, and he had almost taken her. Right there, chained to his bed, he had almost pushed up her shift and taken her as she moaned and squirmed beneath him. Even now, his manhood was so hard it hurt, stretching tight against his borrowed silk pants.

Knowing how close he had come, he felt sick.

An Emp had certain responsibilities in the Karmic cycle of things. One with the ability to create certain desires in others had to exercise the greatest restraint, lest he find himself being used in such a way in the next lifetime. There was a line, and Dragomir had almost crossed it. When he should have been opening her heart rama, so that she could begin to trust him, he had gone directly to her core, freeing her sexual inhibitions so she could lust after him, instead.

Groaning, he let his head come to rest on the wet wood of the fence. *You fool*, he thought. *Why the core first?*

Because he had felt that spark within her, seen the barest hint of desire rise in her core for the first time, and had forgotten himself. In an act of childishness, he had wanted to see what she felt for him without the inhibitions forced upon her by her past.

Now, when their bodies touched, she was going to respond. As long as she experienced no other horror to shut the rama down, she was going to enjoy his touch, whether she wanted to or not.

It was going to make it a thousand times harder for him, when it came time to release the other ramas. Now, it was going to be everything he could do to keep from taking her innocence a second time. Every contact, every brush of skin, every gentle touch…All of it would make her ache to have him. And, having been so long without a woman, seeing her passion arching throughout her body, Dragomir wasn't sure he would be able to stop himself.

Dragomir closed his eyes, brutally letting the icy rain cool his passion. Not yet a day, and he had already failed her. He thought of Meggie, remembered her broken sobs under the Praetorian's body.

That had almost been him.

Realizing it, his disgust was so thick that he automatically glanced at the barn. His eyes found the dark shape of the rope hanging against the wall. In misery, he considered. A few minutes of panic, a headiness in the brain, and then nothing…

CHAPTER 13

Village Life

The sun had gone down outside the window when the Emp came walking into the bedroom with a tray of steaming food.

Victory grimaced when she saw potatoes and a green mass of vegetables. When he set it into her lap, she sniffed. As far as she could tell, it wasn't even spiced. "Where's the main course?"

Dragomir, who had sat down beside her, stopped, potato between his teeth, the fork spearing it still in his mouth. "What?" he asked around the potato. He honestly looked surprised.

Victory gestured at the plate. "Where's the *meat?*"

He glanced down at his plate, then at hers, then back up at her. He took the fork out of his mouth and swallowed his potato. "Um, Princess, welcome to the real world."

She narrowed her eyes at him. "What is that supposed to mean?"

"Well, let's see," Dragomir said. "Between the hawks, the coyotes, the wolves, the martins, the bears, and the neighbor's dogs, I have about thirty chickens I can eat in a year. Any more than that, and I'm eating next year's food supply."

She scowled. "I don't want *chicken*. I want *real* meat. Beef. Elk. Bison. Something with substance. I'd even settle for a moose or deer."

He stared at her, another potato speared and halfway to his mouth. "...you'd...*settle*," he said, sounding utterly flabbergasted.

"Yes," Victory said. "Go get me some steak or something. Doesn't have to be fancy."

Dragomir stared at her. Slowly, the Emp put his fork down and set his plate aside. When he responded, it was slowly, as if talking to a small child. "Princess, this might be a shock for you, coming from a fancy palace where you have people waiting on you hand and foot, but most of the world doesn't eat steak each night." He gestured soberly at the vegetables. "We eat what we can find, and are thankful for it."

Victory snorted. "Surely you have some pork. I'd even settle for duck."

He blinked at her. "You'd *settle?*" he repeated, like a brain-dead ox.

She nodded.

Snorting, he picked up his plate and started stuffing his face again. Victory narrowed her eyes at him. "I'm waiting, slave."

Dragomir looked at her over a forkful of green mush. "If you're not hungry, I'll eat it."

"Please do," Victory said, disgusted. She shoved it across the bed at him. "Better yet, go feed it to your pigs."

Dragomir laughed. "If I could afford to own pigs, Princess, then we'd be eating pork."

Victory scowled at him, sure this was some sort of trick. When he continued eating, however, apparently savoring every bite, she finally began to lose confidence. "You really don't have any meat?"

"Meat's a liability," Dragomir said. "It's the first thing the Imperials take, when they raid a town. Why spend half your yearly income on a flock of geese, when the Imperials are simply going to wring their necks and take them home for dinner?"

Victory frowned. "You said you needed to check on your livestock."

"I have a few goats," Dragomir said. "Turns out, the Imperials generally leave them pretty much alone."

"*Goat.*" Victory scrunched her face. "Goat is unclean."

"And that's probably why," Dragomir said, chuckling at her reaction. He took another bite of potato. "Why's goat unclean?"

"Its flesh is the flesh of demons and succubi," Victory replied. "To eat it is to be inviting the Horned God's Curse."

"I'll have to remember that," Dragomir said. "I was thinking of butchering a buck here in the next couple days, in honor of my guests. Come second thought, might be better not to waste the meat."

Victory shuddered. "Trade it for some pork. Or some beef."

Dragomir eyed her thoughtfully over his meal. "I happen to like chevon."

"Ugh!" Victory cried. "You uncouth barbarian!"

Dragomir shrugged and finished his plate, then started on hers. Victory watched him miserably. "You don't have any cheese?" she asked. "Or bread? Fruit?"

Dragomir grunted and finished the vegetables, then got up and strode from the room, his massive body moving like a big cat. Victory watched him go, mouth open, heat pooling in her groin as she thought of the power that his body commanded…

…and what he looked like underneath the Imperial silks.

Dragomir came back a couple minutes later and dropped a wedge of cheese in her lap. "There," he said, gesturing. "Cheese."

Victory sighed in relief at seeing real food, then frowned. "Where is my knife and fork? My plate? And crackers?"

Dragomir stared at her, obviously trying to determine if she were serious.

When he realized she was, his mouth fell open.

When she continued to wait patiently, he cried, "Oh for the gods' hairy balls." He rolled his eyes and went to retrieve knife, fork, and plate.

"Cad," Victory muttered at his back.

When he returned, Victory delicately cut herself a slice of cheese, wincing at how soft it was. She wondered if peasants even knew how to make cheese properly, and if it was going to give her diarrhea. She tasted a tiny portion between tongue and palate, swishing it around in her mouth warily before swallowing. It had a faint aroma, like the smell of a barnyard. She grimaced, but took another bite. Even a peasant's crude, barnyard cheese was better than plain, unspiced vegetables.

"Well?" Dragomir demanded. "Does it pass with your approval?"

"It's acceptable," Victory said reluctantly, "Though it tastes of tainted milk." She ate quickly, then swished it down with the glass of plain, non-distilled, non-carbonated water that he gave her, barely able to swallow the wretched stuff. Scowling at the empty cup, she said, "That tasted of minerals. Have you put a filter on your well?"

"I got it from the stream an hour ago," Dragomir said. "I don't have a well."

Victory thought she was going to be sick.

"So," he asked, looking at the empty rind. "The cheese was good, then?"

"Like I said," she replied, sliding the plate away from her, "It was a peasant's poor imitation of cheese, not the real thing."

His face darkened. "I made that cheese."

She looked him up and down. "Are you not a peasant?"

"From goat's milk."

Victory felt her gorge rise. Giving him a sweet a smile as she could, she said, "You're lying."

Dragomir gestured at the window outside. "Do you see any cows out there, Princess?" To accentuate his words, she could hear the distant sounds of goats bleating.

I just ate from the body of a goat, Victory thought, staring down at her plate in horror. She waited for the gods to strike her down. When it didn't happen, she cleared her throat. Very politely, she said, "You are a monster."

He chuckled and picked up her plate. He was still laughing as he walked from the room and disappeared down the hall.

When he returned, Victory was still fighting the sick sensation in her stomach. She gave him a sour look as he moved to the dresser and—

Her eyes widened when she realized he was taking off his clothes. "What are you *doing?!*" she cried, scrabbling away from him.

He paused, his shirt half off, arms suspended above his head. "Huh?"

"That!" she cried, gesturing at his rippling stomach.

He looked down, then frowned. "It's not like you haven't seen it before."

"Yes, but now it's…" she hesitated at the way her stomach was fluttering at the sight of his naked skin. He was *beautiful*. "…different," she finished weakly.

"I get hot at night," he complained.

"Keep your clothes on," Victory snapped. "That is a command."

Dragomir chuckled and pulled his shirt the rest of the way off. "You know," he said, as he reached for his waistline, "I was only going to remove the shirt, Princess, but since there's nothing down there that neither of us haven't seen before, I figure I might as well get comfortable." He yanked the waistband off of his hips, and suddenly Victory's heart was hammering at the sight of his naked thighs, the tight swell of his muscled posterior, the dangling flesh at the crux of his legs…

Caught between uncontrollable fear and unreasonable desire, Victory backed all the way to the end of her chain.

It was only for a moment, for in seconds he had crossed the room and was sliding under his homespun blankets, but in that moment, Victory found herself fighting a war within herself. Whatever the Emp had unlocked, it was now working full force, and she felt heat pooling within her where nothing but cold numbness had rested for six years before.

Then she realized he had made no bed for her on the floor, and the extent of the room's carpeting was one small, fuzzy hide that, now that she got a good look at it, looked as if it might have once belonged to a goat.

"Where am *I* going to sleep?" Victory growled.

The Emp opened one eye and cocked his head at her. Then he glanced at the tiny spot beside him. "I made this bed big enough for two," he said, grinning. He patted the blanket beside him. "Hopin' one day I'd need it, ya know?"

Victory scoffed. "That bed is the size of my poodle's mat."

He gave her an irritated look. "This is the biggest bed in my village."

"I'll sleep on the floor," Victory snorted. "Bring me some blankets and some pillows."

Dragomir chuckled, his blue eyes flashing. "Princess, the only blankets and pillows in this entire house are right here beside me." He patted the tiny portion of space beside him. Their bodies, she realized, would probably have to be *touching* for her not to fall off the edge.

Victory's mouth fell open. "You only have a single set of sheets?" The *barbarian*!

"Like I said," Dragomir growled. "Welcome to reality, Princess."

"How do you *clean* them?" Victory babbled.

"You take them out to the stream first thing in the morning, rub them down with soap, shake them out, and hang them out on the line. Then you hope it doesn't rain by the time it's time to go to bed, or you'll be sleeping in a jacket and a double layer of pants."

This is insane, Victory thought. She would have to get her brother to deliver an allowance for the Emp, when he arrived to check on her.

Then she realized how stupid that idea was, considering that the Emp was holding her hostage and abusing her with his beautiful body and performing strange Emp experiments on her. The first thing she was going to do when Matthias showed up was have him cut the chain from the bedpost and get her the hell back to civilization.

"You look a bit dazed," Dragomir noted. He yawned. "You going to be all right?"

"I am *not* sleeping with you," Victory blurted.

"Why not?" Dragomir asked. "Have I molested you yet?"

"Of course you did," Victory snapped. "You chained me to a bedpost, dared to touch me with your body, *kissed* me…"

Dragomir sighed and laid back down, his elbows up, big hands cradling the back of his head as he stared at the ceiling. "Good night." Victory crossed her arms over her chest and snorted her disgust.

Sometime during the night, Victory found herself nodding off. She had eventually settled to the dirt floor with her back against a dresser, knees to her chest, trying not to shiver at the sudden cold in the place.

It has no heat regulator, she thought, disgusted. *I'm living with a complete barbarian.*

"You come over here and I can warm you up, Princess," came a soft voice from the bed.

"Mind your own business," Victory snapped. She started rocking and rubbing her arms, trying to rid herself of the goosebumps. Was that her *breath* she was seeing?

"It's really warm in here. Goose down sewn into the blanket."

"Shut up."

She got up and started to pace, trying to get the blood moving again.

She heard a huge sigh from the bed, then the creak of wood as a great weight slipped from the mattress. Victory turned, frowning. "So, you finally decided to be a decent human being and get me a jack—"

Her words were cut off as Dragomir easily lifted her off her feet and carried her back to the bed.

"What?" Victory screeched, "No! Don't you even *dare!*"

And then he was flipping the cover back, settling her into the mattress, sliding under the covers behind her.

When Victory felt his big body slide up to meet hers, she panicked and tried to scrabble for the other side.

A big arm reached out, grabbed her around the waist, and dragged her back. She felt him settle himself behind her, his body melding to hers. Victory froze, realizing what parts of his naked anatomy were touching where. With only her linen slave-shift between them, she felt every curve of his muscles, every line, every…bulge.

Victory swallowed, hard.

"You don't have to hold me so tight," she managed.

"Making sure you don't run off," Dragomir stated. "It's cold out there, and I don't know if you noticed, Princess, but I'm currently in a state of slight undress. Don't feel like getting up to go after you again."

"You're *naked,*" Victory cried. "And *touching* me." She shuddered, though she wasn't sure if it was from fear or anticipation. Or both. She tried to squirm out of his grip.

He squeezed her closer. "You keep wriggling and I might just have to sleep *on* you, Princess."

Victory went utterly stiff at that thought. With just her shift between her and the large man, she knew that could *not* end well.

Dragomir chuckled softly into her ear. "If you'd gone any quieter, Victory, I'd say your little heart gave out down there."

"Matthias will string you up by your testicles for this," she managed. Her mind was drifting to the muscular arm wrapped around her—as solid as a band of iron—the big legs tight against hers, the ribbed abdomen pressing against her back. She felt the warmth pooling again, despite herself.

"What did you *do* to me," she whimpered. Instead of wanting to be free of him, a good part of her was wanting to roll over, to run her fingers down his muscled chest, to have his big hand stroke her thigh…

She shook that thought out of her head.

He bespelled me, she thought, horrified. Somehow, he had made her crave…*things*…like a wanton pleasure-house slave.

And yet, she found herself realizing, she didn't care. Her body was aching from the contact, yearning to feel his skin on hers, his big form moving over hers, pinning her with his weight. The pressure was growing like a smoldering fire between her legs, and she desperately tried to think of something to put it out.

Instead, her mind kept coming back to the great beast sleeping behind her, and how badly she yearned to feel him moving with her.

She needed release, and she needed it *now*. If she didn't find it, she was likely to lose herself to the creature pinning her in the bed.

She waited until she was sure he was asleep, his breathing deep and even, his arm slightly slack around her torso. Then, as carefully as she could, she slipped her hand down under her shift. As utterly quietly and quickly as she dared, she began to pleasure herself for the first time since that ill-fated ship to the Imperial Academy.

The pressure within her surged, warming until even her hips felt encased in its hot glow. Victory bucked slightly, then bit her lip, terrified that the Emp had noticed. His breathing remained slow and even, and eventually, she found the confidence to start moving her fingers again. It felt good…something that she hadn't even considered doing in six years.

A moan slipped her lips, and Victory froze in horror.

For a long moment, she heard nothing over the pounding of her own heart. Then she relaxed, feeling the Emp's slow, even breaths against her neck. She closed her eyes and decided to finish.

"Do you really want me that bad?" Dragomir whispered in her ear.

Victory screeched and flailed, trying to kick her way onto the floor. Cursing, Dragomir held on, dragging her back to the bed with both hands, this time. "Gods be good, woman!" Dragomir cried, forcing her wrists above her head and settling his big body over her abdomen. "Calm down!"

Victory screamed and arced her back, trying to buck him off of her.

She would have had better luck throwing aside an Imperial tank that had decided to set its treads in her gut.

"I'm sorry!" Dragomir cried, holding her pinned. "Just calm down!"

"You brutish peasant bastard cad you scared the *shit* outta me!" Victory screamed, horrified and humiliated. "Get off!" She renewed her struggles, screeching in shame and frustration.

"Listen," Dragomir said, his blue eyes wary in the moonlight, "I'm going to lie back down. I'm taking you with me. I've gotta get up in the morning and go check on my herd. I'd like to take you with me, but I'm not gonna be able to do that if you don't get some sleep."

"I hate goats," Victory whimpered, but she was relieved he was finding something else to talk about, carefully ignoring the fact that he had just caught her pleasuring herself in his arms.

"I'm going to let you up," Dragomir said. "And lay back down. Please don't run, all right? I'm not going to hurt you."

Victory stared back up at him in silence, seething.

"Okay," Dragomir said nervously, "Laying down now. Just want to sleep."

She turned her head, ignoring him.

As if he were handling a bundle of aged dynamite, Dragomir gently let go of her wrists. Then, pinning her body in place with one arm, he lay back down behind her. Gingerly, he pulled her back to him once more, though not so tightly this time as to give her such excellent mental imagery of what loomed behind her in the dark.

"You all right?" he whispered.

She said nothing.

"Victory?" he asked, softer.

"You tell anyone," Victory grated, "And I will be eating your bloody liver sautéed in butter and shallots."

She could hear the grin in his face when he said, "And you're squeamish about goat."

• • •

Goats, Victory found, had slitty little eyes, cloven hooves, and horns; the very picture of malignant demon-spawn. It didn't help that they tried to eat her hair when she sat on a log to watch Dragomir tend them, or that they nibbled on her shift when she stood up and flailed, absolutely stoic to her shooings.

"Get them *off* of me!" she cried, tugging at the chain that Dragomir had padlocked to his waist.

Dragomir grunted and fell backwards on his rear. The hairy brown goat he had been milking jumped aside and darted away, flicking its tail. The pail, which Dragomir had been collecting for breakfast, went spilling across the yard in a white wave.

"Hmph," Victory said. "Good riddance."

"That is the *third time!*" Dragomir growled, snatching up the empty bucket and jumping to his feet. "You don't *have* to drink it! *I'd* like to have something other than potatoes and eggs for breakfast!"

"And cheese," Victory said. "Don't forget that." She was actually looking forward to the cheese, deciding that, if taken literally, she wasn't eating the flesh of a goat. Besides, the gods hadn't struck her down yet, and with the alternatives being potatoes and eggs…

But Dragomir's face darkened. "I gave you all of my cheese last night. You ate it in one sitting."

Victory's mouth fell open. "That was *it?*" She stared. "But that was just, what, a *pound?*"

"Until you came along," Dragomir growled, "I had been trading it for other things. Like clothes."

Victory snorted and looked away. "When my brother gets here, I'm going to make sure he takes me back to civilization with him. I am in need of a bath and perfume." She glanced down at her feet. "It's going to take my servants a decade to scrub the dirt from beneath my toenails."

He gave her a flat stare. "It's not dirt."

Victory laughed. "Of course it is. What else could it b—" Then her eyes widened at the mangy, flea-stricken animals munching on the bushes growing through the fence, then at the squawking flock of fowl that was pecking at the ground by the hovel's front door.

As she watched, a projectile squirted from one of the feathered posteriors.

"Oh. My. *God*," Victory screamed. "Take me back inside! Now!"

He sighed at her. "Thanks to you, I'm still not done here. I take you back inside, you're getting chained back to the bed until I can finish milking my damn goats."

"Chain me to the bed!" Victory cried, for the first time noticing the delicate texture of the debris between her toes, the slippery feel, the digested bits of grass…"Oh for the love of the gods, chain me to the bed!"

Instead, Dragomir sighed and said, "Fine. I'll just skip milk for breakfast. Come here." Then, to her horror, he started walking *toward* the flock of disgusting feathered cretins. She was given the choice of following or being dragged.

Screaming in dismay, Victory danced over the piles and plops, whimpering whenever she felt something go squish underneath her feet. "What are you *doing?*" she cried, when the numbers of droppings intensified, like entering the center of a minefield.

"I'm getting some eggs for breakfast," Dragomir growled.

"From *where?*" Victory screeched. "The market's back in the town!"

Dragomir came to a sudden stop, then turned, slowly, to face her. After a moment of staring, he pointed at one of the feathered cretins. "What is that?"

"That is filthy."

He narrowed his eyes at her. "What *is* it?"

"It's a duck," she said, disgusted.

"That is a *chicken*," Dragomir said. "What do chickens produce?"

"Meat," Victory said. Then, when he merely frowned at her, she said, "Soup?"

"You are joking," Dragomir said, his blue eyes watching her suspiciously. "Aren't you?"

Victory frowned down at the dirty brown creatures. "Feathers?"

He continued to stare at her.

Now he was just starting to irritate her. "They produce fertilizer," she growled, showing him her foot. "*Lots* of it."

"Eggs," Dragomir said. "They produce eggs."

Victory frowned. "But how would they—" Then she felt her eyes widen, her jaw drop open in horror. "You *eat* that? After it's been… after it's come through…" She pointed a finger at a chicken's butt, wrinkling her nose in disgust. "Never mind on the eggs. I'm no longer hungry."

Dragomir raked his hand down his face, watching her between his big fingers. "Oh my gods, you *were* serious."

"I'll be perfectly fine with potatoes," Victory said. "Sautee them in butter, throw in some onions and rosemary, and I will make do."

Dragomir narrowed his eyes. "Sorry," he said. "I'm all out of rosemary."

"Oregano?" Victory asked hopefully. "Cilantro?"

He turned and started stalking toward the tiny excrement-covered hut.

"Chives!" Victory cried, dancing after him. "Surely you have chives!"

Dragomir wrenched open the chicken-coop door and started plucking eggs from nasty, feather-encrusted wads of straw. "Six eggs this morning," he said, sounding satisfied. "That's enough for everybody to have two."

"I said I didn't want eggs," Victory said, with a grimace.

Dragomir scowled at her. "The alternative is potatoes. With salt."

"I'm not hungry," Victory said.

Glaring, Dragomir said, "Fine. Lion and I will have the eggs and potatoes. You can have water."

Victory thought again of drinking from a raw, unpurified stream and she made a face. "I'm not thirsty, either."

Dragomir made an exasperated sound and dragged her back across the filth-strewn yard to the hovel. Inside, Lion looked up from where she had been standing beside the crude wood-and-pillow couch Dragomir had supplied for her. A goose-egg roughly the size of the Imperium stood out on her temple, apparently, Dragomir claimed, because she refused to sit down when he slid the couch underneath her, choosing instead to topple over backwards. Lion hadn't argued, so Victory assumed it was probably the truth.

Victory went straight to the water bucket beside the stove and stuck her feet inside, rinsing off the grime. "How long are you planning on keeping Lion like that?" she asked, rubbing the nasty accumulation off on the sides of the bucket.

Dragomir's eyes were on the bucket. "That was my drinking water."

"And it's *cold*, too," Victory said, grimacing as she swished her foot around inside the pail. "Be glad I'm not going to make you draw me a bath." She finished, dried her feet on the towel hanging from the stove, then gestured at the Praetorian. "She's only getting madder, you know. Would probably be more survivable for you if you let her go."

"I'll let her go when I'm relatively certain she's not going to try to kill me," Dragomir said, his eyes moving from the grime floating in his bucket to the black streaks now staining the towel. "Until then, I don't want her interfering." He took his eggs over to the frying pan and proceeded to crack them over the stove.

Seeing a tuft of feather and other dubious material still sticking to one of the shells, Victory thought she was going to be sick. "You should wash those first," she managed.

"Maybe," he said, dropping the feather-crusted shell into the disgusting bucket of compost and picking up another. *Crack.* "But, now that you so thoughtfully used up all my clean water, that would mean another trip to the stream, and I'm tired of your complaining." Dump. *Crack.*

"When my brother gets here," Victory said, "The first thing I'm going to do is take me to a decent meal."

Crack. He looked down at her, irritation in his blue eyes. "How do you know it's not decent? You haven't even tried it." Then he frowned. "And I thought the first thing you were gonna do is have him execute me on the spot."

"Lobster. Filet mignon. Wine. Maybe a little shrimp scampi or lasagna." She smiled at him. "I'm going to eat it all in front of you, make you watch every bite. *Then* I'm going to have him cut off your head."

Dragomir rolled his eyes and cracked the last filthy egg into the pan. Then he took a primitive wooden spoon and stirred it all together, until the yolk and white were blended. "And," Dragomir said, reaching for the bag of salt, "since we don't have any cheese…" She watched, horrified, as he dumped nearly a palmful of salt into the eggs.

Then he proceeded to pluck three large potatoes from the pot he had boiled the night before and nipped them into the skillet. Victory felt her gorge rise. "That wasn't refrigerated."

"Nope," he said. Then, as she watched, he built a fire inside the stove using sticks of wood and kindling, then stirred the pan as it started to heat.

"This is taking *forever*," Victory said, finally getting impatient. "Why don't you use a gas stove?"

Without looking up from the eggs, Dragomir said, "Do you see any gas lines running to my home, Princess?"

She narrowed her eyes. "They sell canned gas. I know. It's one of our imports."

"Purchasing and transporting a gas stove costs more than I make in a year. Every *bottle* of gas costs the same price as five goats." He tapped contaminated egg off his spoon and looked at her. "So which would you rather have? Fast-cooked potatoes or slow-cooked meat?"

"Slow-cooked is right." She wrinkled her nose at how long it was taking for the stove to heat. "Is that *ever* going to be done?"

He squatted, opened the stove, blew on the coals, and threw more wood on the fire. "You know," he said, closing the iron door again, "I've been thinking about it, and I think I'm going to do your heart last." He stood, his blue eyes watching her with a calculating look.

"Uh," Victory said. "What?"

He poked a big finger between her breasts. "Your heart rama. That's going to be last. If I open it up now, I'm just going to be leaving you with all sorts of other worries and hang-ups that have built up in the womb and liver ramas, and when you fall madly in love with me, I want it to stick."

Victory jerked away from his touch, horrified at how close his hand had come to her now all-too-sensitive nipples. Then her jaw fell open. "You're doing it *again?*"

"Yep," Dragomir said. "After breakfast." He started stirring the skillet again. "Hungry?"

She backed to the end of her chain. "You can't."

"Why not?" Dragomir asked. "Your brother asked me to heal you."

Victory thought of the way that she had been doing everything she could to avoid thinking about the way his big body moved like a cat, the way his blue eyes danced at her complaints, the way his big hands worked the goat's udders…"Uh," she said, reddening at the warmth that was building at the thought, "I feel completely healed, thank you."

The Emp gave her a flat look.

"I *am*," she cried. Then, at the warmth between her thighs building under his scrutiny, she squeaked, "*Too* healed."

"We're opening another rama. The womb this time. It will help you with your creativity. You like to paint? Sew?"

"Uh," Victory said. "Do I have any say in this?"

"Nope." He went back to stirring his meal.

"Listen, you cad," Victory growled. "I'm a *princess*. I don't need to sew."

He raised an eyebrow. "You want something more than that shift?" He gestured to her linen robe.

"Of course I do," Victory muttered.

"I have goat wool. I know a lady in town who has a spinner and a loom. I can arrange for you to use it."

Victory stared at him so long he had a chance to finish breakfast and serve it up on two wooden plates, carry one of them to Lion, feed her, and then sit back with his own meal with a sigh.

"You have got to be *utterly out of your mind*!" she finally cried.

Dragomir looked up at her over a mouthful of his contaminated egg-and-potato mash. "Winter is coming," he said.

"My *brother* is coming," Victory snapped. "And when he does—"

Dragomir rolled his eyes and went back to his meal.

Victory watched him eat for several minutes before she realized that she was hungry. "I want some of that," she finally said.

Dragomir kept eating.

"Hey," she said, walking up and smacking him on a big shoulder. "Let me try it."

He looked up at her and she saw him deliberate.

"I'm really hungry," she admitted.

Growling, he offered her the plate.

Victory gingerly picked up a bite, tasted it. She took a few more fork-fuls, forcing herself to swallow them. "It's really bland," she said, grimacing. She took another bite.

"Then *give it back*!" he roared, stretching out an arm to take the plate from her.

Victory twisted out of reach and kept eating. "You get hungry enough, you'll eat just about anything." She finished the food, then handed him the plate. "That was passable, considering your resources."

Dragomir sat on his chair and fumed. "That was my breakfast."

She gestured at the unrefrigerated pot on the stove. "Have some potatoes. There were a couple of those left."

He leaned forward, elbows on knees, dropping his face into his big hands. For several minutes, he said nothing, just stared at the floor. Then, with a growl, he got up, grabbed a bundle of twine from the wall, and started walking out the door, Victory in tow.

"Where are you going?" Victory asked, reluctantly following along behind him. Reluctantly because if she didn't stay within chain's-length, she was going to be dragged.

"Getting myself some breakfast," Dragomir growled. He strode out to the yard where the goats were clumped together around a bush that had had the misfortune of growing through the fence, and tied the twine around the neck of the goat he had been milking that morning.

Victory's eyes widened. "You're going to *kill* it?" she gasped, feeling sick.

Dragomir gave her an irritated scowl. The goat on a lead, he went to the small shack beside the house and whistled.

A moment later, a huge black beast came charging up to the yard from the direction of the fields, ebony mane and tail flowing out behind it. Victory frowned. "Is that a *horse?*"

Dragomir petted the animal, greeting it with soothing words. Then he took a set of leather straps off the wall inside the hut and began harnessing the beast.

Victory grimaced. "How primitive."

If he heard her, he ignored her. He set a saddle onto the horse's back and cinched it down. Then he tied the goat's lead to the saddle horn.

"Come here," Dragomir growled, turning to Victory.

Eying the animal warily, Victory backed to the end of her chain. "Why?"

Dragomir grabbed the leash and reeled her in. Then, amidst her flailing and complaints, lifted her off her feet and dropped her onto the horse's back in front of the saddle, alone and unattended.

Victory froze, feeling the great beast move underneath her. "Oh my gods," she said. Inside, Lion had started shouting, the thumps of her body hitting the chain ringing throughout the hovel.

"Better tell her you're all right," Dragomir said, glancing at the open door. "She's going to hurt herself again." Then, to her horror, he swung up into the saddle behind her.

Ducking low in terror on the horse's back, her hands gripping the animal's mane, Victory somehow found her voice long enough to shout, "Calm down, Lion. He's only assaulting me with a horse."

Unable to understand her, Dragomir clucked at the animal and, holding the leather straps, started leading it and the goat toward the fence.

"I'm sorry I ate your breakfast!" Victory cried, as she felt its mass jolt beneath her. "Please!"

"Stop thrashing or you're going to spook Thunder," Dragomir said. He reached around her and patted the horse's neck. To the horse, he cooed, "'Cause he's an ornery old cuss, isn't he?" The horse whickered back.

Grinning, Dragomir patted its side, then looked down at Victory. His grin faded. Straightening, he wrapped an arm around her and kicked the horse forward.

"Where are we going?" She tried to keep the whine out of her voice, but being held this close, it felt like every nerve in her back was afire where he was touching her. And the big arm around her waist wasn't helping matters. That, and this close, he smelled…

…masculine. It wasn't a smell that Victory was used to, and it made her shudder with yearning before she got her instincts under control. *What did he do to me?* she thought again, horrified.

Then she realized he hadn't answered her and a feeling of foreboding began to seep into her consciousness. "Dragomir?" she asked, nervous. Then, when he didn't answer, she scowled and said, "*Slave?*"

He tilted his head to peer down at her, his blue eyes thoughtful. "I thought Imperium Royals were a genetic mutation similar to an Emp or a Psi, but with brainpower."

Victory frowned up at him. "We have photographic memories, among other things. My brain is like yours, except better."

He grunted. "For a super-genius, you're making some very interesting miscalculations."

Victory twisted on the back of the horse to face him. "Like what?"

Still watching the road, Dragomir said, "Oh, I don't know…That I currently have you trapped on a horse, chained to my waist."

Victory scoffed. "We both know how long *that's* going to last, once my brother gets here. I haven't decided if I'm going to sell you off to a fetish pleasure-house or keep you for my own amusement."

He smiled pleasantly. "Or that I'm about three times bigger than you, haven't had breakfast, and am fighting an overpowering urge to make you walk."

Victory's mouth fell open. She glanced down at the rocky ground, then at the skinny brown goat that was fighting in vain against its lead, then back up at him. "Uh."

"But please go on," Dragomir insisted. "You were saying something about a fetish pleasure-house?"

"Uh," Victory said. "You know, that tree is really *green*. I never noticed it before. Is that imported?"

He glanced in the direction of the foliage. "That's an alder."

"Father has to import most of his hardwoods," Victory babbled. "The only ones that Mercy has reliably been able to grow has been oak and maple, and they really only grow on a thin band on either side of the equator—this village is way too far north. There's so much rock and so little dirt on this planet that we really haven't been able to establish any serious tree-farms."

He peered down at her for a long moment. Victory grabbed extra fistfuls of the horse's mane, just in case he tried to fling her off.

"A photographic memory, huh?" he asked finally. "How many potatoes were left in the pot?"

"Seven," Victory said immediately. Then she frowned. "Well, six and a half. You'd cut one up for breakfast."

She heard him suck in a breath behind her. "That's it, isn't it?"

"What?" Victory asked nervously.

"Why you keep being overwhelmed by the visions." He looked down at her, his blue eyes kind. "You're living them over again, aren't you?"

"Part of the Imperial Curse," she muttered.

He nodded in commiseration. "Does the other part consist of being a pampered pain in my ass?"

She glared up at him. "Definitely the fetish house."

"You know, you're right." In an easy motion, Dragomir lifted her up and dropped her onto the ground beside the goat. "Stretch your legs a bit." He never slowed the horse.

"Wait!" Victory cried, running to catch up. "I was only joking about the fetish house! I'm sure we can find you some nice noble family willing to take you on as a personal servant."

Dragomir stopped the horse and looked down at her, blinking. "You are serious, aren't you?"

Victory frowned at his stunned expression. "What, you would rather live in your *hovel?* Raising *goats?*" She snorted. "Personal servants get all sorts of benefits, especially if they are smart—" she hesitated, looking up at him. "Well, you'd get a few benefits. But what I'm saying is you'd have a clean bed to sleep in, nice clothes, a roof over your head that didn't involve grass stuffed between slate…No more of this plain-potatoes-for-breakfast nonsense, either. They'd give you pepper, at the very least."

Dragomir turned and stared ahead at the road for a moment. Then he seemed to shake himself and kicked the beast forward again.

"Wait!" Victory cried. "I'd try to find you a merchant's household. They always have a good spice selection. I spent a night at a trader's house on a journey, once, and they fed us an eighteen-course meal using thirty different spices. And that's the kind of food they ate every day."

"What kind of trader?" Dragomir asked.

Victory reddened. "Uh."

He glanced down at her. "Slaves?"

"My feet hurt," Victory said. "I think they're infected."

"So you would have me eat pepper on my potatoes while serving a man who eats eighteen-course meals on a nightly basis because he's profiting from the sale of honest men and women just trying to make a living on a planet that rightfully belongs to them."

"The chicken manure must have worked its way into the blisters."

He kept the horse plodding down the path in silence.

Muttering, Victory eyed the length of chain, then grabbed it and jogged up beside him. "You really should let me back on the horse," she warned.

"Why?" Dragomir asked, sounding bored. "Because you're going to sell me to a marble mine if I don't?" Then he brought a hand to his face in mock horror. "No wait! Because your *brother* is coming, and if I don't do *exactly* as you tell me, you're going to have him chain me to your bathtub and use me for a footstool."

"Last chance," Victory growled.

"No wait," Dragomir said, still gesticulating at air, "You'll hang me naked in the kitchen and feed me gruel, so that I must live out the rest of my days smelling the wonderful aromas of good food without having the pleasure of tasting any of it." Then he tapped his cheek thoughtfully. "But then again, if you did that, you wouldn't be able to chain me to your *bed* so you can use my naked body to fulfill your newfound carnal urges." He tisked. "That's gonna be a tough one." He held up one hand, palm up, weighing. "Would you focus on torment, getting back at me for all the horrible things I've done to you…" he held up the second palm, balancing them on either side of himself like some thick and muscular statue of a Justicar. "Or would you delight in my helplessness as you pleasure yourself with my inhumanly sexy body? Hmm." He raised a single finger with a shout. "Oh wait! I know. You can chain me in the kitchen during the *day*, and then take me to your *bedroom* at—"

Gripping the chain as hard as she could, Victory took off at a run in the opposite direction of the horse. When she hit the end, she wrenched, hard.

Dragomir made a startled grunt as he jerked backwards off of the beast. He fell into the mud, hard, and the horse whinnied and danced away from him.

For a long time, Dragomir simply lay in the road, staring at the sky. Victory almost felt a twinge of concern, but then realized his chest was moving. His horse, still dragging the goat, wandered to the edge of the trail and started munching on grass.

Seconds passed, then minutes, and still he lay there. Still at the end of her chain, Victory peered at him, wondering if she had somehow disconnected his inadequate brain-cells from voluntary motor control. She tiptoed around him at the full extent of the tether, trying to get a better look.

After a moment, Dragomir lifted his hand and dropped it to the chain around his waist. Tightening his fist around it, he pulled.

Victory stumbled forward.

He grabbed it with his other hand. *Pull.* She cried out and tried to drag him backwards, but she might as well have been dragging a ton of steel. *Grab. Pull. Drag.* Victory flailed and struggled as he pulled her within range, then screamed in panic as a big hand found her ankle. Then he was pulling her down, dragging him down on top of him. She shrieked and tried to wriggle free, but he held her pinned to him with a big arm around her spine, their faces almost touching.

To her surprise, he looked amused. "You," Dragomir said, "Are a pain in my ass."

"Literally, this time," Victory giggled.

Then he was pulling her head down, dragging her forward for a kiss. Victory's eyes went wide, but a moment later, all of her resistance drained from her in a rush of heat and excitement, pooling between her legs in a delicious, tantalizing, overpowering wash. She moaned and squirmed on top of him, enjoying the solid feel of his body beneath her, reveling in the way his big hands felt on her sides, her back. She returned the embrace, digging her hands into his hair, devouring his kiss, slipping a hand under his shirt to feel his rippling chest as her passion built to a crescendo—

"Fancy finding you two here," a deep male voice said, almost identical to Dragomir's.

Victory gasped and rolled off of him—

—or tried to. Dragomir's muscular arm held her solidly in place as he cocked his head to peer around her. "What the hell do you want?" he growled up at Thor. He sounded breathless.

Thor tugged the leash he held. "This little vixen, here, made it pretty clear to me last night that she wanted to make sure her, uh…" He hesitated, eyes catching on Victory, "…*friend* was all right."

Twisting as far as she could in Dragomir's grip, Victory saw Whip standing beside the brute, staring at her as if she'd grown tentacles from her nose. Then she realized that a good portion of both thighs and part of her rear was showing, where Dragomir's hand had been caressing it. Blushing furiously, Victory did her best to tug the shift back down to her knees, as much as she could while hindered by the steel-plated arm that held her.

"We weren't doing anything!" she cried in Imperial. Then, flushing harder, she amended, "I mean, he was accosting me! Didn't you see it?"

Whip, who has always been more softspoken than her sisters-in-arms, lowered her head with a small grin playing on her lips. "Glad to see you feeling better, Princess."

"This was *his* doing!" Victory cried, slapping the brute on his muscular chest. Then, in the native tongue, she snapped, "Let me up! Now! Before I pound your kidneys into pudding!"

Dragomir sighed and released her. "You've got about the best timing on the planet, Thor," he growled, getting up. "The *polite* thing to do would've been to turn the hell around and go back home."

Thor snorted. "I would have, but *this* one, here," he tugged Whip's chain, "wanted to make sure all those weird sounds her very good friend, here, was making weren't somehow caused by you smothering her to death with your mouth."

Victory blushed harder and started wiping the hair back from her face, smoothing down her shift as she tried *very* hard to ignore the stare that Whip was giving her.

Dragomir grunted and retrieved his horse. "How is she…" He gave Whip a wary glance. "…holding up?"

"Oh, I'm pretty sure she'd rip my eyes out of their sockets, if she had her hands free, but other than that, she's been pleasant enough." Thor gave Whip a knowing grin, and Whip narrowed her eyes at him but said nothing. Turning back to Dragomir, he said, "So where were you two headed before…uh…?" He gestured at the muddy patch of ground.

"The market," Dragomir growled. "The wench ate my breakfast this morning."

Thor's eyes widened. "Uh-oh, wench." Thor gave Victory a serious look. "Don't mess with his food. He gets cranky."

"Call me a 'wench' again and you'll lose a testicle, you musclebound oaf," Victory snapped.

Thor raised both brows at her. "Feisty little thing, isn't she?" If he thought it strange she could speak flawless Native Barbarian, he never mentioned it. Victory narrowed her eyes, looking first at Thor, then at Whip, who remained quite thoroughly helpless despite a very docile attitude.

"You *told* him," she cried.

"Of course," Dragomir said, throwing the reins over the horse's head and leading the smelly beast over to her. "He's my brother. You think I would I drop a Praetorian on my brother without so much as an, 'oh, by the way…'?"

"It's my *life!*" Victory cried.

Dragomir shrugged. Thor, for his part, seemed to be looking her over, analyzing her the same way someone would inspect a business partner of dubious intent. "So you fix her yet?" Thor asked. "She certainly looks a bit more…relaxed…than she was when she got here."

Victory choked, even as Dragomir chuckled. "Just one, brother."

"Her core," Thor said flatly.

Dragomir actually got a sheepish look.

"Gods," Thor said. "There are entire levels of hell for what you're doing."

"It was an *accident!*" Dragomir cried. It was the first time Victory had heard the big man get defensive. "She had a spark and I wanted to, uh…"

"…let it out to play?" Thor suggested.

Dragomir shoved a big finger at his brother. "You mind your own damn business. I said I'd heal her. How I go about it's up to me." He shoved past Thor, dragging horse, goat, and human along with him.

"Do you want me to kill him, milady?" Whip called, her voice utterly pleasant.

At this point, Victory would have been happy with a decent pair of shoes. "Just keep your head low, do as your told," Victory said. "Perhaps you can lull the oaf into doing something stupid."

"Already my plan, mistress," her Praetorian said, bobbing her head and smiling like they were talking about bunny rabbits and rainbows. "Perhaps we can add the brother to your collection. He is quite…" she looked up at Thor, considering. "…Pleasing to the eye, milady," she finished.

Victory laughed, delighted. "What a wonderful idea. Perhaps we can teach them to carry a sedan chair."

Whip's smile was genuine. "A matched set, milady." She beamed up at Thor, nodding.

Victory giggled.

"Don't pretend you weren't just discussing how to kill me," Dragomir said, eying her over his shoulder.

"No, something much worse," Victory said. She gave him a measuring glance. "Just how much *can* you lift, anyway?"

Dragomir shrugged. "Two-fifty easy enough, though I can get three and a half off the ground if I have t—" He stopped, giving her a suspicious frown. "Why?"

Snickering, Victory said, "No reason." To Whip, she said, "They would be *perfect*."

"We could hitch them to a cart and dress them in thongs," Whip said.

Victory scoffed. "Thongs?" Smiling at Dragomir, she said, "Why waste the material?"

"Their talking is making me nervous," Thor said. "I think I'm gonna go sit down here a few minutes, let you two go on ahead."

"Agreed," Dragomir said. "I will see you at dinner?"

"That was the idea."

A minute later, they were out of earshot, plodding along beside Dragomir's huge black horse. Irritated, given no other real alternative, Victory trudged along behind the goat, falling into a morose silence. Dragomir tried several times to initiate some form of conversation, but

Victory ignored him utterly, waiting for the moment when her brother and his armada would drop from the sky to ruin his morning.

Dragomir eventually stopped trying, and they walked in silence back to the little cluster of sod-and-stone hovels huddled together along the river feeding out of the valley. Off to one side, there was a smaller cluster of blankets and tables spread out on the ground, with people sitting around them doing various chores like knitting, weaving, carving…

Dragomir went right to the tiny cluster of blankets and stopped at a young boy sitting beside a cluster of cages. Inside the cages were various fowl, mostly unattractive shades of reds and browns.

"I need laying hens, Fell," Dragomir told the boy. "How many you give for a good milk goat?"

The boy—he couldn't have been more than six or seven—got out of his chair and came over to walk around the goat, eying it thoughtfully. "She's in milk right now?"

"Just milked her this morning," Dragomir said.

"Five hens," the boy Fell said.

Dragomir snorted and started walking to another blanket.

"Ten," the boy cried. "And rights to breed her back to a buck of our choice in the fall."

"Twelve," Dragomir said, "And I get to keep a doeling if there's twins."

"You keep a doeling, we'll expect a dozen hatching eggs back in the spring."

"Fine," Dragomir said. He handed over the goat's lead. While the boy was tying the goat to his chair, Dragomir started lashing chicken cages to his horse.

Victory's mouth fell open as she watched the exchange. Never in her life had she suspected that children of that age could make financial decisions, let alone hold his own in a bartering exchange.

"Mom's gonna want the cages back," the boy said, coming to help the Emp.

"Have her send one of you boys over tomorrow," Dragomir said. "Maybe another twelve hens, if she's thinkin' of starting her own herd."

The boy's brown eyes grew suspicious. "You gettin' into the poultry business?"

"No," Dragomir chuckled. He jerked his thumb over his shoulder, indicating Victory. "I just found myself with two more mouths to feed, both of whom refuse to eat goat."

The boy seemed to see Victory for the first time. He gave her a disapproving look. "Won't eat goat? What's wrong with her?"

"A lot, actually." Dragomir shrugged.

The boy grunted and helped him finish packing the chickens. "Could always sell her. I hear they get good money for slaves in the cities."

"Could probably buy a whole herd of goats," Dragomir agreed. He looked back over his shoulder at Victory. "Or maybe even a cow."

Victory felt her face flush and she looked away.

But the boy snorted. "I was thinking five or six cows. Enough to get yourself settled, if you can keep 'em alive through the winter."

Still looking at Victory, Dragomir said, "I'll have to think on it. They cause me much more trouble, though, and I'm going to have to start making other arrangements."

"How 'bout I arrange for you to pull a cart," Victory said in Mandarin, meeting his eyes glare-for-glare. "Minus the thong."

Dragomir frowned at her.

Once the chickens were packed, the boy patted Thunder appreciatively on the rump. His gaze, however, was nervous when he looked back up at Dragomir. "Mom'll probably send Rachel over with the mule. She's been sick real bad. Bad cough. Having trouble breathing. We've been kinda hopin' you'd take a look at her, but Mom didn't wanna intrude, seein' how you just got captured by the Imperium and all…"

Dragomir frowned. "Send her over tonight."

Relief flooded the boy's face. "I'll go tell Mom you said so. It'll take a couple hours to get Rachel wrapped up and on the cart."

"The cart?" Dragomir asked. "Is she really that bad?"

The boy Fell bit his lip, and Victory saw fear play across his honest face. "The gal next door said she thought Rachel was gonna die yesterday. She's doing better now, but she can't really move much."

The Emp glanced off in the direction of the river. "I've got to say a few words to the weaver first, but wait for me and I'll just go with you now. You or your brothers can come get your cages anytime."

The boy babbled his thanks and started packing up the remains of his tiny impromptu shop into the back of a mule-drawn cart.

Looking disturbed, Dragomir led his chicken-laden horse and his barefoot princess back through the cluster of huts, stopping outside a hovel that was a bit larger than the others, rivaling Dragomir's own for size. There was a small, weather-worn blanket hanging beside the front door that proclaimed in faded black letters, WEEVUR. Victory snorted. *Peasants*, she thought.

Beside the sign was a rocking chair with some odd contraption sitting in front of it, wrapped in what looked like primitive yarn.

Inside, Victory heard the sounds of an argument.

Frowning, Dragomir wrapped the reins of his horse around the T-shaped post out front, then ducked inside, giving Victory no option but to follow.

A big man had a tiny woman pinned against a wall, trapping her on both sides with big palms pressed flat against the stone behind her. "Get *off* of me!" she screamed, straining to get around his arms and failing. "Please. I've got friends."

The man was chuckling, his voice low and husky as he said, "Oh, come on, sweets. Everybody knows you ain't got a man…"

Dragomir crossed the living-room in two steps, grabbed the fellow by the back of the neck, and yanked him off of the woman. Completing his turn, he whipped around and sent him crashing into the opposite room, spilling a table of colorful yarn in the process.

"He a friend of yours, Dora?" Dragomir asked, watching as the man got to his feet with a roar.

The woman against the wall, seeing Dragomir, let out a relieved sob and scurried behind him. "Thank you," she babbled. "He's a resistance fighter, passing through. He's been here before, but this is the first time he caught me alone…" Across the room, the man righted himself and picked up a broken chair leg, snarling.

"You better leave," Dragomir growled as the big man approached, the makeshift weapon in his white-knuckled fist. "Now."

"I don't think you know who you're dealing with, man," the man growled. "The lady offered her services. I paid. I was taking what I was owed."

Then, as the man stepped into the light, Victory saw it. She remembered the same exact sneer, as he humped her helpless body in the mud and cold. She gasped and backed to the very end of her chain. When it went taut, she crouched low and wrapped her arms around her ankles, fighting the images that were pounding upwards into her consciousness from the Void deep below.

She caught Dragomir's eyes flicker towards her, a tiny frown on his face, before he glanced back at the man with the club.

"Dora is a weaver, not a whore," Dragomir said. "Whatever she sold you, you obviously mistook her intent."

"I'm a fighter for the Cause," the man growled. "I'm entitled to enjoy myself a little."

"Where I come from," Dragomir said coolly, "We string up rapists by the balls and leave them in a tree for the crows to eat."

The man snorted and gestured at the door with the chair leg. "You think I'm afraid of you? I'm a warrior. And you're what…" He looked Dragomir up and down, disdain clear in his face. "A *farmer*?" He laughed. "Get the hell outta here, man. I've killed a few hundred Praetorian in my life, and I'd hate to have to scatter your brains across the room."

"Really?" Dragomir said, cocking his head. "You must be real proud of yourself, then. I've only ever killed one."

The man gave him an uncertain look. "You're a farmer."

Dragomir just smiled. "Get out of the woman's house. Now."

For a long moment, the man didn't move. Then, slowly, he lowered the club and made a disgusted sound. "The whore's probably diseased, anyway." He threw the weapon aside and started trudging for the door.

He stopped when his eyes met Victory's. "Holy hells," he whispered. "*You* got her?"

"Not sure what you mean," Dragomir said. Even though he spoke pleasantly, Victory felt him tense.

"We just got done with a raid," the man said, lust filling his piggish brown eyes. "I'll give you sixty thousand, cash, for the traitor bitch."

"That's a lot of money," Dragomir admitted. He started helping Dora to right the furniture that had been tossed about in the struggle.

Victory froze at the casual consideration in his voice, every one of her fears suddenly surging into the forefront in a wave. Whimpering, she crawled backwards, away from the man, at the extent of her leash.

"Oh, come on, honey," the big man cooed, coming towards her. He grabbed her by the hair and pulled her onto her feet, shoving her into the wall behind. "Daddy only wants to play." An instant later, he had jammed his hand up her shift, his clammy fingers gripping a breast. Licking the side of her face, the man said into her ear, "You want me inside you again, don't you, honey? Just like last time?" She smelled his rotten breath again, overpowering her, and she screamed.

Victory had never seen Dragomir move so fast.

In one instant, the Emp was standing across the room, righting a table, and in the next, he had the man splayed out on the ground outside, face bleeding, eyes glazed, his arms and legs unresponsive, moaning as he tried to get to his feet. Dragomir kicked him again, all but rolling him under the horse.

"You touch either of these two again," Dragomir snarled, as his big horse danced around the man's head, "And I'm finding you a length of rope and a good solid tree. Now get the hell out of here."

The man rolled, groaning, out into the street, then somehow found his feet and, staggering, wove away from the hovel, looking over his shoulder with a look of real fear pinching his bloody face.

Eyes still on the road, Dragomir helped Victory back to her feet and hugged her close, big arms tight around her back. "You gonna be all right, Princess?" he asked softly, holding her to him. As soon as he said it, Victory felt the warm energy-blanket surrounding her again, and she relaxed into it with a grateful shudder. "You said he's been here before, Dora?" Dragomir asked, frowning as he watched the man limp away.

"Only 'bout three times a month," the weaver said with a grimace. She was still shaking. "Always buys little things, too, like a hat or a pair of socks...kind of like he's makin' an excuse, ya know?"

Above Victory, Dragomir's gaze darkened. He still hadn't released her from his embrace. "How long he been coming to see you?"

"Three or four months," Dora said. "Never thought much of it—I've always had friends over, before. But now…" She wrapped her arms around herself and looked out over the road with a nervous look.

"I should've killed him," Dragomir growled. "He'll be back."

Dora's eyes widened at the Emp, nervousness in her face. "You can See it?"

"You don't get *au* much darker than that," Dragomir said. The Emp cursed. "I'm a coward. I apologize. I would've saved the world a lot of hassle if I'd just quietly finished him and dug him a hole."

Dora scoffed. "A healer doesn't kill people." Then she hesitated, her eyes flickering up and down Dragomir's big form. "Well," she amended, "…in their right minds, they don't kill people. I'll just find someone to stay with me, 'round time for his next drop-in. Maybe get one of the Cooper kids to stay with me…"

Dragomir glanced down at Victory, a thoughtful expression on his face. "I actually think I have something that would work even better than that."

"What?" Dora asked, giving him a suspicious glance. "Look, I told you, Drago, I ain't sleepin' with no Emp in my bedroom. No offense, but that stuff gives me the jitters."

Dragomir heaved a huge sigh. "Don't worry," Dragomir said, "It's someone else. That is, if I can get her to cooperate." He gave Victory a long look, appearing to be in some sort of mental deliberations, then said, "Go get Thor and tell him what happened. Stay with him for a few hours, until I get back. I've gotta go help the Cooper girl. Sounds like she's got pneumonia or something."

Dora cleared her throat, nodded, and ducked into the hovel to grab her coat. As she was leaving, she stopped in the doorway. With a shy grin, the small woman put one hand on Dragomir's big shoulder, stood on her tiptoes, and kissed his cheek. "Thank you, Drago. My Ma always taught me the Universe provides…But I was really getting worried, there for a minute." Then the woman ducked off through the doorway and was halfway out into the yard when she hesitated and turned back, looking at Drago's horse, "So what *did* you come by my place for, anyway?"

Dragomir grunted. "I got two extra people I gotta clothe this winter. Was hoping to come to some sort of trade."

Dora beamed. "I'm always in the market for more wool."

"That's what I was hopin'," Dragomir said, nodding. Then he watched as the weaver turned and disappeared down the road, in the opposite direction as the resistance fighter.

After a moment, still holding Victory tight against his chest, Dragomir looked down at her and said, "You feeling better, Princess?"

"He was one of them," Victory whispered, still holding the Emp tightly around the waist. "One of the ones who paid for…" She swallowed and buried her face in his chest, unable to say it. "…when I was chained to the pole." With his warm arms holding her, Victory felt her terror slowly wash away under her relief, and, still shaking, began to whimper into his shirt. "Please don't sell me to him."

"Gods, girl," Dragomir growled softly, "I'd never do such a thing. You said it yourself. The chain's a show. Keeps your pretty butt from running off and getting lost in the woods, or maybe doing something stupid like freeing Lion before I'm ready. I'd never put you in the hands of that monster."

"You could let me go," Victory whimpered.

Dragomir tensed. "Not yet."

"Why not?" she asked, looking up at him through tears.

"Well, for one," Dragomir said, "If you'd been more than eight feet away just now, that pig might have had his way with you." He wiped a tear from her cheek, his blue eyes kind. "Besides. There's a few things I've still gotta do to you that you're probably not gonna like." He pushed her hair out of her face, helped her re-settle her rumpled shift.

"What things?" Victory asked miserably, her body still trembling with leftover adrenaline and horror.

Giving her a tired smile, he said, "Healing things. I'll let you loose when I'm done. You have my word." Then, carefully setting her upright, he stepped past her and began unwinding his horse's reins from the post. "Let's go check the Cooper kid, okay? That's giving me a bad feeling."

Victory nodded, numbly, and followed him as he collected the boy Fell, his goat, and his mule-drawn cart from the market, who in turn led them to a dirt road that followed the river to the west. She tagged along behind in silence, thinking about what had transpired in the weaver's hut.

"You gonna be okay?" Dragomir asked softly, after awhile. The boy with his mule, easily ten yards ahead, couldn't have heard him over the creaking wagon and the squawking of chickens.

"He recognized me," Victory said, remembering the hunger in the man's eyes, the feel of his tongue against her cheek.

Dragomir sighed and looked at the road. "I should've killed him." He said nothing more until they rounded a bend and she found them approaching a small collection of shacks and lean-tos. Chickens, loose and in cages, pecking at the dirt under the watchful eyes of a dozen children, were everywhere.

"The Cooper place," Dragomir said, by way of introduction.

Once they were in sight of the main hovel, the boy Fell dropped the lead on the mule and ran toward the huts, screaming, "Momma! Momma! I brought the healer!"

And then suddenly they were being overwhelmed by children. At least a dozen of them ran up as they approached, carting toys or chores along with them, laughing and asking questions all at once. With them came a pack of big black mutts, who seemed caught between barking and wagging their shaggy tails, and eventually settled for slinking in and wrapping themselves around Dragomir's feet. It got to be so congested that all forward motion came to a stop, and Victory was finding herself besieged by curious blue-eyed youngsters, all of whom wanted to ask her questions like, "So how did you become a slave?"

A matronly bellow from the front house sent the kids scattering, and Victory found herself able to breathe again as Dragomir proceeded to the front door, leaving his horse to drink from the rain barrel outside.

"Thank the gods," the big, round woman cried, rushing up and slapping into Dragomir with a big-breasted hug. Victory decided she had to be in her late forties, only about five and a half feet tall, and weighed at least two-sixty. "I didn't want to disturb you so soon after you got back," the woman babbled, "But Rachel's in bad need, Mr. Shipborn. Praise Fell, the little devil. I told him not to bother you with it."

"Sometimes Life leads us where we need to go," Dragomir said. "Let me see her."

The big Mrs. Cooper started to lead him inside, then looked down at the chain linking him to Victory. "Will you be bringing the girl with you? Can't you leave her outside?"

Dragomir gave the woman a wistful grin. "Unfortunately, not yet. Maybe in a month or two."

A month?! Victory's stunned mind sputtered. Narrowing her eyes at Dragomir's back, she said in Imperial, "You don't *actually* think you're gonna last that long before Matthias finds me and he hooks you and your brother up to a cart for the rest of your miserable lives, do you?"

When Dragomir glanced back, curious, Victory gave him a smile. She repeated it in four different languages, for his convenience, none of which got more than a blank stare from their recipient.

The dark look that the matronly woman gave her, however, made Victory forget to use the last three languages.

"I don't like her," Mrs. Cooper said, meeting Victory's eyes unflinchingly.

Dragomir sighed. "Many people don't." He gestured into the hovel. "Where is Rachel?"

The woman continued to give Victory a disapproving frown, then turned and led them inside.

In one of the back rooms, surrounded by more worried-looking children, a filthy girl of maybe thirteen or fourteen was lying on a cot, wrapped in too many blankets, her face pale and sweat-slicked, her eyes darting under closed lids. Every breath seemed to be a struggle for her, coming in a low, rattling rasp, and she was shivering visibly.

"Oh gods," Dragomir said, kneeling beside the child. "You should have brought me in here as soon as I got off the ship. She's *dying.*"

Victory saw fear pass through Mrs. Cooper's Life-toughened face before she got it back under control. "Is there anything you can do for her?"

"There is," Dragomir said, glancing at Victory, "But I'm going to need a ride home afterwards and someone to care for my goats for a day or two."

"You've got it," Mrs. Cooper said firmly. "Do whatever you can. I'll send a couple of the boys." Then she rounded on the dozens of faces cramming into doors, windows, hallways. "And the rest of you...*out!* What are you trying to do...smother him? The healer needs his space!" Immediately, the room erupted in shuffling pandemonium as children scattered.

Dragomir took a deep breath and returned his attention to the child. Closing his eyes, he rested one hand on her chest, the other on her stomach. Absolute silence permeated the room, broken only by the rattling wheeze of the girl on the bed.

For a long moment, nothing seemed to happen.

Then, suddenly, the girl choked and went stiff, her breath seemingly cut off in her throat. For what seemed like minutes, the girl didn't breathe. Mrs. Cooper wrung her hands, tears touching her harsh face as she hovered over the bed, waiting.

"Was it too late?" Mrs. Cooper finally whispered, when there was no change.

Dragomir, eyes still closed, frowned and gave a slight shake of his head. He was sweating, his hands starting to shake where he held them on her body.

Then, suddenly, the girl gasped.

It was a deep, gut-sucking wrench of air that was suddenly filling the room with the sound of rattling wet slime. She sat up, suddenly, and started coughing, a deep whooping sound that deposited bloody, yellow-green mucous on the floor beside her bed. And she kept coughing. It came up in waves, like a drowning person spitting out water, hitting the ground in audible *plops*, making a pile of the stuff the size of three of Victoria's fists.

Dragomir watched just long enough for the girl to open her wide blue eyes and give him a startled look before he slumped over backwards, a tired half-smile on his unconscious face.

"Rachel!" Mrs. Cooper rushed forward and pulled the girl off of the bed, into her arms. Cradling her, she started to cry, and the girl weakly reached up and started hugging her back, looking confused and startled and more than a bit frightened.

Victory couldn't take her eyes off of the bloody pile of hard, globular mucous. *That is not possible*, her Imperium-trained brain thought. *Nothing can do that.*

And yet, she was looking at the evidence, right here on the dirt floor of a chicken-farmer's hovel.

When I am Adjudicator, Victory realized, *I am going to hunt down every Emp on the planet…*She looked at Dragomir, who was even then snoring, one knee cocked in a painful-looking angle underneath him.…*and I'm going to have him teach them.*

"Boys!" Mrs. Cooper shouted, making Fell and a younger brother—the only two who had been allowed to stay in the room—jerk. "Get Erik and Todd in here. Tell them they're gonna take Mr. Shipborn back home."

The boys jumped up and darted out, their eyes still wide at the pile on the floor.

A minute later, two lean, yet strong-looking adolescents arrived. They saw the Emp on the floor, then their sister in their mother's arms, and relief washed over their dirty faces. "He healed her, didn't he?" one of them cried, kneeling beside the cot.

"Todd, Erik, get Mr. Shipborn out on the cart and take him home," Mrs. Cooper said. "He's gonna need some rest. Stay as long as he needs, feed his chickens and goats, and don't come back until he tells you to leave." Lifting her voice, she shouted into the hall, "*Boys!* Get your sister some water and eggs! *Now!*"

The one kneeling beside his sister turned and gave Victory a suspicious look. "What do we do with *her*?"

For the first time since she'd used five different languages to tell Dragomir how unpleasant his life would be in the next couple weeks, the Cooper matron turned to Victory. Seeing the coldness in the woman's eyes, Victory cringed.

"Watch her," Mrs. Cooper said. "She runs off—or hurts him in any way—it's your heads."

"Yes, Mother," the boy on the floor muttered, getting off his knees.

Then the true seriousness of the situation dawned upon Victory. She was going to be alone with two young men, without Dragomir or her

Praetorian to protect her. She cringed away from them, her chain yanking her up short.

"And girl," Mrs. Cooper said, looking over the whimpering body of her daughter, "Just to be clear…You hurt that man—in *any* way—and I will hunt you down until my dying day to bring you to justice. He's a treasure. Even a damned Royal Princess would see that."

Victory pretended she couldn't understand, giving the woman as small smile and a nod, but ice was creeping up her spine. She looked again at the pile of mucous on the floor. *She can't know who I am*, she thought. *It's just a figure of speech.* But, looking again into the woman's icy blue eyes, she couldn't be sure.

"Get her out of here," Mrs. Cooper said. "And *boys!*" she shouted into the hall. "*Food! Water!*"

"Yes, Mother!" a dozen voices called in unison.

Then Victory watched as the two adolescents hefted Dragomir off of the ground and carried him out to the cart. The mangy mule was still where the boy had left it, sniffing at a chicken that was pecking at its hoof.

They cleared the chicken cages—and the inevitable chicken fertilizer—out of the cart and gently lowered the unconscious Emp into the back. Then they went and got pillows and blankets and wrapped him up like a baby in swaddling-cloths before grabbing the reins and clucking to the mule, turning it around. One of the boys ran and grabbed Thunder from where he was eating grass at the rain-barrel and came jogging to catch up with the cart.

"And *give his damn goat back to him, for the gods' sakes!*" Mrs. Cooper shouted from the doorway.

Ducking low, the boy leading the mule hurried to snatch up the goat's lead from a couple girls that were trying to force-feed it grass by the river, then tied it to the back of the wagon, beside Victory.

Some of the children followed them to the bend in the road before Mrs. Cooper's bellow sent them scurrying back home. Then they were alone, Victory trodding behind the cart, trying to stay invisible.

After awhile, one of the boys turned to look at her over his shoulder. He nudged his brother, who turned to look with him. Victory froze, and would have yanked Dragomir out of the cart, had he not been so damn heavy. As it was, she stumbled along behind, cringing under their gazes.

But to her surprise, the kid's voice was gentle when he said, "Jeez, she looks like she thinks we're gonna skin her alive."

His brother glanced back and Victory saw compassion there. "Probably does."

"I wonder what she did," the first boy said.

"Taxes, probably." The kid snorted, disgust clear in his voice.

His brother's face grew dark and he turned back to the road. "Poor thing. Wonder what Drago plans to do with her."

"Dunno," the brother said, "But he wouldn't hurt a fly. Probably gonna try to teach her to run goats or something."

Victory shuddered. A goatherd. Right.

They didn't say much of anything else until they got back through the village and were approaching Dragomir's gate. The boy leading the horse came to walk behind the cart with her, looking her over carefully. Victory cringed and backed as far away from him as the chain would allow.

"You, uh, understand me?" the boy asked, his blue eyes looking nervous.

Victory kept her mouth shut, watching him, trying not to let her anxiousness show.

As his brother opened the gate, the boy cleared his throat and continued, "Uh, well, if you can, I wanted to tell you it wouldn't be so bad, if the healer had a girl. He's been, uh, pretty rough since his last girl died. That whole hiker killing her, and all…" He scanned her face, then sighed. "Okay, well, just take care of him. He's a good man." He reached out to gently pat her shoulder.

Victory frowned at him. Reluctantly, she said, "He told me he healed that girl."

The boy's eyes widened, and the brother at the gate stopped to turn back to her in shock. The one standing beside her chuckled nervously and rubbed the back of his neck. "She can talk," he said, making an uncomfortable laugh.

"He said she lived," Victory insisted.

233

The boy beside her glanced anxiously at his brother. "Well, uh, not really. The Praetorian caught him and Meggie on a hillside, beat him half to death and took Meggie in front of him, then shot her in the head. Dragomir brought her back here, tried for days to revive her. Finally went into town, covered in blood, and took Greg Braddock's gun out of his house. Put it to his own head, pulled the trigger before anyone could stop him."

Victory frowned, remembering the streak of white along the side of Dragomir's right temple. "So *that's* what that is..." she whispered. "His scar."

"Shoulda died," the brother at the fence said. "Even Mom said he shoulda died."

"Somethin' kept him alive," the closer brother agreed. "Ma says it wasn't his time." He lifted the gate latch and let them inside.

"And he healed fast, too," the boy beside her added. "Way too fast. Ask Thor. Like you could almost see his head closing up."

"Yeah," his brother agreed. "He was only out a few days, and when he came to, he started healing himself just like he healed Rachel tonight. Real angry-like. Nothing scary as a pissed-off Emp, lemme tell you. That Praetorian only had a week-long head start before Drago was packed up and out after him."

"Brought back his head," the nearest boy said, full of teenage awe. "Killed him with his bare hands."

Victory snorted. "He said he shot him a few times, first."

The Cooper boys looked at her, then both began laughing at the same time. "Uh, no," the one at the gate chuckled. "He didn't."

"Yeah," his brother agreed. "Only gun in the town belongs to Greg Braddock, and Greg had it on him all the time after Drago tried to kill himself. He sure as *hell* wasn't letting him near it again, not so soon after Meggie. I mean, the healer? Killin' hisself on your gun? You'd be thrown outta the village in a second flat."

Dragomir didn't use a gun to kill the Praetorian? Victory frowned. "So he used a bow?"

The closer boy shrugged. "Doubt it. He went up there to die. Everybody knew it, but nobody could stop him."

"All *I* saw on him was a knife," the boy in the lead said. "And he came back with a head."

"Yeah," the boy agreed, nodding, his eyes growing distant as he watched old memory replay in front of them. "Came back with a *head*." He was obviously impressed.

"Braddock made him burn it," the boy in the lead said. "But he had it on his front door for awhile. Let the crows pick the eyeballs out."

The closer boy nodded. "Yeah. The *eyeballs*."

"And he stopped washing or eating, too," the boy leading the cart added, really starting to get into the story, now. "Just came out every morning to sit on the porch and stare at the head. Momma said he was goin' crazy, and Dad had to help Thor and a couple other guys drag him down to the river and bathe."

Suddenly, from the trail behind them, a big male voice boomed, "I ain't gonna have to tell your mother you two boys're tellin' stories that ain't none of your business, am I?"

Both of the boys went crimson and spun to face Thor. "She asked about Drago and the head," the boy at the gate said meekly.

Thor strode up, Whip on the end of his leash. His eyes were fixed on Dragomir, and he was frowning. "What happened to the poor sot this time?"

"He healed Rachel," the boy holding the horse said instantly. "Made her cough up a pile of snot."

"Yeah, *snot*," his brother affirmed.

Thor sighed and put a hand to his brother's head. He winced, obviously not liking what he found there. "Well, thanks for bringing him home. I'll take the fool inside."

"Momma told us to stay," one of the boys said, warily glancing at the other. "To feed goats and such, until he was on his feet again and told us to leave."

"I'm telling you to leave," Thor growled. He reached down and, as easily as if he were picking up a sack of potatoes, threw the huge man over his shoulder. "Go on home. Get yourselves some dinner."

The brother's looked at each other, then the one at the gate said nervously, "Uh, if it's the same to you, Mr. Shipborn, we'd rather just stay here until he tells us to leave. Ma's in a mood." Beside him, his brother vigorously nodded his agreement.

Thor looked at them a long moment, then heaved a huge sigh. "Fine, but you'll be sleeping on the floor. You know the shoddy shape of the place, since he lost Meggie. Probably won't be a spare blanket in the house."

"We brought blankets," one of them said, gesturing to the cart.

Thor grunted, then turned and carried Dragomir into the house. Victory, still attached to the chain around his waist, had no choice but to follow.

Thor carried the Emp through the hovel, down the hall, and into the tiny bedroom. With all the gentleness one would give a sack of potatoes, he dropped Dragomir into the bed, then yanked the cover around him. He gave Victory a warning look. "You be on your best behavior, missy. Just because he's helpless, it ain't mean he ain't got plenty of help, right outside this door." He gestured to the hall leading into the bedroom. "And before you ask, no, I don't know where the fool put the key, or I'd just free your idiot self and let you go run off and get yourself killed in the woods. Save us all a lot of heartache." His blue eyes were intense. "Get me?"

Victory swallowed and nodded.

Thor grunted. "Wasn't my idea to drop you out here, and it sure as hell isn't my idea to keep you, so just be grateful you're alive and breathing, keep your mouth shut, and let him get some sleep. I'll bring in some dinner in a bit." At that, he got up and left, leaving Victory alone with the sleeping Emp.

CHAPTER 14

A Plan Foiled

Adjudicator Keene followed the guards down a long, dark passageway, then waited as they stopped and unlocked a darkened cell. "Lights," he said.

Immediately, the lights flickered on, illuminating the tiny stone cubicle and its bleary-eyed-yet-defiant occupant.

"So, I assume by now that you've figured out that I figured out what you did," Adjudicator Keene told his son. He stepped within the cell walls and leaned against the bars, crossing his arms over his chest. "Did you actually think for a minute that I wouldn't?"

His son stared at him with a look of shock that Adjudicator Keene found amusing. "Then you plan to hand me over to the Imperium?" the boy babbled. More cowardly than Keene would have liked in a son, but at least he would be cooperative.

Idly tracing a finger down one of the grimy cell bars, Keene said, "No need for that. I'll free you the moment you tell me where you're hiding your sister."

"I don't know what you're talking about," Prince Matthias lied. He got to his feet, the chain from his wrist-shackles dragging upon the ground. "My sister is dead." There was an odd tone to his son's voice, and for a moment, Adjudicator Keene had to wonder if this pathetic, scared-looking kid was really his son.

"I think we both know that's not true," Adjudicator Keene said. "Stop wasting our time, Matthias. What did you do with her?"

"She fell in the Boiling Rift."

So the boy *did* know. Smiling, Adjudicator Keene cocked his head. "And how would you know that, if you hadn't conspired to rescue her?"

Matthias quickly looked away. Was he *afraid?* Again, Adjudicator Keene had the odd feeling that he were talking to an imposter, not his strong-willed son. But then again, fear was a welcome sign. There were many things that Keene could do with fear. "So," Adjudicator Keene said, examining his fingernails. "I've had the palace thoroughly searched, and found nothing except a few of her Praetorian, which have been subsequently imprisoned." He gestured at the other cells. "Right down the hall, in fact."

That got through to his son. He saw a flash of despair, then it was quickly hidden again by hot, seething anger. "You'll never find her, worm."

Worm. That was a new one. Adjudicator Keene actually found himself surprised at his son's impetuousness, especially considering his rather hopeless situation. "So," he said, "Since we're both aware that your plans failed, and that your poor, dimwitted sister can no more orchestrate your freedom than she can pop a chambermaid's cherry, it is my hope that you will see the stupidity behind your actions these last few days and simply relent to the fact that I *will* find your sister, and she *will* die, and the sooner she does, the sooner I will let you return to your normal duties."

His son stared at him. "My normal duties?"

"Of course. You are training to be an Adjudicator. I must have someone to take my place when I pass."

But Matthias scowled. "You think I'm betraying my sister so I can go back to being your lap-dog."

Adjudicator Keene gave his son a patronizing look. "Have you ever entertained the idea that you weren't?" He snorted. "Really. I thought you were smarter than that, Matthias."

Matthias looked away, looking almost cowed. "Get out. I'll sit down here and rot before I see Victory killed."

Again, his response set off alarms in Adjudicator Keene's mind. Matthias was smarter than this…wasn't he? Adjudicator Keene frowned at his son, his eyes seeking out the nervous sweat draining down the child's cheeks, his face as open and as readable as a book. Reluctantly, Keene came to the unhappy decision that the boy was not as well-suited to the throne as he had thought. "You disappoint me, Matthias. A ruler needs to know when he's defeated. He must learn to make rational decisions. This…" he gestured at the cold stone around them, the shackles, the bars, "…is not rational."

Matthias snorted and said, "You never understood anything but your accounts."

Which was bothering him. Adjudicator Keene frowned at his son. "Why has she not accessed her accounts?" He could find her in an *instant* if she would just break down and buy some bauble, some tiny luxury…

Despite his fear, Matthias's look gave no more away about his mental state of mind than had Adjudicator Keene been looking into the eyes of a stone tiger. "I'd rather *die* than tell you anything to betray my sister."

And he meant it.

Keene blinked at his son, anger slowly taking the place of surprise. It was unfortunate, but the boy would have to die. Adjudicator Keene couldn't entrust his empire to someone so short-sighted, so wrapped up in emotion that he couldn't observe the obvious. Mercy's economy depended on slavery, and a soft heart would make that system crumble completely. Keene would simply have to find someone else to fill the boy's shoes.

Still, he needed to find the girl and eliminate her, lest she pop back up unexpectedly a second time. He was still trying to understand how she'd survived the first time. If nothing else, it seemed his daughter had a penchant for survival, which was, to say the least, annoying. That he *still* hadn't found her was beginning to grate.

Musing to himself, now, Adjudicator Keene said, "I found the mine where you stashed the passengers and had your co-conspirators in the town executed. I found the ship you used to deliver her to her destination, and while you cleverly removed the locator beacon and all flight recording equipment, it had been recently refueled, and the log suggested that it was some distance away, if the trip to the Boiling Rift was taken into account."

His son's face tightened, but he looked away, saying nothing.

Keene frowned, thinking. "The ship was atmo-only, so unless you delivered her across the planet to some crudely-fashioned space-pad, she is still on Mercy. But where? I found eleven of her twenty Praetorian, and am sure to find the last nine in the next couple days. That means, somewhere on this rock, there is a princess without her royal guard. One would think that such a princess, with nowhere to go, would tap into her old accounts to keep herself surrounded by the luxuries she was used to."

When Matthias said nothing, he gave his son a long, considering look. "Yet she has made no charges to her accounts, and yours have been seized. This means she has a friend upon the planet. A wealthy man—or possibly a woman, considering her condition—who is keeping her relatively comfortable enough that she has not yet attempted to access any of her funds."

"Neither of your children are as stupid as you would assume," his son said.

"Oh?" Adjudicator Keene leaned back, listening, having long ago learned that, rather than pepper the guilty with questions, it was better to allow them to speak their piece. They almost always gave away key facts in their feeble attempts to defend their actions.

"No," Matthias said, smiling. "We're not." He offered nothing more.

Disappointed, Adjudicator Keene nonetheless tried to keep it from showing. "This friend she is staying with. I've already run down the lists and found no one that matches. None of the noble houses have taken a new maid. None of the large merchants have taken on a new trades-woman. It's like she simply disappeared."

Matthias snorted, and leaned back against the opposite wall with a smug look.

Adjudicator Keene found himself irritated with his son's insolence. "You don't actually think that, wherever you have hidden her, she can stay there for long, do you? A princess has expensive tastes. She's going to betray herself sooner or later. The Constable of Numbers has her account flagged. As soon as the soft, silly-minded fool breaks down and tries to improve her lot with a few credits here, a few credits there, she's going to get caught, dragged back to the palace, and publicly executed." He scoffed. "Besides…A noblewoman who is terrified of men will stand out in cultured society. I have my men combing the cities, looking for her. There's nowhere she can hide."

Matthias continued to look smug.

Adjudicator Keene narrowed his eyes. "Regardless of what you think, Matthias, you are not going to be rescued." *Or survive your sister's capture, for that matter.*

His son raised an arrogant brow. "I'm not?"

Adjudicator Keene felt his blood pressure rising. Despite his every efforts to find Victoria, his men had all come back empty-handed, and it made no sense to him. He didn't like it when things did not make sense. Life was a game of math. After all the little additions and subtractions had been tallied together, the sum should remain in balance. This was not balanced. Growling, he said, "You will *die* down here, boy, if you do not help me."

"Oh?" Matthias asked, shifting against the wall. He appeared bored.

Adjudicator Keene snarled a curse at the boy's conceit. "You do not have as much control over your own men as you might think, boy. I have several operatives in high places in your army—one who sits at your very own table. How else do you think I thwarted your plan?"

Matthias only smiled at him. "Who says it's been thwarted?"

For a brief moment, Adjudicator Keene felt a bolt of panic, wondering if there were something he had overlooked. Then he narrowed his eyes, realizing that, chained in his dungeon, the boy could only be bluffing. "I can have my Inquisitors cut the information from your skin, if I need to, boy."

"Father," his son calmly said, dropping his air of sneering arrogance as if it had never been, "In the last ten minutes, you have told me how little you really know about my plan, what crude methods you've used to determine where Victory might be, how many Praetorian are still in the palace, the fact that you have absolutely no idea where my sister is, and that that fact scares the piss out of you."

He played *me?* Adjudicator Keene thought, watching his son's calm confidence in disbelief. *All that was an* act?

Matthias smiled, his green eyes flashing. "Oh, and it also told me that you don't actually plan on letting me out of here. You're desperate because she's eluding you. It's the only reason you'd resort to threats, much less come down here to speak with me personally, when you find the experience so distasteful."

As Adjudicator Keene found himself unable to do anything but gape at his son, Matthias cocked his head at him, smiling. "You always did tell me that silence was more productive than words, Father."

Adjudicator Keene stumbled backwards out of the cage, staring at his son in horror.

The goosebumps on his arms and the odd tingling at the back of his neck made him want to order the boy's execution, *now*. Something was wrong, here, and the feeling that Keene was looking at someone other than his son was a thousand times stronger, now.

You made him, Keene, his own mind chided. *You spent the last twenty-two years shaping him to your image.*

Peering at the boy, Adjudicator Keene again wondered if the boy could possibly have planned everything so far.

He isn't intelligent enough for that, Adjudicator Keene finally decided. It was a shame, but the boy and his sister simply did not have a First Generation's analytical capability. The Royal blood had diluted with his Fourth Generation wife.

Even back then, he had known he should have taken a First or Second Generation Royal to mate, but emotion had gotten into the way and blinded him. Now he was left dealing with the consequences.

Grimly, he decided that it was not too late to find himself a First Generation Royal, certified as a First by the Imperium, rather than a woman whose mother claimed a Third, without even real proof. He was rather sure he could attract a decent mate, even this late in life. Mercy was a miserable ball of rock without even a respectable ocean, but it was lucrative. He could attract a woman on the sheer numbers, alone.

And, once he did, he would go about rectifying the situation with new heirs. This time, of course, he would give her a clinical pregnancy, with male children only. Then, once the new Empress had served her purpose and given him two new children—hopefully in the same birth, to save time—she would have to follow in the footsteps of her prede-cessors. It was a shame to waste the genetic material of a good First Generation, but females, as Victoria and her mother had proven many times, were simply too soft to rule.

Without a word to his guards, Keene turned and stalked from the dungeon.

CHAPTER 15

The Womb Rama

D ragomir opened his eyes to the sound of birds chirping in the trees outside. Sun was streaming through the window, warming the bare earth and shelves that had been cooled by the night before.

Groaning, Dragomir moved his arm to get up, but froze when he found something beneath it. Lifting his head, he gingerly peeled the covers back.

Victory was there, her back to his front, snuggled tight to him, asleep.

By the gods' hairy backs, Dragomir thought, staring at the sleeping princess. He lowered the blanket gingerly, leaving only her face exposed. Settling his head back to the pillow, he watched her, feeling a glow starting in his heart rama, spreading throughout his chest. Even if she didn't want to admit it now, she trusted him.

At least, he amended, getting goosebumps where his arm was exposed to the sharp cold of morning, *Enough to crawl under a cover to stay warm.*

• • •

Victory opened her eyes to sun streaming through the window. She'd been sleeping a lot, lately, with very little else to do. A couple times,

Thor had brought her some project—like washing eggs or pulling brambles out of the woolly fur he had sheared off of one of the fuzzy, long-haired goats—but the majority of her time had been with her sitting on the bed, bored.

That, and sleeping.

She had tried to spend the first night on the floor, but after an entire sleepless night of shivering—and Thor laughing at her for it in the morning—she had finally decided to start curling up with the Emp. The others' somewhat rabid faith that he would never hurt a fly contrasted sharply with the fact that he had apparently beat a man to death with his own bloody knuckles, and then lied to her about it, but in the end, Victory decided to take her chances. It got *cold* in the mountains at night, and these peasants apparently didn't have enough stone to build fire-places in every room.

Or buy window-panes, for that matter. The gaping hole in the wall where a window should have been was irritating to Victory. Why not just wall it off to conserve heat? Why not build shutters, at the very least? If they were going to leave such huge, gaping holes in the walls, why not simply drag the bed out into the fields and sleep with the goats?

She sighed, deeply. Perhaps he simply didn't know how to properly build windows. Perhaps he was just—

"Did you sleep well?" The low, masculine voice came from the pillow not three inches from the back of her head.

Victory shrieked and tried to roll away, but he had locked his big arm around her waist, trapping her to his body. She panted, once again feeling every hard line of his muscular form, and where it touched her, and how. Unbidden, she felt herself shudder at the heat that automatically began to build in her loins.

"You ready for the next rama, Princess?" he asked softly. She felt the gentle rumble of his chest against her back. His big hand settled on her lower abdomen.

"No," Victory whimpered, already acutely aware of the unwanted changes from the first rama. "I'm fine. Really."

"You're not fine," he whispered to her. "I can see that much every time I look at you, and I'm going to help."

As she felt the warmth start to build under his hand, she whimpered.

He made a soft sound, soothing. "Not going to hurt you," he whispered. "It will be like last time. The pressure will build, likely start to hurt, then the rama will snap open. You'll face all those moments that blocked the flow of gi through its center, experience them over again, and then release them. I'll be here the whole time."

"I don't *want* to experience them again!" Victory cried, trying to struggle away again.

But his arm might as well have been made of titanium for all the budge it gave. "It's going to make you feel better, Princess," he swore, "I promise."

After another few moments of struggle, she eventually dropped back to the bed in resignation. Victory found herself staring at the window, tense, as the warmth began to build within her womb, heating and spreading outwards until her whole abdomen felt like someone had dropped a hot coal amidst her guts. "It hurts," she whimpered, but she didn't try to fight him again. The sensation was so deeply intimate, leaving her feeling so terrifyingly exposed.

"I'm a healer," he whispered, as the pressure built. "I'll be here, and this is going to make you feel better. Trust me."

And then, just like last time, the dam broke. She felt the energy rush into her body, the images once again clogging up her mind.

Her father, giving her a disappointed scowl when she showed him her first picture, in wax-stick. *"Don't you have problem sets to be doing, girl?"*

Her father, yanking her half-finished afghan from her lap and throwing it into the fire. *"You will not waste your time on such useless projects in my house."*

Her father, taking her journal from her when he discovered she was writing stories in it. *"Kiara told you no fiction. A ruler does not have the leisure to engage in such frivolousness. Learn that, or you will never touch a writing instrument again."* He had then taken the electronic device and smashed it once against his desk, cracking the screen in half, then threw it out the window, to dash against the Gorgarian Cliffs below.

Her captors, mistaking her poetry scribbles on the sides of her cell for messages for help. Beating her until blood was running from her mouth and she couldn't move. Making her wash them off afterwards with broken fingers.

A stone-faced native doctor, reaching inside her, pulling her baby free, dropping it, still kicking, into the trash.

Like last time, Victory found herself turned to his chest, sobbing in the Emp's arms as the wave of images finally swept away, leaving anguish and horror in their place.

"Why?" she whimpered, as he held her.

"I had to, sweet." There was a tremble in his voice this time. When she looked, she saw tears in his blue eyes. He gingerly reached up and moved a strand of hair from her face. His hand was shaking. She saw the sincerity in his eyes when he said, "I want you to be whole."

He means it, she thought, shocked. Suddenly, all the torments, all the discomforts and inconveniences took on a new meaning. *He wants to help me.*

Then, *Why? All I've done is make him miserable.*

A little discomfited, Victory closed her eyes and just allowed him to hold her, finding strength in the solidness of his body, calm in the rise and fall of his chest. He hadn't really hurt her, she realized. Throughout it all, he hadn't given her any reason to distrust him. And, while the memories had opened a wound in her mind that she had hoped never to revisit, the constant tightness in her lower abdomen was gone, leaving her feeling freer than she had in years.

"Thank you," she whispered into his chest.

She felt him tighten his embrace and let out a breath he had been holding. For several breaths, he said nothing. Then, softly, "Don't thank me until I'm finished. It's going to be…difficult…for you. You have three ramas left. Throat, heart, and liver."

Victory said nothing. She was thinking about the fistfuls of hard, clumpy mucous, sliding from the girl's throat, plopping onto the floor. *He's a healer,* she thought. *He's not going to hurt me.*

Softly, she said, "You can take the chain off, now."

Though she didn't open her eyes, she felt Dragomir look at her. She felt his internal struggle as he considered. Then, like a mountain moving, he rolled, still holding her, and reached under the bed, his fingers following the wooden frame that held the mattress. When he rolled back, he had two tiny brass keys in his hand.

Victory stared at the tiny piece of toothed brass. "You had it all this time…?" Mouth open, she glanced at the edge of the bed. "Right *there?*"

He grinned, his cerulean eyes twinkling. In reply, he stuck the key into the padlock and twisted. The chain fell to the bed between them. Gently, he unhooked the loop of the lock from the collar at her throat, then set it on the bed between them. He then proceeded to remove the chain from his body and set it aside.

"There," he said, sounding nervous. "I'm trusting you, now."

Victory looked up, feeling tears biting at her cheeks. "Thank you."

Then Dragomir's face hardened. "But if you do anything stupid, like try to free Lion—"

She laughed and hugged him, then, relief taking the place of her tears. Reluctantly, Dragomir wrapped his arms back around her, bringing her tight against his chest. "I'm serious," he grumbled. "You're not healed yet, and it would be detrimental to your recovery if your healer suddenly found a sword lodged in his chest."

"From what I hear, you would probably survive it," Victory said, giggling, remembering the gunshot scar.

But Dragomir stiffened above her. "*What* did you say?"

Frowning at his tone, Victory said, "The two Cooper boys were just telling me about how you tried to kill yourself after Megg—"

Dragomir released her with a roar and got out of bed.

"Where are you going?" Victory cried.

But he was already gone, his big back disappearing down the hall. A moment later, she heard him boom, "Todd! Erik! Get your skinny asses back home and out of my house! *Now!* Before I tan the *both* of you, you gossiping little bastards!"

"Sorry, Mr. Shipborn!" Victory heard the thunder of running feet and the startled snort of a mule. Then the cart, creaking as it rumbled over rocks and ruts.

Frowning, she got up and looked out the window.

The Cooper boys were leading the mule toward the fence at a jog, looking over their shoulders like they were afraid Death himself were going to change his mind and come devour their souls. A little curious, Victory followed Dragomir down the hall.

The Emp was pacing the living-room, snarling under his breath, as his brother looked on. Then, seeing Victory, he slumped into a chair beside Lion, gave the Praetorian a dark look, and then glowered at the open door.

"She was going to find out sooner or later," Thor said. He shrugged. "So you lost your mind a little…It happens."

"Shut up," Dragomir growled. Then he lifted his gaze, his blue eyes settling on Victory. "You hungry?" he barked.

A little startled, Victory nodded.

"Eggs or potatoes?" he growled.

The way he said it, he might as well have been asking if she wanted her hand cut off and fed to her in individual digits or in large chunks.

"Um," Victory said, "Large chunks."

Dragomir blinked at her, his anger dropping away suddenly in his confusion. "What?"

Victory, realizing what she'd said, blushed hard. "Um. I mean eggs. Please. Sir."

Dragomir's eyes narrowed at the last. Even his brother's head jerked up to frown at Victory. They stared at her so long that Victory felt squished under their combined gazes.

"Did she just call you '*sir*'?" Thor finally asked. His face was wrought with disbelief.

"It's a form of polite address!" Victory cried, keeping her spine as straight as possible. She also would *never* consider using it on a no-status native covered in dirt and sweat whose greatest asset was a herd of mangy, flea-bitten goats, but quietly kept that to herself. "It connotes respect."

Dragomir continued to scowl at her, as did his brother.

"It's true!" she cried, when it was obvious they did not believe her. She did everything she could not to squirm under their gazes.

Finally, peering at her, Thor said, "I think she's hiding something."

"Damn straight she is," Dragomir said, frowning. "I don't think she's been polite to me since her brother dumped me in her room in chains."

Victory lifted her chin. "We came to an agreement," she said. She gestured at her neck and his waist. "You would stop being an uncouth cad, and I would stop treating you like one."

Thor chortled. Looking at his brother, he said, "Sorry, Princess, but if you think he's given up his cadly ways, you're in for a pretty big shock."

But Dragomir grunted, the suspicion fading from his face. Heaving himself onto his feet, he went to the stove, where there were several eggs sitting on a towel. The ubiquitous boiled potatoes were sitting nearby, along with the sack of salt and a bowl of congealed fat. Dragomir slapped a spoonful of fat into the frying pan. Then picking up an egg, turned to Thor. "You and yours had breakfast yet?" He indicated Whip, who was sitting quietly on the couch, watching the exchange with alert gray eyes.

"Was about to have the boys make us some food," Thor said. "But you got to them first."

Victory caught Dragomir's glance at her over his shoulder, the tenseness in his shoulders before he turned away again. He cracked several more eggs in silence before he growled, "How much did they tell her?"

"From what I heard, most of it," Thor said. He glanced at Victory. "'Cept for the part where you went dangling from a tree. Twice."

"Gods *damn* it, Thor!" Dragomir slammed a big hand into the counter. Scowling at his brother over a shoulder, he snarled, "Go check the herd while I make breakfast." It wasn't a request.

Sighing, Thor eased his huge body out of the chair, gave his brother a shake of his head, and strode out the door, leaving Whip and Lion seated together in the squalid living-room.

Cursing, Dragomir went back to cracking eggs.

"Why were you hanging from a tree?" Victory asked.

Dragomir's hand hesitated above the skillet, the egg in his palm unbroken. After a moment, he cracked it, then dumped it into the pan with the rest. "Not important," he muttered.

Remembering what Dragomir had told the resistance fighter about stringing men up by their testicles, she narrowed her eyes. "You rape a girl?"

Dragomir twisted, eyes wide with shock. "What?"

Victory gestured in the direction of Sodstone. "You said the people of this village hang rapists up by their balls."

Understanding washed across Dragomir's face. He shook his head and went back to preparing their meal.

"Then what?" Victory demanded. "Why would they hang you from a—"

"He tried to kill himself again," Thor said, his big body leaning against the frame of the door. "Only like the tenth time after Meggie."

"*Thor*!" Dragomir snarled at his brother, his gaze deadly.

Thor shrugged. "She's gonna find out eventually." To Victory, he continued, "Your friend the Emp's a coward. I had to cut his ass down twice 'cause he'd decided to stretch his neck."

Dragomir cracked the next egg so hard it spilled its contents over the hot iron stove, then just left it there, bubbling and burning, scowling at Thor.

Thor ignored his brother's glare. To Victory, he said, "He was bad off when your brother got hold of him. So bad I spent the first night with your Praetorian, hunched outside in the rain, watching the house, thinking his newfound interest in Life was some sort of bluff. Didn't wanna show up the next morning and find his stupid ass back in a tree. Good thing I did, too. Lover boy, here, was gonna do it." He gestured disgustedly at Dragomir.

"You *watched* me?" Dragomir sputtered.

Thor gave him a flat look. "You *weren't* gonna do it?"

Dragomir narrowed his eyes. "No."

"Oh?" his brother asked. "And when you wandered out into the rain and leaned against the fence? You were simply contemplating how delightful your current existence is?"

Dragomir turned away from the stove, facing his brother completely. "This is none of your business." His voice was low, deadly. "Get your nose out of it while you still can."

"Imagine my surprise," Thor said, giving his brother a cold look, "When you grabbed that rope out of the barn and carried it over to the base of that big birch. Of course, you must have been planning to hitch

Thunder to it, gonna re-shoe him in the rain." Then he cocked his head. "No, wait. You were making *fence* repairs. That's what the noose was for."

Beside the stove, Dragomir had started to shake. "I'm not going to warn you again."

"But no," Thor growled, "You just threw it over the branch and stood there with it in your hands, staring at it, too much of a damned coward to put it to good use."

Dragomir let out a bellowing roar and rushed his brother, hitting him head-on and carrying them both out into the yard, scattering chickens in all directions. Thor let out a startled grunt when his back connected with the ground, and a moment later, Dragomir was on top of him, aiming his big fist for his brother's face.

Roaring, Thor threw his brother off of him as easily as he was throwing aside a sack of potatoes. As Dragomir rolled aside, he started getting to his feet. "I'm going home, Drago. You wanna go string yourself up?" He flung an arm at the side of the house. "Go ahead. I hid the rope behind the rain barrel." He turned to go.

Dragomir caught him by an ankle and yanked him off his feet.

The struggle that ensued reminded Victory of a fight that she had once witnessed between a couple of male tigers in her father's menagerie. It was brutal, long, and both came out of it utterly exhausted, bloody and panting. They lay in the yard for some time, staring at the sky, bleeding, as chickens warily returned to peck at the scuffed and beaten ground around them.

"Almost looks like it might rain," Thor commented.

"Fields could use it," Dragomir agreed.

"They're forecasting lots of snow this winter."

Dragomir wiped a trickle of blood from his face. "I'll need to get some feed stored up. Little buggers have trouble getting around in the deep stuff."

"Think there's a couple families in the lower valley who have extra feed this year."

"Yep."

"Could call in a favor."

"Yeah."

"You ruined that nice black silk suit," Thor said, still peering at the clouds.

Dragomir grunted. "You check the goats yet this morning?"

"Nah. Wanted to see what kind of lies you were gonna tell the poor wench."

"Well, she knows now," Dragomir said. He heaved himself off the ground with a sigh. "Thanks." He offered his brother a hand.

"She woulda found out eventually," Thor said, taking his brother's hand and pulling himself to his feet. "Figure it's better she knows she's dealing with a panty-waist drama-queen now, before she gets too involved."

Dragomir's eyes narrowed, and his bloody knuckles whitened where they were clenching his brother's hand. "You still hungry?" he grated, squeezing. Victory heard joints pop.

Thor met his gaze over their grip, and his fingers tightened. "Depends," he said evenly. "Whatcha cookin?"

"Eggs." Dragomir bit off the word in a snarl.

"Eggs sound great," Thor growled back. His face, Victory noticed, was reddening. "You using salt?"

"Got some chicken fat in there," Dragomir replied. Blood was dripping from his face onto his arm. He didn't notice.

"Sounds good." More popping of joints.

"Good."

"Fine then. Go cook it."

"I will." But Dragomir made no move to turn, continuing to stare his brother down. His face, Victory noted, was almost crimson, and both of their arms were trembling with the strain, their clasped fists white and shaking.

Suddenly, Thor cursed and loosened his grip. "You prick," he growled, yanking his hand away. He started shaking it out, wincing at the white finger-prints that Dragomir had left behind.

Dragomir grunted and turned back to the house. He hesitated only briefly when he saw Victory staring at him, then, growling, ducked back into the hovel.

Thor sighed, then caught Victory's horrified look. He grinned, wiping a blood smear across one cheek. "Guy stuff," he said. Then he followed his brother inside.

They were savages, Victory decided, watching them with a sort of morbid curiosity. They took turns cooking while they washed and bandaged themselves up. The water bucket was a grisly crimson by the time they had tended to their numerous cuts, wounds, and, in Thor's case, breaks.

The healer, it seemed, wasn't incapable of holding his own.

"By the gods' sweaty nutsacks, Drago," Thor growled, holding his nose in place over a towel. "That's the third damned time."

Dragomir didn't even look up from his food. "Grow a stronger nose."

Thor made a disgusted sound and glanced at Victory over his fingers. "You hear that? You see how unreasonable he is?"

Victory laughed. "I've been dealing with it for a couple weeks, now."

"If only I were that lucky." Thor growled and dunked the towel in the bucket again. Seeing how opaque red it had become, he grimaced and picked it up. "I'm taking this out to the river for fresh. You better have those eggs done soon or I'll come back here and gnaw off your damned arm." Still grumbling, he pushed through the doorway and headed around the house, towards the stream.

"Milady," Whip asked from the sofa, "What just happened?"

"Brotherly dispute," Victory said, disgusted.

"Some dispute," Lion commented. "It sounded like they were killing each other."

"Pity," Whip said. Her gray eyes, however, were amused.

"How has Thor been treating you?" Victory demanded. "If he's been at all indecent—"

Whip snorted. "Lady, even if he were, I could handle it. I was trained as a Praetorian. I can take whatever abuse that I am given."

Victory frowned. "Yes, but—"

"On the subject of the brothers' behavior, however," Whip said, "I would have to say that it has been impeccable, on both accounts. Utterly polite…aside from leaving me in shackles, of course."

"I can try to get them to remove the shackles," Victory said. "Will you promise not to hurt either of them?"

"No," both Lion and Whip said in unison.

Amidst lighting a fire in the stove, Dragomir glanced over his shoulder at her, then at the Praetorian. "You're not thinking about freeing them, are you?" he asked, giving her a suspiciously raised brow.

"Why?" Victory asked. "Are you afraid they might hit harder than your brother?" She found herself irritated with him, but didn't know why.

Dragomir gave her a baffled look. "No, I think they might *kill* me. What's wrong with you?"

"I found that whole display ridiculous," Victory growled. "And next time you and your brother get into a barbarians' brawl like that, I'm going to go find those keys and free my Praetorian to end the matter. Permanently."

Dragomir waved a dismissive hand as he stirred the food. "That only happens once a year or so. It's been a couple years. We were due."

Victory gaped at him. "You were *due?*"

"Yeah," Dragomir said, "Due. Like a big earthquake off of one of those monster faultlines that's been quiet for a few centuries. *Due.*" He jammed the wooden spoon into the eggs, stirring it much more vigorously than was necessary. "He's got big brother syndrome. Every once in awhile, I have to show him he's stepping outta line."

Victory peered at him. "Did you really go throw a noose over a tree?"

"Oh for the gods' puckered asses!" Dragomir cried, slamming his spoon aside. He turned to her, glaring. "That is none of your business."

Victory narrowed her eyes. "I was chained to your bed. My Praetorian was shackled to a timber in your living-room. I think it's my business."

Dragomir suddenly found the iron handle of the spatula extremely interesting. "You wouldn't have been there for long, even if I had." His voice was a mutter. "I had Thor showing up for dinner the next day."

Victory's mouth fell open. "You can't be *serious!*"

When Dragomir looked up, however, there was fury darkening his features. "You don't know what it's like to lose someone that important to you." He made a disgusted gesture at her chest. "Hell, your heart rama has been closed for years. Your womb rama was locked down since before puberty…who's to say that your heart hasn't been locked down at least that long?" He jabbed a thumb in the general direction of the palace, scowling. "And who's to blame you? With that cold bastard for a father, whose ramas *wouldn't* be locked?"

Victory stared at him. "Are you trying to suggest," she managed, only able to produce a whisper, "That I cannot love?" She was so angry that her stomach was clenching and she found her knees starting to shake.

He gave her a searching look. "*Can* you?"

"Of course I can!" Victory snapped.

"Really?" Dragomir challenged. "Who? Who do you love, Princess?"

"My brother," she said, immediately. "I love Matthias. I have since we were born."

Dragomir nodded. "And, as weak and as malnourished as it is, Matthias's is the only active cord still connected to your heart rama. Who else?" He gestured at her guard. "Your Praetorian? They'll give their lives for you. Do you love them?"

Victory frowned. She had, once, but that was before her ill-fated trip to the Academy. Regardless of how much she tried, she could not dredge up the feelings that she had once had for the women who dedicated their entire lives to her protection.

When she did not reply, Dragomir growled, "What about your father? He spawned you, taught you everything he knows. Do you love him?"

"Of course not," Victory growled. "He assassinated my mother and tried to kill me."

"And your chambermaids? Your butler? Your cook? Your vicious little poodle?"

"Not anymore," Victory growled. "But I know what love is. I loved my twin." As soon as the words came out of her mouth, she frowned. *Loved?* "I mean I love him," she growled. "He's my *brother.*"

"And your heart rama is closed," Dragomir growled. "So you *can't* love him. Not until we open it." He yanked the spoon off of the counter and started stirring the eggs that were starting to pop and crackle in the pan. "So you can't understand what I feel."

"That's where you're wrong, brother," Thor said from the doorway. He stepped inside and dropped the bucket of clean water beside the stove. "You said yourself she has a heart-connection. Weak as it is, it was strong once. She remembers the feel of it." He turned and cocked his head at Victory. "Tell me I'm wrong."

"I remember the feel," Victory growled.

Dragomir lifted the skillet from the stove and slammed it onto a counter. "Eggs are done," he said. Then, without another word, he brushed past his brother, out into the yard beyond. Victory watched until he had disappeared around the edge of the house.

Thor heaved a huge sigh. "Well, if we don't find his stupid ass in a tree, then he'll be back sometime after dark." He glanced at Victory, his blue eyes tired. "How about we get you girls fed and I show you around the place?" He frowned in the general direction of his brother's departure. "I get the feeling he didn't take much time giving you the Grand Tour."

Victory frowned. "You actually think he planned on hanging himself? From the moment he stepped off the ship?"

Thor sighed and went to the stove, beginning to serve up the eggs. "You're not the only one who's broken, Princess."

Victory stared at him. "From the *beginning?* He planned to abandon us from the *beginning?*"

Thor grimaced as he loaded the plate with breakfast. "I think he's been struggling with it for awhile, now. Kind of teetering on the brink. Meggie meant a lot to him, and the way she died, well..." he sighed and handed Victory a plate of steaming, half-burned eggs. "He felt responsible, I'm sure. He coulda killed that Praetorian as soon as he saw the bastard hiking across the mountain. He *saw* the darkness of his au, *knew* the guy was a murderer. But he gave him the benefit of the doubt, let the guy get close enough to answer his questions, and Meggie died for it." He started slapping spoonfuls of eggs onto another plate. Face darkening, he continued, "And yes, my brother more than a little lost his mind. He spent three weeks covered in old blood and flies, refusing to take a bath. Me and three other guys finally had to cart him down to the river and scrub him down. When he ate, it wasn't enough. Hell, I saw brains on the ground, from that gunshot he took. It's possible he just lost a screw or two somewhere amidst patching himself up."

Victory glanced at the path the Emp had taken. "Do you really think he's going to kill himself out there?"

Thor sighed and slumped down beside the Praetorian, the plate in his hands. "If he decides to do it, there's nothing you or I can do to stop him. He's a smart guy. Eventually, he'll find a way, whatever we do." He started spooning eggs into Lion's mouth. "Frankly, I was just hoping a pretty little captive princess would keep him interested long enough for Meggie's hurt to go away, but it's looking like that was too much to ask." He finished feeding Lion, then moved to Whip. "And besides. If he is still truly driven to the brink, then we can both agree we really don't want to see him when he steps over the edge, can't we?" He looked up at her. "I love my brother. A lot. He is all the family I've got left." Victory saw Thor's face harden, saw tears before he concentrated again on the fork in his hands. "But he's an Emp. If he can't keep himself from taking that plunge, then I think we're all better off if he goes and climbs that tree."

Victory swallowed. The idea of an Emp that was out of his mind was akin to one of the AIs behind Space-Authority to suddenly losing interest in keeping the net of jumps from being double-booked. For a long time, she only watched Thor feed Whip, unable to find anything to say. Thor seemed satisfied with silence.

"How long you plan on keeping them chained like that?" Victory finally asked, gesturing to her Praetorian.

"If he doesn't show up tonight?" Thor said. He shrugged. "Then they go free tomorrow morning. This was Drago's plan, not mine, and if it's all the same with you, Princess, I'd rather you just take your two friends, here, and find another place to hide." He finished feeding Whip and gave her a flat look. "If the Adjudicator found you here, he'd have every single man, woman, and child in a thirty-mile radius executed for treason."

And, Victory knew, he was right. Her father had a bad habit of annihilating entire villages that had defied him, and this one, after delivering such a grave insult, would be wiped completely off of the map.

"My brother doesn't think about these things," Thor said, watching her expression as he stood and went back for more eggs, "But I do. And we both know I'm not exaggerating. Were you to be found, here, today, everyone from me and my dimwit brother to the Cooper's babies in swaddling-clothes would all be dragged to the center of the town square and shot. For the magnitude of the affront we've caused him by helping you, the Adjudicator's men wouldn't even dig us a grave."

Victory stared down at her cold breakfast, suddenly not hungry.

"Eat," Thor urged, as he sat back into his chair. "If Drago doesn't come back, you're gonna need it. I intend to pack you up and point you toward a hot-springs I know in the mountains, and it's a long walk. Especially with winter coming on." He ate, then, finishing everything that had been left in the pan. Standing, he stretched, slapped his plate on the counter, and said, "I'm going to go check the goats." Then he ducked outside, for the first time leaving Victory completely alone with her Praetorian.

…And her plate of cold, uneaten eggs.

Victory set it aside, carefully, unsure how to deal with the current situation. Dragomir was helping her. She could feel that much, instinctively. He was a healer. He had proven as much. But, if Thor was right, Dragomir was also teetering on the edge of sanity, so consumed with his own loss that it was driving him to the break of madness. If there was one thing that she feared, it was an insane Emp. She had seen what he could do when he was in his right mind, while trying to help. If he were to lose that desire…

"Stay here," Victory told her Praetorian. "I'm going to go see if I can find the Emp."

"Wait!" Lion cried. "Now is your chance, Princess. Set the two of us free, and we will deal with the natives for you."

Victory hesitated, glancing into the bedroom, where she suspected he kept the rest of his keys.

"Just stay here," she said. "I'll be back." She left to the dismayed shouts of her Praetorian.

CHAPTER 16

An Open Heart

Dragomir was seated beside the creek, allowing the smooth flow of energy there to calm him, when he heard footsteps at his back. Immediately, he shielded himself, not wanting to deal with Thor's anger at this point.

"I'm not gonna go swinging from a tree, if that's what you're worried about, Thor," he growled, without looking.

The footsteps stopped, but Thor did not reply.

"That girl…" Dragomir's voice cracked. "That *princess* needs me." He dropped his head to stare at his lap. "She's my soul-half, you know." He made a disgusted sound. "And she hates my guts." Flipping a hand at the trail behind him, he said, "Hell, she's probably back at the house right now, freeing her Praetorian. Didn't hide the key that well—just under the sack of potatoes, 'cause you and I *know* how much she loves those—but she's smart. Probably won't take her long." He felt a sob welling up from within before he fought it down again. "She hates me, Thor. She's the other half of my spirit and she can't even see that I'm trying to help her."

Silence. Not even a snort.

Dragomir sighed. "She asked me to check her past lives. I thought it was a mistake, but it's her. I just haven't been able to *feel* it because her damned *ramas* are blocked, and each one I get open just makes me more and more horny…Like a toad-licking teenager. I feel that energy within her and my heart sings."

Thor continued to wait, his disapproval clear.

"So no," Dragomir growled, "I'm not going to go swinging from a tree. I got that first rama opened and I got scared she was gonna be another Meggie. I can't take a hurt like that again, Thor."

Thor said nothing, waiting.

"But I realized something," Dragomir said, watching the creek. "She's not like Meggie, Thor. She's much, much worse. If I get her ramas open, and anything happens to her, it's going to shatter my very soul." He picked up a rock and threw it into the churning water. He felt his own misery welling up from within. "All that, and I don't even have a guarantee that she's going to like me afterwards. Hell—" he snorted. "She doesn't even like me *now*. Every chance she gets, she tells me I'm an uncouth peasant *cad*." He snorted. "She thinks I've abducted her, and she's constantly complaining about everything—as if I could somehow wave my pretty green Emp magic wand and make the food taste less plain, or the floor to be stone, instead of dirt, or there to be more blankets in the house." He lowered his head again, the misery beginning to hurt. "I can't give her what she grew up with, Thor. If you gave me a thousand years to work towards it, I can't give her that." He drew a shuddering breath at that fact. "She's a princess. I'm a pauper. Once I open her ramas, she's going to move on."

Thor had nothing to say.

"And yet, the moment I open the rest of her ramas, I'm going to lose myself in her. There's a soul-connection there, Thor. I checked. Bigger than anything I ever thought possible. It's why we keep finding each other. But I heal her and it's going to take on a life of its own. It's dormant now, but if she's fixed…That link'll go active, Thor. And for an Emp, that's…" He swallowed, hard. "I'm going to lose myself in her, and she's going to walk away."

Silence.

"And it's going to be bad, Thor," Dragomir said. "There's so much hurt stored in her heart rama…It's gonna be worse than all the others put together." He threw another rock into the creek. "If she even lets me do it."

"I'll let you do it," Victory said softly.

Dragomir froze, his spine suddenly on fire. He watched the creek for several minutes, praying that he had somehow misheard. Very slowly, he turned to look at his visitor for the first time.

Victory stood there, watching him. At his accusing look, she gave him a sheepish grin. "My father taught me that silence was often a person's best tool in a discussion."

Dragomir grunted and turned away, embarrassed and ridiculously joyful at the same time.

To his surprise, she came to sit beside him. Willingly. Not more than two feet away.

Gingerly, Dragomir released his shields so he could feel her.

She was happy…and scared.

Instinctively, he fed energy to her *au* and her womb rama—but *not* her core. The only time an Emp could ever do that, *ever*, without taking a huge black mark in his Karmic tablet, was if she were his mate, and already utterly devoted to him. Which, Dragomir thought bitterly, was a *long* ways off, even in his wildest dreams.

"Thank you," she whispered, once he had finished calming her *au*.

"It's what I do," Dragomir said, returning his attention to the stream.

They sat there together for a moment before she said, "I'm sorry I complain. I'll try to stop."

Dragomir sighed and glanced down at the riverbed between his knees. "Princess, that still leaves us with the fact that your home is a palace, and mine is a stone-and-sod cottage a couple hundred miles from any major road." He hurled another stone, irritated. "I *need* to help you." He turned to look at her. "…but the moment I finish helping you, I'm going to be lost."

She met his gaze, her green eyes beautiful. They were warm with understanding. "You could come back to the palace with me."

Dragomir's heart sang at that simple offer, but he stifled it violently. "And be what? Your manservant? Your *slave?*"

She grimaced and looked away.

Softly, Dragomir said, "Princess, once I get your last rama open and I have direct access to your soul, I'm going to make a connection of my own.

I won't be able to help it. We've had too many lives together for me to fight the instinct." Even then, he could feel the wisps of energy drifting from their ramas, twining down that massive dormant connection, reaching for each other, but with her ramas closed, it was like wisps of smoke trying to knot together. Once she opened up to him, though, the gods themselves wouldn't be able to stop that massive cord that would snap into place between them.

When she looked up at him, frowning, he continued, "It will be like your brother's, but stronger. A *thousand* times stronger, at least for me. You will become my entire world, the other half of my soul. I'd be willing to die for you, in an instant." He hesitated, scanning her eyes. "You, not being an Emp, might not even feel it." He made a disgusted laugh and flopped backwards on the creekbank. He tucked his hands under his head to stare up at the sky. "So there's my dilemma. You need my help. I'm afraid of giving it."

"Well," Victory said softly, "So far, you've been the only man whose presence I can continuously withstand. If I—"

Dragomir shook his head. "No. That's what I'm going to fix." He twisted his head to look at her. "Believe me, Princess, you'd be free to fall in love and make babies with any Royal out there…And it would break my heart." He grunted and turned back to face the sky. "But what can a peasant do about something like that?"

"Nothing," Victory whispered. Whether she was saying it to him or herself, it wasn't clear.

"I'm going to help you," Dragomir said. "I can't *not* help you. It's what I'm here to do, this life. Just, when I *do* do it, don't expect me to stick around for long."

And, by the way her eyes widened, she knew that he wasn't talking about simply walking off to go cool down beside a stream.

• • •

Victory had hesitated, hearing him address her as his brother, but had found his admissions too tempting to resist. She had stayed silent, shamefully, and listened to him pour out his deepest worries to what he thought was his brother.

Now she was sitting beside him, still aglow with the warm energy he had wrapped her in, and he was telling her that he could not only alleviate her fears, but was going to end his own life, once he had.

After several minutes of her silence, Dragomir sighed and got to his feet. "I'll finish with your ramas soon, Princess. Not today—I'm still exhausted from opening your womb rama—but soon. Until then, I'm gonna take those blankets the Cooper boys left and make you a nice bed on the couch."

Then, without another word, he turned to depart.

Victory wanted to call out to him, wanted to say something to reassure him, but she could find nothing. She could promise nothing. She was a Royal Princess of the Imperium. She couldn't make such promises to a peasant.

She sat, watching the stream, wondering why that disturbed her so much. A month before, she couldn't have cared less about the life of a peasant. After all—it was the peasants, in their hatred and ignorance—that had dedicated six years of their lives to hurting her.

But now…

Now, it bothered her beyond reason.

She spent another hour at the stream, picking at the stones, before she finally sighed and got up to go back. She meandered, stopping to look up at big trees, to pluck blades of grass, to kick at dead leaves. Through it all, she tried to think. She knew there had to be a way to satisfy both of them. Yes, he was beautiful, both in body and—she was beginning to think—soul. But a *mate* for her? She just didn't see it. She couldn't picture herself sharing that bond with a man. It wasn't…necessary.

She was a royal, after all. Royals couldn't afford the same emotional attachments as peasantry.

When Victory finally rounded the last copse of trees, she saw the dark shape of a ship squatting behind the stone cottage. It carried no markings, and for a heart-fluttering moment, she thought it belonged to her brother.

Then she saw Thor and Dragomir kneeling in the yard, their fingers laced behind their heads. The three gunmen behind them were *not* of her brother's service. These were dirty, bronze-skinned natives, wearing

motley colors and showing very little discipline. One of the three gunmen was picking something out of his teeth with one hand, his gun limp
in the other.

They made the brothers put their hands behind their backs, then
cinched them together with double bands of zip-ties. They pushed them
forward, chests to the ground, and put their muddy boots between their
shoulder-blades.

As Victory watched, a fourth gunman emerged from the inside of the
cottage, dragging Whip behind him, hand fisted in her short black hair.
As soon as she saw the fourth man, her knees lost their strength. Victory's
stomach twisted with the memories of being chained to that post, and it
was everything she could do not to turn and run at the sight of his piggish face and powerful build.

You have to do something, Victory thought, watching the man drop
Whip down in front of the two brothers, on her knees. He walked slowly
around her kneeling form, grinning as he sized her up like some expensive cow. Victory knew what would come next. She had experienced it
herself, more times than she could count. Quickly, before she could convince herself better of it, she started looping around back, staying out of
sight of the men in the yard, creeping up to the gaping, open windows at
the back of the house.

"Heard what happened to your last girl, Emp," Victory heard the
leader say, so close it made her body jerk with old terror. "Sounded like
fun. Thought we'd give ya a bit of a reenactment. Jog your memory, ya
know?" Several men chuckled, and the surrounding forest rang with the
Shipborn brothers' curses and struggles. "So you just watch the show,"
the leader went on. "Let us know how close we get."

Hang in there, Victory prayed to Whip. She knew that the Praetorian
were sterile—their bodies surgically removed of their ability to reproduce
upon their oaths to their ward—but she knew the horror all too well.

She hesitated beneath a window, then slowly raised herself to look
inside. Lion was still chained to the rafter, the older woman's wrists
bloody from where she was struggling to free herself.

The open portals that had let in the frigid mountain air on so many
cold nights in the past were now her saving grace. Biting her lip, Victory

grabbed the stone sill and, using the rocks in the wall to give her toes purchase, eased herself into the room. Lion heard her and swiveled. Immediately, the Praetorian froze.

Crouched against the wall, Victory had a good view of what was happening in the yard directly outside the door. The man had stripped Whip of her shift, holding her tight to his chest by her collar as he ran his dirty hands down the long curves of her body. Whip, for her part, looked as stoic as if he were a hairdresser giving her a new cut.

He hasn't started yet, Victory thought, utterly grateful, for once, that the beast loved to inspire terror and humiliation in his victims. He would draw it out as long as possible, just to make the two men on the ground scream.

Slowly, eyes on the men outside, she crept across the room, to the burlap sack of potatoes by the stove. She gingerly pulled it aside, biting her lip at the individual thumps of each potato as they slid against the floor, each tiny thud an explosion in her ramped-up senses.

The key was there, right where he had said it would be. Victory's hand was shaking so much that she couldn't pluck the tiny bit of brass from the dirt floor the first time, and had to use both hands and her fingernails to scrape it up into her palm.

Lion was watching her with rapt attention, now, utterly alert, anxiousness lining her face. The Praetorian hadn't spoken, but Victory knew what she was thinking. She wanted Victory to get away from this place. *Now.* Leave the rest of them, just go and save herself.

Trembling, Victory held up the key.

Suddenly, Lion's face changed. She glanced at the scene through the doorway, then her face darkened and she nodded.

It was all Victory could do to crawl on her hands and knees across the room, her terror was so great. Her joints, so pumped full of adrenaline, reacted much like gelatin, and Victory couldn't have run away at that point if she'd tried.

Outside, she heard the sound of a zipper and leader of the group's jeer. "What is it, Ice Maiden? Never seen someone so big before? Scared I'm gonna rip you apart?" The gunmen laughed, and the two brothers struggled on the ground. One of them was crying. "Oh look," the leader said, "The Emp can't watch. Rick, make the Emp watch."

Then she was at Lion's cuffs, desperately trying to get her shaking to stop long enough to insert the key.

She dropped it.

Outside, she heard the man jeer, "So how's the reenactment so far, Emp? Accurate enough for you?" Then a pause. "Is he *asleep?*"

"Passed out," one of the gunmen laughed. "Poor Emp couldn't handle it."

"What a shame. Shoot him."

Victory gasped at the gunshot, at the sound of the body jerking against the dirt out front.

They shot him. Oh gods, they just shot him. Victory scrambled to pick up the key, her every nerve afire at the voices that seemed to be right over her shoulder, but her fingers wouldn't work. They felt like numb, fleshy sticks attached to her hands, and she couldn't force the key into her fingers.

"Hurry, Princess," Lion whispered above her.

"I'm trying," Victory whimpered. She tried again to pluck the key off the ground, but it fell out of her hands again before she got it halfway to the Praetorian's shackles. *I'm not a warrior,* she thought, trying desperately to scrape the brassy bit of metal into her hands. *I'm not trained for this...*

"Please let her go." It was Thor. "You've got no argument with the girl. It's my brother and I that caused offense. My brother's dead. Just kill me and get it over with."

"Oh, we will," the man said. "But she's an Imperial. I think I'll have some fun with her, first."

Victory glanced over her shoulder as she fumbled with the key, her heart hammering so hard it was making her dizzy. She watched the man yank Whip off of the ground by her collar.

"See this pretty little band of metal, here?" the man demanded. "You know what this means, to those bastards? It means, by her own rules, I can do whatever I want to her." He dropped her back to her knees. "And right now, I wanna screw her pretty brains out."

It was then that she saw his pants open, his flesh fully erect jutting from the crux of his thighs. Victory felt her heart clench, felt the memories start to rush up from the depths once more.

A warm blanket of energy settled around her, easing all of her fears, steadying her fingers, slowing her panicked heart. Suddenly, the key went steady in her hand, and it was a simple thing to insert it into the lock, and turn.

Once her first wrist was free, Lion took the key from Victory's hand and smoothly unlocked the rest of her shackles. A moment later, the Praetorian stepped through the doorway and into the light outside, her face a deadly mask.

She stepped behind the man holding Whip by the hair, grabbed him by his chin with one hand while cupping the back of his head with the other, and violently twisted his head up and backwards, making the yard go silent with the loud *pop* of his spine.

She grabbed the man's gun from him as he fell, moving forward without pause, the act only having taken a split second of her time. Whip, who had been watching the process, moved aside with disdain, allowing the body to thump against the bare earth.

The men, startled, peppered the area with gunfire. Lion brought her weapon up and flawlessly executed two of the three gunmen, and, as the third gunman was trying to get his weapon up and ready, she kicked out, caught his weapon as he stumbled, twisted it from his grip, and sent it flying across the yard. He screamed and looked at his fingers, obviously broken from where they had gotten caught in the trigger guard.

Lion brought the weapon to his face and shot him. As he was falling, the Praetorian turned to the two brothers on the ground. She raised the gun up to Thor's head and the man flinched, but didn't look away—

"Lion, *no!*" Victory cried, lunging out into the daylight. "Don't shoot him!"

Lion didn't look up from Thor's face. "He was part of this."

"He and his brother live," Victory ordered. "That is my command."

Reluctantly, Lion glanced at the Emp. "Well, one of them will live, Princess. The other…" She twisted her face as she looked down upon Dragomir's still body. "No one can live through a gunshot like that."

An Emp can, Victory thought stubbornly, but when she looked, she saw too much blood, and white shards of bone and gray matter…

"If your Praetorian isn't going to shoot me…" Thor softly said, eyes still riveted to Lion's face.

Instantly, Lion had the gun leveled between his eyes, waiting.

Carefully, in a very even tone, Thor continued, "…then you should untie me, Victory, so I can help my brother."

Victory frowned at him. "What do you mean?"

Eyes still focused on Lion, he said, "I'm a shifter."

Victory felt her heart give an extra thump. "A what?"

"A Shi. The external kind, not internal." Thor's voice was speeding up. "Can't shape my body, only things outside me. That's how I patched my brother up last time, but I need my *hands*." He nervously took his eyes off of Lion and looked down at his brother. "I never told anyone before this. Hell, Drago doesn't even know. But I can help him, I swear. I just need you to free my hands. I can patch up your Praetorian, too, but I doubt she'd let me get near her."

Victory glanced at Lion, startled, and realized that the spray of gunfire had caught the Praetorian in the shoulder and gut. Even then, a stream of crimson was running down her calf to pool on the ground beneath her bare feet.

"Release him," Victory said.

For a long moment, it didn't look as if Lion would obey her. Then, glaring, her Praetorian lowered the weapon and stalked back to the first man she had killed. She yanked the knife from his belt and walked back over to Thor. She kicked him, hard, in the spine, and Thor fell forward into the dirt with a startled grunt.

"You can tell him that was for his part in all this," Lion snarled. Then she slid the knife blade between his wrists and, with one quick, upward jerk, cut the ties. Before Thor could get back up, she kicked him again in the ribs. "And that was for leaving Whip in chains."

Then, as if Thor no longer existed to her, the Praetorian went and searched the rebel bodies, taking all the weapons and slinging them over her shoulders and hips. Then she stalked toward the ship and up the ramp, passing into the darkness of the hull. There was a moment of silence, then a sharp male cry, cut off suddenly. Two moments later, a dirty male body rolled down the gangplank, sliding to a stop in the dust. It was followed shortly by another.

Victory expected Thor to comment on the Praetorian's ill-bred behavior, but the man was already kneeling beside his brother, eyes closed, hands smeared with Dragomir's blood as his thumbs waded through the crater in the man's head.

Oh my gods, Victory thought as his fingers slid into the hole in his head. She quickly looked away, feeling a pressure rising in her gut.

Whip, who had watched the proceedings with interest, was frowning at the way Thor was running his hands through Dragomir's wound.

"That man's a Shi, ain't he?" Whip asked. There was an intelligence in her eyes that dwarfed Lion's.

"He claims to be," Victory said.

"Makes sense," Whip said, looking intrigued. "The mutations run in families."

Victory ducked into the cottage to retrieve the key to Whip's shackles, but could find it nowhere on the floor. Frowning, she stepped back into the daylight, carefully avoiding the growing patch of blood and brains on the ground under Thor's hands. "Whip, I can't find the—" She stopped when she realized Whip was free of her shackles, and was simply kneeling there, naked, watching, her hands tucked carefully behind her back, chains dangling loose over her ankles.

"Lion dropped me the key, milady," Whip said, without looking up. "For now, I'm just watching. I'm going to have to kill him if he decides to do anything unpleasant, though." She almost sounded disappointed. Then, after she continued observing for a moment, "Does he really think he can *heal* a wound like that?" She didn't sound incredulous, just puzzled.

"He says he's done it before," Victory said. But an anxiety was building in her chest as she watched the big man work on his brother, and the longer she sat there, the more it began to hurt. It was an odd pressure, almost like someone was jabbing her in the chest with a finger.

Stay alive, she prayed, willing the Shi to work faster.

But the body began to pale, the blood oozing from his scalp slowly coming to a stop.

"He's long dead," Whip said, shaking her head.

Even as she said it, Thor pulled his hands away from his brother's head and slumped forward, his big shoulders wracked with slow, uneven sobs.

"That's not possible," Victory whispered. The odd pressure in her chest began to feel like someone was running a stake between her breasts. She rubbed at her breastbone, wondering if she was having some sort of reaction to the excitement. The pressure continued to build, relentless, until it felt like her chest was caught in a giant's fist, its fingers squeezing her lungs to a tiny portion of their former capacity. Grimacing, she sat down against the outer wall of the cottage, her breath starting to come in low, pained breaths.

Whip turned to give her an anxious look. "Are you all right, milady?"

"No," Victory whimpered. Her entire chest was hot and tingly, and it felt like every breath was wedging that stake further between her ribs. "I think…heart attack…" She groaned, sliding sideways along the wall, suddenly needing to lie down.

Whip was on her feet in an instant. She knelt beside her, her gray eyes filled with concern. "We don't have the facilities for you here, milady. The closest hospital is about four hundred miles away, and is run by your father."

Victory closed her eyes against the spike of agony shooting up and down her spine with every beat of her heart. The Praetorian lurched to her feet and ran to the spaceship. She heard her conferring with Lion.

Interestingly, Victory caught sight of Dragomir, standing beside his brother, a hand on his shoulder. He turned, then, and started walking away. The forest beyond was glowing, more alive than she had ever seen it before, every tree seemingly radiating golden light.

Is that the sun? Victory thought, squinting at the clouds. It was, just as it had been all day, overcast. The patch of trees that he was walking towards, however, seemed to be bathed in a pocket of vibrant sunshine.

Go to him.

The voice came from within, and for a moment, Victory thought it was her imagination. She watched Dragomir's back grow distant. *Why is he leaving his brother?* she thought, confused.

Go *to him*, the voice ordered again.

Somehow, Victory pulled herself onto her hands and knees. Every bit of her chest feeling torn and punctured, she crawled over to the corpse beside Thor. She frowned down at it, then at Dragomir's back, almost in the trees.

But she didn't have time to contemplate it. Something was pushing her to flip the Emp over.

Victory wedged her hands under Dragomir's body and, heaving, she began to strain to roll him onto his back.

Beside her, Thor frowned, watching her.

Dragomir's back had almost entered the trees.

"*Help* me!" Victory cried, straining to get the man's big body flipped onto his back.

Reluctantly, Thor did as she asked.

Victory's guts clenched at the great mass of ruined bone and flesh that was Dragomir's forehead. Then he was on his back, and she was crawling on top of him.

"What are you—" Thor asked, frowning. Behind him, Lion and Whip had jogged up, and were watching the scene with confusion.

Instinct had taken over, now. Victory positioned her heart over Dragomir's. Then she closed her eyes and touched the pressure in her chest. It felt like a balloon, stretched to the very limits of its tolerance by hot, energized air. Victory grabbed the straining membrane in her mind and *pushed*.

In the field outside the glowing expanse of trees, Dragomir stopped. He turned, slowly.

A moment later, her heart rama exploded outward like a burst dam.

This time, however, there was physical pain, as well as mental. Victory sucked in a lungful of air and screamed. This time, there was no Emp nearby to help guide the flood. This time, the energy washed through her, hitting the ramas directly above and below, and bursting those dams, too, adding their own stores of horrors to the flood. Then it continued on downward, surging out through her core, and up through the top of her head. The images that it carried with it were an unending stream of violence so shattering that Victory's existence became one continuous vision of pain, horror, and terror.

She screamed until she was hoarse, then screamed until her voice was a whisper, and still they came. Images of her father, mocking her, images of a hundred different men, using her. She felt someone grab her, pick her up, hold her. She felt herself sob until her body shook, until mucous ran freely from her face, until every breath exited in a low moan.

Her cries had finally died to a whimper when she finally found the strength to open her eyes.

Dragomir was cradling her, a circular scar marring his forehead. A few feet away, his brother and the two Praetorian were all standing, faces white, as if they were watching a specter. "Shhhh," the Emp said, still rocking her. "You'll feel better soon, Princess." His blue eyes were filled with tears. "Promise."

When Victory met his gentle gaze, she was lost. Like a hot hurricane passing through her, it bottled in her chest, condensing bolts of energy down her spine, then spread outward, hot and warm and enveloping.

"What *is* that?" she whispered.

In reply, the Emp gasped and dragged her forward, wrapping her in big arms, hugging her to his chest. She felt the pressure building within, but this time, there was no pain, just a gentle current between them.

…between them?

Eventually, Victory pulled herself free, frowning. The feeling of separating made her chest ache, like she was tugging against a wound, and it worried her. She looked down at the place between her breasts, half expecting to find some sort of cord buried in her breastbone. *What did he do to me?*

"Uh," Thor said, clearing his throat. "So." He scratched at the back of his neck and made a nervous sound as he watched his brother. "… you're alive, right?" The way he said it, it almost sounded as if the Shi thought he was looking at a ghost.

Dragomir grunted, beginning to pick pieces of zip-ties from under the newly-scarred flesh of his wrists. When he met Victory's eyes again, she felt all the power of a mountain in his gaze. The hurricane began building within her again, preparing to be swept away, and she instinctively looked somewhere else. She thought she saw Dragomir's face darken with a tiny frown before she cleared her throat. "Well, let's get that vessel out of sight. Those guys' friends might come looking for them. Anyone here who can fly a ship, other than me?"

They couldn't, of course. The Praetorian were not schooled in such things, and the two peasants had never experienced a need to learn.

Sighing, trying to hide the odd sensation she was feeling in her chest, Victory stalked over to the ship and climbed the ramp. She heard Lion bark orders behind her, but continued into the hull, anyway, trying to get somewhere quiet so she could think.

What did he do to me? she thought again. Her chest ached, and again, she felt the odd sensation of a cord. She found the dingy, smoke-smelling cockpit and slumped into the grease-smeared pilot's chair. She heard the others pull the bodies onboard, heard Thor and Whip try to tell each other what to do. Lion emerged in the doorway a few moments later. "Where do you plan to leave it, milady?"

"Somewhere other than here." Victory strapped herself in and began powering up the engines. "Is everyone inside?"

"Everyone but the Emp. He is still sitting in the yard."

Victory felt a spasm in her chest, realizing that she had probably given the Emp the wrong idea in running off. She considered going back, telling him that she just needed a moment to think. Then she put her hand on the throttle, her mouth tightening in a grim line. *A sovereign doesn't have the leisure to waste her time with love. She has to be hard, and cynical, and understand that her life is not her own, that she can not afford the same emotional extravagances as the peasantry she rules.* She pushed the throttle forward and began retracting the gate and landing gear.

She had the ship halfway off the ground before she stopped, shocked to the core.

Those were Father's words. And she had just used them like her own. She was so stunned and horrified that, for several moments, she could only stare at the console in front of her, watching her father repeat them in her mind.

She set the ship back to the ground so suddenly that its entire frame shuddered around her. She was already releasing her seatbelt when Lion ducked her head inside, worried. "Milady?" she asked.

"We're not leaving him behind," Victory growled. She went to the hatch, slammed her palm against the gangplank release, then waited impatiently for the ramp to descend before she stormed down it.

Dragomir was pulling a bundle of rope out from behind the rain-barrel.

Victory slapped it out of his hand, sending it careening across the yard. As he blinked at her, she leveled a finger at his startled face. "You are getting on the ship with me, and you are going to *stay* with me, and you're going to *like* it, and I swear to the gods if you *ever* pick that damned thing up again, I'm going to—"

He dragged her in and kissed her.

Instantly, Victory remembered just how big he was, and just how small she felt with his huge body wrapped around her. Instead of fear this time, however, she felt a tingling at her core, a rush of warmth that traveled all the way up her spine, pooling in her chest. She felt strangely whole as her lips parted to his, seeking. Her heart hammered as his tongue sought out and danced with hers, the heat in her core rising like an inferno from within. She melted into him with a sigh, enjoying the hardness of his body, the solidness of his embrace.

Lion cleared her throat from the gangway. Hard.

Blushing crimson, Victory tried to break away from Dragomir's embrace, but he kept his arms wrapped around her, pinning her to his torso, grinning. Instantly, Lion's eyes narrowed on the Emp, and the Praetorian reached for her sword.

"Oh, calm down, you pinch-faced old prude," Dragomir rumbled at the Praetorian. He grinned down at Victory. "We're not done yet." And he bent down and kissed her again.

This time, Victory went weak at the knees.

CHAPTER 17

A Man Without Mercy

Thor directed them to a hot-springs deep in the mountains where Victory put them down amidst massive, jagged peaks.

Victory glanced at the snow-covered mountaintops around them and grimaced. Lion had taken the boots from one of the dead men and forced them onto her feet when she complained, but even with shoes, she was not looking forward to walking through snow. The valley itself had only received a light dusting, most of which had melted in the daylight hours. The path back, aside for a couple of the higher rises, was more or less snow-free.

"We'll need to be careful," Dragomir said. "Imperial slavers sometimes pass overhead, on their way to the bigger towns on the other side of the range. A group this small, they'd pick us up in a heartbeat."

"You hear something, keep your heads down," Thor agreed, his face grim. "Let Dragomir and me deal with them."

"My Praetorian are perfectly capable of dealing with—" Victory began.

"If we *do* run into them," Dragomir interrupted, his blue eyes catching Victory's in warning, "No offense, Princess, but *we're* gonna deal with them. Sodstone's lost its fair share to kidnappings, and Thor and I would rather just mete out a little justice, okay?" He hesitated, his eyes

276

flickering nervously to her throat. "Besides. You should probably stay out of sight, considering."

Victory unconsciously reached up and touched the collar around her neck. The last—*last*—thing she wanted to do was get caught by slavers. If she was picked up by a sweep, then she could scream that she was a princess for decades, but because she wore the pretty titanium collar around her neck, no one would bother to so much as check her blood type.

"When I'm Adjudicator," Victory said softly, "I'm going to ban them all from the planet."

Both Thor and Dragomir froze, cocking their heads at her like she had suddenly sprouted horns. They watched her so long that Victory's skin began to crawl and she thought maybe she had said something wrong. It was Thor who finally said, "*What* did you just say, Princess?"

"The slave trade," Victory said, fighting embarrassment at their stares. "I'm getting rid of it. Mercy doesn't need it." When they continued to stare at her, she muttered, "It's not a *law* that each planet in the Imperium must deal in slaves. Mercy has other exports, however limited. We can provide top-grade marbles and granites." Then her eyes flickered to Dragomir. "And healing."

Dragomir stiffened. "Healing?" he asked, eying her warily.

"I will grant Emps, Psi, Shi, and Kin amnesty on Mercy. In return, they will help establish hospitals dedicated to the healing arts. I expect we could gain quite a bit of revenue from medical tourism."

"Until the Imperium gets wind of it," Thor growled.

Victory shook her head. "It is one of the beauties of the Imperium. As long as a planet's government pays its tithes and breaks no laws—like the human-rights laws my father is breaking with his slave trade—its Adjudicator is pretty much considered autonomous. I've even heard of a couple planets granting amnesty before. The Imperium as a whole doesn't like it, and often they won't send peacekeeper fleets, if requested, but that's the way it works."

For a long moment, the two brothers merely stared at her in silence. Then, reluctantly, Thor nodded. "I honestly thought you were crazy, Drago, but I can see the method in your madness." At that, he ducked out of the cockpit and started unloading bodies from the hull, leaving Victory and Dragomir alone…

…with Lion.

Her head Praetorian was giving them both a disapproving glare, and hadn't so much as gotten outside visual range since she'd caught them kissing in the yard.

Once again feeling the heat within her building at the Emp's closeness, Victory cleared her throat pointedly. When Lion simply settled against the wall to watch them, missing the point entirely, Victory gestured meaningfully at Dragomir. "Isn't there something you could be doing right now, Lion?" she suggested.

The woman smiled. "I could be gutting the brute, but for some reason you seem to be adverse to the idea."

Victory glared at the older woman. "Thor could use help digging graves for the bodies."

"Whip is helping him," Lion said calmly. "I'm watching."

Narrowing her eyes, Victory growled, "Watching *what*?"

Lion's gaze was icy when it fell on Dragomir. "Watching to make sure a Royal Princess isn't about to be taken advantage of by a peasant."

What if she wants to be taken advantage of? Victory thought rebelliously, feeling the heat of the Emp's body so close. But she raised her head in what she hoped was a commanding manner. "I'm sure you can find something else to do."

"I'm sure I could," Lion agreed.

"Now," Victory growled, feeling her face redden.

"Right now," Lion said, nodding. She didn't move from her spot against the wall.

"What's she saying?" Dragomir asked, watching the Praetorian suspiciously.

"She's saying she bashed her head open a few too many times in Praetorian training," Victory said. She glared at Lion. "Ignore her." Turning to him, she stuck a finger in his chest and said, "Now tell me what you did to me." Even then, she could feel the tug in her ribcage, feeding warmth into her chest.

Dragomir grinned, grabbed her hand where it was stuck to his breastbone, and dragged her close. Wrapping his arms tight around her, he said softly, "I claimed you as my own. Tied a cord between us. As an Emp's mate."

"Your...mate." Even with the warmth tracing through her body, Victory wasn't sure how she felt about that.

He nodded, but his cerulean eyes watched her carefully, obviously expecting her to disagree.

"What...cord?" Victory managed.

"A cord of energy between our heart-ramas, binding us. It will grow, until we will be able to feel each other at a distance." He grinned. "Like I said, Princess. I claimed you." He kissed her forehead. "Made you mine."

The cultured part of Victory sputtered. *I'm a princess. I can't just let this man* claim *me. That's what elk and orangutans do.* And yet, the larger portion of her wanted nothing more than to throw Lion from the room, close the door, and explore his rippling body. So caught between these two emotions was she that Victory just stared up at him, her mind blank of things to say.

Dragomir lowered his forehead to hers. "Will you accept me?"

From the door, Lion coughed loudly.

Dragomir flinched, then glared at the Praetorian, giving Victory momentary freedom from his piercing gaze. She pulled out of his arms and cleared her throat, allowing the shield of civility to once more fall into place around her. "Sir, you've helped me greatly, and I would be honored if you would stay on as a member of my staff, but I couldn't possibly—"

Dragomir tore his eyes away from where he had been matching Lion scowl-for-scowl, and frowned at her. "*Staff?*"

Seeing his scowl directed at *her*, Victory squeaked out, "Perhaps I could hire you as an entertainer. A concubine."

He grabbed her and pulled her close again. In the doorway, Lion growled.

"Princess," he grated, his face only inches from hers, "I bound myself to you. The last thing I'm going to do is watch another man bed you. I'm your mate, or I'm not at all."

"You're not a Royal," Victory managed, feeling helpless under his blue gaze. "You're not certified."

He narrowed his eyes at her for a moment, then released her. "Lion's right. I think my brother needs help digging graves." At that, he turned and stalked from the room. She heard his footsteps thunder on the gangplank and Thor's startled query.

"*Now* do you want me to kill him?" Lion demanded, glancing out the door beside her.

Victory slumped into the pilot's chair, ignoring her Praetorian. She needed to think. An Emp's *mate*? What did he mean by that? Was that somehow different from a normal courtship?

Then another part of her cried, *Courted by a peasant? Are you insane?* The entire Imperium would mock her. The other Adjudicators would snicker at her ill-bred behavior. And, if they were to wed, no other Adjudicators would want her potential children, since they could not be rated as a Generation Royal. Being un-certified, the Imperium would not provide her children with Praetorian, and she would have to hire specially-trained guardsmen.

Then a startled part of her mind babbled, *Children? With a* native? *You have got to be out of your mind.*

"It would be a small thing," Lion said, watching Dragomir go. "Obviously a gunshot won't work, so I would simply cut off his head."

Victory scowled at her Praetorian. "You will do no such thing."

Lion shrugged and turned to go help the others.

Irritated, not sure the woman would obey her, Victory got to her feet and followed.

They were digging graves for the rebels underneath the willow trees, and the moment Victory saw their stiff bodies flop into the graves, congealed blood oozing from their wounds, she grimaced and looked away, trying not to lose the breakfast that Dragomir had made her eat on the flight. She did her best to help, but the corpses' open stares left her with a growing sickness in the pit of her stomach. They were the first dead men she had ever encountered, besides the dead crew of the doomed Academy ship, and while the others simply moved them around like stiff pieces of meat, it was all Victory could do to keep her gut in check.

When Lion started cutting off the index fingers of each of the corpses, however, Victory lost control. She fell to her knees beside the gangplank, retching.

"Or for the gods' steaming piles, woman!" Dragomir snapped, shoving past Lion. "Did you have to do that in front of her?" He knelt beside Victory, putting an arm around her shoulders. Immediately, Victory felt better, and she wasn't sure if it was something he was doing or just the relaxation in her chest, like a cord that had been stretched too thin suddenly going slack.

"Come on, love," Dragomir said. "Let's go get you somewhere else while they finish up."

Victory nodded, humiliated by her lack of control. She let him lift her to her feet and stumbled into the willows with him, shivering with the horrible feeling in her stomach.

Once they were well out of hearing range, Dragomir set her down on a large, mossy rock and squatted in front of her, concern in his eyes. "You going to be okay, Princess?"

Victory wiped tears from her eyes and nodded. "What was she *doing*?" she whimpered.

"Identifying the bodies, I'd suspect," Dragomir said. "It's standard procedure for an Imperial kill. Some Imperial law about—"

"War crimes," Victory finished, in a whisper. She remembered it, now. Rebels, no matter how many of them or how long they've been fighting, had to be identified, their remains eventually returned to their families. She closed her eyes and shuddered. "I just didn't know that's how they're identified."

Dragomir shrugged. "Twice a year, the two sides get together to exchange remains. Too many bodies, really, to realistically pass corpses around, so they pass fingers."

Victory felt her gorge rising again. "I'm going to end this."

Dragomir gave her a long, searching look. "I hope you do, Princess." He reached out and stroked a thumb across her forehead, moving a clump of hair from her eyes. "Mercy's been waiting a long time for someone to make some changes."

Victory met his gaze, held it. She felt her stomach settle under his touch, found her core once again pulsing with warm, insistent energy.

His powerful body was only a foot away, and every inch of her wanted to slip back in his arms to finish what they had started in the cockpit.

Swallowing, she said, "What did you mean, an Emp's mate?"

His smile was sly. "I could demonstrate, if you want."

"No *thank* you!" she cried, though she didn't get up off of her rock. She felt herself leaning into his caress, instead.

"Rather convincing argument," Dragomir chuckled. He pulled her close, his warm breath against her ear. "I'm thinking we'll take our time getting back, while I show you a few things."

"Yes," Victory whimpered, feeling an odd duality at his touch, the sense that she was both the toucher and the touchee. She found her skin start to tingle as he traced his fingers down her face, along her neck, bent to kiss her shoulder. Like a wildfire, heat was rushing upwards from her core, melting her into his body.

Dragomir leaned backwards onto the forest floor, pulling her with him. As soon as her body slid across his, Victory felt a building between her thighs, the hot pressure making her moan, despite herself. His hands swept down her body, slipped under the shift, found the curve of her lower back…

Victory, for her part, was pulling his shirt over his head, exposing the definition of his chest, the hard ribs of his stomach. She moaned again as his big hand swept over her rear, settling into the curve at the back of her thigh, drawing with it a flood of sensations that she knew could not be normal. The skin under his fingers felt electrified, like his touch itself emanated warm sunshine. She shuddered as his hands moved again, slipping under her shift, tracing her ribs as they reached upward, seeking…

A swordpoint came to rest at the Emp's throat.

"Tell him," Lion said calmly, "That he will be trying to figure out how to heal himself a couple of testicles, if he doesn't take his hands off of you immediately."

"Who hired you to be my nanny!" Victory cried, horrified.

"Your mother," Lion said. "Right before she died. Tell him." She pressed the swordpoint deeper into his esophagus.

Without being told, Dragomir slowly pulled his hands free and held them up, eyes riveted to the Praetorian's blade.

"Now get off of him and try to regain some of your dignity." Lion gestured at the way Victory's shift was pushed halfway up her back.

Reddening, humiliated, Victory yanked her shift down and glared at her Praetorian. "Leave. Now."

"Lady," Lion said, "I am your sworn servant, but I am allowed to use my discretion in obeying your commands." She frowned down at Dragomir over her blade. "And, this being an Emp and a native, I am unconvinced that he has your best interests at heart."

"I didn't ask you for your opinion," Victory growled.

Lion shrugged. "I'm giving it." She removed her sword from Dragomir's neck and, stepping back, sheathed it. "We're done with the bodies. We'll be leaving in about thirty minutes."

Cursing, Victory got to her feet. "I can have relations with whomever I please," she growled.

"While this is true," Lion said, examining her fingernails, "I am dedicated to protecting the royal blood from all threats. I would have to say that *that*—" she gestured at the Emp on his back, "—is a threat."

"How?!" Victory cried. "He healed Whip! And the Cooper child."

"I *know* he healed Whip, and that is the reason I haven't killed him yet," Lion growled. The Praetorian looked disturbed. Torn. She turned to give Dragomir another glare. "Your father hunts them for a reason, Princess. Emps have the ability to sway the way a person thinks, one way or the other. I find it *extremely* odd that you were planning his demise not three days ago, yet after your apparent heart-attack this morning—which we *still* haven't figured out the cause, I might add—you've been doing nothing but rubbing yourself against him like a horny puppy."

Victory gasped.

Dragomir still remained solidly on the ground, watching the Praetorian warily. "Am I okay to stand?" he asked, softly.

"He opened my ramas," Victory growled.

Lion's face tightened. "And just what does that mean, milady?" When Victory did not respond, she added, "Because it sounds like he did exactly what I've been afraid of."

"He healed me," Victory snapped.

"Did he?" Lion watched her carefully.

"I feel better," Victory retorted.

"I understand that," Lion said. "And that, too, has kept him alive when all my instincts have been telling me to gut him. But did he *heal* you, or do something else?"

Blushing, Victory glanced down at the Emp on the ground. She *did* feel better. But even before her capture, she had *never* felt so free to let a man explore her…Had he simply removed her inhibitions? And what of that odd tugging sensation in her chest? "He said he bound himself to me," Victory muttered.

"Bound himself to you…" Lion said, raising a brow, "Or bound *you* to *him*?"

Victory hesitated. She honestly didn't know.

"Until you figure that out," Lion said, her blue eyes flat, "You will not be bedding him, milady."

It took Victory a couple of moments to realize that the Praetorian was utterly serious.

Victory gave Lion a disgusted look, then turned and stormed back to the ship.

She paused when she saw Whip pressed up against a cottonwood, Thor's big body pinning her in place as they kissed. Whip was giggling, her borrowed rebel outfit rumpled and bunched under Thor's hungry hands, her body writhing against his.

As Victory stood there in shock, Lion came up behind her.

"You have twenty-five minutes," Lion barked at the two of them, before continuing to the ship.

Thor watched Lion walk off, then renewed his efforts to pull off Whip's shirt.

Against the tree, Whip giggled again.

…*giggled?* It took Victory's brain through a convolution. Whip prided herself on being steely-faced and completely analytical—the perfect soldier. To see her squeal in delight under Thor's advances left Victory in total shock.

Lion stopped on the path ahead, looking back at her. "Will you be coming, milady?" Her voice told her that if Victory didn't follow of her own accord, she would be dragged.

Frustrated, she went with Lion back to the ship, trying not to notice the patches of fresh, overturned earth under the willows. Dragomir appeared from the trail a few minutes later and gave the Praetorian a dark scowl before he settled on the ramp beside Victory.

"What was that all about?" Dragomir muttered, still glaring at Lion.

"She thinks you're using your Emp powers to control me," Victory muttered.

Dragomir turned to look at her sharply. "Do *you*?"

Victory hesitated. She still wasn't sure. She'd never felt so comfortable around a man, even before the rebels attacked her ship. Even as a child, she had maintained a distance, for decorum's sake.

Time passed. From the forest, they heard the unmistakable sounds of lovemaking.

"Are you seriously going to make us wait here while they finish?" Victory demanded, glad for the distraction.

"Whip has had a stressful day," Lion said. "I'm allowing her time to release some tension."

"Release some…" Victory stammered. "And yet you interrupt the Emp and I?!"

Lion cocked her graying head at the sounds. Without turning her attention from the clump of willows, she said, "Unlike you, milady, Whip is sterilized. A little play can't hurt anything. Just relaxing a bit. She'll be done soon."

And, sure enough, Thor and the Praetorian emerged from the willows with flushed faces and disheveled hair. Whip's shirt and pants were rumpled and grass-covered. Thor's pants were inside-out. Seeing the three of them sitting on the gangplank, waiting for them, at least Whip had the decency to blush. Thor just grinned like a fool.

"I've had enough," Victory growled, lunging to her feet. "I'll see the four of you back at the cottage." Lion immediately fell in step behind her, with Dragomir taking a wary distance behind the Praetorian. Behind him, Whip and Thor giggled to themselves, and Victory felt herself experiencing a wave of jealousy as she pushed through the willows. Her body still tingled where Dragomir had touched her, and she couldn't help but wonder what she had missed.

Someday, she thought, irritated beyond reason, *I'm going to be able to tell Lion to mind her own business.*

• • •

Victory crouched beside Dragomir and Lion, peering down at the Imperial ship squatting in Dragomir's front yard. It was small, a modified courier of some sort, but bristling with guns. If Victory had to have guessed, she would have said a personal escort.

As Lion and Whip tried to decide what to do, Victory watched a man in gleaming black House Praetorian armor step off the ship and go walk through the center of the goat herd, speaking into a handheld communications device of some sort. Another cluster of House Praetorian were searching the barn and Dragomir's hovel. When the one on the com turned, still speaking into his handset, she caught a brief glimpse of his face as he scanned the woods. There was a frown on his face.

An instant later, Victory stood up, grinning from ear-to-ear.

"Milady!" Lion hissed. "Get down."

"That's my brother," Victory said. She started down the slope, toward the Shipborn hovel.

Lion gathered her guns and jogged up beside her, glancing around them nervously. "That didn't look like your brother to me, milady."

"He was wearing Praetorian garb and has a haircut, but it's him. Trust me."

Lion frowned. "How can you tell at this distance? I could barely even see his style of dress, that far off. It could be your father's man. I'm pretty sure it was a House uniform."

"It was," Victory agreed. "Dragon and phoenix."

Lion balked. "Then why…?"

Victory never slowed down. "My brother probably got some sort of distress beacon. Probably has a spy in the village or something that called him when the rebels flew over."

"We should be more careful," Lion insisted. "It could be a trap. At least let either Whip or myself—"

A man stepped out of the bushes beside them, a gun in his hand, dressed in Imperial soldiers' camouflage. Lion froze as three more stepped out of the brush beside her, their bodies so well blended with their surroundings that, even standing there, they appeared to be part of the scenery. Only the guns in their hands—and the smiles on their faces—stood out against the woodland shrubbery.

"Evening, Princess," the man said, grinning. His face was dark with camouflage, and he had bits of leaves and twigs sticking from an odd, fuzzy suit he wore to hide his body.

"Lady," Lion said very carefully, "Those are Imperial snipers."

"Yep," the man said. "Six more of us on the hills there and there." He pointed, still grinning. "We watched you guys come in. We were headed up to get a better look when we heard you talking." He pulled a greenish device off of his belt and held it to his mouth. "We've got them," the man said into the radio. "Princess and escort."

"Bring them down," the radio voice ordered. Victory felt a flash of relief when she recognized her brother's soft, cultured words.

The man immediately tucked his gun back into its holster. "So come on, then. Your brother is waiting." He raised his voice to the three who had stopped, stock-still, on the trail behind them. "Come on down, y'all. The prince sends his regards." Then he turned his back to them and started down the path, looking for all the world like a fluffy green-brown teddy-bear who had gotten his fur tangled in bits of brush and leaves.

Victory gave the startled Lion an I-Told-You-So look and followed the man down the slope. He whistled, and four more men appeared out of the brush, grass, and trees overlooking the Shipborn farm, from behind rocks or in bushes that Victory never would have thought could hold a man, much less a man with all of his gear and a five-foot rifle. She saw more shapes coming down out of the hills, their bush-like suits jiggling as they trotted.

"What the hell happened?" her brother's voice demanded, as soon as they came within earshot. He was obviously upset. "There's blood all over the place, and landing-gear divots and exhaust burns over there." He gestured at the place where the rebel ship had squatted the day before.

"We were attacked by rebels," Victory replied. "Lion saved everyone. And the Emp..." She hesitated and glanced back at Dragomir, who was watching the entire exchange warily, "He...Erm...Did some healing."

But her brother was sharp. His gaze flickered toward Dragomir and the Emp stiffened immediately, no doubt remembering the last time her brother had arrived with a group of Praetorian. "He cured you, then?"

'Cured' was a strong word, considering how Victory was still uncomfortable around her brother's men, the memories of her captivity still burning like coals in her mind, but at least the insane, gut-wrenching terror had completely dissolved, washed away by that soft golden glow. Victory lifted her chin and cleared her throat. "I'm standing here, aren't I?" She gestured at the black-clad soldiers clustered around them.

Matthias gave her a considering look, then lifted his gaze to Dragomir again. "You healed her?"

The Emp nodded once, warily.

Hearing that, Matthais strode purposefully toward Dragomir, making the Emp stiffen nervously, then swiftly dropped to one knee in front of him, head down, fists to his thighs. "Give him a blade," Matthias ordered of his Praetorian captain.

The Praetorian stiffened. "But sire..."

"Now, Stone," Matthias growled, head still tilted to the ground, neck bare.

The Praetorian guardsman gave his commander an anxious look, then reluctantly handed his weapon to Dragomir, hilt-first. The Emp took the sword like a man would handle a writhing serpent.

"What is he doing...?" Dragomir asked Victory nervously, glancing between her and her kneeling brother, carefully avoiding looking at the sword in his hands.

In ritualistic High Imperial, Matthias intoned, "You have suffered a grievous injustice at my hands, Dragomir Shipborn. I tortured an innocent man, for no fault of your own. For the wrongs I have done you—"

"Matt!" Victory cried, her heart beginning to pound as she realized what her brother planned. "That is entirely unnecessary."

"For the wrongs I have done you," Matthias went on forcefully, "unprovoked and undeserved, I offer you my life in payment. Do with it as you will." Beside him, his Praetorian captain's breath came in a hiss.

"Ummm," Dragomir said, glancing down at the Praetorian sword, then at the General Commander, "no offense, but you Imperials confuse the hell outta me."

Stiffly, furious with her brother, but knowing that propriety now bade him finish it, Victory said, "He's offering you a choice, Dragomir. Kill him or absolve him. He feels his pride is damaged, and is asking you to cleanse it."

Dragomir blinked up at her over the gleaming blade. "Absolve him of what?"

Refusing to look at her idiot brother, Victory said, "The wrongs he committed you, in taking you from your village. It's an Imperial ritual that was outlawed years ago, because too many Royals were killing each other over slights." She glared at Matthias before returning her attention to the Emp. "Basically, he's asking you to either forgive him or put your sword through his neck."

"Uh. I forgive him." Dragomir, looking extremely uncomfortable under all the stares, dropped the sword and backed away.

Matthias stiffened, and every Imperial in the yard gasped at the insult.

Rolling her eyes, Victory stepped forward and lifted the sword from the ground and shoved it back into Dragomir's hands. As the Emp started to complain, she said, "Don't insult him. *Mark* him. On the neck. Sword tip to the last vertebrae of the spine. Just a little cut, but make it bleed."

"Um," Dragomir said, "Why?"

"It's his *honor*," Victory growled, shoving him toward her brother. "You need to mark him deeply enough to satisfy his honor. Make it a good cut. He will wear his blood-stained clothes as a sign of his penance for seven days."

Looking thoroughly out of his league, Dragomir chuckled nervously. "And you call *us* barbarians." But he scanned the group of Imperials with wary consideration. Then, straightening under the Praetorian stares, he stepped forward, put the tip of the sword to the base of the prince's skull, and hesitated as every Imperial in the yard stiffened. "That gorilla over there isn't gonna rip my arms off if I make him bleed, is he?" Dragomir asked tentatively.

"It's a question of honor," Victory said, catching the Praetorians' eyes. "They will stay out of it."

Dragomir took a deep breath, then sank the point of the blade into the back of Matthias's neck. As Matthias and every Imperial in the yard hissed, Dragomir pulled the sword from the wound and said, "You did what you had to do to help your sister. No shame in it."

Though she abhorred the bloodshed, Victory found herself satisfied with the Emp's cut. It was obviously not the mark of a swordsman, more the ragged, ham-fisted cut of a peasant, but it would suffice. Nodding her approval, she began, "You did well, for a—"

But Dragomir wasn't finished. Leaning down so that he could look into Matthais's eyes, he added, "But you do it again and you're going to find yourself oddly and incurably aroused by the canine form." Then, smiling sweetly, the Emp handed the Praetorian back his sword.

Victory choked. On the ground, her brother looked pale.

"We understand each other, then?" Dragomir asked, still smiling at Matthias.

"Perfectly," Matthias managed, getting to his feet. "My sister and I will take our Praetorian and go. I will see to it you receive suitable payment for your troubles." Turning back to his men, he gestured at the ship. "I just got the call that Imperial investigators have given us the go-ahead to take the palace. Preliminary examination revealed more corruption than even *we* suspected, and they will back our assault to Imperium auditors, but we need to move fast. They fear that Father will get wind of their investigation and begin destroying evidence." Motioning to his men, he started up the ramp of the ship.

"The Emp is coming with me," Victory blurted, before she had a chance to think about it.

"And his brother with me," Whip added.

When the prince hesitated and turned, his brow raised at the two of them, Whip lowered her head sheepishly. "That is, milord, if it pleases you."

"It pleases *me*," Victory stated.

Matthias glanced at the two natives for a moment, then shrugged. "If they're willing to help, we could certainly use them in freeing me from the dungeon."

"Freeing you…?" Victory asked.

Her brother snorted. "Our good Adjudicator Keene has me trapped in his dungeon…Or so he thinks." He grinned. "I'll have to pay David a few extra months' salary, by the end of this. He wasn't too keen on the idea of taking my place in the basement, even if it was just for a few days."

Lion glanced at Matthias with a frown. "David?"

"My brother has a double," Victory said. "Surgically altered. Not even Father can tell them apart, but then again, half the time he thinks he's ranting at my brother, it's actually David. When David lowers his voice and gives his words a bit of a rumble, they sound almost exactly the same. Matthias keeps him on as a Praetorian, but he really found him begging for scraps in a back alley of Cliff City, back when Matthias took his Great Tour of Mercy."

Matthias gave Victory an odd look. "You knew?"

Victory snorted. "You don't think I could recognize my own twin? I caught David wandering the halls with your Praetorian a month or two after your Great Tour. I pulled him aside and confronted him about it. Threatened to call the Inquisitors to come take a blood test on the poor kid. He spilled his guts. Just about peed himself, I think."

Matthias frowned at her. "And you didn't tell me you knew?"

Victory shrugged. "You didn't tell me you were doing it, so I figured you wanted to keep it quiet. Besides. Who *really* wants to sit through Imperial History lessons?"

Matthias looked disturbed. "Well, let's hope that Father never made that connection." Then he shook himself and nodded at his men. "Everything is in place to take the palace at noon two days from now. I have the army and the fleet at ready, despite Father's beliefs otherwise. His agents have all been caught and eliminated. The only real problem will be father's Praetorian in the palace." Matthias sighed. "If I had a choice, I would simply drop a few dozen bombs, level the palace, and build a new one."

"We need him alive," Victory said. "Even with what he's done and the embassy backing us, it would be a crime to kill him."

Her brother grinned, his green eyes flashing. "And so much more poetic to keep the arrogant bastard alive."

Victory raised a brow. "You have plans?"

Matthias pulled a titanium collar from under his jacket. "Already had it made. As soon as the investigation is complete, I'm welding it to the bastard's neck myself." Etched around the outer rim, the collar said, *A Man Without Mercy.*

Seeing it, Victory smiled. "When the time comes, I have just the place for him."

Matthias raised a brow. "Oh? I was going to leave him in a dungeon to think about it for a few decades."

"Oh no," Victory laughed. "A convict of such renown deserves much more than that. Somewhere public, and with a Praetorian honor-guard." Victory turned to Dragomir. Gesturing at the collar, she said, "What do you say? You think Mrs. Cooper could use an extra set of hands cleaning out chicken houses?"

Eyes on the titanium band, Dragomir broke into a slow, malicious smile. "Oh yes."

That night, the ship humming around them as they sped back to the palace, a smith had removed their collars and a blushing young maid dressed Victory in garb that befitted an Adjudicator. At bedtime, Dragomir gingerly lay down on the bunk behind Victory, keeping a wary eye on Lion, who still watched his every movement like a raptor.

"This okay, you old biddy?" Dragomir growled at Lion, over Victory's head. He settled a defiant arm over Victory's stomach.

"Tell him that his manhood leaves his pants and it will be separated from his person," Lion said.

"She says it's fine," Victory said, glaring at her Praetorian.

A few minutes after everyone had settled, Whip and Thor disappeared into the bathroom together and began giggling.

Watching their silhouettes move behind the crack under the door, Dragomir sighed. "They really should use some protection."

"Whip was sterilized," Victory said. Her eyes were closed, and she was soaking up the warmth of his hard body behind her. "They sterilize all Praetorian, male and female, the moment they choose their ward."

"Oh," Dragomir said. She could hear the wince in his voice when he said, "That's not good…"

Victory twisted in her bunk to look up at him. "It's nothing new. They've been doing it for a hundred years. It's part of a Praetorian's dedication to service."

Dragomir blushed, looking almost embarrassed. "Uh. Someone should probably tell her to use protection, then."

Victory frowned. "What do you mean?"

For a long moment, Dragomir seemed to struggle for words. "Remember the nano-poison?" he finally said. "How I even cured her head-cold?"

Victory's frown deepened.

"I wasn't being discriminating," Dragomir said, wincing.

Victory's eyes widened. She glanced at the bathroom door, then back at Dragomir. "You mean you…?"

Reluctantly, he nodded.

Victory fell back to the bed, staring at the ceiling, the possibilities racing through her mind at a thousand miles a second. Finally, she just shook her head. "Definitely medical tourism," she said.

An hour later, just as Victory was beginning to fall asleep in Dragomir's embrace, Thor and Whip opened the door of the restroom and casually stepped out and walked over to their separate bunks, looking as if they were trying to pretend they had not just been the source of the noise that had been keeping everyone else on the ship awake.

Behind her, Dragomir sighed. "Don't bother telling her to use protection."

CHAPTER 18

Trust

"This is it," Matthias said, taking a deep breath as the palace came into view. "Here's where we find out how many of my men were actually mine, and how many were Father's, playing both sides." He lifted the comset to his mouth. Then, glancing nervously at Victory, he said, "Control Tower One, this is Adjudicator Escort Five returning from mission, requesting docking orders."

The entire cockpit remained tense as Matthias held the com, waiting for a response.

A moment later, a man's voice said, "Adjudicator Escort Five, you are cleared to land in Hangar Three. Welcome back, milord."

Matthias let out a huge breath, and Victory relaxed.

"Thank you, Control Tower One," Matthias said. "We shall be docking immediately."

"Good luck, milord."

Matthias put the comset up as their pilot eased the ship into the hangar. The building was empty, as planned, but Matthias had his men spread out upon debarkation anyway.

They met a cluster of her brother's men gathered outside the hangar, along with six familiar female faces, all of whom laughed and hugged Victory, Whip, and Lion the moment they saw them. Then they were moving again, a group of almost thirty, heading for the dungeon. As they moved, they gathered force. It seemed that behind every door, standing in every hall, was another group of men with rifles, ready to fall in behind them. Once they reached the stairs going down, a quarter of the men peeled away from the main body to follow Victory and Matthias to the dungeon, while the rest guarded the path down.

Throughout it all, Dragomir kept close to Victory, his big body within arm's length at all times.

The dungeon itself was guarded by four men playing cards, who stood up with ashen faces upon seeing the flood of armed soldiers.

"Father doubled the guard," Matthias said, looking at the four men with amusement. He gestured at them to open the door.

Hastily, they did so.

As Matthias's men stayed outside, watching the pale guards, Matthias, Victory, the Emp, his brother, and her eight Praetorian entered the cold stone hallway.

Mathias switched on the light.

From down the hall, Matthias's own voice said, "Took you long enough, ass. I've been thinking you forgot me down here."

Matthias chuckled and went down to David's cell and opened it. "Not forgotten," he said, pulling his friend up in a hug. Standing beside him, David was just a fraction of an inch taller, and his face just a shade darker. Matthias unshackled him, slapped him on the back, and gave him a rifle. Then they found their Praetorian, dozens of them, all in one place, several to a cell. Some hadn't even been shackled, just stripped and thrown behind bars.

"Father is too arrogant," Matthias said, shaking his head as they freed their guard. As Matthias's men handed them weapons and armor to dress, Matthias got on the radio with his men deeper in the palace.

"They've got Father and his guard pinned in the dining hall," Matthias said. He turned to Victory. "His chamber should only have a rudimentary guard on it. Get inside, find the documents, and then go to the Constable of Numbers and call for the Embassy. My men and I will keep him situated until we can make his arrest official."

Victory nodded.

"Oh, and sis?" Matthias said, his green eyes showing a hint of mischievousness. "You wanna be there when I do the honors?" He patted the lump under his bulletproof vest.

Victory felt herself smile. "Wouldn't miss it for the world," she said. Then, gesturing at her escort, she led the way deeper into the palace. With her full nineteen Praetorian and the two natives—also dressed in Praetorian armor—in tow, Victory made an imposing image when she arrived at the Adjudicator's office at the very back of the palace, overlooking the Gorgarian Cliffs. The single Praetorian on duty, upon seeing Victory and her guard, looked for a moment as if he would fight.

"Bow to the new Adjudicator, and take your place at her back!" Lion snapped, as he reached for his sword. The man swallowed, then glanced at the two dozen men and women in black, then slowly fell to one knee, head down, fist to his heart.

Victory swept past him.

The papers she sought were strewn brazenly across her father's desk, the utter arrogance leaving her a bit stunned. *He really had no fear,* she thought, disgusted, as she looked through the falsified accounts. Everything she needed to convict him was right here, guarded by a single man. Every document, every ledger, every shred of proof...She didn't even have to go to the Constable of Numbers. It was all on his desk and tucked in binders on his shelves. He even had a pile taking up one side of the bed, still splayed open for perusal.

From her father's private com, Victory made a call to the Imperium Embassy, telling them to send Inquisitors at once, that she and her brother had secured the palace for their perusal, and they had the proof of the Adjudicator's crimes that they had been seeking.

It took four days for the Imperial Inquisitors to make their final case against the Adjudicator, but when they presented it to the Justae in a highly-publicized trial over open com, the verdict came back unanimous, after only ten minutes of deliberation:

Guilty. The current Adjudicator has failed the trust of his people and is hereby removed from service by order of the Grand Justice of the Imperium. His fate is relinquished to the hands of the local Adjudicate from which he hails. May his successor gain insight from his demise. Glory to the Imperium, and wisdom to its Adjudicators.

Victory, who had been confined to her quarters during the Adjudicator's trial—all government officials of Mercy having been given strict orders to cease operations and stay in their homes while the Justices made their decision—had watched all of the proceedings in her personal chambers with her full escort of Praetorian, plus Lion, Whip, Dragomir, and Thor. As the Grand Justice made her pronouncement on public com, Victory slumped to her bed in a mixture of relief and exhaustion.

"That's good, right?" Thor asked. Neither of the brothers had been able to understand the Justices' pronouncement, and Victory had stopped translating for them once she'd heard the very first word.

"Very good," Victory said softly. "It means my father is never going to sit on a throne again."

A moment later, a missive arrived, bearing the Seal of the Imperium. Lion took it from the messenger at the door and carried it across the room to Victory.

"Read it to me," Victory said, already feeling the weight of responsibility settling over her shoulders.

Lion immediately broke the seal and opened it. "By decree of the Grand Justice, Keene Drafton, First Generation Royal, will be stepping down from the throne of Mercy. As his heirs are not implicated in the evidence arrayed against him, his abdication shall be succeeded by one Second Generation Royal, Victoria Drafton. Glory to the Imperium, and wisdom to its Adjudicators."

"Wisdom to the Adjudicator," Lion finished softly, dropping to one knee, lowering her graying head, fist on heart. Whip, too, repeated the hail, dropping to one knee. Behind them, the entire Praetorian Guard fell with them.

Dragomir, who had been frowning at the kneeling Praetorian, looked back at her and said, "I suppose this means you're the empress, now?"

Victory nodded, still too overwhelmed to believe it.

"And that means you can tell anyone on this rock what to do and they've gotta do it?" Dragomir raised a brow in question.

Victory nodded again, the enormity of that fact still settling in her mind.

"Good," Dragomir said. "Get the old biddy and everyone else out of here." He grinned, his blue eyes dancing. "I have something I want to show you."

Looking up at his big body, Victory felt a thrill of mingled fear and exhilaration as she considered what that thing might be. Clearing her throat, she slowly got to her feet. In her most formal voice, she said to the group of women standing behind her two captains, "My friends, as your new Adjudicator, do you swear to obey me in everything I ask?"

Still on their knees, they gave the formal reply in unison, "Until death, milady."

Victory nodded and turned to her youngest captain. "Whip, as your new Adjudicator, and you as my captain, do you swear to obey me in everything I ask?"

Whip responded on cue, her head still lowered to the ground. "Until death, milady." Her voice was low and soft, full of sincerity.

Victory nodded, then turned to Lion. "Lion, as your new Adjudicator, and you as my high captain, do you swear to obey me in everything that I ask?"

"Until *death*, milady," was Lion's firm and heartfelt response.

"Good," Victory said. "Get out. All of you. Whip, go have some more fun with your Shi. Lion, go start drafting an order to halt all slave trade, starting tonight. All slaves on all vessels shall be returned to their homes. Any trader caught disobeying the edict will lose his ill-begotten property and join my father as an Imperial war-criminal to serve penance in native villages across Mercy."

Lion narrowed her eyes, glancing at the Emp. "But milady, another Praetorian could—"

Victory smiled sweetly. "I told *you* to do it."

Lion's face darkened, but only for an instant. Then she stood up and saluted, fist to heart. "As you command, milady." She bowed, deeply, then barked, "You heard the Adjudicator! *Out!*" As the others were quickly filing through the door, Lion gave Dragomir one last frown.

Dragomir grinned at her and waved politely.

Huffing, Lion slammed the door shut behind her, leaving Victory alone with her Emp.

"You know," Dragomir said, scanning the room, "This place looks strangely familiar." He gave her a mischievous look. "You up for a bath?"

Was she *ever.* Victory leapt off the bed and was halfway across the room when she hesitated. She looked up at Dragomir, saw the powerful muscles moving beneath his Praetorian armor, and felt a tingle of anxious anticipation.

"A *good* one, this time," Dragomir promised. He pulled the black Praetorian helmet from his head and set it on the bed. He was grinning as he unbuckled the obsidian breastplate and pulled it from his chest. "One we'll *both* enjoy." He dropped it to the floor, leaving his torso bare.

Victory swallowed, eyes on his big hands, then nodded.

He removed the last of his armor, revealing his homespun peasant's trousers underneath. Then, in a swift forward move, swept her into his arms. Victory gasped as she felt the floor drop away beneath her, and found herself clinging to his strong shoulders as he carried her to the tub.

"Um," she whimpered, as he set her down and started to fill the bath. She had never actually been with a man willingly, before, and now that he was *there*, his catlike muscles flexing in his back as he bent to test the water, her rational mind was having second thoughts.

She watched, nervous, as he filled the tub with steaming liquid and ran his hands through the surface. When he turned and grinned at her, she gave him an anxious smile.

When he stood and reached for the waistband of his pants, however, Victory fell into a crouch and squeezed her eyes shut.

Dragomir might have vanquished her visions, but the memories remained.

"You and your Praetorian are worried I'm controlling you," Dragomir said softly. "So tonight, I will keep my energy to myself." She heard the sound of his pants sliding down his thighs. She felt his heat as he squatted beside her, ran a big thumb along her temple. "I hate to make that promise, Princess, and it's the only time I ever will." He leaned forward, kissed her forehead. Against her ear, he whispered, "After tonight, I intend to use every resource I have to please my mate." Then she felt him stand, still unable to bring herself to open her eyes. "For tonight, though, you're going to have to trust me on your own."

Victory's heart was pounding as she felt his body move, heard water slosh, listened to the tub creak under his weight. Gingerly, she opened her eyes.

Dragomir was sitting opposite her, leaning his head back against the marble rim, shrouded by wisps of steam from the hot water. He lifted his head and gave her an encouraging smile and gestured at the tub. "I think you're right about one thing, Princess," he said, grinning at her over the surface of the bath. "This certainly does beat a splash in the creek."

Victory made a nervous chuckle, her heart lodged in her throat. She glanced at the exit to the bathroom and Dragomir went still in the tub.

"Leave if you have to," he said softly. "I can wait as long as you need, Princess."

Heart hammering, she looked back at him. She bit her lip, debating. Half of her craved to be in his arms, her body tight against his, once more caught up in his embrace.

The other half remembered six years of heartbreak.

"You can trust me," Dragomir whispered, as she hesitated.

Palms clammy with fear, Victory's fingers found the hem of her shirt.

"But before you do," Dragomir said softly, watching her, "I want you to know, Princess, that if you share this bath with me, I will be making love to you tonight." His blue gaze was intense when he said, "Tonight, tomorrow night, and every night thereafter. You will be *mine*, and I will show you the pleasures that you have missed each night for the rest of your life, to make up for lost time."

Oh gods, he had to go and say that, Victory thought, acutely aware of the heat suddenly pooling between her legs. Worse, he finished with such vehemence that, with his sweat-slickened body and the steam rising around him, he reminded her of the visage of an angry god. She almost lost her nerve.

Then her fingers began to move of their own accord. She pulled her shirt up to the swell of her breasts, then hesitated as his gaze sharpened. She swallowed, feeling like a deer caught in a hunter's sights.

I will not be ruled by the past, she thought, meeting his eyes. Shaking, she yanked the shirt over her head and stood. She let her pants fall around her ankles and stepped free.

Dragomir waited.

Trembling, Victory went to the edge of the tub. Her heart crammed into her throat when she saw his manhood within, hard and erect against his flat stomach.

"You can trust me, Princess," Dragomir said softly. "You have my word."

She met his eyes and gave a nervous smile. "It's Adjudicator, now," she said. And slipped into the water with him.

He moved toward her, then, water swirling as he placed a dripping hand on the tub's rim on either side of her. His large body dwarfing hers, he grinned down at her. "Adjudicator," he said, kissing her gently. "That might take awhile to learn." He kissed her jaw, tenderly, then slid down to kiss her neck and throat.

"You can call me Victory," she managed, shivering beneath his great bulk as he brought the heat roiling within her to the surface with every brush of his lips.

"Oh?" he asked, with a kiss. "You told me never to use that name for you, Princess." His lips found her taut nipple just above the surface of the water and he closed his mouth around it, suckling. Victory gasped and arced her back as the pressure built in her core; a warm, aching heat that had already begun to devour her.

He released her nipple and his tongue glided over it in a lazy caress, lapping, bringing a moan from Victory's lips as she reached up and delicately wrapped her hands over his thick shoulders, pulling him closer in her need.

Dragomir chuckled against her breast. "You like that, Princess?"

"Victory," she gasped, as he moved to the other. "Call me Victory." She couldn't think, couldn't do anything but feel his body moving against hers.

He gently took her other nipple into his mouth, drawing searing bolts of passion up from her core, filling her chest, making her heart pound crazily against her lungs. Victory felt dizzy with need as his great hands explored her, slipping beneath the water to glide against her hips, moving inward to part her thighs. She gasped as his fingers slid down to brush her nub, then gently began stroking her there to match the suckling of her breast.

Immediately, a pressure began to build within her core, a searing, demanding heat that left Victory clinging to his body, moaning, as it tried to crest.

Then, unbidden, she thought again of the last man who had been between her legs, of the horrible things he had done. A part of her quailed and she tensed, realizing what he meant to do.

"I can't," she whimpered, feeling the hot, uncontrollable passion throbbing within, knowing what would come. Before it could finish building, she began to crawl backwards out of the tub.

Dragomir's big hand on her shoulder stopped her.

"It's okay, love," he whispered, his hold gentle-yet-firm, his sincere blue eyes only inches from her own. "Trust me."

Victory met his gaze, hesitated. *Could* she trust him? He was bigger than she. He could take her if he wished. And yet, he was giving her a choice. She searched his soul, trying to find some reason to get out of the tub.

He waited, motionless, allowing her to look, bearing his soul for her inspection. And, slowly, she felt her anxiety melt away under the honesty she saw in his eyes. *He could use his Emp powers to calm me*, she thought, *But he's not. He's letting me decide for myself.* Reluctantly, Victory slid back into the water.

He smiled, then, beaming with genuine happiness as he slid back over her. He kissed her gently upon her forehead, then her jaw, then lowered his mouth and worked his tongue around her areola, teasing. She whimpered with the pleasure that once more began to build, over-powering even the fear she carried buried in her past. She once again dug her fingers into his shoulders as the pressure within became unbearable. He tenderly renewed his attentions to her nub, caressing it with expert fingers, stroking and rubbing as he tenderly suckled her breast. Then, gently, he caught her nipple between his teeth and tugged.

Victory cried out as the warmth suddenly exploded within her core.

Grinning, Dragomir wrapped his arms around her and lifted her from the water. As Victory tried to understand that, he took her to the other side of the bath and gently laid her back on a low shelf, so that her body was exposed to air. Laying there, looking up at him, Victory saw his manhood jutting from between his legs, a staff with which to impale her most sensitive parts.

Knowing what he intended to do next, Victory whimpered and tried to crawl backwards, unable to paint a gentle picture of it in her mind.

A firm hand on her thigh held her in place. "Trust me," he whispered again. He knelt in the water, between her legs, watching her face.

Trembling, Victory squeezed her eyes shut, knowing, as she always had, that she had no real choice. She should have known he would take her at his will. What was she thinking when she stepped out of her clothes and—

Her thoughts imploded as she felt his tongue touch her innermost flesh. She gasped and started to sit up. "What—?"

She moaned and flexed back to the ledge when she felt him take her nub between his lips and suckle it. The full-body shudders that wracked her as he alternately suckled, then licked, then lapped at her sensitives left her clinging to the ledge, gasping for air as another, greater pressure built from within.

This time, when he took her over the edge, Victory's back arced and she cried out, wrapping her fingers in his hair and clinging to his head with her thighs. Then she collapsed, panting, staring at the stone ceiling in shock.

To her horror, she felt movement between her thighs as he started working his tongue against her clitoris once more. His big hand slid upwards, tracing the curves of her body, stopping on a breast, kneading it in a tender caress. Even as she was sure she could take no more, he brought her to climax again. This time, she lost herself. Her fears drained away, overpowered by the pleasure that was coursing within her. She bucked and thrashed under his attentions, her sweaty body heaving, her fingers gripping the marble bathtub as he made her world narrow to the overwhelming tide of ecstasy rising within.

When he finally lifted his head and kissed her stomach gently, Victory was in a semi-stupor, still reeling in the washes of pleasure. She groaned and lifted her head to watch as he moved away to let out some of the now-cold water from the tub, then replace it with fresh. Then, as she watched, he lathered a soapy sponge and brought it back to her.

Gently, he eased her down into the water with him, pulling her small body to be enveloped in his own. She felt his manhood, then, pinned between where their stomachs met. He leaned back, so that she was using his stomach as her resting spot and his knees as her backrest, and as Victory looked on, dumbfounded, he began to lather her body with the sponge.

He's not going to take me, she realized, watching him. That knowledge hit her like a concussive blast of relief, and she felt her heart open to him, finally. He didn't seem to notice. She watched his arms work as he finished scrubbing her clean, then began working on himself, following the sponge with his eyes as it traced the chiseled lines of his muscular body.

Without uprooting her from her seat, he reached over with a long arm, grabbed a pitcher from the tub's rim, and filled it. Then, tenderly, he began pouring water over her, careful to keep it out of her eyes. Her heart still pounding from his ministrations, Victory could only stare. He seemed no more concerned about what he had just done to her than he was about the bits of grime and dirt that he was now rinsing away.

She looked down at the hardness she was resting on. She had untold experience with such pillars of flesh, but never had they felt so...innocent...as his felt now, pressed into his stomach with her weight.

Victory swallowed. She had been assaulted a thousand times, by a hundred different men, but never before had she actually had the leisure to explore. Aside from the brief glimpses that she had seen before they were driven inside of her, she had no real idea of what they looked like or even how they worked. She had never been given—nor really wanted—the opportunity to investigate, to learn. And now it was *there*. Hers to examine.

Once he finished the first rinse, Dragomir re-lathered the sponge and started soaping her again. She watched him, still befuddled by his gentleness, his lack of concern for what had just taken place, as he tenderly lifted each of her arms, washing, then gently ran his big hands up her back, rubbing away the grit there. He had finished with her and started again on his own body when Victory's curiosity finally got the better of her.

She let her hands slide under the water to touch the hard flesh against his stomach. Then she froze, biting her lip, wondering if she had gone too far.

Dragomir hesitated for a second, his body going still, before he continued scrubbing, not even looking up at her.

Somehow, his lack of response gave her the courage to continue. Victory shifted, slightly, feeling her way down his length to his scrotum. She touched him gently, there, knowing that it was a man's most sensitive part, that too much pressure could damage, or even kill. She took the tender flesh between her fingers, lifting, cupping the sack with her palm as she examined what it contained, curious.

When he didn't stop her, she slid off of his stomach, into the water, and, when he simply kept cleaning his hands and then forearms, she knelt beside him to get a better look. She lowered her face as close as she dared to the surface, peering into the bath. The water was cloudy from the soap, but she thought she could see lumps…

Clearing his throat, Dragomir pulled himself up onto the ledge she had just occupied, legs spread, dripping. He lifted a knee and started scrubbing, still appearing utterly engrossed in his bath.

Victory bit her lip, watching his face. When he didn't scowl or otherwise warn her off, she slid forward to get a better look. He kept washing, scrubbing the dirt and blood from his scabbed knee.

Heart hammering, now, Victory once again reached out and touched his sensitive flesh. If he noticed, or even cared, he made no sign.

Swallowing hard, she once again pulled at the loose skin of his sack, watching the egg-shaped lumps move within. She singled one out, took it into her hand, pulled it aside.

"Gently," he whispered.

Victory froze. He was looking at her, now, blue eyes kind, sponge still dripping soap from where it rested against his knee. He gave her a sheepish grin and went back to his ablutions.

She almost lost her nerve, then. Her heart pounded in her ears like a faulty engine, hammering at her skull like it wanted to break free. What was she *doing*? He was *male* and males used these parts to hurt people. She swallowed. She looked down at where her hand held him, her curiosity fighting with the instinct telling her to snatch it away.

"Go on," he whispered, still scrubbing.

Trembling, now, she moved her hand back up the shaft. Heart doing tiny explosions in her chest, she moved it between her fingers. She froze when the skin slid down the shaft, revealing an odd, heart-shaped bulb at the end.

She felt his sudden intake of breath, but he didn't look at her. He started scrubbing his calf, then spent extra time on his foot, working the sponge between each toe.

Victory eased closer, until she was between his knees, his manhood displayed for her on the ledge. She looked up at him nervously, then, when he continued washing, pulled the shaft further from his stomach, so that she could see the individual folds of skin, the odd ridges, the veins, the tiny slit at the top.

She gasped and lurched backwards as he switched legs, dropping his soapy foot into the water beside her and lifting his other to the ledge. Dragomir glanced at her, then began lathering that leg, too.

Heart thundering, she laughed nervously.

Dragomir didn't seem to notice.

Victory narrowed her eyes.

• • •

"I know you're paying attention."

Dragomir hesitated in running the sponge across his thigh. Trying not to let his fear show, he looked up at her. He was so terrified that he would make a misstep, that he would return her to that dull-eyed state of shock, that he had almost cried out when he shifted legs and she lunged away from him. He had thought that giving her the opportunity to explore him would help ease her fears.

Now, though, caught under her accusing green stare, he wondered if he had made a mistake. He was just about to apologize when she said, "Lean back." It sounded half-command, half plea.

Dragomir froze, watching her bite her lip, her emerald eyes flickering from his manhood and back to him. She looked like a frightened doe, and he instinctively knew that any stray movement on his part would send her bounding out of the bath. Slowly, he lowered the sponge into the water and leaned his body back against the rim of the tub.

Once he was settled, she slid forward on her knees slowly, making the water ripple around her. Her face was flushed, her breathing elevated. Dragomir had his shields up, but he didn't need to be an Emp to know that Victory was terrified. She kept glancing up at him like she thought he was going to suddenly lunge forward and ravish her.

Deciding to give her all the time she wanted to explore, Dragomir rested his head against the rim of the tub, staring up at the ceiling. He lowered his other foot into the water and spread his knees apart to give her better access. Offering everything, hiding nothing.

He heard water dribble in the bath between his calves, and waited. She settled her hot, wet hand around his width and his breath caught. He remained absolutely still as she started her explorations anew, testing, tugging, teasing. Then she began to stroke the shaft, slowly, and his heart started doing laps around his chest. Realizing the slow, purposeful motions for what they were, his startled mind did a somersault. *She can't be...*He began sitting up before he caught himself.

But her hands began to increase their tempo, sliding up and down his length, gripping it with exquisite firmness as she worked his member. His manhood, already painfully sensitive from watching her body rock with pleasure and from the bounty of her delicate taste, was throbbing for release. His balls, already aching from the pressure of the night's arousal, began to grow heavy as the acute tightness built rapidly under her small, graceful fingers. He felt himself squirm under her attentions, trying not to frighten her, but knowing that he wouldn't be able to hold himself back for much longer. He'd gone too long without release, the thought not even having crossed his mind in weeks.

He strained to hold back the automatic pelvic thrusts as Victory relentlessly massaged his manhood. Sweat began to break out over his body as the pressure became intense, the need to release like a building explosion within him. His heart, already hammering against his ribs, was taking flight, picking up speed with the increasing rhythm of her hands. He felt a tiny moan escape his lips before he clamped his jaw tight, determined not to scare her. He knew, though, that he had to say something, soon, or she would probably never speak to him again.

He opened his mouth to tell her to stop.

"Go on," she whispered. "Let go."

Something about her soft, reassuring voice released all the triggers within him. His spine and hips surged as the pressure in his balls surrendered. His stomach tightened in an unsuppressable groan as wave after powerful wave worked its way up his manhood, spurting his seed onto his stomach in pulsing tides of pleasure.

When it was over, he stared at the ceiling, panting. Between his knees, Victory giggled.

Astonished, he lifted his head to look at her.

"Head back," she growled, though there was a smile on her lips.

A little anxious, he obeyed, once again examining the ceiling as she explored his body. He heard her fill the pitcher, then felt a hot flood of water across his chest as she rinsed his seed away. Then he felt her hands start moving on his shaft again.

Oh gods, he thought. *I can't possibly…*

All thoughts ended when he felt her lips touch his head. His entire world narrowed to the way her tongue slipped out, licked his shaft, the way she took his manhood in her warm, moist mouth and suckled.

"Oh," he whimpered, gripping the rim of the tub to keep from sliding into the water. It was all he could do to keep from moaning, and the strain of keeping his body still for her was akin to moving the Gorgarian Cliffs with his mind. He whimpered as she traced her fingers down his shaft and cupped his balls. He swallowed and tried to keep his hips in check as she pumped her hand down his shaft. He gasped and felt the pressure surging within him again as she worked the head of his manhood with her tongue, suckling.

Thinking about what would happen if she didn't remove her mouth, soon, made him tense. He was not willing to revisit that upon her. Not yet.

"Victory," he whispered. "I can't…"

He felt her grin around his member.

"Sounds familiar," she whispered. But she released him.

Dragomir breathed a huge sigh of relief and slumped against the rim of the tub, grateful for the reprieve…and throbbing for release.

Later, he promised himself, *Once she's asleep, I'll—*

He felt her stand. Felt her touch his shoulders with her hands, place one knee astride his right thigh, then her other knee astride his left.

Dragomir jerked his head up, shocked. Her naked body was positioned over him like a steaming goddess, and it took his breath away.

She gave him a nervous grin. Then, slowly, she reached down for his manhood, to position it beneath her.

Though he wanted nothing more than to show her she had nothing to fear from him, Dragomir sat up and caught her hand. Meeting her eyes, he said, "I can go without, Victory. Not until you're ready."

Victory looked at his muscular arm, holding her tiny wrist, then back at him. "That's why I'm ready," she whispered, meeting his blue eyes. "Besides," she continued, smiling. "You told me you wanted to make love tonight."

"We did," he babbled. "I gave you pleasure. I didn't mean—"

She gently pushed his hand aside.

He released her, but only reluctantly. He felt like a deer caught in the glare of a tank, ready to bolt out from under her at any moment, but unable to find the sense to do so.

Gently, she put a small hand in the middle of his chest and pushed him back to the edge of the tub. He went reluctantly, fighting rising panic. She again found his manhood and settled it between her legs. He felt his head touch her there, felt his balls twinge with anticipation even as his heart screamed for her to wait.

Don't do it if you're not ready, he willed her, meeting her gaze.

Looking deeply into his eyes, Victory settled herself onto his shaft.

Dragomir shuddered in pleasure as she took him completely, enveloping him in her warmth. A moment later, he froze. He anxiously looked up at Victory, watching her face. She was looking at the ledge under his left arm, biting her lip.

Oh gods, he thought. Had she not been sitting on him, pinning him to the ledge, he would have pulled away to give her space. As it was, he remained absolutely still, his heart rama aching to wrap her in his love, but his promise to her before the bath forcing him to rein it in.

Several minutes passed, with Victory looking aside, her breathing jagged, uneven, and with Dragomir staying as quiet and as silent as the wall he wished he could sink into.

After long minutes of nothing, just feeling the silken flesh motionless around his manhood, Dragomir gingerly reached up a hand to her chin. He turned her to face him.

She refused to look at his eyes. He saw tears.

Immediately, he hated himself for allowing her to do it. He started to get up, to set her aside, but Victory caught him by the shoulder suddenly. "No," she said, meeting his gaze with a force that quieted him. "Just…" Her breath caught and she shuddered, looked away again. "Just stay there. Please."

Dragomir sank back to the ledge, watching her. He hated the pain on her face, wanted to wipe it away, wanted to blanket her in his love. Setting his jaw, hoping he was doing the right thing, he gingerly reached out and drew her to his chest, wrapping her in his arms.

She didn't fight him. She laid her head against his shoulder and for a long moment said nothing. Then he felt her body start to quake, heard the quiet sobs. Her arms reached out for him, encircled him.

"Oh Princess," he whispered, drawing her tighter to him. He stroked her hair, feeling tears of his own stinging his eyes. He started to rock her, murmuring silly things that seemed to tumble from his lips. His heart rama was a tortured ball of energy, a hole within his chest. "I'm so sorry," he whispered into her ear, his tears in her hair. "So sorry, Princess."

But when he tried to lift her away from him, she once again stayed his hand.

"But…" he managed, searching her eyes, confused. "Why?"

"Give me time," she whispered. She seemed to tremble, then, holding onto him, and laid her head against his chest, her gaze fixed on a point across the room.

Dragomir doubted she really wanted what she thought she did, but he let her stay, holding her anyway.

Eventually, her shaking stopped. She sat up, met his gaze, and Dragomir almost lost himself in the depth to her ancient green eyes. She gave him a weak smile.

…and started to rock.

"Wait—" he began.

She touched a finger to his lips, and shook her head, her smile still on her lips, tears still in her eyes.

Dragomir reluctantly reclined against the marble tub, still tense, watching her in a mix of awe and heartfelt compassion. He knew what was happening within her. Even through his shields, he could feel it: She wasn't letting her past win. He found himself captivated by her determination, overwhelmed by her strength. He found himself willing her smile to grow, willing her to enjoy herself, willing her to take as long as she needed.

And, to his relief, she seemed to relax. Her movements picked up speed, and the pain cleared from her face, replaced by a slow, sheepish grin. She met his eyes again, smiling, her body moving to its own beautiful rhythm.

It was then, watching her exquisite body moving against his in wonder, that Dragomir realized that the pressure was building again within him, much greater than before. He flinched inwardly, trying to hold it back, trying to remain as utterly motionless beneath her as possible, terrified of ruining this moment for her. Her stunning body, however, twined with his, enveloping him, caressing him from within, was too much. Eventually, his hips bucked of their own accord.

He fought panic and forced his hips back to the ledge.

If Victory noticed or cared, she said nothing. She rocked her head back and closed her eyes, obviously concentrating on the new sensations she was feeling.

Dragomir shook with the need to join with her, to fill her, but he forced his body to hold off as long as it could. He knew it would scare her. He knew it would draw her completely out of the pleasure that she was building. He forced himself to think of something, *anything* but the beautiful woman that was flowering before him.

When she put her feet on the ledge, hands gripping the back of his neck for balance as she started to ride him with abandon, however, Dragomir knew he had lost the battle. He felt the pressure building to an extreme, whimpering as he tried to hold it back. He knew she was close. He could see it in her flushed face, her quick, labored breaths, the sweat gleaming upon her naked body.

It was seeing her pleasure that finally slammed through the barriers he had built up around his own bliss and brought his world crashing down around him.

• • •

Victory had her head thrown back, feeling on the very edge of a great, powerful explosion, when Dragomir groaned and grabbed her hips. She felt his loins thrust beneath her, felt the rhythmic convulsions of his manhood within her.

She gasped and snapped her head back to look at him, startled.

"I'm sorry," he whimpered, his blue eyes wide, his big body going absolutely still beneath her. "I couldn't—"

Heart pounding with sudden horror, Victory started to climb off, but the new warmth he left within her triggered her own body's response. She gripped his neck and cried out as her inner muscles contracted around his shaft, her pleasure taking her fully and completely by surprise. It lasted almost a full minute, arcing her spine with its force, and by the end of it, she was clinging to him, utterly spent.

They sat there like that for several minutes, both panting, neither speaking. Then, slowly, Victory pulled away to look at him.

This time, it was *he* who wouldn't look at *her*. Gently, Victory reached out, touched his cheek. When his blue eyes met hers, there were tears in them.

Victory leaned forward and kissed him. She took the passion that she had felt and worked it into her kiss, stealing the words of apology from his lips, ravishing his fears away. She felt his arms tenderly reach up her back, wrap her again in his embrace. Then he was kissing back, hard and desperate, the kiss of a man who had seen all his fears topple over the edge of the brink...only to have them retrieved and transformed in a breath of love.

She started moving over him again, still wrapped firmly in his big arms. She felt him move with her, tentatively at first, then, as she encouraged him with motion and sound, with more confidence. The passion between them began to build again—Dragomir settling himself deep within her core, Victory accepting everything he had to give. Still kissing, she felt his powerful body move beneath her, taking her completely, and the hot pressure in her core suddenly shattered into another long, powerful climax. Somewhere within, she felt him join her, holding her tight, moaning into her hair as he spilled his seed deep inside her.

They stayed like that for long moments, struggling for air, before Victory, pushed back far enough to grin at him, started moving again.

Dragomir met her gaze, and she saw love within his eyes.

He stood, then, lifting her body with his, her depths still enveloping his rigid shaft. Victory wrapped her legs around him, gripping his hips with her thighs, clinging to his neck as he stepped easily from the tub and carried her to the bed.

He laid her down, gently, and through his kisses, whispered, "I know I said I'd wait. But I've shown you can trust me, Princess. Now I want to show you what an Emp can *really* do." He broke their kiss and met her gaze, then, seeming to wait for her affirmative.

Victory bit her lip, searching his blue eyes, but nodded.

Instantly, her world seemed to wash in warmth. It traced her spine, her legs, her arms, her neck, her ears, her feet. It cradled her, soaked, her, adored her. In a moment, Victory was feeling her orgasm build, a thousand times richer than before.

…And then he began to move within her, and her world crumbled in crashing waves of ecstasy.

CHAPTER 19

An Imperial Decree

When they emerged the next morning, Lion met them at the door. The woman's graying hair was a bit disheveled, her shirt rumpled, and it was apparent to Victory that she hadn't slept. Upon seeing them, her high captain jumped out of her chair beside the chamber exit, looking both exhausted and sheepish. Victory knew why—Praetorian did not use chairs while on duty.

She slept outside my door, Victory thought, both irritated and touched.

Lion gave Dragomir a long, suspicious look. "I take it the slave behaved himself?"

Victory raised a brow. "I thought I told you to write an edict and announce it last night."

Lion flushed. "I did, milady. Slavery has been outlawed. Imperial business has come to a crashing halt."

"We have the treasured Mercy Black," Victory said, shrugging. "We have stone." She glanced at Dragomir, then smiled up at him. "We also have *them.*"

Lion gave the Emp a long look. "Medical tourism."

"From this day forth, Mercy will grant amnesty to all mutagenic anomalies who seek refuge in our system. Put out a notice to the other Adjudicators. We offer open arms and will pay the delivery costs plus processing fees to all DNA-based exiles facing certain extermination in other areas of the Imperium."

Lion continued to scowl at Dragomir for another long moment, then seemingly shook herself and grunted. "As you command, milady. I will draft the orders this afternoon."

Victory glanced up at Dragomir, who was watching the conversation with tense interest. "Further, the Adjudicator has the right to choose her mate." She put her hand on the homespun tunic hiding Dragomir's chiseled chest and smiled up at him. "And, since he has been chosen, his seed already planted, it will please me to know that my children will be able to serve this planet in my passing."

Lion's eyes widened, but she lowered her head in a salute, fist-to-chest. "Shall I write another edict, milady?"

"Write two," Victory said. "The first, stating that Mercerian genetic mutations are to be registered as First Generation Royals and those who survived my father's extermination squads will be given special compensation for stepping forward—I'm certain that it will take some time to convince them of our good intentions, considering the persecution they were subjected to, but perhaps my brother could help. He seems to have created a list of survivors."

"And the other, milady?" Lion asked.

"A wedding," Victory said. "Invite the court—those that were not arrested with my father—and the entire village of Sodstone. Shuttle service provided."

Lion frowned. "An entire *village*, milady?"

"Give them guest quarters in the east wing." Then Victory caught Dragomir's gaze, bathing in the love she found there. She smiled. "And if Mrs. Cooper and her boys have troubles attending due to prior engagements, hire someone to watch her chickens. We have a *special* surprise for her, after the ceremony."

END

OTHER TITLES BY SARA KING

Guardians of the First Realm: Alaskan Fire
Guardians of the First Realm: Alaskan Fury

Millennium Potion: Wings of Retribution

Outer Bounds: Fortune's Rising

Terms of Mercy: To the Princess Bound

The Legend of ZERO: Zero Recall
The Legend of ZERO: Zero's Return

COMING SOON

Guardians of the First Realm: Fury of the Fourth Realm
Guardians of the First Realm: Alaskan Fiend
Guardians of the First Realm: Alaskan Fang

ZERO: Zero's Legacy
ZERO: Forgotten

Terms of Mercy: Slave of the Dragon Lord

Aulds of the Spyre: The Sheet Charmer
Aulds of the Spyre: Form and Function

Outer Bounds: Fortune's Folly
Outer Bounds: Children of Fortune

ABOUT THE AUTHOR

My name is Sara King and I'm going to change the world. No, seriously. I am. And I need your help. My goal is simple. I want to champion, define, and spread character writing throughout the galaxy. (Okay, maybe we can just start with Planet Earth.) I want to take good writing out of the hands of the huge corporations who have had a stranglehold on the publishing industry for so long and reconnect it to the people (you) and what you really want. I want to democratize writing as an art form. Something that's always been controlled by an elite few who have (in my opinion) a different idea of what is 'good writing' than the rest of the world, and have been feeding the sci-fi audience over 50% crap for the last 40 years.

To assist me in my goals to take over the world (crap, did I say that out loud??), please leave a review for this book! It's the first and easiest way for you guys to chip in and assist your friendly neighborhood writer-gal. And believe me, every review helps otherwise unknown books like mine stand up against the likes of the Big Boys on an impersonal site like Amazon.

Also, I have an email! (Totally surprising, I know.) Use it! (Don't you know that fanmail keeps writers going through those dark times when we run out of chocolate???) I love posting letters on Facebook—gives me something fulfilling to do with my time. ;) Shoot me a line! kingnovel@gmail.com

You can also ask to SIGN UP FOR MY MAILING LIST! Seriously, I give away free books, ask people to beta-read scenes and novels, and give updates on all the series I'm currently working on. Stay informed! J

And, for those of you who do the Facebook thing, check me out: http://www.facebook.com/kingfiction (personal) or http://www.facebook.com/sknovel (my author page) or stay up to date on continuous new ZERO publications with The Legend of ZERO fan page: http://www.facebook.com/legendofzero

Made in the USA
Middletown, DE
23 November 2022

15782008R00186